Praise for *Alchemy*

'The clever twists and turns of *Alchemy* are assuredly plotted and Prague, a city in religious and political turmoil, makes for a powerful setting' *The Times*

'Over the past dozen years, S. J. Parris's novels . . . have been among the most enjoyable of all historical thrillers' *Sunday Times*

'Breathless pace and acutely observed detail make for a story that confounds and surprises' *Observer*

Praise for the Giordano Bruno series

'It has everything – intrigue, mystery and excellent history' Kate Mosse, No.1 bestselling author of *The Burning Chambers*

'A delicious blend of history and thriller' *The Times*

'A tight plot combines with subtly realised characters and an omnipresent sense of danger' *Daily Mail*

'Colourful characters, fast-moving plots and a world where one false step in religion or politics can mean a grisly death' *Sunday Times*

'S. J. Parris is one of my favourite authors – and unquestionably our greatest living writer of historical thrillers' A. J. Finn, No.1 bestselling author of *The Woman in the Window*

'Pacy, intricate, and thrilling . . . Full of historical detail and rich with atmosphere' *Observer*

No.1 *Sunday Times* bestseller S. J. Parris is the pseudonym of the author and journalist Stephanie Merritt. It was as a student at Cambridge researching a paper on the period that Stephanie first became fascinated by the rich history of Tudor England and Renaissance Europe. Since then, her interest has grown and led her to create this series of historical thrillers featuring Giordano Bruno, which has now sold over one million copies.

Stephanie has worked as a critic and feature writer for a variety of newspapers and magazines, as well as radio and television. She has also written the contemporary psychological thrillers *While You Sleep* and *Storm* under her own name. She currently writes for the *Observer*, and she lives in Surrey.

www.sjparris.com

f /sjparrisbooks

𝕏 @thestephmerritt

S.J. PARRIS

Alchemy

HEMLOCK
PRESS

Hemlock Press,
an imprint of HarperCollins*Publishers* Ltd
1 London Bridge Street,
London SE1 9GF

www.harpercollins.co.uk

HarperCollins*Publishers*
Macken House,
39/40 Mayor Street Upper,
Dublin 1
D01 C9W8
Ireland

This paperback edition 2024
1

First published in Great Britain by HarperCollins*Publishers* Ltd 2023

A catalogue record for this book is available from the British Library

ISBN: 978-0-00-820857-8 (PB b-format)

Typeset in Sabon LT Std by Palimpsest Book Production Limited, Falkirk, Stirlingshire

Printed and bound in the UK using 100% Renewable Electricity
by CPI Group (UK) Ltd

His Majesty is interested only in wizards, alchemists, Cabalists and the like, sparing no expense to find all kinds of treasures, learn secrets and use scandalous ways of harming his enemies . . . He also has a whole library of magic books. He strives all the time to eliminate God completely so that he may in future serve a different master . . .

Proposition to the Archdukes in Vienna,
on Rudolf II, 1606

I am forced to be brief. That which we suspected in England is also here.

Letter from John Dee to Sir Francis
Walsingham, Prague 1588

Prague Castle

In the late sixteenth century

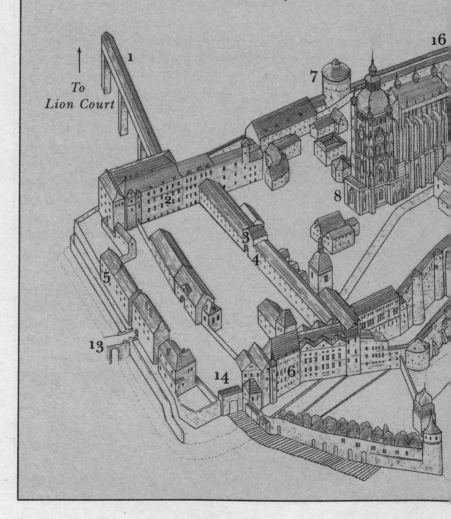

1

To
Lion Court

16

7

2

3

4

8

5

13

14

6

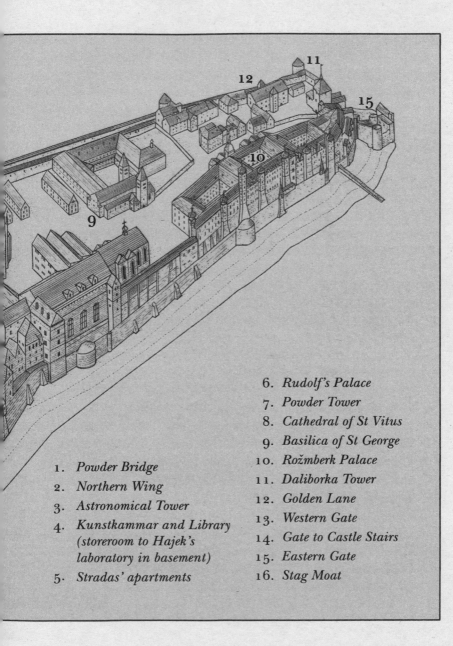

1. Powder Bridge
2. Northern Wing
3. Astronomical Tower
4. Kunstkammar and Library (storeroom to Hajek's laboratory in basement)
5. Stradas' apartments
6. Rudolf's Palace
7. Powder Tower
8. Cathedral of St Vitus
9. Basilica of St George
10. Rožmberk Palace
11. Daliborka Tower
12. Golden Lane
13. Western Gate
14. Gate to Castle Stairs
15. Eastern Gate
16. Stag Moat

PROLOGUE

Seething Lane, City of London
15th day of February 1588

My dear Bruno

I hope Wittenberg is treating you well, and that you have thus far managed to avoid falling foul of the university authorities with your bolder ideas. I know few men who can boast the distinction of being thrown in prison for heresy by both the Catholics and the Calvinists.

I will be brief. I must beg a favour of you, in the hope that your past service to England will incline you once more to our cause. You know that our friend Dr Dee has been at the court of Prague this past while. I have this day received a communication from him, sent a fortnight since, touching some great matter of secrecy that he dared not openly express; yet from his hints, I deduce it concerns the discovery of malign practices against the Emperor Rudolf. If the Emperor's enemies should succeed in his destruction, the tremors will be felt throughout Christendom. I hardly need tell you how vital it is to England, with the balance of power in Europe on a razor's edge, to have a friend in the Holy

1

Roman Emperor, at a time when Her Majesty Queen Elizabeth has few enough of those abroad.

I therefore entreat you: hasten to Prague, and there use all your endeavour and industry to give Dee good assistance and learn more of this affair. There is no man I would trust so greatly in this business, and I have every faith that your reputation as a philosopher will ensure your warm reception in the city, which you might use as cover. Convey to Dee the enclosed cipher; I fear the one he has at present is no longer safe. If that is so, then nor is he. I will send further instructions to you in Prague. But I pray you: as you love Her Majesty, John Dee and the truth, do not delay.

God go with you, along with Her Majesty's good wishes and my gratitude.

Your loving friend
Francis Walsingham

ONE

The alchemist was found hanging from the Stone Bridge at first light with his eyes and tongue cut out. Two sturdy ropes had been slung under his armpits and secured around the plinth of a carved saint who gazed serenely the other way as the corpse swung under the balustrade, dripping its lifeblood into the misty waters of the Vltava. Hebrew letters had been cut into his forehead. This much I had learned even before we reached the gates of Prague, from travellers on their way out of the city, and excitable taverners along the road who delighted in recounting every new detail they gleaned from those passing through. His name was Zikmund Bartos and he had been the Emperor Rudolf's current favourite among the legions of scryers, distillers, prophets, conjurors, star-gazers, physicians and mountebanks who toiled inside and outside the walls of the great castle on the hill, all vying to be the first to succeed in presenting the Emperor with his heart's desire, the Philosopher's Stone. Naturally, there was a surfeit of theories surrounding the gruesome end of Bartos, who had been found on the morning of that chill March day I was due to arrive in Prague. The Ides of March, as it happened, the old Roman deadline for the settling of debts; I wondered if that was significant. By noon, the road was buzzing with definitive versions: he had been attacked by a jealous rival who wished to steal

3

his magical secrets; he had killed himself in despair because he knew his mission was doomed (this one did not find many supporters, on account of the obvious practicalities); he had sold his soul to the Devil in return for forbidden knowledge, and the Devil had exacted his price. This last was seized upon with relish, thanks to the legend of Doctor Faustus, which had been published in the German language the previous year and proved popular with readers. But one word recurred more than any other as we rode those last ten miles towards the city walls in the fading light of the afternoon: *Golem.*

'Maestro? What exactly is this Golem?'

I turned to my travelling companion with my best expression of forbearance. 'Besler. For the thousandth time – don't call me Maestro.'

He blinked his pale eyelashes at me, as if we had not already had this conversation repeatedly along the road from Wittenberg. 'But you are my master, and I wish to acknowledge this by giving you a title of respect and honour, in your own language.'

'I know, but it makes me feel old. And I am not, strictly speaking, your master.'

He leaned back in the saddle to give me an appraising look. 'Well, you are quite advanced in years now, Doctor Bruno. When you do not shave for two days, there are flecks of silver in your beard. More than a few.' He sounded apologetic, as if it were an unwelcome but necessary duty to inform me. 'In any case, I have chosen you to be my master, and therefore you are so.'

'I'm *thirty-nine*, Besler.' I ran my hand across my chin, piqued. 'And that is a quirk, shall we say, of Italian colouring. It's nothing to do with age. At least I can grow a beard.'

His eyes widened as if I had struck him, and his head dropped; he fell silent and I smiled to myself. Besler was twenty-two, with those fair, Germanic looks that meant he appeared barely sixteen and needed to shave once a month at most, a short-coming which made him acutely sensitive; I should not have mocked him. At his age, I recalled, I too had regarded anyone over thirty as half in their grave.

4

'You have really never heard of the Golem?' I asked, to change the subject.

He perked up. 'I know only that it is some kind of Jewish monster.'

'Not a monster. A creature. Like a man, but fashioned from clay, as God made Adam. Only a great rabbi steeped in the secrets of the Cabala can breathe life into it by performing certain rituals and incantations. Then he must carve the word EMET – *Truth* – on the Golem's forehead and it will obey its master in everything. But on the Sabbath, he must erase the word from the creature's head so that it can rest, according to the law.' I shifted position in the saddle and lowered my voice for effect. 'The story goes that once, on Sabbath eve, a rabbi had begun to erase the word but was called away after the first letter, leaving the word MET – Hebrew for Death. The creature went on the rampage, destroying everything in its path, until at the last moment the rabbi was able to subdue it just before the Sabbath prayers began – else it would have been out of his control for ever.'

'Goodness. And the word is that this creature is now loose in Prague, killing people?'

I laughed at his earnest expression. 'It's just a legend, Besler. It's said that the Chief Rabbi of Prague is the only living scholar with the mystical knowledge to create a Golem, but you must know it is all invention. Though it certainly sounds as if this murder is intended to make people afraid of a violent monster.' And point the finger at the Jews of Prague, I realised, with dismay. Even in a city famed for its tolerance, there are those who would try to fuel religious tensions. 'Still – that is not our problem,' I added more cheerfully, nudging my horse to pick up his pace. 'My task is to find my friend John Dee and secure an audience with the Emperor Rudolf. That is all. I have no intention of involving myself in speculation about a killing.'

But the news had made me uneasy. I had seen enough of murder in the past few years to satisfy any curiosity on that score; now I was content to pursue my studies, write my books and teach a select handful of private students, and I had nursed hopes that Prague – that bubbling cauldron of artistic and scientific daring – might prove the home in which my own contentious ideas could flourish. At the university in Wittenberg I met a man who boasted that the Emperor had paid him a salary of three hundred silver thalers for a wholly unoriginal treatise on the music of the spheres; what might this singular prince offer if I could present to him my theory of an infinite universe, free of the confinement of the Fixed Stars, filled with other suns and other worlds? At the very least, I hoped my publications on this subject might not land me in as much trouble here as they had elsewhere in Europe. But there was still the matter of the letter I carried inside my doublet; it pricked me with unease each time I felt it crackle against my side as I moved. I had not told Besler about the letter, and had done my best to hide my apprehension; it seemed wiser to keep him in ignorance.

Towards four o'clock we crested a ridge above the city and the sight caused my breath to catch in my throat, so that I drew my horse to a halt to take in the vista ahead. After so many days' hard riding, I could scarcely believe we had reached our destination: Golden Prague spread out before us, more striking even than the engravings I had seen in Germany. A forest of spires and pinnacles filling the valley, from the ramparts of the great castle on its outcrop of rock, dominated by the tower of St Vitus Cathedral, down through the grand timber houses of the Lesser Town on the slope facing the plain, all the way to the narrow, crowded streets and bell towers of the Old and New Towns across the river. A sharp east wind herded drifts of cloud across a pale sky; the city glimmered in the low sun of late winter, that threshold season that only exists in these northern countries, when spring is not yet on the horizon but offers small intimations of her coming. Through the centre of the city, the wide, gleaming Vltava curved its path, the arches of its ancient Stone Bridge clearly visible from our vantage point. They would have removed the body by now, I guessed, though we were too distant to make out such detail.

'I prophesy,' Besler announced grandly, sweeping his hand from west to east to take in the wide reach of the city below, 'that within a week all of Prague will know the name of Giordano Bruno.'

I gave him a brief smile. 'Careful what you wish for, Besler.'

'Nonsense,' he said with the blithe confidence of youth. 'This city is the very place for your ideas to blossom. It's your destiny. And the Emperor Rudolf was born to be your patron. Your reputation will be made here, you'll see.'

This was more or less what my English friend John Dee had insisted in his letters over the past year as he urged me to join him here, and yet, as his assurances grew ever more confident, so my unnamed doubt deepened. Until Dee's last, enigmatic message a month ago, talking of a fear he dared not commit to ink and paper, urging me to come and find him with all haste. I had havered for a fortnight, knowing Dee's tendency to see conspiracies and persecution where none existed. It was then that I had received the other letter, from England, and made up my mind to depart the next day.

'Of course, they do say the Emperor is as mad as a basket of snakes,' Besler added, sounding more circumspect.

'My ideal patron, as you say. Listen, if I want cheap fortune-telling I can go to one of the booths in the Old Town Square. I hear the place is heaving with soothsayers and card readers ready to promise me long life and riches for a few pennies. Make yourself useful – explain our business to those men.'

'Yes, Maestro.'

I watched him as he rode on ahead to the imposing gatehouse in the city wall, where two sentries regarded our approach with a mixture of boredom and suspicion. Besler's mother was Czech and he spoke the language fluently; it was one of the reasons I had agreed to take him along with me on this journey. The others were equally practical: the boy had money, he was diligent and uncomplaining and had offered his services as my assistant with no expectation of being paid in coin, knowing that any such demand was beyond my means. Altogether the perfect clerk for an itinerant philosopher with a secret purpose. Set against this, he asked incessant questions the way a child would, had little sense of when to preserve a diplomatic silence, and the lack of remuneration left the exact status of our relationship blurry at best; I did not feel at liberty to command him.

For all that, I thought, more generously, I had grown unexpectedly fond of Besler in the past two years since he had presented himself at my door in Wittenberg and announced his intention of becoming my student. 'Disciple' was how he had put it, but I had firmly discouraged any suggestion that I was attempting to convert the undergraduates to my ideas; the authorities were watching me closely enough as it was. He wanted me to teach him my memory system; I feared it was a trap. But in time I discovered that young Besler – whose parents had christened him Hieronymus; the Lutherans have a cruel sense of humour – possessed a sharp intellect and a sincere hunger to understand the mysteries of the cosmos and our place in it. He was also one of those rare people born with unflagging good humour and optimism, which worked as an antidote to my more melancholic tendencies and was welcome in a travelling companion; no amount of bad roads, tired horses, surly innkeepers or obstructive guards could dampen Besler's enthusiasm not merely for our destination, but for every mile of the journey. Officially he was at Wittenberg to study medicine, and had taken to heart the dictum of the great alchemist-physician Paracelsus that a doctor must also be a traveller. This was the first time he had set foot outside the German lands; consequently everything was relentlessly exciting and worthy of remark. It was often a relief when he fell asleep at night.

I watched him now as he engaged in animated debate with the sentries, turning and pointing in my direction. I did not like the sceptical expressions on their faces; I reached into my saddlebag for my letters of recommendation from the university. Besler had begged to accompany me to Prague; he was desperate

8

to see the city and I had agreed because two men are less vulnerable on the road than one alone. Now I hoped I was not leading him into danger. The reports of this murder had done nothing to ease my fears on that score. Zikmund Bartos had been a sometime associate and rival of my friend John Dee. His brutal death cast a worrying light on Dee's recent silence.

One of the guards beckoned me over and addressed me in German with a thick Czech accent.

'You. This one says you are from Italy?'

'That's right. Nola, near Naples. But these past ten years I have lived in England, France, Switzerland and Germany.'

He did not look impressed. Instead he took my letters and affected to examine them closely, though I doubted he could read. 'You move around a lot, then. On the run from something?'

I smoothed my expression. He could not possibly know.

'I am a scholar. I travel between the great courts and universities of Europe to broaden my work.'

'Huh. One of these alchemists, are you?'

'No,' I said, affronted.

'My master Doctor Giordano Bruno is a respected philosopher and the greatest expert on the art of memory in all Europe.' Besler drew himself up indignantly on my behalf. 'His many books are printed in diverse languages across Christendom. His fame has reached the ear of the Emperor Rudolf himself.'

The guard glanced from me to Besler, an eyebrow raised. He had evidently presumed that the young man with the expensive clothes and the better horse was master here, and I some faithful tutor or retainer; he would not be the first to make that mistake. He regarded me narrowly, as if assessing whether I warranted such extravagant praise, before looking back to my letter.

'Lucky for you, then. Dangerous place for those who toy with magic these days.'

'So I have heard. Have they arrested anyone?'

The soldier laughed. 'Don't know what it's like where you're from, but the law doesn't move that fast in Prague. Find someone who wants to kill an alchemist? You may as well round up all his fellows. They'd cut one another's throats or put a hex on their dearest friend soon as look at him. Where do you lodge tonight?'

'With Dr Thaddeus Hajek, in Bethlehem Square.' I hoped this was still true; in the light of Dee's silence, my first steps in the city now seemed uncertain.

'The Emperor's own physician,' Besler chimed in. The guard's mouth twitched minutely. He looked up at me.

'Catholic, are you?'

'Dr Bruno believes—'

'Besler.' I shot him a sharp look. This was not the time to attempt a summary of my thoughts on religion; I had spent the past two years in Germany attempting to set them out clearly in a book, and was still no closer to completing it. 'I was baptised Catholic, yes.'

The guard grunted again and made a show of looking at my papers once more before handing them back to me. 'Good. You're in the domain of the Holy Roman Emperor now. Mind you keep the peace.' He handed the letters back and waved us on our way. As we passed under the gate, the other guard called out something in Czech. I did not understand the words, except one, but I caught the tone of his voice and his grating laughter.

'What did he say?'

Besler dipped his head. 'He said, "Watch out for the Golem".'

We rode along a broad thoroughfare, wide and smooth enough for carts and carriages and lined on each side by handsome timbered houses of three or four storeys, each with the steeply pointed gables I had grown used to in northern Europe. To our left, green parkland rose above the streets on the slope of a hill fringed by woodland and topped by an observatory tower; birdsong carried in the cold air. Ahead, more church steeples needled skywards; not for nothing was Prague known as 'the City of a Hundred Spires'. This quarter – called the Lesser Town – appeared well-kept, the streets swept clean of refuse and ordure, despite this being the main road into the city from the west, so that the wealthy inhabitants of these grand houses did not have to step in filth every time they set foot outside their door.

The road opened out after a few hundred yards into a wide square overshadowed by a tall church of dark stone. Arcades with pillars like a monastic cloister surrounded the square on three sides, set up as shops and stalls selling all manner of goods from leather bags to jewellery and swathes of colourful fabric. Here we turned right and directed our horses ahead towards the turrets of the Stone Bridge gatehouse.

'They say the Emperor Rudolf keeps a lion as a pet in his menagerie, and it eats out of his hand, and a soothsayer has prophesied that if the creature dies, the Emperor's death will follow close behind, so it is treated like a prince of the realm,' Besler informed me as the street grew narrower, overshadowed by high buildings, and the horses' shoes rang on the cobbles.

'I have heard as much.'

'They also say,' he continued, after a moment's pause, 'that in the Great Hall at the castle, the Emperor has commissioned an iron door knocker in the shape of a naked man and woman, and when you knock, it looks as if she is taking his cockstand in her mouth.'

'Is that so?' It did not surprise me that Besler had noted such reports; like all young men who lack experience with women, it was his obsession. I was fortunate that, thanks to his medical studies, he had seen enough of the consequences of a hasty tumble in the stews to act as a deterrent; his fascination was largely theoretical and I had not, so far, had to save him from being fleeced in a brothel.

'I hope we get to see it,' he said, eager as a pup. 'And you know he has the greatest collection of erotic paintings in Christendom. All naked goddesses and fruit. And a book of

Italian prints showing men and women going to it in all the positions you can think of.'

I smiled, wondering how many Besler would be able to think of – three at most, I guessed – but he was lost in his reverie. 'The Emperor's galleries are rightly famous,' I said, instead. 'He brings artists from all over Europe under his patronage. Perhaps you may get to view some of these paintings.'

'Imagine! And there's a prison tower in the castle walls where you can hear the ghost of a young soldier playing the viol, though he died a hundred years ago, and a magic labyrinth in the castle gardens which the Emperor uses to test those who lay claim to the secrets of the universe, and if you cannot find your way out, you will be doomed to wander there for all eternity.'

'Where do you get this stuff, Besler?'

He bristled. 'From a fellow at Wittenberg who studied in Prague.'

'Studied tall tales in the taverns, at least.'

'Maestro.' Besler sounded reproachful. 'You told me yourself that the Emperor keeps the greatest scholars of forbidden knowledge at his court. There is nowhere in Europe more steeped in magic and occult lore. I thought this was why we came?'

I motioned to him to lower his voice. 'Some things should not be spoken of in the streets, Besler. Let us concentrate for now on finding the House of the Green Mound.'

We were forced to pull our caps down against the wind as we emerged from the shadow of the tower on to the Stone Bridge. I drew my horse to a standstill halfway across to take in the view along the Vltava to either side. On the far bank, to the south, three great wheels of a watermill turned steadily, with a mighty creaking; to the north, mounds of earth and the skeletal frames of cranes marked the saltpetre works along the shoreline. Gazing north-west I saw, behind the bulk of the castle on its promontory, a ridge of distant peaks etched hazily against the sky. It seemed months since we had crossed these, though in truth it was only a matter of days; the Golden City had felt like a far-off dream at times on those hard mountain passes, riding with one hand on our daggers and an eye always over our shoulder for wolves, bears or bandits. Now we were here, in the heart of it, and I hoped it would not turn to nightmare. Zikmund Bartos must once have believed he would find his fortune here, as did John Dee, and countless others. A brief shiver ran along my spine; Besler glanced at me with concern, but refrained from asking.

A small crowd had gathered at the downriver balustrade to peer over the side. I dismounted and handed the reins to Besler, before joining them. A man with exuberant grey moustaches gesticulated towards the river. On the other side of the parapet I could see, if I leaned far enough, rust-coloured stains against the mossy stonework. Though I could not understand the animated conversation, I edged my way into the group nonetheless.

'What happened here?' I asked, in German. I knew only a few words of Czech, though I had been assured that Prague was a Babel of different languages, and it would not be difficult to make myself understood. At the court of the Emperor – if and when I should find myself admitted to such heights – I would be able to rely on Latin, Spanish or even my native Italian, since many of Rudolf's favoured artists, musicians and court officials were my countrymen. But among the city's inhabitants, I had been advised to try German, a more formal and often more reliable common tongue in Bohemia than the multiple dialects of Czech.

'You have not heard?' the one with the moustache responded, incredulous. 'A man left hanging mutilated in this very spot for the crows to peck at. A guest of the Emperor! And no one saw or heard a thing – how can that be, I ask you?'

'Witchcraft,' muttered a plump goodwife in a white headscarf, crossing herself. 'That's what you get if you meddle with the Devil's work. One of his fellow wizards did for him with curses, you may be sure of it.'

13

'You talk through your arse, woman,' a stocky, bald man cut in, his lip curled in a sneer. 'It was thick fog over the river last night, that's how no one saw. Oh, there's devilry at work here, to be sure, but we all know who is responsible for this unchristian slaughter.' He turned without pointing, but his gaze was directed upriver, to the jumble of gabled roofs crammed together on the eastern bank, behind the saltpetre works. Again, I felt that twist of my gut; I had studied enough maps of Prague to know that he was indicating the Jewish quarter at the edge of the Old Town. The little crowd affirmed it with nods and murmurs and more signs of the cross, resuming their conversation in a dialect I could not understand.

I sprang back into the saddle and rode across the bridge with a bitter taste in my mouth, nudging my horse to a trot so that Besler had to catch up.

'Maestro? Do you think it is true, that the Jews have done this?'

'I think someone would like to make it look that way.'

'My father told me there were a lot of them in Prague,' he said in an uncertain voice.

'The second largest Jewish community in Europe. Whatever the Emperor Rudolf's faults, he can count this to his credit – he has shown by his laws of tolerance how people of all religions can live prosperously and peacefully as neighbours and respect one another's differences.' I suspected that this admirable legislation worked better in theory than practice, as the crowd on the bridge had implied, but I wanted to believe that proclaiming it might make it true, since it echoed my own philosophy. I turned and noted the small crease of anxiety between the boy's brows. 'Did your father suggest that this should be a cause for concern, then?'

He looked uncomfortable.

'It is only that, in Nuremberg, where I am from, the Jews were not well regarded.'

'Listen to me, Besler.' The sharpness in my tone made him sit up, startled. 'When I was younger than you are now, one

14

of the finest teachers I had in Naples was a rabbi. He was a great scholar of the Cabala and one of the wisest men I have known, to this day. If you have found anything of value in my books and my teaching, know that the best of my understanding came from him.'

He stared at me, his blue eyes wide with amazement. 'This was when you were a Dominican friar? How did they allow you to study with a rabbi?'

'They didn't. I met him in secret. No one knew he was a rabbi – he worked as a goldsmith and did not live openly as a Jew. His community had been expelled from the Kingdom of Naples long before, and those who were left changed their names and converted – at least outwardly. But he preserved the old knowledge, and it was my great good fortune to have learned more from him than all the luminaries of the Dominican order put together.'

Besler fell silent for an unusually long time after this. I could not tell whether he was impressed, or chastened, or silently composing his next letter to his severe Lutheran father back home.

We passed through the gate tower on the right bank and followed the curving street around the Jesuit College and into the heart of the Old Town. Here the atmosphere could not have been more of a contrast with the airy Lesser Town: tall, crooked buildings leaned in on either side, so that little daylight reached the cobbled alleys below; gateways of pitted stone gaped open to reveal murky courtyards; painted signs swung, creaking, in the breeze, showing all manner of fantastical creatures: unicorns, spiders, elephants, leopards and gryphons of every hue. All the houses had been decorated, either with grotesque stone carvings, their features erased by age, or with the ornamentation called *sgraffito*, geometrical and floral designs etched into the plasterwork. We passed a house with a niche on the first floor where a statue of the Madonna surveyed the street, her skin painted black as a Moorish woman's; Besler nearly fell off his horse craning his neck to see it. People watched us from under hoods or hat brims, leaning in doorways as we rode by, somehow more menacing for all their apparent nonchalance.

At length this street debouched into the wide expanse of the Old Town Square with its church and ancient clock tower. We stopped beneath the astronomical clock to gaze up at the dials with their fabled depictions of the planetary orbits and signs of the zodiac. Around the perimeter of the broad piazza, wooden booths had been erected and hordes of people shuffled between them seeking novelty, distracted by puppet plays, peddlers, fortune-tellers, card sharps and tricksters. A babble of music and shouting rose from the throng, so loud that I had to raise my voice in warning Besler to have a care for his saddlebags in the crowd.

There were poets for hire; jongleurs; artists who offered to sketch a likeness in charcoal; vendors of philtres, love-potions and salves of stag-horn jelly all crying their wares; a man playing a viol and another singing a plaintive folk song in an unfamiliar language. By the steps of the great twin-spired church of Our Lady Before Týn, a group parted to allow a tumbler to execute a series of back flips to a smattering of applause, while a woman in tight breeches stood on a wooden box and tipped her head back to swallow a sword whole, as children gasped and young men elbowed and pointed with lewd remarks. Painted girls in low bodices swayed at the fringes of the crowds, scanning for customers; a man in a tall conical hat bustled through a protesting knot of onlookers, pulled by two bull mastiffs dressed in ruffs and tiny scarlet doublets. The air smelled of hot wine and roasting chestnuts.

Besler's head swivelled in one direction, then another, his face alight with the wonder of it all, like a child given his first glimpse of the sea.

'Is it a special festival, do you think?' he asked, breathless with delight.

'I think it is just a Wednesday,' I said, smiling. 'Welcome to Prague.' I shook my head at an old woman thrusting bunches

16

of herbs up at me from a wooden basket; her insistence made the horse jittery and I jerked on his reins to turn him away, when a familiar cold sensation punctured my good spirits as surely as if a blade had been slipped against my skin. We were being watched. I twisted in the saddle, casting around with an eye practised at surveying crowds, but could see no one I recognised, no one who appeared to be paying us particular attention. And yet I knew I had not been mistaken; in all the years I spent on the run from the Inquisition and later, working undercover for the English government, I had sharpened these instincts for survival and learned to trust them. We had been followed, our arrival noted, and I did not think this would prove to our advantage.

'Come,' I called to Besler, who had allowed his horse to amble closer to the sword-swallower. 'We have strayed too far out of our way. Take the next street on the right, and keep your weapon close.'

He turned, surprised at the brusqueness in my voice. I knew he would have liked to linger and soak up the marvels, but that suspicion of a hostile presence observing us had darkened my mood. At our back the astronomical clock began tolling the hour of five, the mechanical figure of the skeleton striking his bell to remind onlookers that we had all moved a step closer to the grave, and I grew conscious of the need to find our lodgings before evening.

TWO

A narrow lane wound between timbered houses, and we followed its twists deeper into the heart of the Old Town, until we emerged into a smaller square and I recognised the distinctive twin pointed roofs of the Bethlehem Chapel to our left, just as Dee had described it in his letters. The House of the Green Mound was easily found on the opposite corner; even without the painted sign showing a bright emerald hill against a blue background, the alchemical and occult symbols decorating the plasterwork around the door would have given it away as the home of an alchemist unafraid to proclaim his art to the world.

'How long since you have seen Doctor Dee?' Besler asked as I dismounted and passed him my horse's reins.

'Five years. He will be sixty-one now. I hope he has learned to take care of his health, but I suspect he still drives himself as hard as he ever did.'

'They say he was the greatest scholar in England.'

'I have not met his match anywhere in Europe. Queen Elizabeth had appointed him her personal astrologer when I first knew him, though his talents extended to every branch of learning.'

'Then why did he leave her court?'

I hesitated. 'As you should know, Besler, those who pursue

knowledge by unorthodox means often arouse the suspicion of conservative minds. For Dee, the study of the heavens and the earth was not enough. He desired to look beyond.'

'Like us, Maestro.'

'In a sense. But Dee believed he could speak with angels. He should have kept this to himself, but he boasted too openly. You see how a man may be wise and foolish at the same time.' I gave him a wry smile. 'And clever men can be mulishly stubborn.'

'I have noticed,' Besler said pointedly. I chose to ignore this.

'Some among Elizabeth's ministers began to whisper against him, and she did not defend him as he would have wished. He felt he might be more welcome here, at Rudolf's court, so he left before the Queen could banish him. Dr Hajek has been a great supporter of his work, I understand, and brought him to the attention of the Emperor.'

I thought back to the last time I had seen Dee, in London, in the autumn of 1583. He and I had been entangled in a messy business involving the murder of one of Queen Elizabeth's maids of honour, which we had been lucky to escape with our lives. How much had changed in our fortunes since then! I thought it best not to mention this to Besler; he did not need to know about that part of my history, when I had earned a wage working undercover for Sir Francis Walsingham, Elizabeth's spymaster, and found myself – never entirely by choice – charged with tracking down killers or conspirators against the Queen. I suspected it might lend me a greater glamour in Besler's eyes; he was already impressed by the fact that I had been excommunicated as a heretic and escaped the Inquisition in my homeland. He admired rebellion, aspired to it, but was cursed with a naturally conformist character; he wanted too much to please his elders. In any case, I had left that life behind to pursue my writing, and had no wish to be reminded of it. So I told myself, anyway. I straightened my doublet and felt the letter crumple against the fabric of my shirt.

'And now Dr Dee has the Emperor's ear, he will recommend you in turn,' Besler said, as if this were established fact.

'Let us hope so,' I muttered as I walked up the short path to raise the heavy brass knocker of Dr Hajek's door. Dee's last, cryptic letter to me was addressed from here. Perhaps the Emperor's physician would be able to throw some light on my friend's mysterious silence. Dee had spoken warmly in his letters of Hajek's hospitality; I hoped we might at least find food and rest at his hearth. I could feel the day's ride in my legs and back, and my gut had begun to cramp with hunger.

I knocked repeatedly, and thought I saw a drape twitch at an upper casement, but otherwise there was no response. I banged again, and rapped with my knuckles on the window glass, until at length the door cracked open an inch and a woman in a white cap squinted out at me.

'Good evening, madam,' I began in my best formal German, sweeping off my hat. I had no idea if she was wife or house-keeper, but a show of respect would serve either way. 'I am Dr Giordano Bruno, a friend of John Dee. I believe Dr Hajek is expecting us?'

A flicker of recognition registered in her eyes, before they narrowed further.

'We know no one of that name.' She made to push the door shut but I sprang forward and wedged my boot in the gap.

'Dr John Dee, the Englishman – I know he was here until recently. Has he changed lodgings? Perhaps you could tell me where I might find him?'

'I told you – we do not know this person, and we are not expecting any visitors. Please leave.'

'May I see Dr Hajek? He has heard of me, I am certain.' Even as I spoke, I felt wingbeats of dread rise in my chest; what could Dee have done, that Hajek's household should deny any knowledge of him?

'The doctor is at the castle.'

I felt the pressure of the door against my foot.

'When will he return? I can wait.'

'No idea. They keep strange hours up there. You would be wasting your time.'

'Madam.' I tried to put as much patience as I could muster into my voice. 'I have ridden for a fortnight from Wittenberg with my young assistant' – I indicated Besler, who widened his eyes in a picture of hopeful innocence as if we had rehearsed it – 'at the invitation of Dr Dee, your houseguest, who wrote to tell me that Dr Hajek looked forward to receiving us. It will be a much greater waste of my time if I do not see your master. If we cannot wait for him here—'

'You cannot, sir.'

'—then we will look for food at the tavern across the square until he returns. You will pass on the message, I trust?'

'If you do not leave our threshold, I will be forced to scream and the neighbours will call for the watch.'

She leaned harder against the door. Her weight was probably equal to mine; I decided not to fight.

'Dr Bruno – you will be sure to give him my name? I promise you, I will keep trying until I find him at home,' I called as the door slammed, leaving me standing on the step like a fool. I looked up at the elegant façade of the house with a plummeting sensation; what if Dr Hajek was at home already, and had given instructions that I was not to be admitted? But that made no sense – what harm had I done Hajek, except to be associated with John Dee? Perhaps that was reason enough now, though I could not fathom it without first finding my old friend.

'Come on – let's eat something and we'll sort this out when we have rested and our minds are sharper,' I said to Besler, leading my horse across the square, where a creaking tavern sign showed a black spider sprawled on its web. He followed behind, the furrow once again etched in his brow. In his unquestioning devotion, he had thought my name would open doors instantly in Prague; he had evidently not considered any other outcome.

'There's been a misunderstanding, that's all,' I said, clapping

21

his shoulder as he dismounted. It was rare that I found myself the one encouraging Besler out of despondency. 'We'll see Hajek soon, have no fear.'

The Spider had a gate wide enough for carts at the side; we led the horses through into the yard, where Besler produced his purse and we passed them to the care of an ostler to be fed and watered. We took a piss in a stinking mound of straw in one corner alongside a couple of other men, and followed them through a wooden door at the rear of the inn into a smoky tap-room.

'But then where is Dr Dee?' Besler asked me as we looked around for a free table. He had not spoken unusually loudly, but it seemed that a tremor passed through the room at the name, though no one made a show of regarding us. And yet I experienced the same needling unease as I had felt in the Old Town Square; that our visit and our conversation were not passing unnoticed.

The Spider was not among the best taverns we had visited on our journey, but neither was it the worst: plain, busy, with more or less clean reeds strewn over a stone floor and blackened beams so low that Besler hit his head. The food and beer I could see on the tables looked passable and the men who huddled over their bowls were dressed respectably enough; I guessed them to be guildsmen for the most part. At one end a large inglenook fireplace belched smoke into the room; the benches nearest its warmth were occupied, so I steered Besler towards a chillier corner by the door and left him to discuss food with the serving girl when she approached.

While we waited for her to return, I leaned across the table. 'Let us speak Latin here.'

Besler looked surprised. 'Do you fear we are spied on? By whom?' He twisted around, swivelling his head left and right to take in the rest of the customers with an accusing glare, drawing plenty of attention as he did so.

'Shh, don't stare. I don't know. But it seems John's name is not the golden key to the city we expected. Some trouble has

22

found him, or else he has caused it, and it would be prudent for us to discover the nature of it before we go around proclaiming ourselves his friends. I hope to Christ it has nothing to do with this murder.' I should not have voiced this last of my fears aloud; Besler's expression froze in alarm.

'But why should you think that? How could they be connected?'

'You're right.' I drew my hands across my face and leaned my elbows on the table. 'Ignore me, I'm tired and my mind leaps to jumbled conclusions.'

'Dr Hajek will see you, surely?' He picked at the quicks of his nails, as I had seen him do before when he was nervous.

'He is our best hope of uncovering the mystery, certainly. If that harridan has not taken it upon herself to guard his door from anyone associated with Dee.' I rolled my shoulders back and leaned against the wall; the aches of the day's riding had grown more insistent. 'But until we can reach him, it seems we must fend for ourselves. When we have eaten, go out and ask around for a halfway decent inn for tonight. One with proper sheets and no lice.'

Besler grimaced, recalling the village where we had stopped the previous night. 'Let us hope they have at least heard of such luxuries in Prague.' He gestured to the ceiling. 'I suppose they have rooms here? You could keep an eye on Hajek's house too, if we take one facing the square. And they have already stabled the horses.'

I shook my head. 'Not here. I don't have a good feeling about this place.'

Besler whipped around again as if he expected to see assassins in the doorway.

'We're too conspicuous here, right by Hajek's house,' I explained. 'We passed a place on the street from the Old Town Square, the sign of the Unicorn. Try there. And if you must give a name, use yours, not mine.' But my name was already known in Prague, I thought; by the soldier on the gate, and the narrow-eyed woman at Hajek's door. I had seen no reason to hide myself here, since I believed I had been invited precisely because of my reputation; too late, I began to think I should have been more cautious.

'I don't understand, Maestro. I thought we were to be Dr Hajek's honoured guests – now you are behaving as if the city is full of enemies.'

I rubbed at the stubble on my chin. 'Here is something you will learn, Besler, if you are determined to read the secret book of nature against all the commands of the Church – every city in Christendom is full of potential enemies. And another thing – a man's fortunes can turn on the spin of a coin, especially when it comes to the favours of princes. It always pays to be careful.' All the more so if you happen to be an excommunicated Dominican heretic known to the Catholic Church as a Protestant spy, I could have added, but the boy looked troubled enough.

The girl brought a stew of white sausage and beans, with coarse dark bread and a jug of beer. It was savoury and filling, if oily, and there was little conversation while we shovelled it down, as we had not eaten since breaking our fast at dawn. Besler finished first, wiped his hands on a kerchief, put on his hat and ducked through the low doorway in search of a lodging for the night. I called for another pot of beer, rested my head against the wall and allowed my eyes to fall shut as I tried to order my thoughts and consider how best to proceed.

I must have drifted into sleep, my muscles still carrying the echo of the horse's gait; a movement disturbed me and when I blinked awake, a man sat opposite in the place Besler had vacated, an urgent look on his face. I started, my right hand instinctively moving to my belt where I kept a dagger of Damascus steel under my riding cloak, but the stranger held up a palm in a discreet gesture. His clothes were good quality beneath a fur-trimmed coat, and he wore his reddish beard close-cropped. The quick glance to either side told me he did not wish our encounter to attract attention.

'Forgive me – I did not mean to startle you,' he said in

English, with the accent of a native speaker. I sat up; it was some time since I had been addressed directly in that language. I thought again of the letter I carried, and said nothing, while I waited for him to reveal more of his hand.

He shifted in his seat and leaned across the table, his voice lower.

'You were speaking of Dr Dee, I think, you and your friend?' When I merely raised an eyebrow, he gave an embarrassed half-laugh. 'My apologies again – but you must realise that Latin is not the most inaccessible language in this city.'

I looked around the tap-room. 'I clearly underestimated the clientele.'

'I know who you are,' he said.

'Then you have the advantage of me,' I replied evenly. 'Tell me, is English any more private in here?'

He gave a quick, practised glance over his shoulder. 'For now. My name is Lawrence Overton. I'm a merchant. I import goods from Bohemia and the German territories, and convey them on to London.' He paused to allow me to understand his meaning, with a look of heavy complicity, but I was not ready to bite yet.

'Have you been following me since I arrived, Master Overton?'

'What? No, not I.' He appeared puzzled by the suggestion.

'So finding me here is pure coincidence?'

'Not quite. I knew you would appear at the House of the Green Mound sooner or later. I have been watching Hajek's for the past few days.'

'You must be a man of leisure. And how did you know this?'

'I was told by our mutual friend.' He reached inside his doublet and I tensed again, fearing he would draw a weapon, but he brought out only a scrap of paper, which he pushed across the table to me under the palm of his hand. I overlaid it with my own and slid the item into my lap, not taking my eyes off his; this was either an elaborate trap or a glimmer of salvation, at least in the short term.

I had expected a note; instead there was only a single mark on the paper.

ㅿ

The astrological sign for Jupiter. I held his look for a heartbeat longer, to make certain, then gave him a terse nod before folding the paper and holding it to the candle flame. We understood one another. He exhaled with apparent relief.

'So you trade in paper and ink, Master Overton?'

'In a manner of speaking.' He offered a tentative smile, and I responded in kind. The symbol for Jupiter was the mark I used to sign my dispatches for Sir Francis Walsingham when I sent him intelligence, first from the French embassy in London, and later from Paris. Merchants made ideal couriers, since they had legitimate reasons to be continually crossing borders. 'Though cloth is my principal business,' he added. 'And I always make time to dine with my friend Dr Dee whenever I am in Prague.'

I nodded again. His words confirmed what I had already guessed from the letter I carried: that Dee had been sending back secret reports to Walsingham from the Emperor's court. Fear pulled my gut tight; had he been found out? Might he, under duress, have given my name as a fellow informer? I reprimanded myself; if Dee had talked, this Overton would not be walking around Prague a free man.

'I had expected to dine with him tonight,' I said, careful to keep my tone neutral.

'I had the same hope last week when I arrived,' Overton whispered, pulling at his moustache. 'But there has been no sign of him. He has not been seen in Prague for at least three weeks, it seems. He appears to have vanished from the earth.'

I leaned in. 'Have you made enquiries?'

Overton drew himself up, ruffled. 'Naturally. I could find out nothing at Hajek's house – whenever I called, I was told the doctor was out and that Dee was no longer there. And from John's acquaintances – I would not call them his friends, exactly . . .' here he paused for weight, with a wry twist of his mouth. 'I mean the alchemists who drink in the taverns on the castle hill, in the Lesser Town – from them I learned mainly that he was not much missed. They felt he set himself above them, you see. It is true, of course, that John did regard himself as a great adept, and everyone else a mere journeyman, toiling in the foothills of knowledge. He did not go out of his way to make friends among his colleagues.' He sighed and shook his head, as if to dismiss the folly of them all. 'But I did discover one thing that may be useful.' Crouching forward, he lowered his voice. 'There was one other among Rudolf's alchemists who considered himself Dee's equal in the occult arts.'

'Zikmund Bartos,' I murmured, and again sensed a kind of frisson in the room, as if someone had attuned his ears to our conversation, though a quick glance assured me that no one appeared to be watching us.

Overton nodded. 'You have heard, then. Who himself met a most unpleasant end during this past night. But the alchemists told me that the day before John disappeared, he had had a public argument with this Bartos in the castle courtyard, in front of the cathedral, where a dozen witnesses heard Bartos accuse John of theft.'

'What was he supposed to have stolen?'

'His life's work, Bartos was heard to say. The holy grail. Which the alchemists have taken to mean the greatest prize of their art – the Philosopher's Stone.'

'So Bartos is supposed to have discovered the secret that has eluded alchemists and seekers for centuries, which John then stole from him – to pass off as his own work, is that the idea?'

'Exactly. You sound as if you find it as improbable as I do.'

I smiled. 'Firstly, I don't believe the Philosopher's Stone is something that can be discovered in a laboratory by distilling schnapps and sheep's urine, or whatever the latest formula dictates, but – more importantly – John would never lower himself to stealing another man's work. He may be susceptible

27

to vanity in some things, but he has an old-fashioned sense of honour and pride when it comes to his reputation.'

'I believe you are right on both counts.' Overton signalled to the serving girl to bring him a pot of beer. 'Except that – while I do not pretend to understand the rivalries among the alchemists, I have the impression many of them would sell their own children if it meant a chance to win the Emperor's esteem. Who knows what John might have been driven to if he feared losing his patron's favour?'

'I still can't believe he would stoop to theft. Besides, he was in good standing with the Emperor, the last I heard from him. Unless you know different?'

Overton shook his head. 'No, but I have not been to Prague for near two months. Much can change in that time when it comes to princes and their favours. This Bartos was said to be a protégé, and look how it has served him.'

'True. How did you know to look for me?'

He dropped his voice to a whisper. 'I took the correspondence from Dee to Walsingham's usual courier the last time I was in London. This was a month ago. The next day Master Secretary sent a fast rider with an urgent response for Dee. I was not due in Prague for another few weeks, but at Walsingham's instruction I came directly here – at the expense of my own business interests, I should add.' He looked briefly piqued. 'I was told that if for any reason Dee could not be found, I was to seek out the Italian Dr Bruno, who would shortly be arriving in Prague, and had ever been a loyal friend to England.' He held out his hands, as if he had nothing more to hide. 'And here we are.'

So Walsingham had assumed I would jump at his command even before the ink was dry on his letter to me, I thought. Of course he had.

'I suppose you do not know what was in the original letter from Dee to Walsingham, that caused such an urgent response?'

Overton gave me a stern look. 'It's considered safer if I do not know the contents of what I carry. Not that such protestations would protect me, mind you, if anyone were to ask.' He averted his eyes and we fell silent, both thinking of the risks we ran in conveying secrets across Europe, and how we might be encouraged to give them up, if discovered. I was inclined to trust Overton; his words chimed with the letter in my doublet, that had also arrived by fast rider and hastened my journey to Prague. It must have been dispatched the same day as the merchant was sent to find Dee or me.

I turned my tankard between my hands. 'Whatever it was, it alarmed Walsingham enough for him to send us both in search of Dee with all speed. I find it hard to believe that was anything to do with the Philosopher's Stone.'

Overton glanced over his shoulder. 'I would rather not know. I am only relieved to have found you – now I can return to Leipzig and my neglected accounts.'

'Was there something—?'

He shook his head minutely to pre-empt the question; his right hand slipped inside his voluminous coat and I felt a tap on my leg under the table. I concentrated on refilling our mugs while my other hand took the proffered paper and tucked it into my sleeve, out of sight.

'For Dee, if you find him,' Overton said. 'If not, I leave it to your discretion. I'll be away at first light tomorrow.'

'Will you not wait for a reply?'

'I have been kicking my heels here for a week already, waiting for one or other of you. My instructions were to leave the business in your hands.' He stood, wrapping his fur collar tighter, and gave me a long look. 'God go with you. Here – for the beer.' He threw a fat leather purse down on the table. I attempted to protest but he merely shook his head again and touched a finger to his temple in a farewell salute. I stowed the money – my expenses from Walsingham, I presumed – inside my doublet and sat for a long moment, staring into my mug, trying to make sense of the encounter. I was eager to read the letter Overton had passed under the table, though sensible enough to realise I must wait for the safety of a private room somewhere. Lost in my thoughts, I only half-noticed a slight man with his hat pulled down around his face rise from a table near the fire and slip out; I started and sat up as the door to the yard banged shut behind him, but I had not seen him clearly. Besides, there was no reason to think that his sudden departure had anything to do with Overton; I reminded myself that I must not fall into the habit of jumping at shadows.

Bells rang out from a nearby church, marking the hour; Prague was not a city where you could ever forget the passing of time. I ordered more bread, and the girl brought it with a lump of strong-flavoured sheep's cheese; I picked at both, watching the door, willing Besler to come back while I attempted to eavesdrop on the conversations around me. But they were conducted mainly in Czech, it seemed, in dialects that eluded me, and this increased my frustration; I have always had a facility for languages and made a point of trying to learn how to speak to people in their own tongue wherever my travels have taken me. I caught only the word 'Golem', spoken by a man huddled on a stool near the hearth; his companion hushed him immediately and both made the sign of the cross. It seemed the stories were spreading fast.

By the next tolling of bells some half-hour later, Besler had still not returned, and I was beginning to worry. I should not have sent him off alone into a strange city, with his trusting face and full purse; the boy would be a gift to those who preyed on inexperienced travellers, and what would I tell his father? I left coins on the table for the food, wrapped the remains of the bread and cheese in a kerchief, and called the serving girl over to explain, in a low voice, that if my young friend should return alone, she must tell him to wait there for me. Her German was halting, but I hoped she had understood. My departure seemed to provoke little interest among the remaining drinkers; one or two raised their heads as I opened the door, but only to mutter about the draught.

Outside, the chill air stung my face and caught in my throat with a metallic taste after the warmth of the inn; I breathed deep, rubbing my hands. Dusk had settled over the square, plunging corners and gaps between houses into blackness and throwing strange shadows along the walls. Overhead the sky was darkening to a deep, clear indigo, pinpricks of stars already visible. Lamps had been lit in the upper windows of Hajek's house opposite; I wondered if this signalled that someone was now home, or if the housekeeper was merely going about her duties. I walked briskly across to the lane that we had ridden through from the Old Town Square, in search of the inn I had mentioned to Besler. Here, between the high walls, darkness closed in fast; the spring had been cold so far and an early frost was beginning to harden the rutted mud underfoot, so that my boots crunched as if over glass. After a few minutes the lane narrowed further and I had still not passed the sign of the Unicorn. I glanced up at the houses on each side, beginning to doubt my direction. Perhaps I had mistaken the street; these gabled fronts with their leaded windows all looked the same in the half-light. I pulled my cloak tighter, thinking of how Besler would laugh if he knew I had managed to lose myself within a few yards of the inn – the master of memory misremembering which street he had taken an hour earlier. The lane curved to the left, almost completely sunk in shadow by now, and I caught a tang of river silt on the breeze, which made me pause. I should not have been heading for the Vltava; it was clear that I had taken the wrong path. I turned to retrace my steps, and jumped to see a man standing in front of me, twenty paces away, blocking the street; he must have been following close behind. As I reached for my dagger I sensed a minute disturbance in the air at my back and by pure instinct born of years on the road I feinted to one side, not quickly enough to dodge the blow that landed on my left shoulder from behind, though at least it missed my head. I cried out, almost knocked off-balance, and wheeled around to see my assailant raise a wooden stave to strike a second time. I dropped to the ground and rolled so that his weapon swung through empty air; the force he had thrown behind it caused him to stagger forward, giving me time to draw my knife and lunge at the nearest part of him. I drove the blade through the flesh above his knee, but he was a thick, bullish man built of solid muscle; though he roared, it was more in rage than pain and the wound did not seem to have slowed him. He loomed over me; I aimed a kick towards his groin but he anticipated the move, catching my ankle in one meaty hand as he brought his foot down on my wrist and ground the bone into the dirt until, against my will, my fingers loosened around the handle of my knife and I heard it fall from my grip.

At this, the second man, the one who had been blocking my way back to the square, approached and crouched beside me. He was small and nimble, though, like the man who kept his boot pressed against my arm, this one also wore a cap pulled down tight over his ears and a kerchief tied around the lower half of his face. Above it I could see he had a distinctive scar running from the corner of his right eye along his cheek. His eyes glittered blackly as they met mine for an instant, while he scrabbled for the purse at my belt. Dull relief washed through me; they were no more than common robbers, picking off a foolish lone traveller in the hope of a few coins.

'Take it,' I said in German, thinking only to get out with as little damage as possible; if I let him have the purse I carried openly, he might not search further. He kept his gaze fixed on me as he untied the strings, rifled through the contents with growing impatience, then tossed it on the ground with a sound of contempt.

'No more,' I said, holding up my free hand in a gesture of surrender. The pain in my right wrist ebbed away as I began to lose feeling; the bigger man increased the pressure of his foot until I cried out. 'It's all I have, I swear.'

The smaller man hesitated, then swiftly patted me down along each side of my torso until he found something that piqued his interest; I saw him glance up and exchange a brief nod with his companion, and in that moment I jabbed my left hand up and poked a finger into his eye. He howled in outrage,

32

clutching his face, spitting '*Hijo de puta!*' through his teeth, but before I could move, his comrade had snatched up my knife and held it against my throat. I froze, while the man with the scar – one eye now screwed shut – tore at the laces of my doublet, all the while swearing at me in Spanish under his breath. I knew then that my first suspicion had been correct; I had been followed, and these men were not here for my money, but the papers I carried inside my clothes. Had someone watched Overton pass me the letter in the Spider? I thought of the man who had slipped away, his hat pulled down, and cursed myself for not taking greater care. Now I was in danger of losing not only Walsingham's money but the letter Overton had entrusted to me, that urgent message from Walsingham to Dee, without even learning its contents, which might hold the key to my friend's disappearance among God knew what other confidences.

I lay unmoving, feeling the tip of my own knife pressing against the skin of my throat every time I swallowed, trying to keep my breathing steady while my mind raced through any possibility of saving the letters, as the Spaniard slipped his hand inside my doublet. I could come up with nothing that would not immediately forfeit my life. As I lay weighing up my potential moves, the sound of approaching hooves clattered across the hard ground and the wavering light of a lantern picked out the alarmed expression in the eyes of my attacker as he straightened to see the interruption. Twisting my head to the side, from my prone position I could make out only the figure of a man in a broad-brimmed hat astride the horse. I couldn't see if he was armed, but he shouted a command in Czech in a voice used to being obeyed; in response, the scarred Spaniard pulled a knife from his own belt and stood, pointing it at the newcomer. From where I lay, I could see the light glinting along the edge of its curved blade. I tensed, fearing that this interference would only make my situation worse, but before I could protest, the most extraordinary intervention occurred. The man on the horse raised his arm and with a smooth, graceful movement, lobbed an object towards us. I saw a brief glitter in the lantern light as it described an arc through the air, before it landed to our left with a tinkle of breaking glass and a violent explosion of green smoke and flame that caused my assailants to jump back and cry out to Santa Maria. In the commotion, I snatched up my knife and heaved myself to my feet, rubbing my bruised wrist.

The two men had partially recovered their wits; the larger one lunged at me, while the smaller took a step towards the horseman, who calmly raised both hands above his head and muttered an incantation in no language I recognised, as tongues of flame appeared to leap from the ends of his fingers. My two attackers exchanged a look, then fled into the night, crossing themselves, the smaller man yelping about *brujería*.

THREE

I thought I knew what I had seen; nonetheless, I sheathed my dagger and limped towards my rescuer warily as he sprang down from his horse and removed his hat with a curt bow, revealing a weathered face framed by sandy curls receding from a high forehead, wide-set eyes and a neat, full mouth above a pointed beard.

'I see *you* have no fear of witchcraft,' he said in Italian. I stared at him, and he laughed. 'Party tricks. Basic chymical reactions, though colourful enough to fool children and simpletons. But you know this, of course. Are you injured?'

I tried to flex my right wrist and winced. Was this another trap? Impossible to know, but he had saved me for now, and since he addressed me in my own language, I replied in kind. 'I've had worse. They caught me off-guard.'

'Did they get what they wanted?'

I watched him, not wanting to give myself away, as I began to lace my doublet, adjusting my clothes so that the papers inside stayed hidden. His eyes followed my fingers; I was suddenly conscious of their tell-tale tremble in the aftermath of the shock. 'I think they left my purse.'

He stepped forward and retrieved it from where they had thrown it aside, picking up the handful of coins that had spilled. 'No interest in your money, then. They must have had clear instructions.' He nodded as he spoke, as if confirming a theory of his own, peering into the gloom where the two men had disappeared towards the river. 'We should not waste time loitering here.'

I glanced behind. 'I had not thought these were such dangerous streets.'

'I'm afraid every street is dangerous for you,' he said. 'Come – you'd better let me look at that wrist, you'll need something for the swelling. We'll do it inside. You can sit on the horse if you prefer?'

'I'm sorry, I don't— who *are* you?' I shook my head at him, confused.

'My apologies, I assumed you knew me. Thaddeus Hajek.' He jerked his head down in an approximation of a bow. 'And you are Doctor Bruno. I've been expecting you.' He grasped me by the shoulders and placed a brusque kiss on both cheeks. I bit down a cry as he squeezed the bruise where the cosh had landed.

'But – how did you know to find me here? I was lost—'

'Magic.' He looked at my expression and let loose a hearty laugh. 'I only just missed you. My housekeeper, Greta, told me you had called, the girl at the Spider said you had gone in search of your servant, he told me you had not appeared at the Unicorn. Together we reasoned you had taken a wrong turn. Not such a good memory for directions, eh?' He chuckled again.

I acknowledged the joke with a tired smile. 'Besler is safe, then?'

'He waits for you at my house. Come. You are better off on foot, I think, with that shoulder.'

'He had a stick,' I rubbed the bruise. 'They came out of nowhere.'

'I doubt that,' he said grimly, leading his horse, but he did not elaborate.

'I did not hope to find you,' I said after a while, as we neared the lights of Bethlehem Square once more. 'Your housekeeper was keen to keep you from us. When I mentioned Dr Dee—'

He held up a hand to pre-empt me. 'She is overly protective

of my privacy, I'm afraid – I am never sure if she has appointed herself a substitute for my mother or my bodyguard. Though I cannot fault her loyalty – the world is suspicious of progress, as you know well, and many good Christian women would not keep house for an alchemist, for fear of their reputation or their immortal soul. Not to mention that it is a devilishly messy profession.'

I thought of Dee's laboratory at his house in Mortlake: the acrid smoke and curious smells, the explosions and accidental conflagrations, and the time he tried to distil horse dung to find its essential properties. The stink had lingered for months. He was lucky to have found a patient wife. 'A dangerous profession too, in Prague, from what I have heard,' I ventured as we crossed the square towards the House of the Green Mound.

He glanced down and his expression darkened. 'So it seems. I suppose they are talking of nothing else in the taverns?'

'And the marketplace, and the Stone Bridge, and all along the road since early morning.'

'Hm. Of course the tale would spread like plague. There are plenty who would delight in an alchemist meeting such an end, and relish it as divine justice.'

'He was widely hated, then, the dead man?' I could not help my curiosity, though I had vowed not to involve myself in this murder in any way. Hajek turned to me.

'Bartos? Not especially, as far as I know. At least, not personally. But this is a deeply divided city, for all the Emperor's talk of tolerance.' He lowered his voice. 'Those who are more *conservative*, shall we say, in matters of religion, view the science of alchemy, and the Emperor's generous patronage of it, as tantamount to necromancy and communion with the Devil. Or with the Jews – for some there is hardly a difference. They will use the alchemist's death as proof that Heaven will not bless the godless Rudolf, nor his empire, while he turns his face from the Catholic Church to pursue the occult arts. But this murder was no divine judgement, I can tell you that.'

'How do you know?'

'I have spent the day examining the body.' As we arrived at his house, he put his fingers between his lips and gave a shrill whistle; immediately a boy ran around from the side entrance to take the horse. 'But let us speak of these matters inside.'

'You are certainly not afraid to advertise your profession,' I said, indicating the carvings and symbols decorating the façade as we walked up the path to the door.

He smiled, evidently pleased. 'You like it? This was the house of my father, Simon – he was an alchemist too, and made good money from it, as you see, though to my sorrow he didn't live long enough to watch me rise so high in the Emperor's service. When I was a boy, my father's dinner table hosted the most learned men in Europe. Many of them your countrymen.'

'Was that where you learned to speak my language so well?'

'You are generous – I fear my Italian grows as creaky as my knees. I studied in Bologna and Milan as a young man, among other places. But the seeds of many languages were planted in childhood, I'm sure. Our house was a Babel and it fascinated me, even as a boy – the ways in which we strive to make our thoughts known to one another. Wait till you see inside.'

He opened the door and the housekeeper, Greta, appeared instantaneously, as if she had been standing behind it, awaiting us. She helped the doctor off with his cloak and hat, though her expression when her eyes fell on me was no less hostile than before; perhaps more so, as she took in my dishevelled appearance and the blood and dirt on my clothes. I was ushered through to a grand receiving room with a high beamed ceiling, the lower half of the walls panelled in wood, and understood what Hajek had meant about the interior; every inch of white plaster was painted with colourful designs of birds and leaves, while letters and astrological symbols were picked out in silver and gold. Above the hearth a Latin inscription read:

This art is precious, transient, delicate and rare. Our learning is a boy's game, and the toil of women. All you sons of this art, understand that none may reap the fruits of our elixir except by the introduction of the elemental stone, and if he seeks another path he will never enter nor embrace it.

'First words I learned to read,' Hajek said, nodding to the wall. 'Near sixty years ago now. I could recite them before I ever knew my letters. This was my father's old laboratory. He was keen I should learn ambition and humility in equal measure.'

'Did it work?'

He smiled, creases fanning at the corners of his eyes. 'You would have to ask my friends. Or perhaps my enemies. But here, talking of friends—' He gestured to a pair of high-backed chairs by the fire; Besler sprang from one and rushed over, arms spread as if to embrace me, then remembered his place at the last moment and instead hopped from foot to foot, looking me up and down, his hand to his mouth.

'Maestro! What happened? Oh God, you have been set upon! I should never have left you – this is all my fault. Are you hurt? Did you lose your purse? I came back to the Spider and met Dr Hajek, who said you were nowhere to be found, and I was afraid the Golem had taken you—'

I suppressed a smile at the idea that my attackers might have been deterred if this skinny youth had been there to defend me.

'Besler, please. I am fine, as you see – hardly a scratch.'

'We'll see about that,' Hajek said, switching to German for Besler's sake as he rolled up his shirt sleeves and nodded me to a chair. 'Let's have a look at that shoulder and wrist. Take off your doublet and unlace your shirt.' He caught my hesitation and his gaze flickered briefly to my chest. 'Or perhaps you would prefer a little more privacy to undress. Greta – bring a basin of hot water and a jug of spiced wine. And find ice from the cold store if we still have any, and all the necessaries for swelling and bruising. You, lad,' he ordered Besler, as if he were any other serving boy, 'go and help her. We'll need clean linens.'

39

Besler, too much in awe of Hajek's reputation, simply nodded open-mouthed and followed Greta obediently from the room.

'Whatever you are carrying on your person, Bruno, I will hold it to be none of my business unless you wish to share it,' Hajek said, returning to Italian and lowering his voice. 'But someone else clearly wants it enough to have it taken by force. And you must know that Dee has told me something of your history. So you may wish to keep your cargo more secure.'

'Where is Dee?' I began to undo my doublet, avoiding a direct acknowledgement of his words. Dee had trusted Hajek, whose reputation as Prague's greatest scholar was equal to Dee's own in England. My friend had written to me of the Czech with unequivocal warmth and admiration, but now Dee had disappeared, and he had not always proved himself the shrewdest judge of character, so I was inclined to keep an open mind about the Emperor's physician. I was fast learning that the court of Prague was as full of factions, spies and conflicting loyalties as any other in Europe. I wondered what exactly Dee might have told him about me.

'Ah. That is the question on everyone's lips.' Hajek watched, his eyes sharp, as I carefully checked the pocket sewn into the lining of my doublet before hanging it on the back of the chair. 'Shall I fetch you a strongbox?'

'No – thank you. I have one in our luggage. Besler will know.'

He nodded. 'You are wise to be cautious, Dr Bruno – I would be too, in your position. I hope once we are better acquainted you will see that the trust your friend Dee placed in me was earned. He called me his "comrade in the pursuit of truth".'

'I know. His letters have been full of praise for you. He told me your table was as lavishly stocked as your library, and your generosity as liberal with both. He spoke especially highly of your learned treatise on Czech beer.'

Hajek rolled his eyes, laughing. 'A lifetime devoted to the study of astronomy, medicine and alchemy, and that is the only thing anyone remembers of all my writing.' His expression turned serious. 'Well, I hope you will regard me as your friend in Prague. You will have need of one.'

I could not work out if this sounded threatening or reassuring. He stood behind me, easing the cloth of my shirt down over my shoulder before pressing both hands firmly around the bone and feeling along it until I yelped.

'Tell me what you know about John, then,' I said through gritted teeth. 'How long has he been gone?'

'I have not seen or heard from him these three weeks. I don't know where he is.' He hesitated, as if weighing up how much to say. His thumb pushed into my collarbone. 'I'll make a poultice to bring down the bruising, but it should mend quickly.'

'Aren't you worried?'

'No, no – it's not broken.'

'About John, I mean.'

Hajek's hands stopped moving.

'I assume he had good reason for making himself scarce.'

I twisted my head around to look at him. 'What reason? It must have been something serious for him to leave without warning?'

He sighed. 'There had been some trouble at court. Let us see the damage here.' He moved around to the front of my chair and took my right hand gently between his, turning my palm upwards. I tried not to flinch away.

'What manner of trouble?'

'He was worried about his standing with the Emperor. Can you flex your fingers? There – and again?' He felt along the tendons in my wrist as I curled my fist, nodding as if to himself. 'John had made enemies in Prague, and they had begun to turn Rudolf against him.'

'Zikmund Bartos, you mean?'

Hajek straightened, stretching his back.

'I was not thinking of him. Dee and Bartos had their differences, and of course they were in fierce competition to be the first to give the Emperor his heart's desire, but I did not suppose there to be any serious enmity between them. Dee always spoke

41

of Bartos with a grudging respect, and vice versa, as well-matched rivals often will.'

'But the day before Dee vanished, they had a public altercation in which Bartos accused John of stealing his life's work. That sounds more than professional rivalry.'

Hajek raised an eyebrow. 'You are well informed for a man who has not been in the city half a day. Who told you that?'

I shrugged. 'I asked around in the taverns after Dee. I was told by someone who heard from a witness.'

He nodded. 'I also heard the story second-hand, though I didn't take it too seriously at the time. Ziggi Bartos was hot-headed and prone to think the world set against him because he was of humble birth. But he had a strong sense of shame precisely for that reason, and an acute sensitivity about the way he was viewed by others – it was most unlike him to draw attention to himself by turning a private grievance into a public spectacle. Later, after John vanished, I wondered if Bartos was being used.'

'To slander Dee, you mean?'

'The enemies Dee had made were considerably more dangerous and more powerful than Ziggi Bartos. Men who could easily have bought Bartos, either with coin or with promises, to accuse Dee publicly of the one thing that would end his favour with the Emperor for good.'

'Might they have gone further, these powerful enemies? Beyond spreading slander. Did you have the sense that John was afraid?'

Hajek gave me a sharp look. 'Afraid for his safety, you mean? Not in that sense. John's greatest fear was that the Emperor would give credence to the lies that had begun to circulate and draw up a decree of banishment. He had asked me to intercede for him with Rudolf. Why do you ask?'

'Because you're talking as if you're certain John disappeared of his own volition. But do you know that for a fact?'

'I have no reason to think otherwise. Do you?'

I thought of Walsingham's letter. 'No. But we must consider

the possibility, surely. Did he mention going away? What was your last conversation with him?'

He shook his head. 'So inconsequential, I don't even remember. John lodged here, but we could often go several days without coinciding, if we were both busy with our work. I was at the castle the night he had his altercation with Bartos, but Greta said he came home late, around midnight, and went up to his room. A short time later, he came down again. She was still in the kitchen, and called out that there was pie if he was hungry, but he said there was no time and left again. It took us another couple of days to realise that he hadn't returned.'

'Did she notice if he'd packed for a journey?'

'As far as she could see, he took nothing except that old leather bag he carries with him everywhere, containing his journals. You know the ones I mean.'

I nodded. Cold spread through my insides at the thought; the notebooks in which Dee recorded all his supposed conversations with angels and spirits.

'He even sleeps with them,' Hajek added. 'He lives in terror that they will fall into the wrong hands. Not without reason – they would condemn him for necromancy in a heartbeat, if the Church laid eyes on them.'

We exchanged a glance in silence, weighing the possibilities.

'Three weeks is not such a long time, Dr Bruno,' he said, aiming for reassurance. 'And you know John – he is often impulsive. My guess is that he decided to lie low somewhere until the Emperor's ire had blown over. His Majesty's moods are notoriously capricious.'

'So – John disappeared the night of his public argument with Ziggi Bartos,' I said, 'and three weeks later, Bartos is murdered. It's a devil of a coincidence. Do you suppose the connection is these powerful enemies you mentioned?'

Hajek cracked his knuckles. 'You are running ahead of me,' he said, fixing me with a stern look. 'I have concerned myself today only with the manner of Bartos's unfortunate death. I have not had time to consider who might be responsible, or their motives. Ah, here is Greta with our supplies – I want to get that wrist of yours in ice without further delay.'

The door had been nudged open as he spoke and now Greta entered bearing an armful of heaped cloths and clay pots, a leather pail hooked over her elbow. Behind her, Besler balanced a tray holding a steaming jug and three glasses, his face a picture of frowning concentration; I guessed he was wondering how he could best impress our host with his willingness to help, while also making clear that he was not that kind of servant. Hajek had turned away to relieve the housekeeper of her burden and our conversation appeared to be over for the present, though I watched his face closely as he lined up a series of jars; I did not believe that he had not considered a link between Dee's vanishing and the murder of Bartos. I wanted to ask him who these powerful enemies might be, but his closed expression told me this would need to wait.

Greta plunged my hand into the pail of ice with a marked lack of gentleness and held my arm fast lest I try to escape. I clenched my jaw as the cold began to burn the torn skin on my wrist until it turned numb, the pain a reminder that I too appeared to have made enemies in Prague before I had even arrived. I wondered if they were connected with Dee's; it seemed clear enough that my Spanish assailants had been after the letters I carried. Hajek poured me a glass of hot wine and set about preparing a salve, tipping his ingredients into a stone mortar, judging measurements with a practised eye, while Besler stood at his elbow, watching with rapt attention. Hajek noticed the boy's expression and turned to include him. 'Tincture of arnica,' he said, indicating the bottle he had just corked. '*Fallkraut*, in your language, the fall herb. Works wonders for bruising – not to be taken internally, except dilute, unless you want to make your patient sick. There is an apothecary in the city who climbs the mountains every year to collect the flowers – charges a fortune for his trouble, but take note, this is one of the most useful potions a doctor of physick can have in his cabinet.'

Besler nodded avidly and his enthusiasm made me smile, though it was replaced by a grimace as Hajek began to apply his bitter-smelling ointment to my shoulder with firm circular strokes. While he worked, he asked after acquaintances at Wittenberg, and questioned Besler about his medical studies, as Greta silently cleared up and packed away the pots and jars; I had the sense that Hajek was carefully keeping his talk light in her hearing, and wondered if this was out of consideration, in order not to worry her, or because he did not entirely trust her. When he deemed my wrist had been in the bucket long enough for the ice to take effect, he lifted my arm out – I could barely move it myself by now – patted the skin dry, applied more of the arnica salve and bound the whole tightly in a stiff cloth.

'You'll feel the difference tomorrow, I assure you,' he said, reaching for his wine and sinking back into a chair. 'Still – you could have had a great deal worse. Lucky you know how to fight.'

'You think they meant to kill me?' I asked, trying to shrug my doublet back on with only one useful arm. Hajek gestured to Greta and gave a minute shake of his head. She stood with her back to us, still tidying away ingredients, but I thought I saw her shoulders stiffen. It occurred to me that I had given the housekeeper my name and told her where I could be found barely an hour before I was set on by those thugs. One of the first things I had learned in Walsingham's service was never to speak of important matters in the hearing of servants; you never knew who was buying their loyalty on the side. He himself had placed agents in every Catholic house in England, watching, listening, biding their time in the shadows while they poured drinks or emptied chamber pots, because those who are used to servants often pay them no more heed than their dogs, and frequently treat them with less respect. I squeezed my eyes shut and pressed my fingers to my temples, reminding myself that caution was a virtue, but – as with so much else – in moderation. Hajek would surely not employ a woman he mistrusted, and her evident dislike of me was most likely prompted by her loyalty and protectiveness towards her master. I waited until she had finished bustling about and made to leave the room with her arms full; Besler held the door open with a show of gallantry that earned him a roll of the eyes from under her coif. When he had closed it behind her, I saw the alarm in his face when he looked at me.

'Maestro? Who is trying to kill you?'

I turned to Hajek. 'You said you didn't think they came upon me by chance. Since we arrived in this city I have felt I was being watched. If you know who sent those Spaniards, I think you should tell me.'

The doctor walked over to the hearth and stood with a hand on the mantel, his eyes fixed on the flames.

'Spaniards?' Besler said, incredulous, looking from one to the other of us.

I waited. Hajek rubbed his thumbnail along his beard.

'I don't know for certain,' he said eventually. 'But Dee has spoken about you to the Emperor. Bragged, I should say. Of your books, naturally, and your prodigious memory, but also of your other talents.'

A shiver ran through me, as if my bowels had been plunged into an ice bucket. 'Such as?'

'He told Rudolf how greatly you were valued by Elizabeth of England for your ability to uncover treachery and corruption, and that you could find out a killer faster than a pig after truffles.'

'A flattering image.' I flinched as sensation returned to my bandaged hand in a thousand burning needles. 'Alas, he exaggerates. She did not value me enough to give me a stipend.' I could not keep a note of bitterness from my voice; after two years, it still rankled. In spite of the work I had done for the Queen, she had not found a way to allow me to stay in her realm, though it would have been no hardship to her; I knew how to live modestly. Walsingham said it was because I was more use to her elsewhere, but the truth he did not need to

46

voice was that, for all my service to England, I was the worst of all worlds: a Catholic in the eyes of her Protestant ministers, and a heretic to her Catholic enemies in France, Spain and Rome, whom she could not afford to provoke any further.

'Dee has a tendency to speak too much, and without due care,' Hajek said, poking a log, which shifted and resettled in a bloom of sparks. 'I'm sure he thought he was doing you a favour, building up your reputation for the Emperor. He may not have considered who else might be listening.'

I drew closer to the fire, intent on the dance of the flames, not meeting his eye.

'Who do you mean?'

He sighed, seeming reluctant to voice his suspicions.

'Who do you think, Bruno? Who is it always, casting her long shadow?' He looked at me with a trace of impatience. '*Rome*. You of all people should know. The Catholic Church. Those for whom it is not enough to have faith of their own – they must eliminate or forcibly convert anyone whose beliefs veer even slightly from their dogma.' He spoke with such controlled anger that I understood he must have been targeted by the zealots, as I had.

'But I had thought that here, in Prague—'

'What? That His Majesty had created a promised land of tolerance and equality, where a man may worship God according to his conscience, where Jews and Catholics and Protestants break bread together and astronomers strive to expand the limits of the cosmos, unhindered by petty bigotry and fear?'

'Well – yes. So I had been led to believe.'

'That was the dream.' His voice was tart with disappointment. 'That is why scholars and artists flock to Prague from all corners of Europe – they have been promised a city where unorthodoxy and a hunger for knowledge are positive virtues. But Rudolf forgets sometimes that his title is Holy Roman Emperor – or else he has too little regard for what that means. His role is to hold the Eastern half of Christendom for the

47

Catholic Church – at least according to his uncle and the Pope. And if he will not apply himself to that task, it is quite possible that they would seek to replace him with someone who will.'

'His uncle.' I grimaced. 'King Philip of Spain.' The man who dreamed of returning a purged and united Europe to the rule of Rome, with all heresy and dissent persecuted into extinction for good, no matter if it took a century of bloodshed and destruction. Even in Wittenberg, I had picked up rumours that he was building an Armada designed to rain fire on England until Elizabeth Tudor surrendered. 'I can imagine how Philip regards the idea of his nephew's domains being famed as the home of religious collaboration.'

'Exactly.' Hajek's expression mirrored my own. 'And you must understand that the Emperor is a contemplative man, given to frequent bouts of melancholy and introspection. He would have been better suited to the life of a scholar than a ruler, but for the accident of his birth. He would rather spend days on end in the Powder Tower with his alchemists, or in his library, than dealing with affairs of state, and often he does. Daily, the Spanish ambassador and the papal nuncio send dispatches home questioning his state of mind and his fitness for the office God has ordained, while they sweet-talk his younger brother Matthias, who waits in the wings with the Inquisition like hungry wolves at his shoulder . . .' He allowed the thought to fall away. 'I'm sorry, Bruno. I wish I could paint a prettier picture of my city, but the truth is that the Emperor's throne balances on a razor's edge.'

I dropped my gaze to the fire again. It sounded too much like the French court under King Henri; I had been driven from there, too, by determined Catholics who feared my ideas would lead the king away from God and the Church.

'I suppose the same is true of every monarch in Europe – except Philip,' I said. 'These are the times we live in. So those Spaniards who attacked me—'

Hajek held up a hand for silence; I stopped, as we both became aware of a soft purring sound from behind us. He nudged me, nodding with an indulgent smile towards the chair where Besler had fallen asleep in an improbable position, the way children do, gently snoring with his head lolling in mid-air.

'We should find him a bed,' Hajek said. 'You must be tired too. We can talk more when you're rested. I'll ask Greta to make your rooms ready.'

He left, and I shook Besler by the shoulder. He jerked awake, eyes wide. 'What about the Spaniards?' he said, as if the conversation had never been interrupted.

'Never mind them for now,' I said. 'Bring our bags up and get a good night's sleep for once – we're safe here.'

He rose to his feet, rubbing his eyes and yawning. Hajek showed us to our rooms; I was to have Dee's, in his absence, since he had been given the finest guest chamber. Besler was put in a small garret on the top floor. He didn't complain; only fell on to the bed without another word. I was secretly delighted, and fought to contain my impatience as I looked around my quarters. If Dee had been forced to leave in a hurry, he might have left behind papers or letters that would offer some clue to his disappearance, or more detail about the warning he had sent to Walsingham. It occurred to me that Hajek may well have thought of that already, but it was also probable that the physician did not know what to look for.

Greta brought hot water and clean linen; I had begun undressing when she returned again with fresh candles and logs for the fire, and a third time with extra fur covers for the bed in case the night turned colder; she hung by the door, eyes lingering on the doublet in my hand.

'I can take that down and brush the dirt from it if you like, sir,' she said. 'Looks like you've been rolling down the street.'

'Something like that.' I smiled, but my expression remained wary. Her tone was more carefully respectful than before; that might be because I was now approved by her master, or because she was hoping to get her hands on my clothes and whatever they contained. 'There's no need to trouble yourself. It will clean up better in the morning when the mud has had a chance to dry.'

'Then I can hang it in front of the kitchen fire with the rest of the laundry,' she said, still pleasant, eager to help. 'It's kept stoked all night. No trouble at all.'

'It will be fine here.' I smiled harder. 'But I thank you for the offer.'

We looked at one another a moment longer, before she bobbed her head and backed away.

'As you wish, sir. Give you good night.'

The door clicked softly behind her. I listened for the sound of her footsteps retreating along the landing, but heard nothing except the tell-tale creak of a floorboard. I allowed myself to exhale slowly as I sat on the bed, noticing that my hands were still trembling. Was it merely because I was shaken by my encounter with the Spaniards that I suspected even the house-keeper of treachery? I raked my fingers through my hair and mastered myself; the wine had brought the full weight of my tiredness crashing over me and I could barely keep my eyes open. But I could not allow myself the luxury of sleep yet.

Under the window that looked out over Bethlehem Square stood a table piled with books that Dee had evidently used as a writing desk, and tucked beneath it a chair, which I carried as silently as possible to wedge against the door, as there was no key to lock the room from the inside. I crouched to squint through the keyhole, half-expecting to see Greta's eye peering back at me from the other side, but as far as I could make out the corridor was empty. She must have perfected the knack of appearing and disappearing without a sound, like the best servants. I rummaged in one of the bags Besler had brought up earlier and found a spare kerchief, which I stuffed into the keyhole, to make certain, before I emptied the purse Overton had given me on to the bed and counted the contents. One hundred thalers – the equivalent of twenty-five gold sovereigns, or twenty-five English pounds. A significant amount, suggesting that Walsingham thought this mission would be costly or of long duration, perhaps both. I wondered if Overton had paid it out of his own coffers with the promise of reimbursement

– that was often Walsingham's way, his network of informers and espials scattered across Europe so unofficial that Queen Elizabeth rarely acknowledged our existence, much less provided a budget from her treasury. I scooped the coins back into the purse and tucked it under the mattress, relieved that it would at least cover the costs of my journey from Wittenberg.

Finally I brought two candles over to the desk and took out the letter Overton had passed under the table at the Spider, now somewhat creased and spotted from my brush with the Spaniards. The seal was unmarked; as I broke it open, I realised how long I had been holding my breath.

The writing inside brought a pang of memory so sharp it was almost painful; rows of letters, numbers and signs in the small, precise hand of Thomas Phelippes, Walsingham's scribe and master of ciphers. The mere sight of a code, like a lock waiting to be picked, seemed to collapse time, jerking me back to those years in England in a rush of sensation that only now made me acknowledge how much I missed it. Not just the place, but the work; that constant prickle of danger at the back of the neck, the sense of being at the secret centre of the war between freedom and tyranny that was being fought in the shadows all over the continent.

I rubbed my eyes; perhaps that was too grand a description of what I had done for Walsingham. But I could not deny, faced with this glimpse of a life I thought I had turned my back on, that I had been fooling myself for the past two years, thinking I could be content solely with the life of the mind. The challenge implicit in those rows of apparently meaningless characters spiked my blood like strong drink; my pulse quickened as my eyes skated over the paper, searching for patterns to be shaped into meaning. I had felt a sense of purpose when I was working for Walsingham, that was it; though he had drawn me into a world of mistrust and dissembling, he had also made me feel I was part of a greater cause, and the value of that to a man who lives in exile, belonging nowhere, dependent on the whims of others – it cannot be underestimated. It was a feeling I grasped at when I wrote, striving to set down what no one had dared say about the universe and our place in it, and yet in the solitude of my study it had always eluded me.

I supposed Dee had felt the same. I wondered how long he had been sending intelligence to Walsingham. The two men had known each other for decades; perhaps this had been the whole covert motive for Dee's journey to Prague. So what could he have stumbled upon now that had prompted such an urgent response from England? Hajek's mention of Dee's enemies had troubled me further; if conservative Catholic emissaries from the Vatican and the Spanish court had taken it upon themselves to keep the Emperor from heretical influences, that did not bode well for my chances of patronage, and the last thing I needed now was to find myself in the sights of Rome again.

I smoothed out the paper and rolled my shoulders, cursing the cracks of my joints and the ache in my muscles. Besler was right, damn him; I was past my youth, no matter how I might try to deny any waning of my powers. The intellectual thrill of a puzzle like the cipher before me was one thing; the prospect of deliberately putting myself in the way of paid brawlers like those Spaniards was a different game altogether. I retrieved the cipher Walsingham had sent me for Dee and laid it next to the letter Overton had brought. But as I bent over the table, my eyes flicking from one to the other, it struck me how few papers there were in the room.

Dee was no fool, of course; at least, not in matters of security. So much of his work was potentially incriminating that he had learned not to leave it lying around for curious eyes, as Hajek had mentioned; if he made sure to carry with him the notebooks detailing his seances, I guessed that any secret correspondence from England would be guarded with equal care. Whatever letters he might have received from Walsingham would have been quickly committed to memory and destroyed. But Dee was messy, too, or had been when I knew him. At his home in Mortlake, every surface had been a riot of scribbled notes and scattered sheets with fragments of ideas, snatches of conversation and esoteric diagrams jotted at random; it seemed obvious to me now, looking around the room, that it must have been cleared since he vanished. By whom – Hajek? If so, why? Was he searching for clues to Dee's disappearance, keeping his guest's writings safe, or had he passed them to some other hands?

Besides a small pile of books on the desk, there were only a few leaves of blank paper; any letters Dee had written here had vanished with him. I stood with my fingertips resting on the topmost page, my vision blurring with tiredness, when I realised that I could feel indentations on the surface of the paper. I held it up to the candle and made out faint lines; this sheet must have been under one Dee had written on, and he had pressed hard enough with the quill for the markings to have come through. I grabbed the poker and edged a piece of charcoal out of the fire; when it was cool to the touch, I rubbed it lightly over the paper and lines of script began to appear as white marks. At first I could not make sense of the symbols, until I turned the paper and realised I was looking at Hebrew characters. This was not so unusual: Dee, like many of the more open-minded Christian scholars in Europe, could read and write Hebrew fluently and believed there was much to be gained from studying the texts of Jewish mystics and adepts, but as I worked to interpret the words (many of the letters were too faint to make out clearly), I realised that I was looking at a letter. It began:

Most Worthy Maharal,
    I write in haste, to warn you of [here there were a couple of words I could not read] *to come. For I fear our enemies suspect, if not all then part. Vile slanders are spread against me, the which, if they be believed, will mean banishment or prison, though I fear it would go worse for you and your* [again, illegible] *if we are discovered. I send this by way of B; if anything should happen to me, it will fall to you to tell him of the danger to his—*

I flipped over the sheet urgently but there was no more; either Dee had begun a new piece of paper or he had been interrupted. My thoughts scrambled to catch up. So Dee had believed himself in serious danger – a fear his subsequent disappearance seemed to justify. Who were these enemies he spoke of, and what did they suspect? 'Vile slanders' – could he mean the public denunciation by Ziggi Bartos? Hajek thought that Dee had fallen foul of the Catholic authorities; it would appear that, whoever these enemies were, they were also a threat to the intended recipient of the letter, who – given the Hebrew – must be a fellow scholar or, more likely, someone in the Jewish quarter. Who was Maharal? A name or a title? Either way, it was not one I had encountered before. And who was this B? Bartos? *Bruno?* Had he been waiting for me to arrive and deliver this letter for him? Surely not; it had been written at least three weeks ago, before he had any knowledge of my coming. And 'tell *him*' – who was the recipient supposed to warn of danger? The mysterious B? If Dee had meant Bartos, it was too late for warnings.

I stowed all the papers in the hidden pocket of my doublet and sat heavily on the bed to unlace my breeches. My mind was too fogged with tiredness to attempt the deciphering of Overton's letter; I decided to work on it in the morning when I had slept and could think more clearly. I must also try to find this Maharal, the person Dee had been writing to. There was no way of knowing whether he had finished the letter and sent it, or if he had been interrupted in the writing, and who else might have seen it; either way, it appeared that at least three people were potentially in danger, and the nature of that threat might lead me to John. I would go to the Jewish quarter and make discreet enquiries.

I snuffed the candle and lay down with the blanket pulled up to my ears. With such a swarm of questions buzzing around my head, I feared sleep would elude me, but I must have dozed because I was startled awake by the clatter of hooves on the cobbles under the window and a hammering at the door. I sat up, straining to listen, but I could only catch a murmur of male voices and then a thunder of footsteps on the stairs followed by a knock at my own door. I hesitated a moment then swung my legs out of bed; wincing at the chill, I shifted the chair out of the way before opening it a crack. Hajek stood on the landing, fully dressed, a cloak in his hand.

'I've been summoned to the castle,' he said. It was so cold his breath made clouds in the air. 'There's news in the Bartos business. Get your clothes on. Clean ones, if you have them.'

'What? Why?'

'You're coming to meet the Emperor.'

'But – I'm not prepared,' I said, drawing a hand across my stubble.

'Doesn't matter. He's heard of your arrival and he thinks you might be of use.' Noting my reluctance, he added, 'This is an honour, Bruno. I've known him to keep credentialled diplomats waiting eight months for an audience, and you've not been in the city eight hours. You don't want to miss this opportunity, trust me. I'll see you in the yard.'

An honour. Perhaps, though this was not the glorious first encounter with His Majesty that I had envisaged. What could be so urgent that the Emperor had called us out in the middle of the night? I pulled on my breeches and doublet, snatched up my cloak and ran down to join Hajek. It did not feel much like an honour at that moment; in truth, it felt more like a potential trap.

FOUR

I held tight to Hajek's back as we cantered through the dark streets of Prague with the court messenger leading the way. At the checkpoints each side of the bridge and at the castle gate, the seal he carried allowed us to pass unhindered. We rode under the gatehouse into a broad cobbled courtyard lit by torches, though I could make out only indistinct shadows of buildings on all sides; towering above them, the spire of the great cathedral within the walls. The horses were led away by silent servants the moment we dismounted, and the messenger vanished into the interior. I hurried after Hajek, who was already striding away across the courtyard.

Ahead, a door swung open and we were met on the steps by a slightly built man who exchanged a few words with the physician and, turning, greeted me in Italian with traces of a Mantuan accent.

'Ottavio Strada,' he said with a brief bow. 'His Majesty's court librarian. I have long wished to make your acquaintance, Dr Bruno – though perhaps not in such circumstances. Follow me, if you please.'

He led us up a flight of stairs, along a corridor and into a well-lit chamber, where I saw that he was around my own age, good-looking with prominent cheekbones and cropped dark hair (no threads of silver in his beard yet, I noted), and carried himself with a nimble, upright grace, like a fencing master. But I was too entranced by the room to dwell long on his appearance. All the walls were painted with bright images illustrating the four elements, a frieze around the upper parts depicting the twelve months of the year and their astrological symbols. I thought I recognised the hand of my countryman Giuseppe Arcimboldo in the profusion of fruit and vegetables, but before I could ask about the paintings, Hajek had drawn closer to Strada with a glance at the far door.

'How is he?' Hajek asked, in a low voice.

The librarian grimaced. 'Greatly disturbed. You know how he can be. Much talk of dark forces. But then His Majesty has had a terrible shock tonight.'

Hajek raised an eyebrow but Strada shook his head. 'He wishes to tell you of it himself. I hope that you can allay his fears, God knows I have had no success.'

'Is anyone with him now? Your sister?'

'Not tonight. I stayed with him myself a little while at first, but he wants no one except you, Thaddeus. And your visitor, apparently.' He glanced at me with a degree of reserve; I couldn't tell if he resented my presence, despite his effusive words earlier. 'I offered to fetch the Lord Chamberlain, but His Majesty insisted on being left alone until you arrived. Go quickly now – I don't like to think of him being in there unattended with – *that*.'

'With what?' Hajek asked with evident alarm, but Strada only knocked on the far door of the chamber and opened it for us.

It took a moment for my eyes to adjust to the dim light of the space we entered, but as the door clicked shut behind me and I realised where we were, I exclaimed aloud. A vast, vaulted gallery stretched out before us, tall glass cabinets lining the walls on either side and smaller ones displayed down the centre of the room. Much of it was sunk in shadow; only one wavering bank of candles on each side provided light, most of those already burned down to stumps, but it was enough to discern sculptures, coins, enamelled bowls, exotic musical instruments, astrolabes and stuffed animals, curiously embellished daggers with jewelled hilts and curving blades, shining reliquaries, bright feathers and corals, glowing lumps of amber showing dragon-flies preserved perfectly within, bezoars, stones with runic carvings and a row of skulls of all shapes and sizes, animal and human. I snatched up a candle from the nearest rack and held it out to take in this cavern of wonders, the original purpose of our visit almost forgotten.

Like Besler, I had heard reports of the Emperor Rudolf's *Kunstkammer*, his extraordinary collection of artistic, scientific and natural curiosities, said to be the greatest in Christendom; unlike my assistant, I counted myself well-travelled and had stepped into the heart of the grandest courts in Europe, so I had not expected to be so quickly rendered speechless by the variety of treasures on display. It reminded me of the chambers of Catherine de Medici, dowager queen of France, though on a much larger scale. I progressed slowly, shielding the flickering light, trying to absorb the extent of the riches amassed here.

'Bruno,' Hajek called, impatient. I turned and something brittle hit me in the face; with a start, I raised my head and realised it was a skeletal human foot. Craning my neck, I saw that the rest of the skeleton was attached, the bones held together by invisible wire in the correct anatomical position, the whole suspended from the ceiling by silver chains like a macabre marionette, swaying and grinning down at me.

'All of art and nature is here,' I breathed, gazing up to see a whole new menagerie of stuffed birds, bats and flying creatures affixed to the roof beams. As I stepped back for a better view, I became suddenly aware of a tall figure standing behind me in the window embrasure. I whipped around and almost collided with a brown bear rearing up on his hind legs, his mouth fixed in a snarl, teeth bared, eyes of black glass glinting. I let out a shaky breath and patted his shoulder by way of apology.

'*Vanitas vanitatum, et omnia vanitas*,' said a lugubrious voice from deep in the shadows. 'All is vanity,' it added helpfully, in

German, in case the meaning was not clear. I stopped still; ahead of me, Hajek held up a hand to indicate that I should not move.

'Your Majesty?' he said gently, peering into the dark.

'*Oculos habentes non videtis?* Having eyes, see ye not?' said the voice.

'What is it you wish me to see, Majesty?' Hajek said in that same firm, kindly tone, as if soothing a frightened horse or a child.

'Come here, Thaddeus.' The voice sounded petulant now. Hajek beckoned to me and we followed the sound to a corner of the room, where a high-backed wooden chair with intricate carvings had been wedged between two display cases. Huddled into the seat was what appeared to be a bundle of fur with a hat. Hajek kneeled and I hurriedly followed suit.

'Yes, all right, get up.'

I lifted my head; the fur shifted and as my eyes adjusted I made out the figure of a small man wrapped in an enormous cloak, his feet tucked under him like a child. He wore a shapeless woollen cap and as he moved I saw – with some alarm – that he was clutching in his lap a six-foot-long horn that tapered to a vicious point. This, then, was the Invincible Emperor of the Romans, His Everlasting and Most Benevolent Sovereign and Majesty Rudolf II. He looked down at me with dark, hooded eyes. I recognised in him the long Hapsburg nose and full lips, but his skin was pale and his face pouchy; it was hard to believe that he was only thirty-seven, two years younger than me. I could already see what he would look like as an old man.

'You,' he said, levelling the implement at me. 'You are the Neapolitan with the memory system?'

'Yes, Your Majesty,' I said, keeping my eyes lowered. 'Giordano Bruno of Nola, at your service.' He had addressed me in German so I replied in kind. It was hard to imagine a less regal figure than the one curled into the chair in front of me. Even his voice quavered.

'We'll see about that. You know, John Dee insists that your talents are unequalled and that I must take you to the imperial bosom.'

'Well, I—'

'But then John Dee is an agent of the Devil.'

'You are mistaken there,' I said, raising my head to meet his gaze as I felt Hajek's sharp glance in my direction. It was no doubt unwise to contradict an Emperor so bluntly, especially one who is agitated in the middle of the night. But I had started so I may as well continue. 'I mean to say, I know John Dee to be a seeker after truth, and a man of honour. I do not believe he wishes harm to anyone, least of all Your Majesty, whatever is said of him.'

Rudolf sniffed. 'Tell that to Zikmund Bartos.'

'John Dee did not kill Bartos,' I said hotly, before I had time to consider the wisdom of such an assertion.

'Then who do *you* think killed him?' Rudolf leaned forward and pinned me with his intense stare. Behind the veil of melancholy I sensed a shrewd intelligence. 'The Golem?'

'I – I do not know, Your Majesty. I only arrived in your golden city yesterday. But I would wager all I own that John Dee would never murder a man, least of all in such a barbaric way.'

'I may yet take your wager,' the Emperor said thoughtfully. 'Unequal though it is. I don't suppose you own much, and I own all this, as you see.' A slender white hand emerged from his voluminous sleeve and waved around to take in the room before retreating. 'My *theatrum mundi*. But the killing of Bartos is a message to me, and I cannot read it clearly. Thaddeus, see if you can do better. Or you, Neapolitan, since you are so certain of your knowledge.'

Hajek rose to his feet. 'Tell me, Majesty. Strada said only that something had occurred to disturb your peace of mind?'

Rudolf gave a hollow laugh. 'What peace of mind? I have had none since I was crowned in '76. *There*.' He pointed with his narwhal horn to a small table a few feet away. Its surface was a mosaic of tessellating gemstones and on top sat a wooden casket with a paper wrapped around it and tied with string. 'Go on,' he urged, when Hajek hesitated. 'This was left on the palace steps some time before midnight, outside my private residence. The fools that serve me were too afraid to look inside, so it was passed from hand to hand until it reached Ottavio, who recognised the writing of Bartos. He brought it to my chamber, and – well. See for yourselves.' He shuddered.

Hajek unwrapped the paper attached to the casket. It read, in Latin:

For His Imperial Majesty, the final fruit of all my labours. A curse on anyone who breaks the seal before my sovereign lord.

The doctor handed me the paper and glanced at Rudolf. 'What did you expect to find?'

The Emperor shrank back in his seat. 'I thought perhaps he had discovered the goal of our striving after all, and found a way to smuggle it to me before he was killed.'

'You thought this contained the Philosopher's Stone?' Hajek could not keep the scepticism from his voice. He flipped open the casket's lid and moved closer to the candles to see the contents. I leaned over his shoulder, careful not to block the light. The box was lined with red satin and contained a square of oiled leather, such as jewellers use to wrap precious stones, though I caught a sharp scent that made me think of an alchemist's laboratory. Hajek lifted a corner of the material and I heard his quick intake of breath echoed by my own. Inside were two severed eyeballs.

For a moment, no one moved.

'*Dio mio*,' I whispered. Whatever I had expected, it was not this.

'You see? Devilry,' Rudolf said with an air of satisfaction. He seemed pleased by the effect of his little drama. 'You understand now why I must keep my talismans about me.' He swept his horn through the air around him as if drawing a protective circle and fixed his beady stare on me again. 'You know what this is?'

'It's a narwhal tusk, Your Majesty,' I said.

'*Wrong*. It is the horn of a unicorn, obtained for me at great expense by Signor Strada, most rare and precious and efficacious against maledictions.'

'Of course,' I said quickly. 'Hard to see in this light.'

Hajek composed himself and closed the lid, though I noticed a tremor in the hand that held the casket. 'May I take these to examine, Your Majesty?'

'Please do. Take them as far as possible. This too.' He drew out a piece of paper from the folds of his cloak, holding it between his first two fingers as if it might contaminate him. 'It was inside with them.'

As Hajek had his hands full, I took the paper and unfolded it. Written in the same neat, spiky writing as the note that had wrapped the box, it read,

Oculos habentes non videtis?

'Gospel of Saint Mark, chapter eight, verse eighteen,' I said, showing Hajek. That explained why the Emperor had quoted the verse to us when we entered. 'And you are quite sure this is the writing of Zikmund Bartos, Your Majesty?'

'I know his hand all right,' Rudolf said, nestling his chin deeper into his furs. 'He has written me enough begging letters.'

'Then someone took these from among his papers after his murder,' I mused.

'Or he was forced to write it before he died,' Hajek said with a wince. 'Either way, someone meant to alarm you, Majesty.'

'Well, they succeeded,' Rudolf said with feeling. He shifted his legs and I saw that he wore jewelled velvet slippers in the Turkish style. 'But why is the message so oblique? What do they think I am failing to see, Thaddeus? My whole life is a

62

quest to look beyond the visible, to read the secret writing in the Book of Nature. Who would dare accuse me of blindness?'

'I do not know, Majesty. But I can't believe that damned fool Strada did not look inside the casket before he allowed you to open it,' Hajek said, in a harder tone. 'He should be more cautious – it could have been a scorpion or a poisonous snake for all he knew.'

Rudolf's eyes widened in horror. 'Do not blame the boy,' he said, though I guessed the librarian was near enough the same age as his master. 'He feared the curse. He also feared my anger, if the box had contained what was promised.'

'I will speak with him,' Hajek said with an angry glance towards the room where we had left Strada. 'For now, Your Majesty, I counsel you not to open any more letters or packages that have not first been checked. Particularly if they come from dead men.'

The Emperor shivered. 'Yes, Doctor,' he said meekly. 'Have you brought something to help me sleep? I have terrible palpitations here' – he laid a hand over his heart – 'and I doubt my eyes will close tonight for dread of Bartos coming to me in my dreams, staring with his empty sockets.' He cast a fearful glance towards the casket.

Hajek patted his leather satchel. 'I will see you settled, Majesty,' he said, his tone soothing again. 'You shall have a dreamless sleep. Bruno, take that' – he gestured to the wooden box – 'and wait for me in the antechamber. Make sure no one interferes with it.'

Rudolf pushed himself to his feet, still clutching his tusk, and I saw how small he was; no more than five and a half feet. He fixed his brooding gaze on me again.

'Dr Bruno. John Dee says you saved the life of Queen Elizabeth more than once through your ability to sniff out a killer where her wisest advisers could not,' he said.

My first instinct was to deny it, since I was not sure I liked where this was tending, but then it occurred to me that I was already embroiled in this murder whether I wanted it or not, as it clearly involved Dee and perhaps Walsingham. Besides, it never hurt to impress powerful men with patronage in their gift.

I bowed. 'I have used what humble talents I may possess to render Her Majesty some small service on occasion.'

'Don't fawn,' Rudolf said with a spinsterish tut. 'I can't bear false modesty. Very well – tomorrow we will speak again. If you are so convinced John Dee is innocent, you will use these humble talents of yours to discover who did kill my alchemist.'

'Majesty—' I straightened. 'I am not sure that I am qualified – I do not know your court or your city—'

'Hajek will tell you all you need to know.' He pointed the horn at me. '*Quid pro quo*, Bruno. You Italians understand that readily enough. Because you may be sure that I will find Dee, wherever he is hiding, and if his innocence cannot be proven, he will hang.' He looked down at the object in his hand. 'A narwhal tusk, you say? Really?'

I took a deep breath; if he valued plain speaking, I may as well start now. 'I'm afraid so. Unicorns are a myth.'

He nodded sadly, though he did not let go of the horn as he held out his other hand to Hajek, who offered his arm to lean on, as if the Emperor were an elderly woman. At the end of the gallery Rudolf stopped and turned back to me. 'The Golem,' he said. 'Is that a myth too?'

I hesitated, and caught Hajek's warning look over the Emperor's head.

'I do not believe the Jews would make any creature that would visit destruction on others, Majesty,' I said carefully.

'I should hope not.' He sniffed. 'I have been extremely generous to them here in Prague. As was my father.'

I felt my expression grow rigid. I have always bristled at the idea that one group of people must be grateful to another merely for being allowed to go about their lives unmolested; growing up in an Italian kingdom occupied by the Spanish, I had learned this resentment from my father. I was glad the Emperor was too far away to see my face as I worked to keep it neutral.

'But is it possible,' he persisted, 'think you, to create a being without the need for a woman, and breathe life into it, as God did with Adam?'

'Anything is possible with the right knowledge, Your Majesty,' I said.

He weighed this up for a moment, considering. 'Interesting,' he said, nodding, as Hajek held the far door open for him, and they left me there, holding a casket containing a dead man's eyeballs.

FIVE

Ottavio Strada was still pacing the antechamber when I closed the gallery door behind me. His gaze homed straight to the box in my hands and I saw him flinch.

'How is His Majesty?' he asked, twisting his fingers together.

'Disturbed, as you said. But Dr Hajek seems to have soothed him.'

He nodded. 'I suppose Hajek is furious with me for letting him open that?'

'I think he feels it would be prudent to check first, in case anyone wishes to send the Emperor something more dangerous than eyeballs,' I said, aiming for diplomacy.

'Easy for him to say,' Strada muttered. 'If I had opened that casket and it had proved to contain whatever Bartos claimed he had discovered – the elixir of life or some such – His Majesty would have accused me of taking a draught to make myself immortal and challenge his throne. He suffers from notions of persecution,' he added with a note of weariness. 'Did he threaten you with his narwhal horn?'

I looked at him, surprised. 'He said you assured him it came from a unicorn.'

Strada laughed, and for the first time I saw his features relax. 'Not I. He would have meant my father, Jacopo. He has been court antiquary to this emperor and his father Maximillian

66

before him. My father travelled all over Christendom acquiring treasures for them – much of what you see in the *Kunstkammer* was collected by him. And you are right – he was not above presenting the goods in the most pleasing light. He was nothing if not shrewd in his dealings with princes. They say that is characteristic of Mantuans,' he added with a touch of pride, 'though I am not qualified to say – I have never lived there. My sister and I were born at Maximillian's court in Vienna. Service to the Hapsburgs is in our blood.'

I recalled Hajek asking if his sister were with the Emperor; from that I could guess at the nature of her service. I assumed from the way Strada talked of his father in the past tense that Jacopo must be dead, but he shook his head.

'No, he is still with us,' Strada said, 'but he is seventy-three and ailing. I carry out most of his duties now, though I have not been formally appointed in his place. Officially I look after the library. His Majesty has agents all over Europe buying precious manuscripts and books to send back – part of my work is to catalogue those that come in, look through them and write a précis for His Majesty so that he can decide which to prioritise.'

'That sounds like an enviable job,' I said, thinking how much I would give to be let loose on the Emperor's collection of rare books. 'You must be familiar with many languages.'

'I get by,' Strada said with an affectation of modesty. 'But the reality of my work is not as exciting as it might appear, I'm afraid. For every truly original treatise that passes across my desk, I must plod through forty that are either dull as rain or downright preposterous. And it is not without an element of risk. If I should miss something the Emperor later decides to be vital to his quest, I would lose his favour in an instant.'

'His quest?'

He laughed, but uncertainly, as if he wasn't sure whether I was joking. 'Surely you must know, Dr Bruno, what His Majesty seeks? The purpose of all this accumulation?' He swept a hand around as if to encompass the *Kunstkammer* and the entire castle. 'All that industry out there in the Powder Tower and the laboratories underground?'

'You mean the Philosopher's Stone?'

He nodded. 'Whatever that may be. His Majesty remains convinced that somewhere out there is a manuscript or a formula or a distillation waiting to be discovered, that will hold the key. So he spends a fortune in pursuit of it, and a great many chancers flock in hope of a share.'

'The key to what, though? Turning metal into gold?'

'Oh no. He has more than enough gold, though if someone were to effect that miracle, I don't suppose he would refuse it. No – Rudolf seeks nothing less than immortality,' Strada said with a short laugh that conveyed exactly what he thought of that idea.

I smiled. 'You do not share his conviction, I see. Then you think the alchemists toil in vain?'

'I didn't say that.' He lowered his voice. 'There are those among the alchemists engaged in valuable work on the properties of metals and minerals, the development of medicines, and in the sphere of optics and astronomy, the movement of the planets. Hajek is one. Any investigation that allows us to understand the world better is worthwhile, of course. But if you ask me whether I believe there is a book or a tincture that will equip a man to cheat death, I must confess to a certain scepticism that I would not voice to my master. And the frauds in the Powder Tower far outnumber the true seekers, in my view, though it is Hajek's job to sift the wheat from the chaff.'

'Which was Bartos?'

He looked away to the window. 'I used to think he was a man of science. He was committed to experimentation and observation when he first arrived. He had a keen interest in mathematics and often visited the library in search of the treatises of the Arabs.' He leaned in, and his eyes brightened. 'It was an enthusiasm I shared, and we often conversed about it. The Arabs are a long way ahead of us in their understanding of geometry, and I am certain that this knowledge could be harnessed to design machines and structures of far greater sophistication than we have now. When I can snatch a few moments to myself, I make drawings—' He broke off, lowering his eyes.

'I should be interested to see them,' I said. 'And the manuscripts.'

'You are welcome any time, of course.' He glanced up with a shy smile. 'It would be a pleasure to show the collection to someone who would appreciate it.'

'I will take you up on that,' I said. 'But you changed your mind about Bartos?'

He shrugged. 'You are no stranger to the courts of queens and princes, Dr Bruno, so you will understand how these things go. His Majesty the Emperor is capricious with his favours, especially where the alchemists are concerned – there are so many of them, and new hopefuls pouring through the city gates every day, full of grandiose promises. Those who wish to retain his good opinion – and their stipend – must tell him what he wants to hear or risk being displaced. That is not a climate in which to foster true scientific enquiry, where one must be willing to fail in order to reach the truth. These last months, Bartos had devoted all his energies to confected mysticism and flattery, and it was making him bitter.'

'Was that why he had begun to slander John Dee?'

'Possibly. Also, he had fallen in with . . .' He hesitated, his expression sour.

'With whom?'

Before he could answer, the door to the gallery was flung open and Hajek strode through with his medical bag. He came to an abrupt halt and glared at Strada.

'Dear God, what were you thinking, boy?' he barked, in Italian. 'Nothing comes into His Majesty's hands that has not first been examined inside and out. *Nothing*. There are poisons that work by contact with the skin, you must know that. One piece of cloth impregnated with such a solution, that's all it would take. Or some biting creature – a snake or spider.'

'I'm sorry, Thaddeus. It was only— that message, in Bartos's writing – I thought—'

'You did not think at all. You're a damned fool,' Hajek said, as if pronouncing definitive judgement. 'Your father would not have made such a mistake,' he added darkly.

Strada flinched at this. 'Do not tell him, I pray you,' he said. 'It would cause him distress. I swear nothing like this will happen again.'

Hajek jabbed a finger close to his face. 'It cannot. One incautious moment like that, and—' He drew the flat of his hand across his throat like a blade. 'I should not have to spell it out to you, Ottavio. If we lose His Majesty, we are all dead men.'

Strada swallowed and nodded. His complexion had subsided rapidly from flushed to deathly pale.

'Come, Bruno,' Hajek said, still brusque, sweeping past me towards the stairs. 'Let us take a closer look at this grisly gift.'

SIX

'Now then – bring that light closer. What was the first thing that struck you when we opened the casket?' Hajek pushed up his shirtsleeves. Trying not to crowd him, I held up the lantern and peered down at the severed eyeballs he had placed on the slab. He had adopted – perhaps unwittingly – the attitude of a teacher instructing a student, but I didn't mind; it took me back to my days as a young friar in Naples, when I had worked as assistant to the brother infirmarian, who taught me most of what I know about anatomy and how to analyse the signs of unnatural death.

'The smell of distilled spirits,' I said, keen to please. 'And the absence of blood.'

'Exactly. Which points to what?'

'Well, alcohol is a preservative. It seems likely that these specimens did not come from the dead man.'

'Very good. In fact, I would go further. I would say, by the shape of them, that these did not come from any man at all. Look, here.' He poked one with the tip of his knife. I winced; I had seen enough of death and mutilation to consider myself fairly strong of stomach when it came to the human body, but the way the jelly quivered made my gut tighten.

'An animal, you think?'

He nodded. 'Most likely a sheep. And you see how carefully the nerves have been separated and kept intact here? That speaks of careful anatomisation, by one who knows what he is doing and wishes to study the function of vision. Whereas if you were to look at the body of Bartos, you would immediately see that what was done to him was not the work of a skilled physician but a butcher. In fact—' He turned to me, an idea dawning plainly on his face. 'Why don't we take a look at the corpse now? I should be glad of your insight.'

I tried to blink away tiredness and my longing for the warm bed I had enjoyed for less than an hour; the last thing I wanted was to examine a butchered corpse, but I could hardly refuse to assist, and I knew from experience that murdered men and women can tell you a great deal more than their killers expect about what was done to them, if you know what to look for. While Dee remained under suspicion of this murder, I had a chance to clear his name and impress the Emperor with my abilities at the same time.

I agreed; Hajek took the lantern and led me out of his laboratory and along a chilly unlit passageway. We were deep in the bowels of the castle here; Hajek, as the chief court physician, had his own consulting rooms near the Emperor's private quarters, but a separate laboratory in the cellars to conduct his experiments, reached by spiralling staircases, away from the communal space of the Powder Tower where lesser alchemists were obliged to share workshops.

As we approached a heavy door at the end of the passage, Hajek reached into his doublet and drew out a kerchief, which he tied around his mouth and nose.

'You may wish to do likewise,' he said. 'He doesn't smell too good.'

I had left the kerchiefs I wore for riding in my bag, so I pressed a sleeve to my face as he unlocked the door.

'You are keeping the body here?' I asked, surprised.

'It's cold, as you've no doubt noticed. The temperature will delay decay to an extent, until I have finished my examination. I thought it prudent not to keep him in the city morgue – the townspeople were muttering of dark magic and curses, and the presence of the corpse might have provoked unrest. When I am satisfied that there is no more to be learned, I will have him taken outside the city and buried quietly where he is unlikely to be dug up.'

'What about his family? Will they not wish to bury him?'

'He has none that I know of. Or if he does, it would take too long to track them down. I want him in the ground as quickly as possible. People are superstitious here, and credulous with it.'

I understood his motives; even so, I was surprised by the apparent lack of feeling. I hoped Bartos did not have a mother somewhere waiting for him to write.

'I heard muttering of the Golem as well,' I said, recalling the talk in the Spider.

He frowned as he pushed the door open. 'Exactly. There are plenty who seek any opportunity to slander the Jews, and this murder is a gift to them. Come, now.'

The stench of old blood hit me like a punch the moment I stepped inside; the climate in this underground chamber was not doing much to limit putrefaction, whatever Hajek said. As my sight adjusted, I saw that we had entered a small room with a low, vaulted ceiling, bare except for a makeshift bier comprised of planks laid over trestles. A channel cut into the flagstones sloped down towards an iron grille set into the floor, and I guessed that Hajek used the room for dissection.

A shape lay on the planks covered by an oilcloth, and I shivered as Hajek passed me the light and drew back a corner; no matter how many times I confronted the spectacle of violent death, I had never yet learned to look on it with detachment, and in that I found some confirmation of my humanity.

The face was monstrous. I saw immediately what Hajek meant: the mutilations done to Zikmund Bartos were not made by a practised hand. Though the body had evidently been cleaned for examination, the ragged holes where his eyes had been showed signs of frenzied gouging with a blade, as if his attacker had been possessed by fury or extreme haste. The carefully preserved eyes in the box could not possibly be his. I hoped to God the

73

poor man had been killed first. His lips were drawn back in a horrible rictus and his jaw had fallen loose, revealing the empty cavern of his mouth, black with dried blood. Cut into his forehead were the Hebrew characters מ ו ת – the word for Death.

'He was young,' I said through my sleeve. From Hajek's description of Bartos as Dee's chief rival among the alchemists, I had imagined someone of Dee's years and experience. But the man on the table could not be out of his twenties – possibly only midway through.

'Yes.' Hajek sounded regretful. 'Twenty-seven, but exceptionally gifted, in my opinion. I had predicted great things for him.'

Twenty-seven. The age I had been when I first fled my religious order, escaping over the convent wall at San Domenico Maggiore under cover of darkness. The age at which I felt my life had truly begun.

'How long had he been at court?'

'Less than a year. He became Rudolf's obsession at first. I fear that was my fault – perhaps I over-praised the boy, created expectations he could not meet. But I was so struck by his quick mind, the breadth of his knowledge. All the more remarkable because, by his own admission, he had not studied at a university.'

'How came he by his skills, then?'

'He claimed to have been apprenticed in boyhood to an apothecary in his home town on the borders of Bohemia. I say claimed, because many of those who arrive here invent a new history for themselves – you know how appealing that can be when one travels, the idea of shedding one's past self like a skin. Bartos said he had learned the essential properties of plants and minerals from the apothecary and progressed to his own experiments.' He lifted a shoulder in a gesture of helplessness. 'The Emperor, though he is a great patron of knowledge, is an impatient man, as you will find out. He does not fully grasp, I think, the long and painstaking path that any worthwhile endeavour must follow, the manifold failures and disappointments along the road. His way is to seize upon every newcomer, as if this one might give him overnight what all the others have yet failed to achieve, just as some men will take a new mistress each time the one he has turns out to possess the same faults as every other woman. Which, come to think of it, is also the Emperor's way with his mistresses.' He grimaced and returned his gaze to the ravaged face of Ziggi Bartos. 'His delight is all in novelty. I suppose that is the prerogative of princes. I told Bartos only to persist with his work, that the apparently miraculous breakthrough is always built on a foundation of diligent application. But he saw his star fading with Rudolf and he began to panic.'

'Ottavio Strada said that Bartos had lately turned towards mysticism,' I said, lowering my arm as I began to acclimatise to the smell.

'In the same way that a woman will employ whore's tricks to revive her man's flagging interest, so the alchemists know that a smattering of magic will always whet the Emperor's appetite in the short term.' There was disapproval in his expression, though whether for women or alchemists I could not tell. 'But that is a fine line to tread. Rudolf desires magic and secret knowledge, but he dreads anything that smacks of demonic powers.'

I wondered if Bartos had inadvertently crossed that line. Rudolf had accused John Dee of being an agent of the Devil, now that he was out of favour.

'Was Bartos interested in the Cabala?' I asked.

'Anyone in this city who seeks to interrogate the mysteries of the universe has at least a passing knowledge of the Cabala,' Hajek said. 'There is not much regard among scholars here for the Inquisition's Index of Forbidden Books, you'll be glad to hear. You ask because of the letters?' He gestured to Bartos's face.

'His killer clearly wanted to draw attention to that connection,' I said. 'Perhaps he wished to imply that this is the consequence of involvement with the Jews, or Jewish books?'

'That would be a reasonable conclusion – except that, as far as I'm aware, Bartos had no especial connection to the Jews. I had surmised that the killer's aim was to be rid of Bartos and cast aspersions on the Jewish community at the same time.

Which is why – as I have tried to explain to His Majesty – it is unlikely to be John Dee, even supposing him capable of such violence. He may have the first motive but not the second – quite the reverse.'

I thought of the correspondence in Hebrew I had found in Dee's room. I had no way of knowing if the original had been sent, or if Hajek had found and removed it after Dee's disappearance. Until I was more certain, I decided not to mention it.

'Dee was close to the Jewish community, then?'

He gave me a narrow look over his kerchief. 'He respected their learning and culture, as I'm sure you know. Now, look here. What do you make of this?' He drew the cloth further down to expose the corpse's torso and I held the light closer. One single wound on the left side of the chest, below the nipple, gaped like a lipless mouth.

'Is that the blow that killed him?' I asked.

'As far as I can see. What interests me is the contrast between this and what was done to the face.'

'The precision, you mean?'

'Exactly.' He beamed across the corpse at me, as if I were a precocious student. 'A single entry wound between the ribs, straight to the heart. It would have been the work of a moment. He may not even have realised he had been stabbed at first, but death would have been extremely quick. And that level of precision, as you say, speaks to me of a killer with some degree of experience. You would expect an amateur to slash at their victim, to deal a number of blows in the hope that one would do the job. Whoever murdered Bartos knew what he was doing.'

'A professional assassin, you mean?'

'Certainly someone who has killed before. A soldier, perhaps. Even someone with a sound understanding of anatomy who knew where to aim. Which also suggests to me that Bartos did not suspect violence from his killer. You could not get a knife in so accurately if your victim was running away, or attempting to defend himself. I would say it was done face to face – a concealed weapon, one swift move – before Bartos had a chance to anticipate danger.'

'Then you think the mutilation was done after death?' I asked hopefully.

'On balance, I would say so,' Hajek said, 'and not merely because the alternative is too dreadful to contemplate. These abrasions under the arms – look, here, and here – fit with being hung from the bridge, but if he had been alive while someone gouged his eyes and tongue out, you would expect to see injuries on his hands and arms where he tried to protect himself.'

'Unless his hands were tied.'

'True, but there are no ligature marks on the wrists – only where the body was suspended.'

'That's another thing – how could someone hang a corpse from the Stone Bridge without being noticed?' I said, incredulous. 'Surely passers-by would have seen?'

'There was thick fog – you could barely see more than a few feet ahead. And not many people crossing at night.'

'That should make it all the easier to get a description from the guards. They must have noticed someone carrying a body.'

Hajek made a dismissive noise. 'I can tell you are a stranger to Prague. Those guards are easily bribed, especially in winter. They take the coin offered and stay in the warmth of their guardhouses in the towers at either end, seeing and hearing nothing. I'm afraid we can't expect any useful testimony from them, they will be too busy covering for one another.' He shook his head. 'This business with the eyes. I think the Emperor is right – someone is trying to make a point about blindness, about his failure to see. But to see what?'

'And his tongue,' I said, pointing to the corpse's lolling mouth. 'Can we expect that to be delivered to the Emperor at some point, with another cryptic verse?'

'Let's hope that damned idiot Strada opens the box first, if so,' Hajek muttered.

'You are certain Bartos wrote those notes himself?'

'It was his hand, I'm sure.'

'So – Bartos wrote out that verse about eyes and seeing, then lost his own eyes. I can't make sense of it. Have his lodgings been searched?'

'I have not had time today – I have been too busy with the body and trying to calm His Majesty. I don't know if Rudolf sent anyone else, though I doubt it – he was too distressed by the news, even before he received the casket tonight.'

'Someone took those papers from Bartos's rooms, either before or after his murder,' I said, thinking aloud. 'If there was anything else of value there, or anything that might explain why he was killed, they may have taken that too. But we should search as soon as possible, to make sure.'

Hajek smiled briefly as he drew the cloth back over the alchemist's sightless face. 'Dee said you were like a truffle pig when you caught the scent of a murder,' he murmured. 'You are quite right, of course. But would you not rather go back and sleep, and we can search in the morning when you are rested?'

I can't pretend I was not tempted. But I thought of the letter that had wrapped the casket sent to Rudolf – the claim, in Bartos's own writing, that he had finally achieved his goal and found what he had sought. Was it that boast that had signed his death warrant? Or was it just possible – though I found it hard to credit – that he had truly discovered something that would have made him pre-eminent among the alchemists? His death had been common knowledge in the city since he was found; his killer would have had plenty of time to pillage his lodgings and remove anything that might have linked them, or any such discovery Bartos might have made. But it was worth a try. It also struck me as a little odd that Hajek, who had been so eager to drag me from my bed, was suddenly solicitous about returning me to it. Surely he could have no reason for wanting to delay a search of the alchemist's rooms?

'*Carpe diem*, Hajek,' I said with determination.

'*Noctem*,' he said with a faint smile. 'Very well. Then we shall pay a visit to Golden Lane. Keep a hand on your dagger.'

SEVEN

He led me across the first courtyard and into the second, where torches flickered in wall brackets with little effect on the thick shadow cast by the tower of the cathedral. The castle appeared quiet: sentries yawned and slumped at their posts, making a brief show of alertness as we passed and relaxing again when they recognised Hajek, though I had an impression of unseen activity in the background. Now and again hooded figures scuttled around the edges of buildings and disappeared through hidden passageways. But there was no time to stop and wonder; Hajek kept up a brisk stride – the man seemed indefatigable, though it was gone one o'clock – and I hastened to follow him, when a sudden piercing howl cut through the still air, disconcertingly close, and my blood froze.

Hajek turned, amused. 'The wolves in Lion Court,' he said, gesturing to the northern walls. 'The Emperor's menagerie, over there in the gardens. The animals grow restless at night. I'll show you some time.'

He led me on around the cathedral, past a smaller chapel and into the mouth of a narrow, cobbled lane that ran parallel to the castle's north wall.

'This is not a place to come alone after dark, Bruno,' he said. I had no desire to do so; the street seemed to brood with a menace that I could not imagine would be much improved by daylight, and I found myself glancing uneasily over my shoulder, one hand on the knife at my belt as he had instructed. I had to assume that the name Golden Lane was ironic. The place reeked of poverty; small, ramshackle houses crowded in on both sides, so that the path itself was barely ten feet across. Acrid smoke drifted from chimneys, mingling with baser smells of refuse. Dim tallow lamps glowed in a few windows, but the glass was too soot-blackened to see anyone inside, or what they might be doing at this hour.

'These dwellings were originally built for soldiers of the castle guard,' Hajek informed me in a low voice as the lane curved downhill. 'Some say the name came about because they used to piss copiously in the street.'

'That would make sense,' I muttered, trying not to think about the slippery cobbles underfoot.

'After proper barracks were built outside the walls, the guards moved out, and gradually the alchemists took their place. Which is why you see so many windows lit – they keep unusual hours and entertain motley company.'

'Then surely there will be witnesses to what happened last night,' I said, brightening. 'If Bartos had a visitor, or if he left with someone, or his body was carried out – in a street this size the neighbours must have seen something. Have you made enquiries?'

He motioned to me to speak quietly. 'There is no guarantee that witnesses would be willing to come forward. The alchemists exist in a strange relationship to the law, Bruno. They are tolerated because the Emperor indulges them, but Prague is a Catholic city, in name at least, and plenty in the town regard alchemy as tantamount to witchcraft or black magic, so they like to keep a low profile. Now and then, if one of them draws unwelcome attention to himself, the city authorities will haul him up on charges of necromancy and the Emperor will not stir to prevent his banishment, because to allow the occasional successful prosecution helps preserve His Majesty's own reputation. That way he can insist that his patronage of the alchemists is not at odds with his faith – the way you might sacrifice a pawn for the sake of the long game. So while you may well be right that someone saw what happened, I would be most surprised if any of them were willing to admit to it, much less testify publicly. There is more advantage in silence. Here we are.'

We had reached a narrow house that appeared even more run-down than its neighbours, if that were possible. The latch had rusted and the wooden door looked half-rotten, the tiny window beside it grimed with dirt. As Hajek tried the handle, I sensed that prickling at the back of my neck that I had experienced in the Old Town Square, the feeling of being watched. I whipped around, at the same moment a lamp was extinguished in an upper window of the house opposite. I thought I saw a fleeting movement behind the glass, but I was distracted by Hajek's oath.

'Locked,' he said, rattling the iron ring. 'How frustrating. No matter – we can come back tomorrow with a locksmith. At least we know no one else can access the place in the meantime. You must be tired.'

'I had not thought a man who can make fire leap from his fingers would be so easily deterred by a locked door,' I said, affecting a jauntiness I did not feel. Hajek's attitude was beginning to trouble me. Despite professing his belief in Dee's innocence, he seemed determined to find obstacles to the most obvious lines of enquiry about Bartos's murder. I shunted him aside and tested the latch for myself. The lock was of a basic kind; the only challenge was how badly it was rusted. In truth, the whole door looked as if it would give way to one good kick, but I could see how that might be difficult to explain away. 'Hold the light closer, will you?' I asked him.

Hajek lifted his lantern, curious despite his objections. 'You think you can open it?'

'If you would give me the pin from your cloak.'

'Try not to break it,' he said, unfastening the clasp after a moment's hesitation. 'It was a gift.' He passed me a handsome brooch wrought from gold in the shape of an ouroboros, the serpent devouring itself. Two emeralds sparkled in its eyes. I crouched and fitted the pin into the lock, inserting the tip of my knife alongside it, trying to proceed by touch as the candle in Hajek's lantern burned lower.

'An unusual skill for a philosopher,' he remarked, holding his cloak together with one hand while he kept the light steady with the other.

'When I fled the Dominican order without permission,' I said, tentatively feeling for the pins inside the mechanism, 'I spent many months on the road north through the Italian states. You would be surprised at some of the things I learned from the people I met along the way.'

The lock took some work; I could feel him jiggling his leg impatiently at my side and feared he would insist we give up, but at last I felt that satisfying moment of congress as the bolt yields. I stood, returned the brooch to him – its pin only a little crooked – and held the door open with a small flush of triumph. He stepped through, looking grudgingly impressed.

Someone had beaten us to it. The initial impression, as I closed the door behind me, was that a hurricane had torn through the cramped room in which we found ourselves. Shards of glass and pottery lay scattered over the dirty rushes on the floor, where jars and alembics had clearly been dashed from the shelves, now almost empty, that ran along two walls. Shreds of paper were strewn over the stones by the hearth, and more charred fragments lay in the grate, though the ashes were long cold. The spilled contents of the jars gave rise to a peculiar mix of smells that reminded me of the time I had spent in John Dee's laboratory in Mortlake: preserving alcohol mingling with dried herbs, sulphur, wax, vitriol, vinegar, urine and decaying flowers. I picked my way gingerly across the floor – the chamber was so small it took only a few steps – and retrieved a half-burned candle from the chaos, which I lit from Hajek's dying lantern. The physician looked shaken; he cast his eyes around the devastation, hunched into the collar of his cloak. The ceiling was so low that even I had to stoop; only a man of the Emperor's size could have stood at his full height without hitting his head on the blackened beams.

'Do you think he tried to fight off his assailant?' Hajek asked.

I stepped back for a better perspective and heard something crunch under the heel of my boot; looking down, I saw the desiccated carcass of a lizard. A dark red stain leached across the flagstone beneath. The dampness of the room had prevented it from drying completely; I crouched and touched a finger to the substance, then sniffed it.

'Tincture of red lead. I see no sign of blood, and you said yourself, the fatal wound was not inflicted during a fight. Wherever he died, it wasn't here. But someone clearly wanted something they believed was in this house.'

'The news of his death was all over town by this morning,' Hajek said, bending to retrieve an object from the floor. He held up a small round nugget of silvery metal, its surface etched with a star pattern. 'See, here – antimony. Alchemists' ingredients don't come cheap – perhaps his competitors saw their chance to loot his belongings.'

I shook my head. 'Then they would not have left the antimony, for a start. This was not some opportunist robbery – all his jars have been smashed and trodden underfoot. No alchemist would waste valuable substances so casually. No – whoever did this was looking for something in particular.'

'Bartos's writings, perhaps? If he truly had made some chymical discovery, that would be worth a great deal to his rivals.'

'Possibly. Or else Bartos had something in his possession that could link him to his killer, and the killer wanted to remove that evidence.' I shone the light slowly around the room again. In one corner there was a rickety table and chair, and beneath it a chest with its lid hanging open. On closer examination, I could see that the wood around the lock was splintered where it had been forced. A few scraps of paper remained inside the chest; I lifted them out to find notes in the same distinctive spiky hand we had seen in the casket letter: alchemical formulae and astrological observations in Latin, other jottings in Czech which I would have to leave to Hajek to interpret. 'I think you're right – this was in pursuit of papers,' I said, passing him the bundle of pages. 'We should look through these in case the looter missed anything, though I doubt it – he seems to have been thorough. Some pages have been burned – we should sift through the ashes, in case any scraps escaped the flames. Whoever it was entered with a key, too, which argues that it was the killer himself – he must have taken it from the body.'

'Unless he possessed your familiarity with locks.'

'Much harder to lock a door without a key than to unlock it. And by the state of this place, he was not in the mood for patience. I think he had the key.'

'What puzzles me,' Hajek said, tucking the papers into his medical bag, 'is the way the finger seems to point in two directions at once.'

'How do you mean?'

'Well – the Hebrew letters cut into the dead man's flesh suggest the killer wanted people to make an immediate association with the Jews and the Golem. And yet, at the same time, there is also this peculiar business of Bartos's altercation with John Dee – his very public accusation of theft and plagiarism. I didn't witness it myself, but those who did said it had the air of a performance, as if Bartos wanted to plant the idea that Dee was his enemy.'

'But Bartos could not have anticipated that he would be murdered, could he?' I asked. 'If he was trying to tarnish Dee's reputation, it must have been for some other reason.'

The doctor rubbed a hand across his forehead. 'I cannot fathom it, Bruno. Let us go home and rest, and we can apply ourselves to all this in daylight. I have a busy day tomorrow and my bed is calling.'

I nodded reluctantly, taking a last look around Bartos's devastated room. I felt sure there was more to be discovered

84

here; I would have liked to make a thorough search now, especially since whoever had extinguished that light in the house opposite had certainly seen us enter, and may be inclined to warn someone. But I could hardly insist on staying without Hajek; I did not like my chances of making it back to the House on the Green Mound alone with those Spaniards waiting for me somewhere out there in the dark streets.

'Talking of beds,' I said, 'where did he sleep?'

Hajek nodded to the ceiling, and I noticed in the far corner, opposite the table, a narrow ladder leading up to a hatch.

'Give me two minutes.' I stepped over broken glass and began to climb. 'Perhaps you could see if there is anything to be salvaged from the papers in the hearth before we go.'

If he resented me giving him orders, he made no objection. I pushed open the hatch and poked my head through the small gap, giving thanks – not for the first time – that I had the wiry build of a Neapolitan and not the bulk of these northern Europeans I had lived among for the past few years.

The upper floor was little more than a crawl space, with barely room for a man to enter on hands and knees; I winced as I leaned my weight on my bandaged wrist. Something brushed my face as I wriggled in; I flicked it away and glanced up to see a rosary hanging from a nail in one of the beams, over a straw pallet whose innards were now scattered across the boards where it had been slashed with a knife down each side. I dripped a few spots of wax and stuck the candle carefully to the floor – with all this loose straw and the flammable liquids downstairs, it would only take an instant to send the place up like a tinder-box – so that I could feel around in what was left of the mattress. I had little expectation of success and was on the point of giving up when my fingers closed on a metal disc. I drew it out and in the light I saw that it was a gold coin. Impressed on its face was the shield of King Phillip II of Spain.

'Nothing in the grate. Anything up there?' Hajek called from below.

I slid down the ladder and held it out on my palm. 'Look

at this. A gold escudo. Hidden inside his bedding, though the searcher had torn it to pieces. I wonder if there were more, and this one escaped?'

Hajek took the coin and examined it, his mouth set in a tight line.

'It seems you were right,' I prompted, when he didn't reply. 'Bartos *was* taking Spanish money. But what for? To accuse John?'

He turned the coin between his fingers as if considering how much to say. 'I do not know, Bruno, but this troubles me. It suggests that Bartos's death was bigger than a rivalry between alchemists.'

'The two men who attacked me were Spanish,' I said, rubbing my wrist. 'Could that be connected?'

'Again, I cannot say. I know only that Spain is no friend to the Emperor, whatever they might pretend. Nor to the likes of you and me,' he added with a note of warning.

'You don't have to tell me that,' I said, recalling the many times I had found myself pitted against Spanish interests in the course of my work for Walsingham. I knew all too well what dangerous enemies they made.

'Which is why I counsel you to be careful,' Hajek said, looking me sternly in the eye. 'I know you are keen to prove Dee's innocence and win the Emperor's favour, but if this murder is anything to do with the Spanish, you would be inviting danger, and I do not know if I can protect you.'

'I have not asked you to,' I said, piqued, though my fingers strayed to the bandage on my wrist, a sharp reminder that he had already done so.

'No, of course. But I can't help feeling a certain responsibility. I have read your books, Bruno. Men such as you do not come along often, and it would be a great waste of your genius if you were to be extinguished by one blow of a cudgel from brutes like those we saw off tonight, simply because you had gone about asking awkward questions. I felt the same about Dee, and look where that has ended.'

'You don't think Dee is dead?' I asked, as a chill rippled through me.

He pressed his lips together. 'I think there are those in Prague who would like him dead, given the work he was engaged in. The Spanish chief among them.'

'What do you mean?'

He made an impatient little noise through his nose and dropped his voice to a whisper. 'Let us not pretend, Bruno. I know he was sending ciphered letters back to England. And if I knew it, there's a good chance the Spanish did too. So if you are here for the same purpose' – he gave a pointed glance to my doublet, where I had tucked the papers – 'I strongly advise you to take more care that you are not observed.' He slipped the gold escudo inside his bag and rolled his shoulders. 'Let us go home and sleep. Tomorrow I will consider whether to approach San Clemente.'

'Who?'

'Don Guillén de San Clemente. The Spanish ambassador.'

'You think the *ambassador* is involved?' As soon as I had spoken I realised I was not at all surprised; I had had my own run-ins with Spain's ambassador to London and Paris, who had been enthusiastically active in conspiracies on King Philip's behalf.

'As I mentioned before, Philip of Spain is keen to steer his nephew the Emperor back to a more orthodox Catholic faith,' Hajek said. 'The ambassador's purpose here, along with the papal nuncio, is to put pressure on Rudolf on behalf of Spain and Rome. Wherever there is intrigue in this court, you may be sure it leads back to San Clemente and Montalcino. What is it?' He caught my expression. 'Are you all right?'

I blinked, incredulous. 'Did you say *Montalcino*? Not Agostino da Montalcino?'

'That's right. He is the Pope's envoy here in Prague. Why – do you know him?'

I nodded, leaning heavily against the wall. 'Our paths have crossed. He was head of the Dominican order in Rome when

I was a young friar. He accused me of heresy in front of the Pope.'

'Ah. Then it would be safe to say you are not on friendly terms.'

'I think he would burn me as soon as look at me,' I said. '*Dio porco*.' I made my tone light-hearted – Montalcino could have no authority here in the Emperor's domains, and I would not have Hajek thinking I was afraid – but when I tried to swallow my throat had dried. If Agostino da Montalcino learned that I was in Prague, he would do everything in his power to bring me down one way or another, especially if he was connected to this murder and Dee's disappearance. Even at twenty years' distance from our last encounter, the memory of his fleshy face with its bristling wart and searching eyes made the hairs on my arms stand up. The last I had heard of him, he had become an inquisitor, which had not surprised me in the slightest. So he was papal nuncio now; well, he had always been ambitious, though I doubted his move into diplomacy had lessened his old taste for inflicting pain.

'All the more reason for you to keep away from this Bartos business,' Hajek said firmly. 'Come. Time for bed. We can talk further in the morning.'

I disliked leaving Bartos's house unlocked, but I reasoned that the searcher had probably taken what he wanted already. As I closed the door behind me, I glanced across at the house opposite and again thought I saw a shadow move behind the window. Whoever lived there was clearly taking an interest in us. I decided I would return and speak to them, and even the thought of Agostino da Montalcino would not deter me.

EIGHT

'I can't *believe* I slept through the whole thing,' Besler exclaimed, for about the twentieth time, his mouth full of bread. 'Did you see the door knocker with the cockstand?'

'No, Besler, it was dark. I was not there for sightseeing.' I took a draught of warm milk and flexed my bandaged wrist. Hajek's salves had done their work; already it felt less tender, my bruised shoulder too. I saw why the Emperor valued him as a physician.

We sat at Hajek's kitchen table the morning after my visit to the castle, as a weak sun filtered through the latticed panes and dust motes circled like flecks of silver. I had woken late, to find Hajek already gone and Besler making himself at home by the kitchen range, tucking into a plate of warm bread and butter, continually replenished by Greta, who seemed to have taken to the boy; at least, she was markedly less frosty with him than with me, and I noticed they now spoke to one another in Czech. In the rare moments when she left the room, I had given Besler an edited version of the night before, leaving out the fact that the papal nuncio in Prague was an old enemy who would like to see me burned for heresy; I didn't want to worry the boy more than necessary. Not that he looked as if anything would trouble him; he had the bright-eyed, fresh-faced appearance of someone who has slept almost twelve hours. I had barely managed two, and in my dishevelled state I resented his chirpiness.

'But, really, you should be honoured,' he continued, still chewing. 'That the Emperor wants you to look into the alchemist's death. Although it is a strange request to make of a philosopher.'

Greta was busying herself at the stove with her back to us, but I saw the way she stilled at the mention of the murder. I motioned for Besler to be quiet. Finally, she disappeared into the yard and I leaned across the table.

'The fewer people who know what the Emperor has asked of me, the safer for us,' I hissed, gesturing to the door.

He frowned. 'But she is only an old servant.'

'Servants have eyes and ears, and she takes a good deal of interest in our conversations.' I propped my elbows on the table and ran my hands through my hair. 'Look, Besler – this trip is shaping up to be quite unlike what I anticipated. I mean to look into this death because it seems the only way to clear John Dee's name—'

'And because the Emperor will reward you,' he added.

'Possibly, though there is no guarantee of that,' I said, thinking again of Queen Elizabeth. 'But I must be completely honest with you – in my experience, a killer will go to any lengths to avoid discovery, so there will be danger. I can't put you in that position.'

His face took a moment to catch up with his understanding; when it did, it crumpled almost comically with disappointment.

'Do you mean to send me back?'

'I have been thinking.' I had done little else all night, lying awake in the dark because to close my eyes meant seeing Ziggi Bartos's ruined face, or the malicious sneer of Fra Agostino da Montalcino. 'There is an English merchant I know, leaving Prague imminently for Leipzig. You could travel safely that far with him, and I could ask him to make provision for you onwards to Wittenberg. I'm sorry, Besler' – his lip was trembling like a child's – 'but your father would—'

'My father is not here,' he cut in hotly, 'and I will not be packed off like a boy to school with some merchant. I am in your service, and I will stay at your side regardless of the danger.'

I half wanted to laugh; he sounded like a knight in a courtly tale, swearing allegiance to King Arthur.

'But you're not really, though, are you?' I pointed out. 'In my service, I mean. I have no right to risk your safety, it would be wrong.'

'You also have no right to make choices for me,' he said, drawing himself up. 'I may not need to shave often, but I am a grown man, Dr Bruno, and besides, I have my own money. If you send me away, I shall simply find lodgings in Prague at my own expense, and begin making enquiries into the murder to help you.'

'Christ, no – please don't even think about it,' I said, pressing my forehead into my hand. I didn't want to picture the consequences if Besler took it upon himself to run around town knocking on doors with his guileless questions. I sighed; I could see he was not to be deterred. 'All right, but listen. I saw what was done to the alchemist. This man – whoever he is – has no mercy. So if you insist on remaining here, you must trust my judgement, and promise to do exactly as I tell you, even if that is to stay home and keep out of harm's way. Understood?'

His eyes lit up with delight and I felt a sinking in my gut; I could only hope I was doing the right thing, and that my judgement was up to the task.

'I will follow your instructions to the letter, Maestro,' he said, knocking back his bowl of milk and wiping his mouth on his sleeve. 'I only want to learn from you.'

'There are some lessons you would be better off without,' I said, thinking again of Montalcino.

'Anyway, how do you know it is a man?' he asked.

'What do you mean?'

'Well, you said "this man is without mercy". But how are you so sure it is a man who killed Bartos?'

'That is a very good question.' I pointed at him, nodding

my approval. 'See – you are thinking like an investigator already. You're quite right that a woman could be capable of murder – I have seen it before. But in this case, it would have taken some strength to heave the body over the bridge. I doubt a woman could do that alone – even a strong man would struggle. And the nature of the killing blow – Hajek believes it was dealt by someone familiar with a dagger. Perhaps someone who had learned on the battlefield, or a practised assassin. That also argues against a woman. What?' I added, catching his anxious expression.

'I was not suggesting a woman.'

It took me a moment to figure his meaning. 'Are you still thinking about the Golem?'

'Greta says it has killed before.'

'For the love of God, Besler – the Golem is a myth. And you should know better than to listen to old women's stories. Although – now that you are such friends with Greta, see if you can find out – subtly, mind – what she has heard about the murder. Servants' gossip can often be instructive. Now, get your cloak and gloves, it's cold out.'

'Where shall we start?' He jumped up eagerly, as if I had promised a great adventure.

'The Jewish quarter. How is your Hebrew?'

Consternation briefly dimmed his bright look. 'Not so good. My father didn't approve of me learning. What do we seek there?'

'Anyone who might know what has happened to John Dee.' I had not told Besler about the letter, but I felt certain that somewhere in the Jewish Town I would discover the identity of the mysterious Maharal, and perhaps learn from him the nature of this danger Dee anticipated.

'Should I make the horses ready?'

'No, we'll go on foot. Less conspicuous, and we won't have to worry about leaving them.'

He paused at the door; I could see him wrestling with another question.

'Courage, Besler,' I said, patting him on the shoulder as I passed. 'I don't think the Golem comes out in daylight.'

We took the street north from Bethlehem Square, following the curve of the Vltava and skirting the grand complex of the Clementinium, the Jesuit College that stood between the river bank and the Old Town Square. I had heard it boasted a fine library, but my last encounter with Jesuits in London was not an experience I wanted to repeat, and had left me with the desire to keep a healthy distance from them wherever possible. Besides, I reminded myself, I had an invitation from Ottavio Strada to visit the imperial library at the castle – one I meant to take up as soon as time allowed. A sharp breeze off the river chivvied scraps of cloud across a blue sky; I struck a brisk pace so that even Besler, with his long legs, had to scurry to keep up. I remained alert as we walked, but I was fairly confident we were not followed this time; perhaps the Spaniards had been frightened off for now, though I doubted that whoever had sent them would be deterred for long.

Beyond the Clementinium the streets grew narrower until we passed through a gate between high walls, into a town within a town. Here the houses were built of wood, smaller and more tightly clustered; despite the sense of overcrowding, I could see that front steps were neatly swept and windows kept clean, unlike the dwellings I had seen in Golden Lane the night before. There were carved mezuzahs affixed to the doorposts, a display of faith that would not be seen openly in many European cities.

I was uncertain, now that we were here, of how to proceed. I needed to find the man Dee had written to, but I was reluctant to walk up to a stranger and ask directly; from the snippet of the letter it sounded as if Dee's association with the person he addressed as Maharal was a matter of secrecy, and clearly there was some degree of danger involved. We turned on to a street with a row of shops along each side, ware-benches with goods for sale outside each one. Women in headscarves browsed the trestles of clothes, shoes, hats and pottery, eyeing us with curiosity and a measure of wariness as we passed. I felt Besler at my back, tucked in close, his head darting to either side as if he anticipated an ambush at any moment. Whatever reservations I may have had about involving him in a murder enquiry, I could at least persuade myself that this excursion was a valuable part of his education. I hoped that meeting people face to face might go some way to counter the pernicious ideas that the Lutherans had put into his head about the Jews.

At the end of the street we turned a corner and saw, directly ahead, a buttressed building of pale stone with a roof of red tiles rising to a high point. Outside, two men with brooms and a pail of water scrubbed at words that had been crudely painted on the façade. The writing was in Czech, though one word needed no translation. I nudged Besler.

'What does that say?'

He gave a little cough and looked uncomfortably at his boots. 'It says "Christ-killers out, Golem out".'

I cursed under my breath and shook my head. I had not expected to see such open displays of ignorance and hatred in Prague. I had been naïve, I realised; the attitude of the crowd on the bridge yesterday should have taught me that already.

The two men cleaning the wall were conversing in a language I recognised as Yiddish, though I could not understand it. The older one – a short, balding man in his forties – noticed us watching and his expression grew guarded. He called something in Czech. I looked at Besler.

'Uh – he asked if we have come to gloat,' he murmured.

I stepped forward and greeted the man in formal Hebrew with a brief bow.

'Who has done this?' I asked.

He looked surprised to hear me speak the language, then shrugged and turned back to his cleaning. 'Does it matter? They won't be punished.'

'Does it happen often?'

94

The younger man turned and appraised us. His coat and shoes were patched and worn, the red scarf around his neck was fraying, but he had a handsome face, lent a touch of melancholy by his large brown eyes. The fingers and thumb of his right hand were stained with ink; I recognised a fellow scholar and hoped he might be more inclined to talk to us. He leaned on his brush and pushed his dark curly hair out of his eyes.

'Too often,' he said with a grimace of resignation. 'But it's worse since—' He stopped abruptly.

'Since the murder yesterday?'

He nodded. 'We have to hope they will find the killer soon, so that these absurd rumours can stop. If painting is the worst that happens, we will count ourselves lucky. Sometimes they break windows, spit at women in the street . . .' His voice tailed off and I heard the weariness in it.

'I'm sorry,' I said. I knew, from my time in London, what it was to be spat at in the street because of the assumptions people made about my religion, but it was nothing compared to what the Jews endured all over the continent. He must have heard my sincerity, because he looked up and met my eye with a sad smile.

'Thank you,' he said. 'How do you know Hebrew so well?'

'I have studied your Scriptures,' I began, with what I hoped was appropriate humility, but the older man gave a loud snort of contempt and resumed his scrubbing more vigorously.

The young man darted an apologetic look. 'My cousin does not think Gentiles have any business with our books. For myself, I believe learning should be shared, otherwise how will we ever hope to understand—'

'Because it is not a question of sharing,' snapped the older man, turning and levelling his broom handle at me. 'There is no reciprocity, only theft. Christian scholars cannibalise our wisdom, picking and choosing from our sacred texts, appropriating the parts that suit them, thinking they can make it their own. They talk of the Christian Cabala, as if such an entity could even exist – as if all our centuries of learning are a mere stepping stone to their own superior enlightenment.' He let out a scornful laugh. 'The entitlement of it! Meanwhile, they don't do a damned thing to stop *this* from happening, over and over.' He indicated the writing on the wall.

'David,' the younger man said in a warning tone, but David was not to be diverted now that he had begun.

'That alchemist who died, he was one,' he continued. 'Came here looking for books, demanding access to our libraries, pestering our teachers – not from respect, but in pursuit of secrets he could turn to his own advantage.'

'You knew Ziggi Bartos?' I said.

'I knew he was one of those who believed he could understand in a matter of months the mysteries that have taken our rabbis and scholars a lifetime to comprehend. And if you ask me, the Englishman is no better, even if the Maharal likes him.'

'David, *enough*.' The young man spoke sharply this time, and glanced at me. 'Forgive me, but we must finish this job. We can't leave the synagogue like this.' He picked up his brush and turned away.

'Wait,' I said, clasping him by the shoulder. 'What Englishman?'

He stepped back, alarmed by my urgency. 'An older man. Long pointed beard. His name is John Dee. He comes often to study with the Maharal, they spend hours together in conversation. Or at least, they used to.'

'When did you last see him?'

He frowned. 'A month ago, perhaps. Do you know him?'

'He's my friend. I am trying to find him. Tell me of this Maharal? Might he know something? If it is a he.'

He smiled. 'It's a nickname for our rabbi. An acronym – from *Moreinu ha-Rav Loew*. It means "Our Teacher Rabbi Loew".'

'Not Rabbi *Judah* Loew?'

'You know the rabbi?'

'I know his reputation, of course.' I could not keep the excitement from my voice. 'He is one of the leading scholars of the Cabala in all Europe, I have read his commentaries. I thought he lived in Poland?'

'*The* leading scholar,' the man called David said, and his expression softened a little. 'He was in Posnan, he returned to Prague two years ago.'

'And Rabbi Loew knows John Dee? I didn't realise. What did they talk about?'

David shook his head and turned his attention back to the wall.

'It was all very secretive,' the younger man confided. 'There were those in the community, like my cousin David here, who were concerned that Rabbi Loew was over-friendly with a Gentile, particularly one known to be a seeker of hidden knowledge. People feared Dee was a spy for the Emperor, sent to find evidence that could be used to make accusations of conspiracy.'

'And now there is a murder designed to turn the city against us,' David said, his voice hard again. 'So perhaps, Benjamin, you concede we were right to be suspicious.'

'Might I speak to the Maharal?' I asked. 'He may have some idea of where I can find Dee.'

The young man, Benjamin, looked at me uncertainly.

'Well, but – who are you?'

'Forgive me.' I bowed again. 'Dr Giordano Bruno of Nola, and this is my assistant, Hieronymus Besler.'

Poor Besler had not understood a word of the conversation so far, but he perked up at the mention of his name and followed my example, bobbing his head in a bow.

'We're guests of Dr Thaddeus Hajek,' I added, since Benjamin was still looking at me expectantly. 'I understand he is known to your community.'

'Dr Hajek has been a friend to us,' Benjamin said, nodding slowly. He appeared to be weighing up the possibilities. After a moment, he held out his hand to me. 'Benjamin Katz,' he said as I shook it. 'Well, I will take you to the Maharal, though I can't promise he will see you. He has a lot to contend with right now.' He glanced back at the writing on the wall.

'We can speak in Czech if it's easier for your friend,' he

97

added as he led us past the synagogue and down a twisting side street. 'Or Italian?'

'You know my language?'

He nodded. 'I studied in Padua.'

'Really? That's a long way to go.'

He gave me a sidelong look. 'Surely you know, we are not permitted to enter the universities in Bohemia or the German lands. Your country has been more accepting in that regard – there have been a number of Jewish students at the medical schools in Padua, Pisa, Ferrara. I was fortunate that members of the community raised funds for me to travel.'

'That's your profession – medicine?' I said. 'Besler here is a medical student too, in Wittenberg. It might be easier for him if we spoke German.'

'Of course,' he said, switching. 'I must apologise for my cousin David. He takes the view that we protect ourselves by looking inward, preserving our traditions by keeping the rest of the world out, the way the ghetto is contained within its walls. He regards every outsider as a potential enemy.'

'I can't fault him for that, in the circumstances,' I said. 'But you disagree?'

'I do.' Benjamin darted a quick glance at me. 'I think prejudice is broken down by opening up, not shutting ourselves away. I would like to see the walls torn down altogether. All manner of walls, visible and invisible. We must be part of the world we live in, else how will the Christians know that we are men and women like them, and not monsters who drink the blood of children? Rabbi Loew feels the same, I believe – at least, he is always willing to listen and converse with men of all religions. But this murder of Ziggi Bartos will be bad for us. You could feel it yesterday, as soon as news spread of what was done to the man. Some people boarded up their shop windows in anticipation of reprisals. Here we are.'

He stopped in front of a timber-framed house, broader and taller than its neighbours, the window frames freshly painted, silver candlesticks visible on the sill through the glass. He knocked and stepped back; I glanced at him, surprised to see that he seemed nervous, twisting his hands and shifting from foot to foot as we heard steps approach from inside.

The door opened and immediately I understood the cause of his disequilibrium. On the threshold stood an exceptionally beautiful young woman. She was tall and slender, with pale skin and long black hair tied back under a scarf; as her clear gaze alighted on me, it stirred a memory of a Jewish girl I had known in Naples, long ago.

'Ben?' She greeted him with a questioning smile, which faltered as she took in Besler and me. They exchanged a few words in Yiddish, in which I caught John Dee's name. Eventually she nodded.

'I'm Esther Loew,' she said to me, in German. 'My father is not at home, but I expect him back any moment. You can wait if you like?' She opened the door wider and gestured inside.

I thanked her and introduced myself and Besler, hiding a smile at the way the boy was helplessly staring as if he'd had a divine visitation. I could hardly blame him; her beauty was so arresting, it was all I could do to keep my own face steady.

'I'll wait with you,' Benjamin said, almost aggressively. Esther held up a hand to forestall him.

'There's no need, Ben – the rabbi will not be long and you must be needed at the hospital. I will be quite safe with these gentlemen, I'm sure.'

He said something else in Yiddish, low and impatient as if he were angry with her; she responded calmly with a shake of her head and nodded to me.

'Please, come in.'

'Close your mouth, Besler,' I hissed as we followed her into the entrance hall. I turned back to thank Benjamin, but he was glaring at us with a stony expression and I could see that he was reluctant to leave Esther alone in our company. I wondered if this was a general wariness of strangers, or some more specific reason.

Esther showed us into a comfortably furnished parlour with

a fire burning in the hearth and we took a seat on a wooden settle, its arms worn smooth and shiny with age.

'Benjamin is protective of you,' I observed, taking in my surroundings. The furniture was simple, but well-made; Rabbi Loew evidently had money. Esther gave me a sharp look.

'He is devoted to my father,' she said, 'and so he worries unnecessarily about our family. He knows I can look after myself.'

'I think it is more than that.' I caught her eye. 'I think his concern is all for you.'

She blushed at this, and for the briefest moment I saw a shadow cross her face, as if she had allowed herself to remember an old sorrow. In the next instant she shook it away and smiled briskly again.

'So, you are looking for John Dee? We have not seen him here for some time. My father has been concerned.'

'He seems to have vanished,' I said. 'I was hoping Rabbi Loew might have heard from him, or know where he has gone?'

'What makes you think my father would know?' she said, and I caught a note of defensiveness in her voice.

I hesitated, but decided not to mention the letter except to the rabbi himself; I did not want to worry her.

'Only that I believe they were in touch. I wondered if John might have confided in him. I think he was afraid of something.'

She glanced at the door. 'Everyone is afraid of something in this city. You saw what was written on the Old-New Synagogue today, I suppose? This murder was intended to stoke fear of us, with the result that we now live in terror of mobs burning our houses and looting our shops.'

'Your father knew the dead man, I understand?'

Her face tightened. 'Not well. My father has nothing to do with this.'

'I didn't mean to suggest – it's only that John Dee knew Bartos too, I wondered if he might have discussed him with the rabbi?'

'You would have to ask him. You don't believe Dr Dee is

connected with the murder, though?' She frowned, as if she found it hard to credit.

'I don't, but there are rumours of a dispute between them that would make him a suspect, and his disappearance has only compounded that.'

'I don't understand.' She shook her head. 'I thought, from what they said was done to the body, that the killer wanted the world to think it was the work of the Golem. Which would be ironic.'

'Ironic, how?'

She hesitated. She had remained standing, one hand resting on the high-backed chair next to the hearth that I guessed was her father's. 'Because Ziggi Bartos was obsessed with the legend of the Golem. He was constantly pestering my father, offering him money, demanding to know how one might go about generating such a creature. He believed it was another version of the alchemists' quest to make a homunculus. You know what that is, I presume?'

'Of course. The idea that a human-like being can be created in a laboratory, in a glass vessel,' I added for Besler's sake. John Dee had once experimented with making a homunculus, I recalled; it had involved burying quantities of his own semen in a bed of moist soil and heating it in an alembic for forty days, waiting for it to show signs of life. Needless to say, it had never worked and the smell was diabolical.

Esther gave a dry laugh. 'It is a desire common to men of all religions, it seems. God has given them a perfectly efficient way to make new people' – she patted her own stomach – 'and yet they remain convinced that a better means must be possible, one that removes women from the equation altogether.'

'It is my understanding that both the Golem and the homunculus have the advantage of unfailing obedience to their creator,' I said.

She smiled. 'Yes, the same certainly cannot be said of children. Do you have any?'

'Children?' I hesitated. 'No. Do you?'

'I am not married. Yet,' she added more quietly. 'But my sisters have plenty between them, so I can understand the attraction of making a being that would obey your every word – although in all the legends, the creature longs to escape its master's control, so perhaps not so different from parenthood.' She reached up to tuck a loose strand of hair into her scarf and I noticed the curve of her throat, her fine jaw and cheekbones, how she wore her beauty so unselfconsciously. 'It began as a joke among friends, you know, or at least a hypothetical discussion,' she continued, 'this idea that my father had the knowledge to make a Golem, and somehow the story grew in the telling, until all over Prague it was the one thing everyone knew about him. Ziggi Bartos refused to believe that he didn't possess the secret, and I'm afraid the Maharal can be mischievous – it amused him to tease Bartos with the idea that he was not ready to be inducted into such powerful mysteries.'

'Why was Bartos so determined to make a creature?' I asked.

She let an impatient huff of air escape her lips. 'Why do any of them pursue their mad ideas? To please the Emperor. It is all anyone thinks of in this town.' There was bitterness in her tone, but before I could ask another question, she said, 'Are you an alchemist, then?'

I straightened. 'I am a philosopher.'

'How grand.' She didn't trouble to hide the twitch of amusement at the corners of her mouth, and I saw, too late, that I was no better than Besler or Benjamin, puffing myself up like a foolish youth to impress a beautiful girl. Though she was hardly a girl; I guessed her to be in her late twenties. I felt the colour rise in my face – not something I had experienced for some time – and glanced away in confusion.

'Well, Master Philosopher,' she said, moving towards the door, 'and your silent friend, I should offer you some refreshment. Will you take wine?'

'A little early for me. If you have any fresh water or small beer, I would be grateful.'

She nodded. As she was about to leave, we heard the sound of the front door opening.

'Ah. There is the Maharal – wait here.'

She left, and I caught the cadences of a murmured conversation from the hall, before the parlour door opened again and a stately figure appeared in the doorway.

When I was a young friar in Naples, one of my mentors, Giambattista della Porta, had believed firmly in the science of physionomonics: the idea that a person's character can be read in their face. I had always disagreed with him on this point – even at twenty, I thought it self-evident that all of us dissemble in our different ways, and some are highly skilled at hiding their true natures – but now and again I encountered an exception that made me concede his point. I liked Rabbi Judah Loew immediately. He could not have been far off seventy, but there was a vigour about him that belied his years, from the thick mane of white hair swept back from a high forehead, to the bushy grey beard, and the bright, shrewd gaze that assessed me and Besler with friendly curiosity. He was not especially tall, but he was broad-chested and hearty, creating the impression of a big man, and I saw an essential goodness in his expression, as if he went through life determined to find the best in everyone he met until they proved otherwise. His face was lined with the creases that come from years of laughter, not the pinched expression that some old men acquire from disillusion, though he must have carried more than his share of care on his shoulders over the decades.

'Well, well,' he said, addressing us in German, extending his arms as Esther took his coat. 'Dr Bruno – John Dee's illustrious friend. We've been impatient to meet you, haven't we, Esther? John spoke of you so often with admiration, he was so hoping you would find the time to visit. Come – welcome to Prague.'

I stood and he wrapped me in a bear-like embrace, then turned to Besler.

'And you, my young friend. My home is your home for as long as you are here.' He grasped Besler by the shoulders and planted a kiss on each of his cheeks; the boy looked too astonished to speak. 'Daughter, fetch beer and cakes, if we have any.' He shook out his jacket and settled himself in the chair by the fire.

'I fear my arrival in Prague has come at a bad time,' I said, when Esther had left the room.

His expression grew serious, and he made a gesture with his palms spread wide. 'When is it not? But you've seen already how this murder ripples back to us. Ziggi Bartos will not be widely mourned for his own sake, poor man – the alchemists are not much liked by the townspeople – but you will be amazed at how hotly they defend his memory if they can be convinced that I sent my creature to kill a Christian.' He shook his head at the folly of it. 'I have just come from my Talmudic school, where two windows were smashed last night and human excrement left on the doorstep. The young scholars are understandably afraid.'

'But that's terrible,' Besler burst out, his face a picture of outrage. 'Who would do that to a *school*?'

The rabbi studied him from beneath his thick brows. 'Stories are powerful, you must know this. And those we learn from the cradle and hear repeated often by the ones we most respect – our mothers and fathers, our teachers and religious leaders – those are the most potent of all. Sadly, there are many in Prague who have grown up being told that my people are a threat to them, that the Emperor gives us too much liberty, that we will never be satisfied until we have taken all business and coin and land away from good Christians. You know, perhaps, that there are near ten thousand of us here in the Jewish Town, and the Emperor has given us self-rule? That is too much for some, who fear we want to replace them altogether. And they repeat these falsehoods to their children, who pass them on, and so the stories become hardened, as if written in stone. It takes a strong intellect and a degree of humility to pause and question what we learned from our fathers, do you not agree?'

Besler gaped at him as if the rabbi was reading his mind. I bit down a smile; we are making progress, I thought.

'Your daughter mentioned that Bartos visited you here,' I said.

Loew nodded. 'Regularly, for a while. My door is open to anyone who wishes to learn, if he is sincere. Although for every alchemist who ventures down from the castle with a genuine desire to understand, there are ten who treat the Cabala as a magic trick they want me to teach them, and others who come only to try and catch me out in some manner of heresy that will give them something to report.'

'Was Bartos sincere?'

He considered for a moment. 'Bartos was desperate,' he said. 'He was a gifted young man, that much was clear from our first meeting, intelligent and well-read, but he feared he was failing. He had been in Prague a year and had not succeeded in his experiments with the Philosopher's Stone. He was deeply in debt – much of it to our moneylenders – running out of credit, and he feared the Emperor had lost patience with him. So he came to me, frantic for something that would capture His Majesty's interest. He felt it was his last chance.'

'He wanted you to share the secret of creating a Golem?'

He allowed a faint smile. 'It is an old legend, and one that has somehow attached itself to me. But there are versions of it in many cultures, as I'm sure you know – man's desire to create a being without the need for a womb, the way God formed Adam from clay.'

'Paracelsus believed that the homunculus would be a perfect being, because it would be free of all taint and corruption by female elements,' Besler piped up.

Loew laughed softly. 'Exactly. Do not let my daughter Esther hear you say that; she has strong views on such matters. I'm afraid I entertained myself at Ziggi Bartos's expense, but he was so persistent – he refused to accept that I could not teach him how to make a Golem. He offered me money I knew he did not have, so in the end the only way I could dissuade him

105

was to tell him he was simply not ready, and to come back when he had studied further.'

'What made him think that making a creature was the key to the Emperor's favour?' I asked, puzzled.

'Well – it would be a novelty, and Rudolf does love wonders. But consider also that His Majesty has no heir. No legitimate one, anyway.'

'You think Bartos wanted to make an *heir* for the Emperor in his laboratory? That's insane.'

'It is not the most outlandish idea to come out of that castle, by a long way,' the rabbi said with equanimity. 'But as I told you, he was grasping at straws.'

I pressed my fingers to my temples; the lack of sleep was beginning to catch up with me as I tried to process this new information. So Ziggi Bartos had been deeply in debt – and yet I had found Spanish gold in his bed chamber. A man with creditors is easily manipulated. What could Bartos have sold the Spanish faction, or promised them, in his desperation? The idea that he was attempting to create a homunculus for the Emperor was preposterous – but, as the rabbi said, no more preposterous than the pursuit of an elixir that would make men immortal, or turn base metal to gold.

'Pardon me, Dr Bruno, but why do you concern yourself so with the death of a man you never met?' Loew asked gently.

'Because the Emperor is convinced that John Dee is involved, and told me that he will hang for it if he ever returns to Prague, unless I can prove his innocence.' And Dee had found something to trouble him here, something he had written of in great haste to Sir Francis Walsingham in England; shortly afterwards he had been falsely accused of theft and disappeared. Now his accuser was the victim of a brutal murder, so it was not unreasonable to surmise that the two were connected. I didn't think the rabbi needed to know this yet.

'Hm.' Loew sat back and pulled at his beard. 'So. The murderer wishes to incriminate John, and also to show clearly to the good Christian citizens of Prague what comes of meddling with the Jews. It seems to me, therefore, that we must look for a common enemy.'

I thought of Dee's letter; he had used the phrase 'our enemies' as if it were a shared persecution. 'Yes – that is what I wanted to ask you—'

At that moment the door opened and Esther entered with a tray of glasses and a plate of honey cakes. The rabbi smiled at her.

'My dear, I wonder – since the sun is almost showing its face, perhaps you would like to take our friend Herr Besler for a walk around the garden? I fear it is rather tedious for him to sit here listening to his elders.'

'Father, I have things to do,' Esther said, giving him a pointed look as she set the tray down on a small table beside his chair. 'Besides, it's freezing.'

'I'm not bored,' Besler said, glancing anxiously from me to the rabbi, though I could see he was torn; half-afraid of being excluded from an important conversation, the other half keen not to miss the opportunity of time with Esther. For myself, I was bristling at the implication that I was of an age with her father – that was not how I wished her to regard me – but I understood his intention.

'It's not a large garden,' Loew said, 'but it might be pleasant for you to take the air a while. Put a coat on if it's cold.' And he gave Esther a look that reminded me of my own father; one that said this was not up for discussion.

'Very well,' she agreed, with a trace of impatience. 'Come and see our modest garden, Master Besler, though it is mostly mud this time of year. Bring your beer.'

'Sometimes I wish I *could* make a Golem,' Loew murmured, his eyes on the door as it swung shut behind them. 'It would be a lot less trouble than a daughter. And I should know – I have six of them. For now we have a few minutes' privacy to speak more plainly, Dr Bruno.' He leaned forward and passed the plate of cakes. 'You came to me with a specific question, I think?'

I unlaced my doublet and withdrew my charcoal rubbing. 'I found this in Dee's chamber. I hoped you might be able to tell me more?'

The Maharal took the paper and retrieved a pair of reading lenses from somewhere inside his jacket; I bit down my impatience as he fussed about adjusting them on the bridge of his nose and squinted at the letter.

'I never received this,' he said. 'I wonder what happened to the original.'

'If it wasn't sent to you, then either Dee took it with him, or Hajek removed it after he disappeared,' I said. 'But you know what he refers to here?'

He twisted his mouth, a non-committal expression. 'I would like to know what more he said. I hope it has not fallen into the wrong hands. You haven't asked Hajek?'

'Not yet. I wanted to find you. Who does he mean by "our enemies"? You spoke of a common enemy just now?'

Loew sighed. 'Surely you must have guessed? Who would like to limit the influence of John Dee, an English Protestant, and me, a German-born Jew, on the man who is charged with holding the eastern half of Christendom for the one true Church?'

My heart sank; of course I knew. 'The Catholics.' Everything came back to Rome.

He nodded slowly. 'They have spies even here, in the Jewish Town, among my own community, it grieves me to say. But it's the same all over Europe. Rome feels her power weakening, and the best way for her to claw it back is through succession. In England, Queen Elizabeth has no heir. In France, King Henri has no children and has named a Protestant as next in line. Here in Prague, the Emperor is nearing forty and has refused all matches made for him with Catholic princesses who would secure the imperial throne, so Rome looks now to his younger brother for their best hope. There are rumours that his uncle Philip of Spain, together with the Pope, means to depose Rudolf, excommunicate him, have him declared mad – any excuse to

108

replace him with Matthias, who is a devout servant of Rome and would be zealous in purging Bohemia of all other faiths.' He grimaced, and reached for a cake. 'Unless Rudolf makes a sound Catholic marriage and produces a legitimate heir in the very near future, I fear they will find a way to succeed. Matthias has hinted that he would bring the Inquisition to Prague. And I do not need to tell you where that would leave the likes of you and me. Expulsion would be the best my community could hope for.'

I thought of Hajek's anger at Ottavio Strada, his remark that if anything happened to the Emperor, they were all dead men. Was that what he meant? Did the doctor fear that Rome would not stop at excommunicating Rudolf – that they would be willing to remove him by more extreme means? It would not be the first time they had tried such stratagems: there had been multiple plots against the life of Elizabeth of England, tacitly sanctioned by Rome and Spain – I had been caught up in two of them. The Protestant Dutch prince William of Orange was murdered on his own stairs by a fanatical Jesuit. In Paris, the moderate King Henri III lived in fear of assassination by his hardline Catholic enemies. Rabbi Loew was right; everywhere you looked across Europe, wherever the succession was in doubt, there was a Catholic waiting to grab the throne and stamp out any threat to Rome's power.

'But what has this to do with John?' I asked, indicating the paper in his hand. 'He is only one man, and from what I understand, his influence with the Emperor was not so great lately. This letter hints at a joint enterprise – he says your enemies *suspect*. Can you tell me what?'

There was a long pause. I watched him as he re-read Dee's words, his eyes flicking right to left while he weighed up how much to say. Eventually he folded the paper in half, smoothed his fingertips along the crease and fixed me with a direct look.

'John was sending letters back to England,' he said, lowering his voice further. 'I assume you know this already. He believed he had uncovered a conspiracy at court, and he wished to

109

dispatch intelligence about it. But he had lately begun to feel unsafe at the House of the Green Mound – he mistrusted Hajek's servants. He feared someone was looking through his things whenever he was out – he said one of his notebooks had been stolen. So he asked me if he could keep certain papers here until his courier arrived. That is all I can think of.'

I looked at his open face and a finely honed instinct, finessed through my years of working for Walsingham, told me he was keeping something back. Yet what he said rang true; I thought of Greta and her assiduous desire to relieve me of my doublet the night before. Surely John Dee could not have suspected an old Czech servant of having the capacity to read ciphers devised by Francis Walsingham's own codebreaker? But of course not; she would be working on behalf of someone else. I needed to find out more about Greta's background and her connections; that would be a job for Besler.

'You don't have those papers, I suppose?' I asked.

Loew shook his head. 'John took them back the last time I saw him – about three weeks ago, this was. I assumed he was expecting his contact.'

I remembered Overton saying that he had waited in vain for Dee. Whatever had become of those letters, he had not handed them on.

'And this conspiracy – do you know any details?'

Again, he paused. 'I believe it was tied up with these vile slanders he mentions. The Catholic faction at court have tried many times to accuse the Emperor of black magic as grounds for excommunication, and goodness knows, with his taste for forbidden books and bizarre experiments, they are not short of ammunition. If they put about the rumour that John summons demons and prophesies the downfall of the Church, they taint the Emperor by association and hope to be rid of two enemies at once. It is a ploy they have tried before, without success so far. It is no small matter to level such accusations at the anointed Holy Roman Emperor and make them stick. You would need incontrovertible evidence.'

'Then why was John so worried about it now? Did he fear they had some compelling evidence? Was it connected with Ziggi Bartos?'

Loew puffed up his cheeks and blew out air through pursed lips, exactly as Esther had. 'Oh, these petty rivalries between the alchemists – I told John to rise above it, but he could not resist. He envied Bartos's youth and promise, Bartos envied John his experience and connections, and John enjoyed antagonising him. I knew it would not end well. One of the moneylenders here in the Jewish Town told me that, a few days before he was found dead, Bartos had come to him to exchange a significant quantity of Spanish escudos for thalers. Naturally, I wondered what a man who was constantly lamenting his debts had done to come by that kind of money from the Spanish. If I had to guess, I would surmise that he had been paid to falsify evidence that could be used against John and by extension the Emperor, but I don't know for certain. If that was the case, poor Bartos did not live long enough to carry out his side of the deal.'

'But – if Bartos was a paid pawn in a Catholic plot, why would they want to kill him?'

I pushed my hands through my hair. The more I tried to follow one thread to its end, the more tangled the whole cat's cradle became.

'Perhaps he reneged on their terms. Perhaps he became more trouble than he was worth.' Rabbi Loew helped himself to another cake. 'Would you take a word of advice from an old man, Dr Bruno?'

'From one elder to another, you mean?'

He smiled. 'Yes, sorry about that. I wanted your boy to go without protest. My advice, for what it's worth – leave this murder alone.'

'But—' I stared at him, amazed. 'Don't you want to know who did this, and why?' I pointed to the window. 'What I saw just now, what was done to your synagogue – if the killer is brought to justice, then the Jews will be free from suspicion.'

111

He gave me a weary look. 'You think? In your experience, do people in thrall to their prejudice readily change their minds when they are shown evidence that contradicts those assumptions? Do they not rather find a way to twist that proof to suit their original belief? If the murder is proven beyond doubt to be the work of a man and not a Golem, do you honestly imagine people will leave us alone, even if that man is strung up in the Old Town Square for all to see? You know better than that, Dr Bruno.'

I turned my glass between my hands; he was right, of course. 'For John Dee's sake, then. The Emperor challenged me to clear his name. I thought he was your friend.'

'He is. But the best thing any of us can do for now is to lie low and wait for the storm to pass. Clean the walls, repair the windows. We have weathered worse, and people have short memories, even emperors. Something will come along to distract them soon enough. As I said, it is not as if Ziggi Bartos was deeply loved.'

'Then – you think his murder is the end of the business?' I was not convinced; in my experience, a killing – especially one so deliberately intended as a public spectacle – often led to more, if the killer felt his message had not been heeded.

He spread his hands wide. 'I can't foretell the future. But I do know that there are powerful forces in conflict with one another at Prague Castle, and you are one man with no one to protect you. Besides, you are already an enemy of the Church. Courage is a virtue, Bruno, but so is self-preservation. A wise man knows which is better suited to the moment. Sometimes we must take a longer view.'

'Longer than an innocent man accused of a murder that is also being used to incite hatred of your community?'

'If you want to put it like that. Take a lesson from John.'

'You speak as if you know something. Tell me – is he safe?'

He dipped his head piously. 'I pray that he is.'

It was not an answer. If Loew knew Dee's whereabouts, it was clear that he was not going to share them. I could not deny the good sense in what he said, especially if the Catholics were behind Bartos's murder, but I baulked at the idea of sitting back passively while the synagogue was defaced and Dee falsely accused. I also had to admit that Besler was right: I liked the idea of impressing the Emperor, ensuring his favour by serving up the killer to him on a platter. Perhaps the rabbi was genuinely trying to protect me from walking into danger, but I was more certain that he had not told me the whole truth.

'Well, I must get on,' Loew said, slapping his hands purposefully on his knees. 'It has been good to meet you, Bruno, and your young student, who is, I think, astonished to find that we do not have horns and tails.'

'He has only lately escaped the influence of his father,' I said, smiling. 'He has much to learn about the world that he won't find in books.'

'From what I hear, he could not have a better teacher. Well, you must come for dinner, both of you, when we can talk of more cheerful subjects.'

'Thank you. One last question, before I go.' I saw his face grow guarded again. I gestured to the letter. 'Who is "B"?'

He glanced at the door. 'He means Benjamin. The young man who brought you here. He carried messages between me and John.'

'So why would he be in danger?'

The rabbi shook his head. 'I can't know without the rest of the letter.'

'But you must have some idea? John asks you to warn him. Perhaps Benjamin will know?'

'You can leave that with me,' he said, and I caught in his voice the same paternal sternness with which he had spoken to Esther, the tone that clearly said this was not a matter for argument. I nodded, deciding immediately that I would speak to Benjamin Katz privately.

'I suppose I had better find young Besler,' I said as I stood, 'before he falls hopelessly in love with your daughter.'

I had meant it as a joke, but the rabbi looked grim.

'*That*,' he said, 'is the last thing we need.'

'I have never met a woman with so much learning,' Besler said, his face rapt, as we wound through the narrow streets towards the Old Town Square. It seemed I had arrived too late to prevent him from becoming smitten. 'She knows six languages! My father always told me—'

Here we go, I thought, steeling myself.

'—that I should avoid Jewish women, because they are lascivious and want to lure Christian men into wickedness.' He looked as if he couldn't imagine anything he'd like more.

'Did your father actually know any Jewish women?'

He frowned. 'I doubt it. But Esther is not like that – she is modest and gracious. And she has read books on mathematics and astronomy, which I always thought beyond a woman's capacities.'

'It's nothing to do with capacity, Besler – it's a matter of opportunity. I have known educated women who would have been a match for any man if they had been able to progress into the law or medicine or philosophy. As things stand, their only chance to pursue learning is by taking the veil, or being born a queen, and in this I think we wrong them.' I couldn't help a flash of envy, and wondered how I might engineer an opportunity to discuss astronomy with Esther Loew. I intended to take the rabbi up on his offer of dinner as soon as possible.

We had followed the way back past the Old-New Synagogue in the hope of encountering Benjamin Katz again, but he and his cousin had evidently finished their cleaning while we had been with Rabbi Loew; only a ghostly outline of the slogan remained on the side of the building as we passed. I would have to come back and find him; I was convinced that Dee's fear for Benjamin's safety was connected with Dee's own disappearance and whatever their enemies suspected. If the rabbi wouldn't tell me, perhaps Benjamin would be easier to convince.

Besler walked deep in thought, considering my words. 'My

father always said too much learning was undesirable in a wife. She should be able to read her Bible and know enough of writing and arithmetic to manage the household accounts, but if she yearns for knowledge outside her sphere, she should be avoided at all costs, for then she will never be satisfied with her wifely duties. A woman who is not content with her lot is more trouble than she is worth.'

'That's your father's view, eh?' I found myself forming a clearer picture of Herr and Frau Besler's marriage. 'How does your mother feel about it?'

He frowned, puzzled. 'I never asked her.'

'No, I don't suppose you did. And what are a wife's duties, then, in your view?'

He glanced at me, unsure if this was a trick question. 'Well – to take care of the home, organise the servants and so on. And of course to have children and raise them correctly. To obey her husband. Why – do you disagree?'

'Would you not rather have a wife you can talk to? One you can share ideas with? Who makes you laugh? One who has something more to discuss over supper than whether the butcher is overcharging for beef?'

'I – I had not thought that was an option.' He looked confused, as if I had asked him whether he wouldn't like a talking dog. I could just picture the kind of pinkly scrubbed, modest, practical Lutheran girls his father would have pushed into his path: schooled in their Scriptures and the preparation of good plain food, none of the fire or ambition that appealed to me in a woman. Not that that had done me much good, I reflected.

'What did you talk about with Esther Loew?' I asked.

'Medicine. She asked about my studies, and we discussed Avicenna and Galen.' The reverent expression had returned to his face. 'She is very beautiful, don't you think? It's a wonder that she is not married, at twenty-eight. I suppose, because she is the youngest daughter, it falls to her to keep house for the rabbi, but what a waste.'

115

'Perhaps *you* should ask her, Besler. Imagine your father's delight.'

He flushed to the tips of his ears. 'I don't mean – that could never – in any case, I can't marry yet. I have to finish my studies and establish myself in my profession before my father will grant me the funds to support a family.' He sighed. 'And I couldn't marry a woman like Esther.'

'Because she is Jewish?'

'Well, of course. And because she scares me a little.'

I laughed. 'If you want my advice, never even think of marrying a woman who doesn't scare you at least a little.'

'What would you know of it?' he said with a sly glance. 'You have never married.'

'You're quite right – I am in no position to offer advice. In my defence, I was in holy orders until the age of twenty-seven. After that, I was on the run from the Inquisition, and whenever I found a place of safety, I was always dependent on patronage, which is unreliable when you have a reputation like mine. I have lived in exile for twelve years – that's no kind of life to offer a woman.'

He fell silent for a moment. It was the most I had ever told him about my life before Wittenberg. 'But did you never fall in love?'

'That's a different question.' I thought of the woman I had loved in England – and loved still, in some deep secret part of my heart, though I tried to keep her from my mind, because the memory was painful, and because I doubted I would ever see her again. 'I did love someone. She had all those qualities – courage, spirit, a quick mind. But she would not have married me. She disliked the idea of marriage.'

'Then it is her loss,' Besler declared, with touching loyalty. 'You are still quite handsome.'

'For an old greybeard, you mean?' I cuffed him on the arm and he gave me a sheepish grin. 'Talking of women – when we get back to Hajek's, I want you to use your charms on Greta. Don't look so appalled – this is part of our investigation.

116

You'd be amazed how much servants see and hear. Offer to help her in the kitchen, carrying heavy sacks or something. Befriend her.'

'But – *why?*'

I laughed at the expression of utter horror on his face; this was not how he had envisaged his trip to Golden Prague in the company of a renowned philosopher.

'Dee feared someone in Hajek's house was looking through his private papers. Hajek obviously trusts Greta, but people can have old loyalties that run deep. I want to know her background, her faith, who she is friends with in Prague. She likes you – you can ask her guileless questions in her own language. She is more likely to let something slip.'

'And what will you be doing while I'm fetching and carrying in the kitchen?' he asked, with an air of resentment.

'Reading,' I said, tucking my right hand into my left armpit to feel the outline of the letters in my pocket.

NINE

Back at the House of the Green Mound, in what had been John Dee's room, I sat at the desk and leaned my head into my hands. My eyes ached from staring at Thomas Phelippes's cramped letters and symbols, and I was no closer to unlocking its meaning. I should have realised that Walsingham would be too clever to send a direct substitution cipher, in case it should be intercepted. The numbers in the code I had brought from Wittenberg did not refer directly to the writing in the letter Overton had carried; instead they would relate to a third text, most likely a book, that both sender and recipient owned in common. It was a favourite method of Phelippes's, but without knowledge of which book, the message was impenetrable.

The years of studying by candlelight were beginning to catch up with me; I had suspected for some time that I would benefit from a pair of reading lenses like Rabbi Loew's, but vanity deterred me – as if holding the page at arm's length and squinting made me look any less ridiculous. From the courtyard downstairs, snatches of Besler's bright chatter drifted up to the window as he helped Greta with baskets of laundry; the image would have made me laugh, if I were not so frustrated with myself.

I blinked hard, pinching the bridge of my nose. I had once been admired for my facility with cryptography; why could I not now summon it? I had allowed it to grow rusted with lack of use. For that I had only myself to blame; after my last experiences in Walsingham's service two years earlier, during the summer that had finally brought Mary Stuart, Queen of the Scots, to the block, I had chosen to retreat from political intrigue. My own life had almost been forfeit then, as well as the lives of people I cared about; the business had ended with watching six men die a brutal traitors' death on the scaffold, disembowelled alive, as a result of my actions. I could not regret that they were caught, but their dying screams still haunted me. That, together with the pain of losing the woman I loved, had led me to seek the safety of a university cloister. Wittenberg allowed me to live quietly; I taught, I wrote my books, I attempted to avoid controversy as far as was possible for someone like me (at least the Inquisition had no jurisdiction in the German lands), and I felt my edge growing dull. It was there that I had received word, in the autumn of 1586, that my dear friend Philip Sidney, Walsingham's son-in-law, had died of an infected wound in the Low Countries during a military campaign he had insisted on joining because he too had tired of a quiet life. He was thirty-one and never met his infant daughter. Though I had not seen him for almost two years by then, the news of his death had affected me deeply, and seemed to draw a line under that time I had spent in England, where I once hoped I might make a home. I dedicated the books I wrote in London to him, and in return he had given me volumes of his poetry, which I took out and read in my cold lodgings in Wittenberg when I wanted to indulge in melancholy. Perhaps Besler was right; I was growing old. Almost forty, no wife or family, only a shelf full of published books and a series of rented rooms to show for the days I had lived. My own father had died at fifty-six, a fact I pondered these days with increasing frequency.

I slapped my hands on the desk, making the inkpot jump, and pushed the chair back. Enough self-indulgence, Bruno; this would get me nowhere. I stretched, paced the room, cast my eyes around for some inspiration, and my gaze fell on the pile of Dee's books that I had moved to the floor beside the desk.

Thinking of Sidney and his poetry had given me an idea. I sifted through the stack and sure enough, wedged between a volume of Cornelius Agrippa's *De Magia Naturalis* and Trithemius's *Stenographia*, I found a slim bound manuscript similar to the one I owned: Sidney's *The Arcadia*. John Dee had been Sidney's boyhood tutor; of course Philip would have given Dee a copy of the book he had circulated privately among his writer friends – a book which was also a link to Walsingham.

As I pored over the pages, cross-referencing between the cipher I had carried, the letter Overton had given me and the page numbers of the book, sifting out the nulls and blanks scattered through the text to foil attempts at deciphering, I knew that my guess had been correct. It was as if a heavy mist began to lift; words took shape out of the general haze, and at length I experienced that beautiful moment, as with picking a lock, when the mechanism aligns perfectly, every part engages and you feel it begin to yield. Once this happened, in a short while I had a transcript – complete with my guessed-at punctuation – of Walsingham's urgent words to Dee:

I mean to acquaint Her Majesty with the content of your letters. However, if what you suspect be grounded in truth, and the principal agents of this business directed as you believe, it falls to you to act swiftly. I am sending the Nolan to give you good assistance – he has ever been a faithful servant to Her Majesty and is a useful man – but there is no knowing how long the journey will take or when you might expect him. In the meantime, if this danger be imminent, you must intercept it by any means necessary, for the good of the Emperor, the Queen and all those who share our faith, but let no suspicion fall on you and take every care of your person.

In haste I commit you to God, who will forgive what is done in His Name.
Your loving friend,
FW

I stared at the page for a long time. It was infuriatingly vague, as all secret correspondence must be, and yet its substance appeared beyond doubt, confirming in its outline what Rabbi Loew had already told me. If Dee had written to England of his fears about a plot against the Emperor, Walsingham's response read as an instruction to do whatever was necessary to prevent it. Including murder? The old spymaster's words about God's forgiveness could imply as much. Then was it possible that Dee had killed Ziggi Bartos after all? The facts would fit: Bartos, deep in debt, had taken money from the Catholics at court, either to concoct evidence that could see the Emperor excommunicated, or some worse deed. I thought of the note I had seen, in Bartos's writing, wrapping the grisly casket sent to Rudolf the night before – 'the fruit of all my labours'. An alchemist creating an elixir for a man desperately seeking immortality would have the perfect opportunity to slip him poison. By some means, Dee had found out Bartos's intentions, and sought to save the Emperor's throne – perhaps his very life – by killing the alchemist before he could act.

I looked down at the paper in my hand. Absurd: there were too many holes in this explanation. Dee had never received this letter, with Walsingham's tacit approval of assassination. In any case, the form of the killing was all wrong. John Dee was a gentle soul; I could just about believe him capable of giving a man poison in the name of a greater good, but I could not picture him dealing a fatal knife wound to the heart, face to face, still less carrying out the vicious mutilation I had seen on the alchemist's body. And the Golem connection made no sense at all: John was a friend to Rabbi Loew, he would never knowingly direct the city's anger towards the Jews. The one thing that seemed beyond doubt was that Dee had uncovered a plot that threatened the Emperor. I scanned my deciphered copy again, committing it to memory before I held the corner to the candle flame and let the paper burn, allowing myself a brief flush of pride at Walsingham's reference to me as 'a useful man'.

I was watching the original letter curl to ash in the grate when there was a furious thumping at the door and Besler blustered in without waiting for an invitation, as was his habit.

'There's a messenger arrived from the castle,' he said, breathless from running up the stairs. 'You've been summoned.'

'Good.' I nodded; if I wanted to know what Dee had suspected, the answers were surely to be found at the castle. 'You can come with me. You might want to change your jerkin. I'll go down and see the horses saddled and on the way you can tell me how you have spent the afternoon.'

He grimaced, wiping soapsuds from his front. 'I am only grateful none of my fellow students could see me heaving barrels of washing about like a kitchen skivvy. Give me one moment. Are we going to see the Emperor?'

'I presume so. Wash your face as if you are – make your mother proud.'

'Bit late for that,' he said, laughing, 'since I took up with you.'

'Greta is quite interesting actually,' he told me as we rode across the Stone Bridge. The breeze off the river had grown keener, the sky darkened with low cloud, as if winter had decided it was not yet ready to cede its ground. 'She's lived in Prague all her life – fifty-eight years. Her father ran a tavern in the Lesser Town, and her husband was an alchemist. He was apprentice to Hajek's father.'

'Really?' That at least explained Greta's willingness to keep house for the doctor. 'What happened to him?'

'He blew himself up,' Besler said cheerfully. 'It was fifteen years ago. He was experimenting with the manufacture of gunpowder and – BOOM.' He took his hands off the reins to mime an explosion, in case I had failed to picture it. The horse jerked back in alarm, its ears twitching. 'Anyway, Hajek took her in after she was widowed. Apparently he felt guilty.'

We passed under the tower on the north side of the bridge, watched by laconic guards lolling at their posts. I returned their scrutiny as we rode by, wondering if any of them had been on duty the night Ziggi Bartos was hung from the parapet, and how much might persuade them to talk.

'Why?' I asked, turning my attention back to Besler's story as we began the ascent up the cobbled street to the castle. 'How was Hajek responsible?'

'She didn't say. But the husband had no money, so she would have been destitute if Hajek hadn't invited her to work for him. Her father left her nothing because he disapproved of the marriage. Her sister and brother-in-law run the tavern now.'

'And her religion?'

'Her family was Utraquist, she said. I have no idea what that is.'

'Moderate Protestants,' I told him. 'Descended from the Bohemian reformer Jan Hus. Like your lot, but less puritanical.' This revelation was a flaw in my theory about Greta; if she was a Protestant, she would hardly be spying for the Catholics at court.

'I'm *not* a Puritan,' Besler objected. 'I'm the one who wants to see the Emperor's door knocker, aren't I?'

'Who knows, perhaps your wish is about to be granted,' I said, smiling, though I was still thinking about Greta. If Dee had been right to suspect her of looking through his papers, who could she be working for?

I put this question aside as we dismounted at the castle gatehouse and I announced myself. A boy took our horses while the guards on the gate conferred in low voices, checking a list. One of them snapped something in Czech and Besler turned to me apologetically.

'He says he has to search us. No weapons inside the castle grounds.'

I thought about protesting that this had not been demanded of me the night before, but then I remembered that I had been with Hajek and that visit was hardly orthodox, so I held out my arms obediently while the soldier patted me down and removed my knife.

'He says you can collect it when you leave,' Besler informed me.

From the Lesser Town below a series of church bells struck the hour of three as we stamped and shivered at the entrance. I tucked my hands inside my riding cloak and asked Besler to explain again that the Emperor had specifically sent a messenger for me and would be angry if I kept him waiting; the guards looked confused at this, discussed it some more in murmurs and told us to wait before one of them trotted away to fetch someone, or so I hoped.

After a quarter hour had passed, I turned to Besler. 'This messenger – did he actually say he came from the Emperor?'

He looked at me blankly. 'I can't remember. I think he just said you were wanted at the castle. But who else would be summoning you?'

I was about to remonstrate with him on the importance of details, when a servant dressed head to foot in black arrived, nodded in acknowledgement and gestured to us to follow him.

Instead of leading us towards the *Kunstkammer* or the Emperor's private apartments, the man took us through the first and second courtyards, past the great Gothic basilica of St Vitus, to a smaller, less imposing church behind it, built of white stone in the Romanesque style. He pushed open a small door set into the main entrance and I saw Besler hopefully scanning the knocker as we passed through.

'They're not going to put it on the church, are they?' I said.

'You never know with the Catholics,' he whispered back, grinning, and I laughed softly, glad of the distraction as the door slammed hard behind us, because I had begun to feel distinctly uneasy. We found ourselves at the end of the nave, looking towards the apse. The basilica's interior appeared ancient and austere; round-arched windows set high in the walls let in little light. Shadows stretched down the length of both side aisles; the air was chilly and smelled of old incense and damp stone. Our breath clouded around our faces. After the bustle of the courtyards outside, the place appeared abandoned and unnaturally silent, the only sound the click of our boot heels on the worn flagstones.

The servant led us halfway along the nave, where a stone staircase curved around on the right and left sides, leading to a kind of viewing platform above an archway barred by an iron gate. He lifted the latch, issued a curt instruction in Czech and slipped away.

'He said we should go in,' Besler translated, glancing around uncertainly; I could see his initial wonder giving way to nerves.

'Come on then.' I squeezed his shoulder to offer encouragement. 'Don't worry – the Emperor is a man like any other, only shorter.'

A shallow flight of steps led down into a vault lit by candles in wall brackets. It appeared empty, but I progressed with caution, knowing how Rudolf liked to conceal himself in the shadows. As I approached what looked like an altar at the far end, I sensed a figure standing motionless to my right. I turned, and could not help crying out at the sight: a decaying corpse rendered in blackened bronze, sightless sockets fixed on me, its flayed torso gaping open to reveal a coiled serpent in the cavity of the belly. Besler collided with me as I leaned one hand against a pillar to catch my breath, berating myself for being so easily startled. Behind us, the iron gate clanged shut, the sound reverberating through the crypt, and I heard a soft laugh at my back.

'*Qué belleza de mujer, verdad?* Her name is Brigita. A local legend. Her lover was an Italian sculptor. He murdered her and thereafter he was cursed – whatever image he tried to create, the only thing he could carve was her rotting flesh. The moral, I think, is that Italians must be very careful who they upset in this city.'

I faced the man who had addressed me in such a refined Castillian accent. He was tall and athletic-looking, his close-cropped hair and beard black with threads of silver, though the deep-set lines on his face put him closer to fifty than forty. He had a sallow complexion and searching eyes that assessed me with one practised glance. The half-smile on his lips suggested he was reserving judgement.

I had walked into a trap, and my best recourse was to say nothing. I hoped Besler would follow my example.

'Dr Giordano Bruno,' said the Spaniard, with a curt bow. He wore a leather doublet and a short cape with sable trim, which he drew around himself, keeping his hands out of sight. 'Forgive the cloak-and-dagger nature of this invitation, but we were not sure you would come willingly. I am pleased to make your acquaintance.'

I kept my head raised; damned if I was going to bow to him.

'Don Guillén de San Clemente, I presume?'

'Correct.' He stepped forward and, to my surprise, grasped my shoulders to greet me with a brisk kiss on both cheeks. 'Ambassador to the Emperor from His Catholic Majesty King Philip of Spain. Tell me, how do you like Golden Prague?'

'I have hardly been here long enough to form an opinion,' I said, keeping my expression neutral.

He nodded to my bandaged wrist. 'But you are injured. I hope you have not come to serious harm in the short time you have been here.'

I touched the dressing. 'No harm done. Not everyone was so eager to welcome me. A couple of your compatriots, as it happens.'

'How unfortunate,' he murmured. 'I'm afraid this city attracts brigands and thieves from all over. The streets can be dangerous after dark – your friend John Dee should have warned you. But I hear you've had a warmer reception from the Jews.' He raised one carefully plucked eyebrow.

'You're well informed,' I said, recalling Rabbi Loew's confession that there were paid spies in his own community.

San Clemente fetched up a thin smile. 'You can hardly expect the arrival of a man such as you to go unnoticed, Dr Bruno,' he said. 'It's a small city, after all. And who is this young gentleman?' He turned his keen gaze on Besler, who was hopping from foot to foot at my side as if he needed to relieve himself; I realised belatedly that it was because he spoke no Spanish and was terrified of missing out.

'My assistant, Hieronymus Besler, from Nuremberg,' I said. The Spaniard looked him up and down and spoke to him in German.

'Your father is a member of the town council there, is that right, boy?'

Besler nodded, surprised.

'What does he think of you attaching yourself to a notorious heretic?'

Besler glanced at me. 'Well, my father would consider you a worse heretic, sir,' he said politely. 'At least Dr Bruno has been excommunicated by the harlot Rome, so there is some hope for him.'

There was a long silence, before San Clemente let out a burst of laughter.

'An honest reply,' he said. 'I see you have not yet taught the boy your talent for dissembling.'

'Hm. I dissemble, you practise diplomacy,' I said.

'Precisely. And speaking of diplomacy,' San Clemente added, 'you're acquainted with my colleague. In fact, I believe you were once brothers in Christ.'

He turned his head expectantly as a figure in a long black robe stepped out of the shadows from behind a pillar – he always did like to indulge a taste for the theatrical – and our eyes met. It was almost twenty years since I had last seen him, and the passage of time had evidently not diminished his hatred for me. Fra Agostino da Montalcino, former head of the Dominican order in Rome, scourge of heretics, enemy of free thought and scientific enquiry. He had never forgiven me for ridiculing him in a debate at my convent in Naples when I was a hot-headed youth of twenty; I believe he considered it his divinely appointed mission to bring me down, one way or another. He was the very last person I would have wished to run into in a city where – as Rabbi Loew had shrewdly reminded me – I had no powerful patron for protection.

Montalcino continued to scrutinise me. The years had not been kind to him; he was heavy-set, but his excess weight seemed to drag towards the earth now, his jowls and the pouches beneath his eyes sagging, giving him the air of a melancholy mastiff. He wore his habit too tight at the collar, so that he appeared to be in permanent discomfort, continually tugging to loosen it with one finger, and the mole on his cheek, repellent and fascinating in equal measure, still bristled with coarse hairs, though these were white now, while the hair on his head had turned iron-grey. He must be approaching sixty, and he looked as if he carried his advancing age like a cumbersome burden.

'Frater,' I said, addressing him by the old title we had used to one another as Dominicans. I dipped my head in a reluctant show of respect that I knew he would take for mockery.

'No longer your brother, in point of fact, Bruno,' he said. 'You abandoned the order, remember?'

'That can't have surprised you. I'd have thought the Dominicans were glad to be rid of me.'

'What surprises me is that you have managed to escape the flames so far.' He compressed his lips into a thin line. 'I have read your books, you know. It was among the more distasteful of my duties as inquisitor to compose reports on heretical texts.'

'I'm flattered. I can write a dedication in them if you'd like?'

'Only in England could you publish such monstrous heresies and not face retribution. But I hear the English didn't want to keep you.' He stroked the mole on his cheek with the tip of a stubby finger. 'Too much a Catholic for Elizabeth's more puritanical advisers, am I right? And neither did the French – too much a heretic for Catherine de Medici.' He shook his head with affected regret, as if at a wayward child who had been warned where his follies would lead. 'It seems that you are too much and not enough all at once, Bruno. A man who belongs nowhere.'

That stung – a touch straight to my most vulnerable flank – but I would not let him see that he had scored a hit. I was grateful that he had spoken in Italian so that Besler could not understand.

'I live in Wittenberg now,' I said, standing straighter. 'I teach philosophy at the university.'

'Oh, I know. But I hear there are murmurs against you even there,' Montalcino said in his low insinuating voice that always felt like being caressed by a spider. 'They say you seek to establish a secret sect of believers in your own ungodly philosophy of an infinite universe and a religion that would make no distinction between Catholic and Protestant, Jew and Turk. And you have no shortage of gullible youths such as this one eager to spread your lies.'

Dio mio, he had been thorough in his research; that should not have shocked me. It was true that the theories put forward in my books had given rise to concerns about my influence on the students; the rest was malicious rumour. It was almost a compliment to learn that Montalcino had gone to such lengths to keep a watchful eye on me.

'I am not responsible for what stupid people say about matters they do not understand,' I said as nonchalantly as I could manage. 'For my part, I did not expect to find you turned envoy, Brother. I always thought you had found your true calling with the Holy Office. Surely diplomacy is a little tame for your tastes?'

'Two sides of the same coin, Bruno.' His black eyes glittered. 'Both diplomacy and the regrettable business of correcting misguided beliefs are, in the end, concerned with the art of persuasion, are they not? With a greater or lesser degree of subtlety.'

I was the first to look away. 'Well. I don't suppose you brought me here to discuss my books. What is it you want?'

'We want to know why you have come to Prague.' San Clemente had been observing our exchange with amusement, but now he spoke crisply, as if he had indulged our sparring long enough.

'I am here at the invitation of my friend John Dee,' I said.

'Why now?'

'It is the first opportunity I have had to take time away from my work at the university.' Could he know that Walsingham had sent me? Surely not. I kept my expression clear.

'Then where is Dee?'

'That's a good question. I arrived yesterday afternoon, as I'm sure you know, to find him long gone. So your guess is as good as mine. Perhaps better.'

'He is suspected of theft and murder,' Montalcino said dispassionately. 'That makes him a fugitive from justice. So if you know his whereabouts, you are guilty of assisting him.'

'If I knew his whereabouts, I would have gone to find him, and as you have clearly had me followed since I arrived in Prague, you would have us both by now. What evidence do you have that John had anything to do with this murder?'

'The dead man accused your friend of theft shortly before he vanished,' San Clemente cut in.

'A desperate man may say anything for a few escudos,' I said pointedly. 'Besides, as I understand it, three weeks passed between John's disappearance and the killing of Bartos, during which time John has not been seen in the city.'

'With his contacts, he could easily have slipped through the gates unnoticed to commit the crime.'

'Or he could have had a proxy,' San Clemente suggested. 'Someone to carry out the deed at his instruction.'

'Or some*thing*,' Montalcino said darkly.

At this I laughed. 'A Golem, you mean? Come now, Fra Agostino, you are not a small boy to be frightened by nursery tales. Whoever killed the alchemist was as much flesh and blood as I am. Or even you.'

'And yet, that is not what they are saying in the Old Town Square,' he murmured. 'What did the old Jew tell you this morning?'

'If you mean Rabbi Loew, he was no help,' I said. 'He doesn't know where John is either.'

'I don't believe you,' San Clemente said. 'They are practised at spiriting people away under cover of darkness. It is their way.'

'That Jew knows where Dee is,' Montalcino agreed. 'And I think he told you.'

'He told me nothing,' I insisted, but I remembered my conviction that Rabbi Loew had been keeping something back. I wondered if they could be right, and if he knew what had happened to Dee, or even assisted in hiding him.

'We could of course *encourage* you to tell us what you know,' Montalcino said quietly, in Italian, casually examining his nails. A cold sensation washed over me, leaving my fingers numb.

'The Holy Office has no licence here,' I said, keeping my voice firm and my back straight; he wanted me cowed, and I would not give him that. He met my look with a small, private smile, conveying a horrible kind of intimacy. I knew he would not care about legitimacy; all he needed was for those two Spanish thugs to catch me off-guard one night and carry me to some quiet out-of-the-way place where he could practise all the persuasive tricks of his trade. 'I am a guest of the Emperor,' I added.

'That's not strictly true, is it?' San Clemente replied. 'You've caught his attention, granted, but please do not delude yourself that you have any special standing at court. If you were to disappear the way John Dee has, I don't imagine Rudolf would put himself out to find you. And your English friends are a long way away – not that I imagine they would trouble themselves overmuch either, since you are not Her Majesty's subject, however useful you make yourself.'

I looked from the Spaniard to the nuncio and folded my arms; I had had enough of their games, and I could see that Besler was growing scared, though I doubted he had been able to follow the detail of the conversation. 'You can threaten me all you want, Ambassador, but I am not clear what you hope to gain. I can't tell you where John is, and if you believe that Rabbi Loew knows, why don't you ask him yourselves? We are leaving.'

I saw them exchange a glance, and guessed that pressuring the most senior Jewish leader in the city was a line even they dared not cross.

'We would not dream of bothering the good rabbi,' San Clemente said smoothly. 'And I have made no threats, Dr Bruno – I have simply pointed out the truth of your situation. But it occurs to me – there is something you can do for us that would help to keep things harmonious during your stay in the city.'

Now we come to it, I thought. 'What is it you want?'

'You've been asking questions about the alchemist's murder,' he said.

'If you're going to tell me to stop, that does rather imply that you have a reason for keeping the truth hidden.'

'On the contrary,' Montalcino said. 'We want you to find out.'

'What?' I stared at him, wondering if I had misheard.

'Presumably your aim is to clear John Dee's name so that he can return to court?'

'Yes, but—' I glanced again at the Spaniard, confused. 'I would not have thought you shared that ambition?'

'We simply wish to know one way or another,' San Clemente said.

'Then – what are you saying – you *don't* believe John killed Bartos?' My mind was scrambling to catch up; if Rabbi Loew was right and the Catholic faction had been using Bartos in some kind of plot, either to defame or to assassinate the Emperor, surely it was in their interest that the blame for his death should fall squarely on Dee, who was already their enemy and was not here to speak in his own defence.

'I find it the most likely explanation,' San Clemente said. 'The two were well-known rivals. But if you should uncover anything that suggests someone other than John Dee was responsible, we would like that information before you pass it to anyone else.'

'So why don't you go out and look for it?' I asked. 'You clearly have a city full of informants.'

He gave me a tight smile. 'Oh, you may be sure we are making our own enquiries. But we would like to be kept abreast of anything you find out.'

'And if I refuse, on the grounds that I don't trust you?'

Montalcino let his appraising gaze fall on Besler. 'Then this young man's family would have good reason to rue the day he fell under your spell.'

'What will you do – hang him off the Stone Bridge too?' I tried to maintain a note of defiance, but I felt my gut clench; I knew Montalcino well enough to know he was capable of carrying out a threat purely in order not to lose face.

He lifted one shoulder in a dismissive gesture. 'You can gamble with your own reputation and safety, Bruno, you have always found some dubious childish thrill in doing that. But to risk the safety of others – that strikes me as extreme self-ishness.'

Besler was looking at me in alarm; Montalcino had spoken Italian so I doubted the boy had understood the nature of the threat, but he was no fool – he could see the nuncio was talking about him.

I gritted my teeth and battled to control my anger that even here, in the most tolerant court in Europe, the emissaries of Rome and Spain should feel so confident of their power that it was clear I had no choice but to do their bidding, else put Besler's life in danger. I was considering how I might make a suitably ambiguous reply when we all started at the metallic clang of the gate and the sound of quick footsteps on the staircase.

Ottavio Strada stepped into the circle of light from the candles. He took in the little tableau before him and his expression briefly darkened as he looked from the ambassador to the nuncio, before he assumed a courtier's smile.

'Gentlemen,' he said, addressing us in German. 'Here you are. I had been growing concerned – the messenger I sent for Doctor Bruno returned almost an hour ago with assurances that he was on his way, so I began to fear that something had happen to divert him.' He turned to me. 'Fortunately, I learned from the guards on the gate that you had in fact arrived and mistakenly been shown to the basilica of St George.' He glanced at San Clemente as he said this, but the Spaniard only returned his smile with equal insincerity.

'Forgive us, Signor Strada – Fra Agostino could not pass up the opportunity to renew acquaintance with his old colleague from the Dominican order, and for myself, I have heard so much about Dr Bruno that I insisted on meeting him in person. I hope we have not delayed whatever business you have with him.'

'Well,' Strada said, steepling his fingers, 'we are all pressed for time, and I see these gentlemen have not been offered any refreshment, so if you have finished here . . . ?'

'I think we have finished, for now,' Montalcino said, stepping forward to take me by the shoulders and plant a kiss on both cheeks; I had to fight not to recoil. 'It is indeed a marvellous thing to find you so unchanged, Brother,' he said with a fulsome smile. 'Reassuring, in a way.'

'Likewise,' I managed, nodding to San Clemente as Strada ushered me and Besler to the stairs. I did not miss the warning glance he sent the two Catholics; it was a look that said, I'm watching you.

TEN

'They bribed one of the guards on the gate to inform them if you arrived,' Strada told me as he led us back through the courtyards to the Emperor's private apartments. I could hear the anger straining his voice. 'It's not unusual – information is currency here and most of the watchmen are for sale. I've reported the man to his commander, but I doubt anything will come of it. What did those two want with you?'

I hesitated before deciding to leave the complexities of the murder aside; I was still trying to understand the Catholics' position. 'Fra Agostino da Montalcino has hated me for the best part of twenty years. I think he just wanted the chance to remind me that he still does. He once tried to make me condemn myself as a heretic in an audience with the Pope. I only narrowly talked my way out of it.'

Strada laughed. 'That sounds like a story my father would enjoy hearing. And what do you make of San Clemente?'

I shrugged. 'A career diplomat, I assume. I have met the type before. Charming, clever – well-born, no doubt. Ruthless too, I imagine.'

'Extremely. And unlike many career diplomats, a man of action as well as words. He's a decorated soldier – he fought at the Battle of Lepanto in his youth. Be careful of those two,

Bruno – they are dangerous men singly, and even more so when they work together.'

'Why so?'

He lowered his voice and leaned closer, so that his shoulder touched mine as we walked. 'Because they are both failing in their missions. Montalcino has been in post less than a year, but he is the latest in a line of papal nuncios who cannot do the job they have been sent to do, which is to impose the will of Rome on the Emperor. Rudolf is his own man, and increasingly disinclined to obedience. He no longer takes the sacraments, and when he makes his confession now, he instructs his confessor to leave out the phrase about *auctoritate apostolica*.'

I whistled softly. 'I imagine that would not sit well with the Pope.'

'As for San Clemente,' Strada continued, 'his task – which has been his sole focus from the beginning of his embassy – is to secure the marriage between the Emperor and his cousin the Infanta Isabella, Philip of Spain's daughter. But Rudolf prevaricates and dithers, he promises and reneges, and the matter has stretched out over years, with no official betrothal as yet. Philip is on the point of losing patience altogether, and it will mean the end of San Clemente's career if he is recalled without achieving his prize. So you see why they are both hostile to anyone who might distract the Emperor from his religious and dynastic obligations.'

'It sounds as if there is not much love lost between you.'

'Well, you must know,' he said, holding open a door into the wing I had visited last night, 'there has always been a degree of resentment about my family's status at court, and the extent of our influence.' He could not disguise a swell of pride as he said this. He set off up a staircase lined with tapestries as Besler and I followed.

'How so?' I asked. 'Are the Stradas not Catholics? Or – what *is* your religion, then?'

He gave me a sidelong glance and smiled. 'Pragmatism, Dr Bruno. You understand that, I think? We are Catholic by

136

baptism, of course, but we tailor our faith to the Emperor's. We do not share the zeal of a man like Montalcino, for instance. I could not do the work I do in the library if I were concerned about knowledge corrupting my immortal soul, and I am happy to converse with men of all religions and none. But it is not simply a matter of creed.'

'No?' We reached the top of the stairs and progressed along a carpeted corridor towards another set of painted doors. It occurred to me that in the shock of confronting Montalcino and his threats, I had not yet asked Ottavio why he had sent for me.

'My sister, Katherina,' he said with a confidential air. 'She is the Emperor's preferred companion, and has been for seven years now. That breeds envy and ill-will in some quarters, as you can imagine.'

'Ah. I had heard Rudolf was fickle in his affections?'

Strada sighed. 'He can be easily distracted. But Katherina is the one he always returns to. I do honestly believe he loves her, in his way. Witness how he will not marry, though most of the eligible princesses of Europe have been offered at one time or another. San Clemente chooses to see my sister as the obstacle to King Philip's marriage plans – rather than acknowledge the bald truth, which is that Rudolf has no love for Spain and no wish to tie himself more closely to her crown.'

'Your sister must be a great beauty,' Besler said with a flourish of gallantry.

Strada glanced back at him, his smile restrained. 'I am hardly the person to judge. I think it is more that she has the knack of soothing him. But you can decide for yourself.' He paused at my puzzled expression. 'Forgive me – I thought the messenger had explained? It is my father who wished to see you. Here – these are my family's private quarters.'

We crossed a large, comfortable chamber and Ottavio opened a door into a smaller room, the light dimmed by heavy drapes pulled across the window. I followed him in and caught the close, musty smell of a sickroom. We found ourselves in a bedchamber, a carved four-poster dominating the space, its curtains drawn back to reveal a white-haired man propped amid a complicated scaffolding of pillows. On a chair beside the bed sat a young woman, a book open in her hands, though she had paused in her reading to look up as we entered.

'*Ecco*, my father Jacopo Strada,' Ottavio said, gesturing to the bed. 'And my sister Katherina.'

The woman stood up and bobbed a brief curtsy. I imagined Besler would be disappointed. She was a few years younger than her brother, who appeared to have inherited all the looks in the family. Katherina was well into her thirties, tall with a flat, boyish figure and brown hair caught up in a twist under a linen cap; her long, straight nose mirrored that of the man in the bed. True, she was no striking beauty in the manner of Esther Loew, but there was a gentleness to her face, especially in her wide brown eyes, that made me see how a man with the cares of empire on his shoulders might want to lay his head in her lap while she stroked his brow.

'We were just having some Dante,' she said, raising the book.

'That would make anyone feel better about his ailments,' I said, and she smiled shyly.

'So this is the famous Neapolitan,' said the old man in the bed, pushing himself upright. 'Come here and let me look at you.'

His chest rose and fell effortfully as he breathed, but his voice was firm and the dark eyes that settled on me unnervingly bright; nothing wrong with his mind, I thought, seeing the way he appraised me. I took the arthritic hand he extended and kissed it respectfully.

'My father particularly wanted to make your acquaintance,' Ottavio prompted. He seemed ill at ease in the old man's presence, and I wondered if he was embarrassed by Jacopo's presumption in dragging me across the city at his demand.

'Signore Strada,' I said. 'It is an honour.'

'Pardon me for greeting you in this state, Dr Bruno,' Jacopo said. 'On a good day I get up and dressed, but today is not such a good day. I had hoped to show you around our collection of treasures – my son tells me you are greatly interested in the *Kunstkammer*.'

'I could spend a month there and not stop marvelling,' I said.

'A *month*?' He laughed, which turned abruptly to a coughing fit; Katherina leaned forward anxiously with an enamel bowl for him to spit into. 'You could be shut in there half a year and not scratch the surface,' he said, when he had recovered. 'Once I am well enough, I will give you a tour,' he added. 'More than fifty years of collecting, and each object with its own story.'

'I would like that very much, signore,' I said, 'and so would my assistant, Besler.'

Besler stepped forward with a neat bow; Jacopo eyed him briefly and nodded.

'Well, young man,' he said in German, 'if you wish to see the *Kunstkammer*, I'm sure my son can spare a few moments to show you now, eh Ottavio?'

'Yes, Father.' Ottavio shot me a complicit look; evidently his father wanted to speak to me alone.

'There is one thing Besler is particularly keen to see,' I said. 'A certain celebrated door knocker?'

Ottavio smiled. 'Ah. Of course. If you would care to follow me, Herr Besler, I'm sure we can find plenty to entertain you while they reminisce about the old country.'

'You don't mind if I go with him, Maestro?' Besler asked.

'On the contrary, I'm delighted for you,' I said with something of the relief a mother feels when the nursemaid arrives to take the child off her hands.

'I shall tell you all about it later,' he assured me.

'I don't doubt that for a moment.'

Ottavio put a hand on Besler's elbow to steer him to the door, when the silence was shattered by a bestial howl from somewhere outside the room, causing us all to leap a couple of inches in the air. I felt the hairs on my arms stand up; it was not quite human, nor quite animal.

'*Madonna porca*, Katherina,' Jacopo cursed. 'Go and tend to that creature.'

Katherina bowed her head and hurried from the room. Ottavio muttered something I could not catch, but which sounded very like '*diavolo*', and ushered Besler into the corridor so that I was left alone with Jacopo.

'You sent for me?' I prompted.

'Put another log on the fire, will you?' he said, slumping back in his nest of cushions.

The room was already overheated, the air thick, but I obeyed, wondering at the ease with which he issued commands from his sickbed as if I were his underling, and my own willingness to do his bidding. Strada senior had a natural air of authority about him, even in his present state. I poked the fire to stoke it, waiting for him to come to the point. As I did so, I glanced up to see a grand portrait mounted above the mantel.

'This is you?' I asked, stepping back for a better look. The subject was a self-possessed man in his early fifties, his beard and moustache full and fox-red, his shrewd gaze trained on an object outside the frame. He wore a doublet of black velvet with peach satin sleeves, a gleaming chain of office wound around his neck and a cloak of thick grey fur over his shoulders. The artist had shown him surrounded by the spoils of his profession; in his hands he held a marble statue of a naked goddess, while antique coins and parchments were spread on the table before him. The clothing and the expression were so exquisitely rendered in oils that it had to be the work of a master.

Jacopo gave a rasping laugh. 'More than twenty years ago, when I still had a full head of hair.'

I peered closer at the artist's signature and turned back to him, amazed. '*Tiziano?*'

'Yes. I sat for him in Vienna. That was the year the Emperor Maximillian appointed me court antiquary. Interesting man, Tiziano. Though it is a mixed blessing to lie here looking at my younger self as I waste away.'

'What ails you?'

'Sit.' He indicated the seat Katherina had vacated and sighed. 'Dr Hajek says there is a growth in my stomach. Like a malign

140

pregnancy. So I suppose I have that in common with my daughter. That monstrous noise you heard just now?'

'What *was* that?'

'Her child. A boy of three years. There's something wrong with him,' he added with a marked lack of compassion. 'She won't hear it, of course, but I saw it straight away. Doesn't speak, you know – never has. Just makes those noises. He catches birds to break their wings for pleasure. And it's in the family line, you know.'

'What is?'

'*Madness*.' He levered himself forward and took hold of my sleeve. 'His Majesty's great-grandmother was famously insane, spent her life locked up. Juana la Loca, they called her.'

'You mean . . .' I paused. Juana la Loca was the grandmother of King Philip of Spain, and therefore also of Rudolf's mother Maria. 'Katherina's child is—'

'The Emperor's bastard, obviously. I doubt he'll be the last she gives him, either.'

'Does Rudolf acknowledge him?'

'He provides for him. The boy has no formal title as yet – I suppose His Majesty is waiting to see how he turns out.' He grunted. 'He'll be waiting a long time, if you want my opinion. But we have to nurture the feral creature and hope for the best.'

I bet you do, I thought. So Rabbi Loew was wrong; the Emperor did have a living heir, albeit one who was illegitimate and possibly not right in the head – although in my limited experience all three-year-olds displayed traits of lunacy, so it seemed unfair to write the boy off just yet. And a bird in the hand was something, as the old proverb said. His existence bound the Strada family to the Emperor. I recalled what Ottavio had said about the Catholic faction resenting the influence of his family at court; suddenly his meaning became a lot clearer. I looked at the white-bearded man in the bed, whose sunken face still held a vestige of the strength and purpose that Tiziano had captured in the portrait, and felt a wave of distaste at his willingness to pimp his daughter for the sake of his own status.

141

'But I didn't ask you here to talk about my bastard grandson and his strange ways, nor to admire my portrait,' he said. 'Ottavio told me what happened last night. The eyes in the casket.'

I grimaced. 'Someone wished to send a very literal message to His Majesty.'

'So it seems. Someone who clearly knew the effect it would have. Rudolf is—' he searched for the right word as he resettled himself among his pillows. 'I do not say he is unstable, mark you, but the balance of his mind is delicate. A shock like that – it is guaranteed to throw him into a state of fear and melancholy, where all he thinks of is retreating from the world.'

Pointedly saying Rudolf was not unstable strongly implied that he was, as Jacopo knew.

'Is that something he does often?' I asked.

'Increasingly.' The old man let out a laboured sigh and shook his head. 'He is tormented by the idea that his advisers are conspiring against him – even old and trusted counsellors like me and Hajek, who have known him for years. He mutters of curses and poisons, he fears his subjects will rise against him, so he locks himself away with his treasures and will see no one, not even his valet. The servants have to leave food outside his door. In these moods only Katherina can coax him back to himself, and often he refuses to admit even her. I fear that this murder and that vile gesture with the eyes are designed to plunge him into despair. There are those who would profit from his incapacity.' He fixed me with a meaningful look, as if he expected me to divine who he meant.

'Who deals with affairs of state when the Emperor shuts himself away?' I asked.

'Count Vilem von Rozmberk. He is the Supreme Burgrave of Bohemia, the highest official in the land, and president of the Privy Council. You'll see his palace on the other side of the castle complex, behind the cathedral.' He paused for a prolonged bout of coughing, gesturing for me to pass him the bowl for spitting. 'He avoids the city if he can – spends most of his time at his castle in the south. But when Rudolf falls into one of his black

142

moods for any length of time, Rozmberk is summoned back to manage affairs. You see how precariously Bohemia stands, Dr Bruno?' He gave a dry laugh and closed his eyes, as if the explanation had exhausted him.

I sat back, trying to fit this new information into my picture of the Prague court. 'So this Rozmberk effectively rules whenever the Emperor falls prey to one of his fits of melancholy?' I said. 'Was that what you meant about profiting from his incapacity?'

'I was not thinking of him so much,' Jacopo said. 'I do not believe Count Vilem has any interest in governing – he is another who spends all his vast fortune pursuing the secrets of the alchemists. Although he has an ambitious new wife, so perhaps that will change. I had one of those myself, so I pity the man.' He chuckled softly. 'No – I meant the emissaries of Rome and Spain, the hardline Catholics. They want Rudolf declared unfit to rule so he can be legitimately deposed – I would not put it past them to carry out tricks like this one with the eyeballs, knowing how it would affect him.'

'Then you think the Catholics ordered the murder of Ziggi Bartos? San Clemente and Montalcino, you mean?'

He sucked in his cheeks. 'I'm saying it would be in keeping with their longer purpose, certainly. Naturally, one cannot entirely rule out the Jews either.'

'What? You don't believe in the Golem, surely?' I said, surprised.

'Ha. Of course not. But the Emperor does, and I believe in the existence of a man who is ruthless in the defence of his people's continued independence and rights.'

'You mean Rabbi Loew? But you can't think he would have someone murdered and make it look like the work of a Golem? That makes no sense.'

'Oh, but it does. If you can't make people respect you, make them fear you, no?'

'The Jews are already experiencing reprisal attacks because of this murder.'

'A double bluff. You think they couldn't have done that

themselves, to make their innocence the more convincing? They look to their own interests as much as anyone. More so – they are notorious for it.'

'I find the idea highly unlikely.' I was beginning to wonder if Jacopo's mind was ailing as well as his gut; either way, I did not want to spend any more time in his company. I shifted in my seat as if preparing to take my leave.

'I am simply saying,' he continued, motioning for me to stay, 'that you should consider every possibility. My son tells me the Emperor has asked you to find the killer?'

I pushed a hand through my hair. 'I told His Majesty that John Dee could not be responsible, and in doing so it seems I volunteered to prove to him who was. But I confess, I feel at the moment like a man lost in a dark wood. There are so many competing factions in this city, all wanting to cast blame on one another, and I am a foreigner here with no knowledge of how to sift truth from falsehood.' I had not meant to express myself quite so forcefully to him; perhaps the comfort of relaxing into my own language had lulled me into confidences.

'I understand. I have been in Prague eight years, since Rudolf first moved his court here, and I still do not know who to trust. But in my experience, the most obvious explanation is usually correct, no? *Cui bono.* Who stands to gain?'

'That is the problem. There seem to be any number of people who would have liked Ziggi Bartos dead and their enemies blamed.'

'Yes, but the manner of his killing. The eyes and the tongue, the inscription. If you simply want rid of a man, you dispatch him and bury him where he won't be found. So you have to ask yourself – who benefits from making his death a personal message to the Emperor? I have already given you two possible answers.'

'Have you told His Majesty of your suspicions about the Catholics?'

'He has not asked my advice,' Jacopo said, and I heard a note of pique in his voice. 'Speak to Ottavio. He can help you navigate the tangled connections at court,' he added when I didn't respond. 'He's a good boy – a quick mind, though his mother cosseted him, against my better judgement.' I noted the twitch of disdain at the corner of his mouth. 'He could do with learning a few worldly skills from a man like you, Dr Bruno.'

I gave him an opaque smile. I was not sure what he meant by this; did he want me to teach his son how to hold his own in a bar brawl? Or did he want to make sure that I kept Ottavio informed of whatever I discovered about the murder? Jacopo was certainly very keen for me to look at San Clemente and Montalcino; naturally I was not going to tell him that they also wanted to find out who had killed Bartos. As for the idea that the Jews wanted to stir up belief in a vengeful Golem, I dismissed that as pure prejudice. I shifted the chair back and with startling speed he grabbed my wrist in his gnarled fingers.

'If you will take one more piece of counsel from me, Dr Bruno,' he said, drawing me close so that I could smell the sickness on his breath, 'you are right to be wary of who you trust. And you would do well to start with your host.'

'Hajek?' I stared at him. 'You can't think he had anything to do with the murder?'

'I didn't say that, precisely. I am simply urging you to see that most people in this city, whoever they claim to serve, are usually serving themselves foremost. There is no man closer to the Emperor than Thaddeus Hajek, or so he believes, and he wants to keep it that way. He did not climb so high by being meek and self-effacing.' The very idea of Hajek possessing these qualities sent him into another bout of laughing and coughing. I felt that Jacopo was unintentionally revealing himself with this observation, but my heart sank nonetheless; I had chosen to be persuaded of Hajek's integrity because John Dee had been convinced of it, and because the doctor shared so many of my own interests, but Jacopo had a point: all I knew of Hajek was what he allowed me to see, and Dee was, after all, missing.

'Ottavio told me what was written on the paper that came

with the casket last night,' the old man continued, his chest rasping with the effort of speech. 'Let us suppose, for a moment, that there was truth in it. Ziggi Bartos had made some momentous discovery in his alchemical experiments. Who would he tell first?'

'The Emperor, I presume.'

'My guess is that he would not be able to resist telling his mentor, the man who has nurtured his talent since he arrived in Prague. The man who is responsible for overseeing all the alchemists. And if Hajek recognised that Bartos had genuinely stumbled upon something worthwhile, might he not wish to take the credit himself?'

'And then draw attention to his theft by taunting the Emperor with a note written in Bartos's own hand, boasting of his discovery? That seems no more plausible than the idea that John Dee did the same.'

'Ah, I don't know, Dr Bruno.' Jacopo let his head fall back, his eyes fixed on the canopy overhead. 'I am deeply unsettled by this business and I am clutching at straws in the wind. The one thing that seems certain is that the manner of the alchemist's cruel death was designed to sow fear, and a fearful populace quickly loses patience with a weak leader.' His grip on my wrist loosened. 'Above all, I fear for my daughter.'

'You think she's in danger?'

'She has not confirmed it to me, but she has another one in there, I'm sure of it.'

'Another child?'

He nodded. 'That makes her a greater threat to those who have other plans for the Emperor's affections, and if this killing is part of some scheme to destabilise his throne . . .' He let his hand fall to his side. 'I have done my best to protect my children, Bruno, and perhaps they are somewhat naïve as a result. I fear they do not comprehend how deeply our family is resented in some quarters. If your enquiries should uncover anything that places Katherina in jeopardy, you will tell me, won't you? Or Ottavio?'

146

'Of course,' I said, standing. It seemed everyone at court was taking an interest in my investigation; no doubt because they all had secrets of one kind or another and feared exposure. Whether those secrets were connected in any way to Ziggi Bartos and John Dee remained to be determined.

'I read your book,' Jacopo said as I bowed farewell. 'The one you published in England.'

'*The Ash Wednesday Supper?*'

'That's the one. Ottavio bought John Dee's copy from him for the imperial library. I admired it greatly.'

'Thank you,' I said, my initial dislike of him thawing a little.

'You are a bold man, Bruno. I salute you. Not many would dare to posit the idea of an infinite universe in print.'

'There are not many printers who would have risked it, that's for sure. I was fortunate.'

'As we are fortunate here to have a sovereign who defends free thought and intellectual courage. You see why those of us who value such things are concerned by any events that upset the equilibrium and give ammunition to Rudolf's enemies. Find this killer,' he said, levelling a bent finger at me, 'so that we can put a stop to all the rumours. I know you will. Send my daughter in to me now. And come back soon – I would be glad of the chance to talk further.'

I assured him that I would, and found Katherina in the outer chamber, gazing out of the window, one hand resting speculatively on her flat stomach. She started when I cleared my throat, and forced a smile.

'I hope he has not tired himself,' she said. 'He very much wanted to meet you, but this business with the alchemist has so troubled him, he does not sleep or rest as he should, and I'm afraid the worry will hasten the progress of his illness.'

'He seems like a man of strong constitution,' I said, conscious that I had little to offer her by way of comfort. She shook her head sadly.

'Dr Hajek says there is no fighting it,' she said, dropping her voice and glancing anxiously at the bedroom door. 'He says the

147

best we can hope for is to manage his symptoms so that he does not suffer too much.'

'Does Hajek say – how long?' If Jacopo Strada was dying, that would explain his anxiety for his daughter. Those who regarded her as an obstacle to Rudolf's marriage would surely not dare to touch her while her father remained one of the Emperor's most trusted officials, but in his absence she and her son would be significantly less protected. Although I had to wonder whether her father was worrying unnecessarily; it was hardly unusual for a sovereign to have mistresses and bastards in the background, and these were not considered impediments to a dynastic marriage and legitimate succession. Unless, of course, there had been some suggestion that Rudolf wanted to make Katherina his wife.

She lifted one shoulder unhappily. 'He said at first that the tumour was slow-growing, and that in the best case it could be a year or more yet. But my father seems to have taken a turn for the worse overnight, and I'm sure it's the distress. Hajek gave us a tincture to relieve the pain, but my father will not take it because he fears the doctor is trying to dull his wits.' She appeared to be half talking to herself; after a pause, she turned to me with an apologetic smile. 'Forgive me – I don't know why I am telling you this. Only that if he said anything foolish to you in there, I hope you will not take offence. He is not quite himself.'

'Not at all – he was most gracious. So he mistrusts Dr Hajek?'

She lowered her gaze. 'He mistrusts most people, Dr Bruno.' She seemed about to say more, but it appeared a sudden cramp or gripe took her; she reached out and placed a hand on the wall for support.

'Are you all right?' I asked, guiding her to a chair. Her face was wan.

'Thank you. I must have eaten something that has troubled me.' Her gaze swerved away from mine as she said this.

'How many weeks since you ate it?' I asked, with a meaningful glance at her stomach.

Her face flushed and she rested a hand there. 'You have sharp eyes for a man. I think eight. Please don't say anything to my father or my brother. I wanted to wait until I was sure it would stay. There have been others that . . . did not.'

'Of course not,' I assured her. 'It's not my business. Does His Majesty know?'

She raised her eyes to me and I saw a kind of pleading in her expression. 'I have not yet had a chance to tell him,' she said. 'He has not sent for me since—' She looked down at her lap.

'Since it happened?'

She nodded miserably.

'Because he is melancholy?' I asked.

She made a gesture of helplessness. 'His moods are so changeable. I never know if it is I who have displeased him or something else entirely.'

I felt again that surge of irritation: at Rudolf, for treating the mother of his children like one of his collectable *objets*, to be picked up and discarded on a whim, and at her father and brother for putting her in that position to further their own ambition, regardless of her feelings. I thought of the shrunken, lugubrious figure I had encountered the night before in the *Kunstkammer*, and wondered if she felt any genuine attraction or affection for him. It was not impossible; women and their desires were unfathomable.

I moved to lay a hand on her shoulder in a gesture of reassurance and withdrew it before I made contact; better not to risk accusations of over-familiarity with the Emperor's mistress.

'Your father asks for you,' I said.

She nodded, placing her palms flat on her knees and inhaling, as if taking a moment to compose the face she must present.

'Thank you again for your discretion,' she murmured, without looking up.

ELEVEN

In the courtyard, the light was fading early. A low lid of cloud had settled over the city and a pervasive damp spread through the air; nothing so substantial as mist, but seeping determinedly into my clothes and hair all the same. There was no sign of Besler; I hoped he was still having a marvellous time looking at paintings of naked women. I decided to profit from his absence by making another trip to Golden Lane, on the far side of the castle complex; I wanted to know who had been watching out of the house opposite Ziggi Bartos's lodging, and what they might have seen. It was only as I approached the old convent of St George behind the cathedral, where Montalcino and San Clemente had issued their earlier threats, that I remembered I had handed in my dagger at the gatehouse. If the watcher behind the window resented me asking questions, I had only my fists for defence – and they were not in the best shape after my encounter with the Spaniards, despite Hajek's ointments. I thought resentfully of those two hired thugs as I passed the basilica; there was no doubt in my mind that they had been sent by the ambassador to intercept any letters I carried. The Catholic faction must surely have known, then, that John Dee was sending dispatches back to England; clearly, they wanted to find out what he might have said, and the response – though how they were primed to expect me was a mystery. I had only sent word to John that I was on my way to Prague the same day I left Wittenberg, and he would not have received the message. But did they really not know who killed Bartos, or was that merely a ruse to keep me answering to them, to make sure they were the first to know if I came too close to the truth? Either way, Montalcino was not one to make empty promises; there were countless ways he could arrange for Besler or me to come to harm and make it look like the kind of accident that befalls unwary travellers in a strange city. I hurried on, keeping extra vigilant in case he or San Clemente were still in the vicinity.

Dusk seemed to come prematurely to Golden Lane, or perhaps the place existed in a permanent penumbra, built as it was in the shadow of the high castle wall that ran along its northern boundary. Though there were few people about here, I felt less confident than I had in the dead of night with Hajek, whose official status within the castle had at least given the illusion of protection. Now I was alone and unarmed, probing into matters that everyone in Prague appeared determined to warn me off. I had the unnerving impression that the small houses had moved closer to one another since my last visit, as if to hem me in, as my hand strayed impotently to the empty sheath at my belt.

I found the door of Bartos's house still unlocked; as I turned the handle I assumed it must have remained undisturbed since the previous night and no one had yet discovered my tampering with the lock, but as soon as I stepped inside, I saw that this was not the case. The place was transformed; every shard of broken glass and pottery had been cleared away, the floor scoured of all traces of spilled liquids and the grate swept clean of charred paper. It was as if the house had never been inhabited, much less been the scene of a frenzied search. I cursed under my breath, bitterly regretting that I had not pressed Hajek to make a more thorough investigation with me before we left. The haste with which the place had been stripped bare and scrubbed down was suspicious too; had our visit put someone on the alert? Someone who had returned after our search last night to ensure there was not one speck of dust or scrap of writing that could tie them to Ziggi Bartos. In which case – how had they known about the search? It could only have been the watcher in the window opposite. *Or Hajek*, said a voice in my head that I tried to ignore. He had been reluctant to enter the house; he had claimed to find nothing when I asked him to check the burned writings in the hearth. I thought about Jacopo Strada's warning as I climbed the ladder in the corner and poked my head up into the sleeping loft; this, too, had been emptied, every last strand of straw from the ruined mattress swept away. Even Bartos's rosary had gone from the nail above the bed.

I stepped out into the lane, closing the door behind me with a growing sense of foreboding. It was as if Ziggi Bartos had never existed. I glanced up at the house opposite and caught again a flicker of movement in an upstairs window. Turning my collar against the damp, I strode across the cobbles and rapped firmly on the door, tensed for a hostile reception.

I waited a few moments, as it occurred to me that if the occupants spoke only Czech I would be at a loss and would have to return with Besler. I was about to knock again when the door swung open to reveal a tousle-haired child of about eleven or twelve, with a striped woollen shawl wrapped around her shoulders and an expression that suggested I had better not waste her valuable time. She raised an expectant eyebrow, leaning on the door as if poised to slam it in my face.

I removed my hat and swept a bow. 'Good evening, madam.'

She looked me up and down as if deciding whether to laugh at my exaggerated gallantry, and said something in a language I did not recognise, though it sounded like one of the Nordic tongues.

'German?' I said hopefully.

'I said, *what do you want*?'

I smiled at her, relieved. 'Is your mother or father home?'

'My mother is dead,' she said bluntly. 'My father is in the Powder Tower. Or more probably in the Blue Elephant. Does he owe you money? I don't have any here.' The resignation in

152

her tone implied that I was not the first to knock at her door with this purpose.

'Oh – no, nothing like that. I don't know him. My name is Bruno,' I added, hoping to put her at ease.

'Yes, and . . . ?' She folded her arms. 'Wait, I've seen you before. You were here last night.' She pointed across the lane at Bartos's house.

'That's right,' I said. 'Do you keep an eye on the place, then, Mistress—?'

'Moller,' she said. 'Susannah Moller. I was reading in my room. Sometimes I happen to look out of the window.'

'I'm sure. Are you a good reader?'

'You don't have to talk to me like I'm three. I'm a very good reader, as it happens. In Danish, German and a little Latin. My father taught me.'

'My apologies. I did not mean to insult you.' I added another clumsy bow; I realised I was out of practice at talking to precocious children. 'Your father is an alchemist, then?'

'He's an *inventor*,' she said, pulling her shawl close with an effort at dignity, then added, 'Supposedly. What's funny?'

I was smiling because she sounded exactly as I had when insisting to Esther Loew that I was not an alchemist but a philosopher.

'Nothing. So you're Danish?'

She nodded, and for the first time her air of confidence faltered and she looked down at her shoes. 'But we haven't lived there since I was little. After my mother died we came here. My father said there would be *opportunities*.' The savage disdain in her tone suggested that he had mainly found opportunities to visit the taverns. 'What did you want him for, anyway?'

'Actually, I'm hoping you might be able to help me, Susannah Moller.' I reached into the purse at my belt and withdrew a couple of coins; she eyed them with wary interest. 'I wondered if I could ask you some questions about the house across the street, and the man who lived there. I imagine you see a lot from your window. You seem to be a very observant girl.'

She gave me a narrow look and I saw that flattery was not the way forward with her. 'Why do you want to know?'

'Someone killed him,' I said. 'You've probably heard. I'm trying to find out who. The Emperor asked me to,' I added, wondering if that would carry any weight with her. She quirked her eyebrow again, though I couldn't tell whether she meant to look impressed or sarcastic.

'All right,' she said, after brief consideration. 'But I can't invite you in. Far says I mustn't let anyone in the house while he's out.' She sighed. 'He thinks they'll come and take our stuff.'

'Who will?'

'His creditors.'

'Ah.' I watched her as she shifted from foot to foot, her gaze fixed on the coins in my hand. I noticed how patched her skirt was, how worn her shoes, the way she wrapped the ends of her threadbare shawl around small hands white with cold. She had a sweet, round face and clear hazel eyes, but there was a line etched between her brows, the legacy of a burden of worry that no child her age should have to shoulder, and beneath the too-big dress her bones jutted sharply. 'Look,' I said, changing tack, 'are you hungry? I haven't had supper yet – you could join me, if you know of anywhere that would serve a good bowl of hot stew.'

She weighed up the possible pros and cons and tilted her head to one side. 'How do I know you are not going to kidnap me?'

'I suppose you don't,' I said. 'But why would I want to do that?'

'There are men who look for girls my age,' she said matter-of-factly. 'Goodwife Huss told me. She's my neighbour,' she added, glancing down the street. 'I help her with chores some-times and she gives me bread, if Far has forgotten to buy any. She's warned me about men.' She scuffed her foot against the step as she said this, and I saw again the acute shame of poverty; I remembered it too well myself.

'Well, Goodwife Huss is right to look out for you,' I said,

154

'but I am not one of those men. I'm looking for information, and I'm prepared to pay for it. Do we have a deal?' I held out my hand; she raised her head and met my eye.

'All right,' she said, shaking my hand, her fingers icy and fragile in mine. 'There's a good place not far from here. They know me, so if you do try anything, they'll witness where I was last seen.'

'Fair enough.' I waited while she locked the house behind her and slipped the key into the folds of her dress.

'Do you work for the Emperor, then?' she asked as she led me back past the cathedral to the main gatehouse.

'Not really,' I said. 'I'm a writer.'

She skidded to a halt and stared at me as if I had finally said something worth her attention. 'A real one? Have you printed books?'

'Yes. Several.'

Her mouth dropped open. 'What are they about?'

'The cosmos,' I said, gesturing vaguely at the sky. I had no idea what religion she might profess, and therefore whether she would consider my writings heretical, so I opted for caution. 'And the art of memory. That is my chief subject. But I have written plays and poetry too.'

'I've never seen a play,' she said thoughtfully, resuming her pace as we crossed the square in front of the castle and turned into a narrow street running steeply downhill. 'Except the puppet shows in the Old Town Square, but they're for little children. I think I should like to see a proper play. Is yours funny?'

'It's meant to be.'

She nodded, as if this was the right answer. 'They're the best kind. Come on.'

We passed down a flight of steps into a small square, one side occupied by a tavern under the sign of the Winged Horse. The tap-room was spacious, if hazy with woodsmoke from a chimney that needed a good sweep. Groups of men huddled along trestle tables, but Susannah showed me to a nook by the fireplace, where she held her hands out to the meagre warmth. I felt a sudden stab of anger at the father who had brought her to a strange land and apparently drunk away the money that could have bought his daughter a proper coat and gloves.

'The food's not bad here,' she informed me. 'This is where the alchemists drink, mostly. Far's barred,' she added as a tall woman in her fifties appeared and cast a sceptical eye over me.

'You all right, Sukie?' she asked, her voice heavy with implication.

'Don't worry, Magda,' the girl said, pointing at me. 'He's paying. He's a writer.'

'Is he now.' The tap-woman pursed her lips. 'And why's he paying for you?'

'I'm a friend of the family,' I said. I resented her tone, but supposed I ought to be glad that there were people keeping an eye out for the girl.

'Right.' She wiped her hands on her floury apron and lowered her voice. 'Well, you tell that useless fuckster Erik Moller next time you see him that he owes me ten thalers from four months ago, and he's not setting foot through those doors again except to settle his account. Unless that's why you're here,' she added, glancing pointedly to the purse at my belt.

Something in the woman's bearing and her manner of speaking struck me as familiar. I studied her more closely and all at once I realised: she reminded me of Greta. The resemblance was there in the furrowed brow, the look of instinctive suspicion. I was sure this must be the sister Besler had mentioned, who had inherited the family tavern, but I decided not to mention the connection for now. Instead I counted out eleven thalers.

'Extra for your trouble,' I said with my most charming smile. 'Now, I'd like a pot of beer, some bread and whatever the girl wants.'

Sukie asked for a beef pie, assured me that I should have the same, and when Magda had gone, she rested her chin on her hands and fixed me with a stern look.

'So I suppose you think I'm in your debt now,' she said. I spread my hands wide.

'*Quid pro quo*. Do you know what that means?'

'Of course.'

'Well, then. As I told you, I need information.'

'To catch the person who killed Ziggi?'

'I hope so,' I said. 'If you can help me.'

'Good. He was my friend.'

It was the first time she had mentioned this; I must have looked surprised because she offered a shy smile. 'I used to go over and help him sometimes when Far was out,' she explained. 'Measuring ingredients for his experiments, washing up the equipment, that kind of thing. Far didn't like me spending time there, but he didn't know Ziggi. He was kind. We used to lie for each other.'

'How do you mean?'

'If the debt collectors came. I'd say I hadn't seen him, and he'd do the same for me.'

'So Ziggi had money troubles too?' That confirmed what I had learned from Rabbi Loew.

'All the alchemists are up to their necks in debt,' she said, as if this were common knowledge. 'But Ziggi—' She stopped, chewing her lip.

'What?'

'He said his fortunes were about to change. He was going to make a lot of money. He promised to buy me a rabbit fur hat, and a new doll, although I've outgrown dolls, really.' She smiled sadly. 'I thought it was too good to be true. Next thing I know, Goodwife Huss is running up and down the street telling everyone the Golem has ripped him to pieces. Far went to the Stone Bridge to see for himself, but he wouldn't let me go with him.'

'I think that was wise,' I said, picturing Bartos's mutilated face. Perhaps her father wasn't entirely irresponsible after all. 'Did Ziggi tell you how he hoped to make this money?'

In her hesitation I saw that she had a good idea, but at

that moment the innkeeper returned with the pies and I had to curb my impatience while Sukie attacked hers as if she had not seen a hot meal in days – which I suspected might well be the case.

'It was something to do with his experiments,' she answered, when she finally paused to draw breath. 'He wouldn't say what exactly.'

'But you knew what he was aiming for, if you were assisting him?' I prompted.

She shrugged. 'Ziggi said the Philosopher's Stone was not something that would turn iron into gold, only fools without the imagination to see further thought that. All I know is he was teaching me about distillation. He wanted to produce a kind of liquor – he said I must never touch it because it would make me very sick. Only adepts could drink it safely.'

'Did he say what it was for, this liquor?'

'He said when he had finessed it, it would make you transcend your mortal body. It had gold in it, I know that. He needed to melt quantities of gold to make it, that's why he had to borrow so much from the Jews. And he said' – she dropped her gaze to her trencher – 'that if anyone knew what he was working on, they would try to steal it. He made me take an oath not to speak of it.'

I nodded. All this made sense; the pursuit of *aurum potabile* – drinkable gold – was yet another goal of the alchemical art, related to the elixir of life. For centuries, alchemists had believed that if gold, being incorruptible, could be distilled into a liquid through the correct formula, it would cure all diseases by transferring its properties of perfection. The Arab physician Geber had been the first to discover that certain forms of acid could liquefy gold, and Paracelsus was convinced that *aurum potabile* was viable, but he never claimed to have produced it. Did Ziggi Bartos believe he had succeeded where they had failed? I tried to process this new information without saying anything that might alarm Sukie or cause her to clam up.

'After Ziggi was killed,' I said, turning my tankard between my hands, 'his house was searched. Before I came last night, I mean. Did you see who did that?'

She turned her attention back to the remains of her pie, eating more slowly this time. 'A man. That's all I can tell you. He came in the night, before the news broke at dawn that Ziggi was dead and everyone ran down to the bridge to see. I could hear the sounds of breaking glass from my room.'

'You didn't tell your father, or go to see what was happening?'

She took a moment to answer. 'I just assumed . . .' A lift of one thin shoulder. 'These things happen, when you owe money. Sometimes they come to give you a warning. People don't get involved.' From the set of her mouth, it was clear that such things had happened in her own house. 'My father slept through it, of course.'

'This man who smashed up the house – did you get a clear look at him?'

'He had a cloak with the hood up.'

'And then he came back to clean up after I was there last night?'

She shook her head, her mouth full. 'Maybe. I don't know if it was the same person. But the second time there was a woman too.'

'A *woman*?' I stared at her, the tankard halfway to my mouth. 'What did she look like? Young, old?'

'Tall. Apart from that, I couldn't see much. They came just before dawn today. She had long skirts and a hood. The man wore a cap pulled low and a kerchief tied around his mouth like this.' She indicated the lower part of her face. It sounded very much like one of the Spaniards who had attacked me. 'He brought a little handcart. When they came out, they loaded it up with sacks and took them away. I went over to look after they'd gone, and there was nothing left.'

Greta? I wondered. Could Hajek have sent her with another servant to strip the place bare, knowing I would want to go over it again in daylight? I took a drink, silently cursing Jacopo Strada for planting that suspicion in my head. I would have liked to believe that Hajek was the one person in Prague I could trust.

'So I suppose,' I said carefully, setting my pot down, 'that the searchers must have found whatever they were looking for. This potion he was making, I presume.'

At first she didn't respond; all her concentration was very deliberately on mopping up sauce with a piece of bread. After a moment she raised her eyes to meet mine, and I saw in her expression an internal struggle, which I divined to be a conflict of loyalties. All at once, I thought I understood, but it was a matter of persuading the girl to confide in me.

'Listen, Sukie,' I said, leaning across the table. 'Ziggi is dead now, so you are released from any oaths you made to him. Secrets he asked you to keep, for example.'

Her gaze darted away; I could see her biting the inside of her mouth as she tore the bread into ever-smaller pieces and rolled them between her fingers.

'What if they didn't find it?' she whispered, confirming my guess.

'In that case . . . I'll be frank with you – I think your friend was killed precisely because of that substance he was working on.' I was not at all sure of this, but she did not need to know that. 'That man who came to search his house – I have an idea who he is, and he is dangerous. So if, by some chance, Ziggi feared people might come looking for it, and he gave the potion to someone he trusted to keep it safe – well, then, that person might also be in danger. The searcher will have been asking around, as I am, to find out who he associated with. One of your neighbours might have mentioned you spending time at his house.'

The colour drained from her face as she stared at me, though in an instant her expression hardened to a frown. 'How do I know you are not also trying to steal his work? You were searching his house too.'

'True. But I did not smash the place up. I have settled your father's debt here, haven't I?'

She let out a dry laugh that belonged to someone older and

world-weary. 'Yes. Thank you. That just leaves all the other taverns in the Lesser Town.'

'I'll do what I can. In return, I'm asking you to trust me. Sukie – I saw what was done to Ziggi Bartos,' I added quietly. 'Your father saw it too. These are people you don't want to cross. You say your father didn't like you spending time with Ziggi – how would he feel if he knew you were keeping the very thing that got him killed? What if – God forbid – that man suspects you have it and breaks into your house?'

She poked miserably at her pie and pushed away the remains, as if my threats had ruined her appetite. I felt bad for frightening her, though only a little.

'But Ziggi said' – she flicked one of the miniature balls of bread on to the floor – 'it was going to make his fortune. He was so sure. So I thought, after he died, maybe if Far took it to the Emperor, he could claim he discovered it and that would solve all our problems.' She would not look at me and she sounded close to tears; I understood how desperately she wanted to believe that she had inherited some miraculous cure-all from the dead alchemist, and why she was reluctant to let it go.

'If your father had made that claim and then been unable to replicate the substance, he would have been revealed as a fraud and punished,' I pointed out. 'The Emperor has banished alchemists for less. And as you saw for yourself, this elixir or whatever it is did not bring Ziggi riches – it brought him a violent death.'

'Doesn't that prove it was valuable? If that man wanted it so much?'

'Not necessarily. Look, why don't we try this,' I offered, grasping at incentives. 'If you let me take the substance and test it, I can tell you if it's worth anything. If it is, I will arrange for you to bring it to the Emperor in person and I'm sure there will be a reward, especially if it helps us to catch Ziggi's murderer. At least that way it will not be hidden in your house, putting you and your father at risk.'

I had no idea whether I could make good on this promise;

I would worry about that later. Sukie weighed up the offer and eventually nodded. 'All right. But you have to do something for me in return.'

'Name your price.' I fervently hoped she would not ask me to settle all her father's debts in one go; the purse Overton had given me from Walsingham would not stretch to that.

She picked at a splinter on the tabletop. 'I want a book.'

'Which book?'

'Don't mind. But Far has sold all of his, except a couple I managed to hide, and anyway I have read them many times. You're a writer, you must have books.'

'Oh. Well, I do, but—' But none of them suitable for an eleven-year-old girl, I almost said, stopping myself before I offended her. 'What kind of books do you like?'

'Adventures,' she said without hesitation.

'You mean, courtly tales? Like the knights of King Arthur?'

'I don't mind King Arthur.' She wrinkled her nose. 'Or the Norse gods – Far has told me those stories. Are there any adventures with girls in?'

I considered. Not enough, I realised. 'Do you know the tales of the Greeks?' I said. 'Plenty of heroines in those.' It occurred to me as I spoke that most of them ended up raped, dead or transformed into inanimate objects, but she could find that out for herself.

'All right, I'll read those,' she said, brushing crumbs neatly into a pile with the side of her hand as if the matter were now settled.

'Shall we go back to your house now, and you can give me whatever Ziggi left in your keeping?' I said, afraid she might change her mind. 'I'll bring you the book as soon as I can find a good one,' I promised, seeing her hesitation. Hajek surely had a translation of Homer or Ovid; failing that, perhaps I could persuade Ottavio Strada to raid the imperial library. When she answered with a reluctant nod, I pushed my chair back. 'Let me pay a visit to the yard and settle our bill. Wait here for me.'

I left coins on the serving hatch and slipped out of the back door. Darkness had fallen while we were eating, and the yard was sunk in shadow, barely lit by lanterns on poles flanking the rear gate. I passed under the leafless branches of a chestnut tree in the centre of the yard and stopped to piss in a mound of straw by the stables, breathing through my mouth to avoid the smell. I was lacing my breeches when I heard the sound of male voices from around the side of an outbuilding. They caught my attention because, although I couldn't make out all the words, I recognised from the cadences of their speech that they were conversing in Hebrew; unusual enough here, so far from the Jewish Town, to be worth remarking on. I crept closer, curious to know what was being discussed.

There were two of them and they spoke urgently, in whispers; I pressed my back against the wall and strained to listen, though it was impossible to hear clearly until one raised his voice in frustration.

'But I could not have known it would come to this,' he protested, 'or I would never—' and I heard his interlocutor hiss at him to be quiet. A muted exchange followed, until the first man spoke louder again.

'Then it ends here,' he said with evident agitation. 'I cannot have that on my conscience. Are we agreed?'

I heard a rustling and the chink of coins; money was changing hands. I inched towards the corner of the building, hoping for a look at them, but I had not reckoned on a wooden pail that had been left by the wall; my foot struck it and sent it rolling over the cobbles with a clatter that sounded loud as gunshot in the silence. For a moment, there was only the stillness of held breath; I stepped out from the shadows, clearing my throat and making a show of adjusting my breeches, to see one of the men already hurrying away under the broad arched gate. I glimpsed only an impression of height and the whisk of a cloak as he disappeared, the sound of his quick footsteps carrying through the night behind him.

'Evening,' I said, nodding to the remaining man, who appeared rooted to the spot with fear; I looked a second time, more closely, at the same moment that he tilted his hat back and said, amazed, '*You?*'

It was David, the cousin of Benjamin Katz who I had met that morning, wearing a large hat with a rabbit fur trim pulled low to hide his face. He clasped an object between his hands; on recognising me, he stuffed it hastily inside his jacket and I heard again the soft jangle of metal. Even in the dim light I could see the colour burning in his cheeks; he had not expected his transaction to be witnessed by anyone he knew, and his mouth opened wordlessly as he formulated an excuse.

'I was just having supper,' I said pleasantly, to spare him. 'This place was recommended to me for the food. Are you a regular here?'

'I – no. Not at all. I was just – I don't know about the food,' he finished lamely. 'I can't eat it.'

'It's that bad?'

He allowed a nervous smile. 'No – I mean, it's not kosher.' He hesitated, then grasped at my sleeve. 'Listen – would you mind not mentioning to Rabbi Loew that you saw me here? He – he wouldn't approve. Nor would my cousin.'

'Why not? Oh—' I gave him a sly nod. 'Women, is it?' I had noticed girls in the tap-room who were clearly for sale, though they went about it more discreetly than in many such places.

David flushed a violent red and looked appalled. 'Absolutely not! I'm a married man. I sometimes—' he hesitated, glancing over his shoulder.

'I won't repeat a word,' I said, leaning in to encourage confidences.

'I sometimes take a drink with the alchemists,' he said, not meeting my eye. 'Some of them are learned men with an interest in the Cabala, and they wish to acquire books. That is all. But Rabbi Loew wouldn't like it, so I would really appreciate—'

'Why not?' I asked. 'I thought he was all for sharing knowledge. He told me the alchemists often come to him.'

'Well, exactly,' David said, his eyes flicking past me to the gate. 'They go to him. He does not frequent Gentile taverns.'

I gave him a long look. 'I thought you were the one who disapproved of outsiders dabbling in Jewish learning?'

He let out an impatient sigh. 'I have four children, Dr Bruno, and another on the way. I'm a bookseller – I must supplement my income however I can, and here is a ready supply of men who will pay well, especially if they believe they are purchasing the only available copy of a rare work.' He shook his head, and pulled his hat down further to hide the shame in his eyes. 'I envy you if you have never had to compromise a principle to put bread on the table, but the rest of us do what we must.'

'Oh, I'm the last person to judge a man for his need to make a living,' I said, surprised at his defensiveness. 'In fact, I would be curious to see your shop – I have a little money put by for books myself.'

He weighed this up briefly and nodded; I could tell he was in a hurry to be gone. 'I'm sure I can find something of interest. I'm in the street behind the Old-New Synagogue – Maier and Sons. And you won't mention seeing me here?'

'Where you do business is no concern of mine.'

'Thank you, sincerely,' he said, though he didn't look wholly convinced. 'Well, I must go.'

'Take care out there with such a full purse,' I said as he turned to leave.

He snapped back to look at me. 'What?'

'You've clearly had a profitable night.' I nodded to his chest, where he had tucked away the pouch. 'And I've learned the hard way that these streets are full of thieves.'

He gave a thin smile. 'I'm sorry to hear that. But I have known these streets all my life, and you have not. I appreciate your concern.' He shifted his jacket uncomfortably; I could see he did not like me drawing attention to the money he had received. It was not for dealing books to alchemists, of that much I was certain; the few who could afford specialist works of Jewish mysticism would hardly be trading them like contraband by a tavern privy.

He nodded a curt farewell and hurried away through the

gate, into the maze of back streets. I wondered if the man in the cloak was waiting for him somewhere. If not for Sukie and the promise of whatever Ziggi Bartos had left in her keeping, I would have been tempted to follow him.

Instead I returned to the tap-room to find Sukie gone and the table wiped clean.

TWELVE

'*Merda*.' I kicked the table leg, looking around the tavern, furious with myself for allowing the girl to slip away; I should have realised her acquiescence had come too easily. The other drinkers were busy talking or occupied with their food. 'Where did the child go?' I asked a couple of men in shabby smocks at the bench closest to us. 'The girl who was sitting here?' They paused long enough to give me a cursory glance, before shrugging and resuming their conversation in Czech. I swore again under my breath and crossed the room to bang on the serving hatch until Magda appeared.

'What now?' she asked, glaring at me. Definitely Greta's sister, I thought, seeing her expression.

'Where did Sukie go?'

'How should I know?'

'I was only outside for five minutes. You shouldn't have let a young girl like that leave on her own.'

'What am I, her nursemaid?' She pushed her sleeves up with a combative air and I noticed a dark bruise around her left wrist. 'That child's more than capable of looking after herself – she's had no choice, poor little cow. So if she's slipped away when your back's turned, I'd say that's because she didn't care for your company any longer.' She caught me looking at her arm and tugged her tunic down again. 'Now – do you want to order something else?'

I shook my head. She was right; Sukie had evidently had second thoughts about the terms of our agreement, despite her handshake. Her loyalty to Ziggi Bartos – or perhaps her faith in his mysterious discovery to change her family's fortunes – was clearly greater than her desire for a new book. Maybe it was simply that she didn't trust me, for which I could hardly blame her. But although I had exaggerated the threat to press her into confiding in me, I now found myself concerned that she might genuinely be in danger if she was holding on to Bartos's secret elixir.

I returned to Golden Lane without much hope of finding her home, though I hammered on the door until a middle-aged woman in a white coif stuck her head out of the next house and barked something in Czech.

'Goodwife Huss? I'm looking for Sukie,' I said in German. 'I was supposed to meet her here.'

'My arse you were,' she said, folding her arms beneath her formidable bosom. 'Haven't you people any shame? They've barely anything left for you to take. Have a scrap of Christian charity.'

'Oh – no, I'm not here for money,' I said quickly. 'I specifically wanted Sukie. We had an arrangement.' The goodwife looked like the kind of neighbour who didn't miss a thing that went on in her street; I was fairly sure she would have watched me and Sukie leave together earlier. She gave me a long look and her eyes narrowed further.

'She's *eleven* years of age,' she said with undisguised contempt. 'Do you know what her father would do to you if he found out about your *arrangement*? I ought to report you to the castle guard.'

'Please don't,' I said hastily. 'It's nothing like that. Although maybe her father could try staying home with her more often if he's worried about her safety,' I added under my breath.

Goodwife Huss sniffed loudly. 'Well, you'll have no disagreement from me on that point,' she said, surveying the lane. 'Though he's not a bad fellow underneath, you know, Erik Moller, whatever they say. Head in the stars, but he loves that girl more than his own life. And if she doesn't want to be found, there's no point you looking. She's run from you for a reason.'

I peered up at the dark windows of Sukie's house, clenching my fists in frustration. It would have been no trouble to pick the lock on the front door or force one of the windows open, but I could hardly do that with the goodwife standing over me.

'Sukie's father is protective of her, then?' I asked as a thought occurred.

'Well, he's not a fool, whatever else he may be,' said Goodwife Huss, leaning against the frame of her door as if we were settling in for a chat. 'He knows as well as anyone what can befall young girls, and she's too trusting, Sukie, with no mother to advise her. So I've taken it upon myself to tell her what's what when it comes to men and their ways.' She looked me up and down as she said this, as if I were giving off a bad smell.

'That's very neighbourly of you,' I said, and she allowed a grudging nod. I gestured to the house opposite. 'Did the man who lived there keep an eye on her too?'

'Ziggi Bartos?' She made a noise that could have meant any number of things, none of them complimentary. 'I suppose you might call it that.'

My stomach clenched. 'He didn't – you don't mean to say there was something improper in their friendship?'

'Oh no, not in that way,' the goodwife said, looking across at Bartos's house. 'He treated her like his apprentice. Had her running errands all over the place, fetching and carrying materials, using her pretty smile to beg extra credit with the apothecaries when he'd used up his own.' She tutted in disapproval. 'She'd come back stinking of sulphur and smoke, her hands all discoloured from whatever muck he'd had her mixing up for him. I'd hear Erik giving her an earful about meddling with

169

people like him, but it didn't deter her. Never saw the child happier than when she came out of that house.'

'People like him? Erik disliked alchemists?'

'Well, he disliked that one,' she said darkly, with a meaningful look at Bartos's door.

'Why?' I asked, but she was prevented from answering by a loud bellowing from somewhere inside her own house.

'Now there's my husband waking up,' she said, making a face. 'No rest for the wicked.'

'If you see Sukie,' I said quickly, 'tell her I'll be back with her book. Remind her we had a deal.'

Goodwife Huss gave me a pitying chuckle. 'Good luck making a deal with a Moller,' she said, and closed the door.

I made my way back up Golden Lane plagued by a sense of frustration; I had come so close to finding something useful and instead was left to fill in the gaps with guesswork. I tried to comfort myself with the thought that at least I knew more than I did this morning: it seemed likely from what I had seen at the Winged Horse that David Maier was one of the spies Rabbi Loew had mentioned, informing on his own community. I wondered what his motive could be. Perhaps it was no more complex than a need for coin, but I suspected there was more to it; information is currency, as Ottavio had said earlier. David had struck me as an upright man, but a man of strong principle might stoop to underhand means if he could convince himself that he was acting for a greater good. I wondered who, among the competing factions at court, would pay for David's secrets, and whether Rabbi Loew had any inkling. Either way, it seemed that David had had a fit of remorse over his actions. I kicked at a loose stone, muttering a string of reliable Neapolitan curses to myself; if I had known Sukie was planning to run out on me, I would have followed David to find the man in the cloak. It might be useful to know who was paying him, and for what. But then, I reflected, if I had known Sukie was going to renege on our agreement, I would not have left her in the tavern in the first place. It was a much greater frustration that I had not been able to get my hands on whatever Ziggi Bartos had entrusted to her; surely this elixir he had been finessing held the key to his murder. I determined to call on her first thing the next morning.

I was crossing the courtyard beyond the convent of St George, brooding on the evening's failures, when I heard the ripple of girlish laughter nearby. I turned to look and, on the far side, in the shadow of the private residences that lined the southern perimeter of the castle precinct, I made out a couple standing close together, murmuring softly, their silhouettes outlined in the flickering light of a wall-mounted torch. Though I couldn't see their faces, the young man's stance – awkward, lanky, trying too hard to look casual – struck me as familiar. I took a step towards them, peering into the gloom.

'Besler?'

He started as if he had been poked with a stick and peeled himself hurriedly away from the wall.

'Maestro! I was just looking for you. Where have you been?' His tone was overly bright; he was clearly embarrassed to have been caught dallying. I moved closer and took a look at the girl beside him. She was about his age, small and sharp-featured, with fair hair piled in an elaborate braid under a jewelled hood. A fur-trimmed cape hung around her shoulders, over a gown cut low in the bodice. I surmised, from the knowing way she let her gaze roam over me from head to foot, that she was probably a courtesan. The obvious quality of her clothes and the large pearls in her ears suggested she was a woman of means; perhaps the mistress of some nobleman. If that were the case, I needed to get Besler away as quickly as possible, before he made a fool of himself. She cocked her head to one side and regarded me with a pert smile.

'You must be the famous Dr Bruno,' she said. 'Your friend here has been telling me how you have won the Emperor's favour.'

'I don't know about that,' I said, bowing as I shot a stern

glance at Besler; I would speak to him later about proclaiming our business to any pretty girl who simpered at him. There was a good reason why Catherine de Medici of France employed a bevy of young women as spies at the Parisian court: some men will say anything to impress if they think there might be a tumble in it. More than one courtier in Paris had literally lost his head over Catherine's girls. I saw from Besler's expression that he had registered my annoyance.

'I was only saying, Maestro, that His Majesty has already sent for you to ask your counsel, such is his esteem,' he blustered, unwittingly making it worse.

'On what matters does the Holy Roman Emperor seek the counsel of a renowned thinker like yourself?' the girl asked, coiling a strand of hair around her finger.

I straightened. I had more practice than she could know at resisting the tricks of women like her. 'Oh, dull philosophical matters,' I said. 'But I'm sure a young lady can have little interest in the affairs of a couple of travelling scholars. Come, Besler – we must go. Madam. A pleasure to make your acquaintance.' I nodded a polite end to the conversation and turned away; she responded with a fluttering laugh as she laid a hand on my sleeve.

'But you have not, yet,' she said, the tips of her fingers lingering on my wrist. 'Made my acquaintance, I mean. Will you not ask your friend to introduce us?'

I moved my arm away, though not so abruptly that it would look like a rejection. 'Besler?' I said reluctantly.

'Oh – Dr Bruno, this lady is Polyxena von Rozmberk,' he said hastily.

The girl held out her skirts and executed a slow curtsy, not taking her pale blue eyes off mine. 'You can call me Xena,' she said.

'Rozmberk?' I took a step back. Not a courtesan, then. 'Are you perhaps Count Vilem's daughter?'

Xena laughed. 'I'm his *wife*,' she said with a hint of reproach.

'My apologies, my lady – I had not thought—'

'No need, it's a common mistake – there are more than thirty years between us. I'm the fourth. No doubt the fifth is not yet born.' She let out another peal of laughter, but I caught a forced note in it. 'I'm joking, of course. There will not be a fifth, because I will be the one to give him an heir where all the others failed.' She smiled briskly. 'My husband will be so jealous when I tell him of our encounter – he has been longing to meet you.'

'Has he?' I wondered how the highest noble in Bohemia had heard of me, and what he might want.

'Oh yes. John Dee has sung your praises to the count since he arrived. Oh, I know!' She clapped her hands together suddenly, as if she had just alighted on an idea. 'You must come and dine with us. Both of you.' She gestured to the elegant building behind her, one of a row that lined the south wall of the castle precinct. 'This is our palace. I will send a messenger – Besler tells me you lodge with Dr Hajek?'

'That's right. You know John Dee, then?' I asked.

'The count does. He has been a guest at our table on occasion, though I must say I find his manners unrefined.' She wrinkled her nose. 'He talks with his mouth full and sprays half-chewed meat over the board.'

I smiled; she was not wrong. 'He feels he must express an idea the minute it strikes, lest it slip his grasp. Have you seen him recently?'

'Not for some time. I don't know if the count has – he has not spoken of him lately, at any rate.' She sounded as if the topic hardly concerned her. 'Come tomorrow for supper, then. It is so nice to have some new blood in this town – I grow tired of the same old faces.' She pouted prettily, making sure to meet my gaze as she held out her hand for me to kiss. I took it warily, my lips barely brushing her skin, careful to be neither too enthusiastic nor too cold. I had some knowledge, as Besler did not, of what could happen when bored noble-women set their sights on a man as a distraction from the tedium of having everything they could want except their

173

husband's attention, and I could see from the way Xena von Rozmberk was looking at me that she had already decided I might provide amusement. I did not flatter myself that this was on account of my personal charms; it was more probable that, like the Emperor, she simply craved novelty. Either that, or she had a more subtle motive; it was not impossible that, like everyone else at Rudolf's court, she was trading in information. For her husband, the second-most powerful man in Bohemia? It would be unwise, I thought, to accept her invitation, though perhaps equally undiplomatic to refuse. Her reference to us as 'new blood' was not reassuring.

'My lady. Come, Besler.' I turned to him; he was still gazing at her as if he would scale the cathedral spire if she asked him to. I wished again that I had persuaded him to return to the German lands with Overton.

'Xena is excessively beautiful, is she not?' Besler said as we waited at the gatehouse for the boy to bring the horses.

I gave him a sidelong look as I strapped my knife back on to my belt; its reassuring weight at my side immediately put me in a better humour. 'Have you forgotten Esther Loew already? I thought you were besotted with her this morning. The affections of youth are so fickle.'

He blushed. 'Go ahead and laugh at my expense. But I do not have the chance to meet many women at the university, as you know, and I feel the lack. Besides, Esther is too old for me.'

'And the Countess von Rozmberk is too married,' I said pointedly. 'Do not even think of her. How did you come to be in conversation with her, anyway?'

'She was in the *Kunstkammer* looking at the curios when I came out of the library with Ottavio Strada. He introduced us. Xena said the Emperor allows her to visit on occasion, to pass the time. Then she asked me to walk her through the castle grounds to her own house as she doesn't like to be out in the dark, and I thought it would be unchivalrous to refuse.'

'Hm. If you should find yourself in that situation again, set

174

your gallantry aside. You must not be seen alone with her, Besler – do you understand? Her husband is an important man, and the last thing we need is for him to challenge you to a duel in defence of his wife's honour.' He looked suitably horrified, and I judged that the threat had hit home. 'Tell me of your afternoon, then,' I said, more gently. 'Did you see everything you'd hoped?'

He nodded, ducking his head with a bashful smile. 'The door knocker is quite realistic. I will draw it for you from memory when we get home. *And*' – he continued, before I could tell him there was no need for a sketch – 'Ottavio allowed me to see the Emperor's private collection of books, that are kept in a secret part of the library. I never would have thought—' He broke off, and even in the dusk shadow I could see that his face had turned fiery red.

'What?' I asked, tamping down a smile. He put me in mind of me and my fellow novices when I had first joined the Dominican order, the way anything to do with women was an inexhaustible topic of fascination and guilt – though we at least had the excuse of being barely seventeen at the time.

'That there were so many ways to go to it,' he said with an expression that suggested he could not decide whether this was wonderful or terrifying. 'Do you think Rudolf has tried them all?'

'I have honestly not considered the matter,' I said, though now he had put the image in my head, it was hard to imagine the lugubrious little man summoning the energy for any contortions of that nature. 'It may be one of the perks of being an Emperor.'

'No wonder Ottavio's sister looks so worn out,' Besler said, his frown deepening. 'But, Maestro – do all women expect such things? I mean, that you would turn them every which way on your yard? Upside down and backwards and I don't know what? Because, some of those pictures, I can't imagine how you are supposed to keep your balance. But I would not like to disappoint – *what*?'

I had surrendered all pretence of suppressing my laughter; I had to lean against the wall to hold myself up. This was not the kind of counsel I had pictured myself dispensing when I took Besler on as my student. For a moment he looked offended, before he began to laugh himself.

'I'm sure you will work out the logistics when the time comes,' I said, clapping him on the shoulder when I had recovered enough to speak. 'What the devil have they done with our horses? I'm beginning to think they must have stabled them in Vienna.'

As we looked across the courtyard in the vain hope of seeing the animals appear around a corner, a sudden commotion broke out; a group of armed guards came running through the gatehouse and passed us in haste, heading in the direction of the cathedral court. A woman's scream carried through the air, joined by others until the sound rose like the chorus of a Greek play. The men on duty at the gate called out to the soldiers as they rushed past; one barked a terse response over his shoulder. I looked to Besler for a translation.

'He said the Emperor has been attacked.' He stared after the soldiers, eyes wide with shock.

'Come on.' I grabbed his wrist and ran, before the guards on the gate had time to notice that I still had my dagger.

We followed the soldiers to the interior courtyard, to find a crowd already gathered outside the South Door of St Vitus's Cathedral, jostling and talking over one another as the armed men pushed them back with difficulty. I recognised the febrile excitement that feeds off anticipation of drama, but I also sensed a current of alarm, as speculation and fear mounted. I plunged in and shouldered my way to the front (you don't spend the years of your youth negotiating the streets and markets of Naples without learning how to move through crowds; you have to give as good as you get if you want to avoid being trampled). Most of the people around me appeared to be castle servants speaking fast in Czech dialects and I could not catch enough to grasp their reports. As I was edging past a large woman in a headscarf who had planted herself at the front and was not to be displaced from her prime vantage point, the captain of the guard blocking the door barked an order that was relayed back through the crowd in both Czech and German: 'Make way for the doctor!'

The mob parted – unwillingly and barely a couple of feet, but enough for me to see Hajek pressing through the throng, arms wrapped protectively around his medical bag at his chest. I called his name and he turned; catching my eye, he jerked his head for me to follow. I ducked under the woman's outstretched arm; Hajek grabbed my sleeve and pulled me after him into the space the soldiers had cleared around the entrance. He exchanged a few words with the captain, who shot me a suspicious look before opening the door a sliver to allow us in. I glanced back to see Besler's anxious face peering over people's heads; he had not been sharp-elbowed enough to reach us in time. I pointed to my ear to indicate that he should use his time to pick up what he could from those around him, as I slipped through the crack after Hajek and into the cool, dark hush of the cathedral.

'What's happened?' I asked him in a whisper as the door closed behind us with an echo that rang down the empty nave.

He shook his head, his lips pressed tight together. 'I was in the Powder Tower when someone burst in and said I should come immediately, the Emperor had been attacked at prayer. There was such an uproar, I couldn't glean any more details. It seems—' He broke off and held up a hand for silence. From the depths of the vast interior we heard a soft keening.

Hajek glanced at me, puffed out air through pursed lips, steeling himself as he nodded towards the source of the sound.

As we approached the altar, a figure in black appeared suddenly from behind a pillar on the left-hand side of the church, making us jump. I realised he was dressed in a priest's robes and there was blood on his hands.

THIRTEEN

'Where is he?' Hajek snapped.

The priest appeared so shaken he could not form a reply; he only pointed with a trembling hand to an ornate chapel off the south aisle of the nave. Banks of candles cast their light on richly coloured frescoes that decorated every wall to the height of the vaulted ceiling; every pillar and rib glinted gold.

But there was no time to admire the surroundings; Hajek rushed forward and I followed, to see a crumpled heap of robes on the carpeted step in front of the altar. I watched as the physician froze for the space of a heartbeat, and my throat seemed to close; if the Emperor was dead, the repercussions would be felt throughout Europe, the way the tremors of Vesuvius echoed around the Bay of Naples.

Hajek knelt by the prone figure and peeled back a corner of his cloak.

'Majesty?'

There was a dread silence, while the priest muttered incantations in Latin behind me. Just as I could bear it no longer, a small voice came from inside the jumble of velvet and fur.

'God is punishing me, Thaddeus. *Mea maxima culpa.*'

Relief coursed through me, as Hajek spoke in the same soothing voice I had heard him use the night before.

'Can you sit, Majesty?'

He glanced up and motioned to me, snapping his fingers. I understood his urgency; it was an offence to touch a sovereign, but the present situation appeared to trump the observation of such niceties. Between us, we guided Rudolf to an upright position, resting against the altar. I stepped back to show the proper deference and Hajek opened the Emperor's cloak to examine him. Flecks of dried blood darkened the hem of his shirt. The doctor's jaw tightened as he began to feel along Rudolf's sides.

'Where does it hurt?'

The Emperor shook his head, his eyes fixed glassily on the chapel ceiling. 'My own curse has rebounded to pierce me,' he moaned. 'The sin is my own. I rue the day Zikmund Bartos set foot in this city.'

Hajek caught my eye; I made a face of incomprehension. He unlaced the Emperor's shirt.

'What happened here, Majesty? Tell me slowly, so that I can help.'

Rudolf let out a dry laugh. 'You have no remedies against this evil, Thaddeus. I am the author of my own misfortune.'

The priest was still muttering in the background, wringing his hands; Hajek clicked his tongue and turned to him.

'*You.* Stop your damned noise and tell me what you witnessed.'

The priest glanced at the altar as if at some terrible spectre that only he could see; he made the sign of the cross and his gibbering grew more incoherent.

'Bruno,' Hajek said quietly, motioning with his head.

I grabbed the priest by the shoulders and shook him.

'Get a hold of yourself, Father,' I said. 'His Majesty is injured – we need to know how this came to pass, when he had an armed guard. Did you touch him?'

The priest squeaked and flapped his arms, frantically shaking his head, so I gave him a sharp slap for good measure, which seemed to bring him to his senses.

'It was there when I came in.' He pointed at the altar. 'I

179

don't know how it could have got there – the chapel was locked, it's always locked until His Majesty wishes to confess. I had no idea. Before I knew what it was, he had already—'

'*What?* How what got there?'

'He just sort of collapsed,' the priest offered, with a helpless gesture. 'As I was approaching – no one touched him.'

'I don't think he *is* injured, you know,' Hajek said, puzzled, as if the Emperor couldn't hear us. He sat back on his haunches and frowned.

'Then where is the blood from?' I asked.

'From *that*,' Rudolf said ominously, and we followed the direction of his gaze to see a wooden casket lying open on its side, half-hidden under the altar cloth. My stomach lurched; I recalled the doctor's warning to Strada about snakes, scorpions, poison, the manifold dangers that might be concealed in such a box. How had it come into the Emperor's private chapel?

Hajek was still taking Rudolf's pulse; he nodded to me to retrieve the casket. 'Careful,' he added, and I pulled the sleeves of my doublet over my hands as I picked it up, only to find it empty. I lifted the altar cloth and saw beneath it a sheet of paper that had fluttered to the ground. It was stained with blood at the edges and read, in the writing I now knew to be that of Ziggi Bartos:

Os justi parturiet sapientiam; lingua pravorum peribit.

'The mouth of the righteous brings forth wisdom, but the perverse tongue will be cut out,' Rudolf said, as if it were his sad duty to clarify.

'Book of Proverbs, chapter 10, verse 31,' I said, crouching again to look for the inevitable contents of the box. I could see nothing on the floor around the altar; I turned back to the priest.

'Did you see what was in there?' I asked. He nodded towards the Emperor and I saw that Rudolf's right hand was bunched against his chest. A dribble of blood ran down his wrist from between his clenched fingers.

'Majesty?' Hajek said, coaxing Rudolf to unfold them. A grotesque pink object flopped out of his palm, freshly congealed blood around its severed root.

'I tried to use this tongue against my brother, and you see how it returns to accuse me,' the Emperor said, holding it out.

'Your brother?' Hajek took the grisly trophy, frowning. 'What does he have to do with it?'

'I asked Bartos to put a curse on Matthias,' Rudolf said. 'It was a grievous sin, I grant, but I feared he was plotting my death.'

'Bartos?'

'*My brother.*' Rudolf tutted irritably. 'Bartos assured me he had the knowledge to direct dark powers to strike Matthias down. Not to kill him, you understand. Just to afflict him with a wasting sickness, to rob him of any power to harm me. But as you see, God is punishing us both. The curse has turned against me. *The perverse tongue will be cut out* – and yet he uses it to accuse me from beyond the grave.'

'This is a dog's tongue, Your Majesty,' Hajek said firmly. 'See how long it is – and it has been only recently severed. It is nothing to do with Bartos, I assure you.'

'It is a warning to me,' Rudolf said, undeterred.

'Well.' Hajek indicated for me to hold out the open casket, dropped the tongue into it and wiped his hands on his apron. 'It is certainly a warning to improve the security in your private chapel. You—' he snapped his fingers at the priest, who had resumed his anxious incantations. 'Who has access to this place?'

'No one, Dr Hajek,' he stammered. 'That is to say – the door is locked and I keep the key. When His Majesty feels moved to hear Mass or confess in the splendour of God's house rather than in his own quarters, a messenger is sent to me. Guards come in to clear the building of other worshippers, while I unlock the chapel and make ready the sacraments.'

'And all this happened as usual today?'

The man nodded, his Adam's apple bobbing above his collar as he swallowed nervously.

'Then how the devil did someone get this casket on to the altar without you seeing?'

'There was . . .' the priest hesitated, evidently afraid of the consequences. 'A sudden noise.' He ran his tongue around dry lips. 'The soldiers had given the all-clear so I locked the West Door first and set about preparing the host and the wine when I heard a loud crash, like something falling, from the other side of the cathedral. I rushed across to see what had happened, and found a statue had toppled and smashed in the Hora Chapel – you know, by the West Door. I stopped to clear the worst of the damage, but then I heard footsteps along the nave, so I returned with haste here, to the Wenceslas Chapel, but His Majesty had already entered with his bodyguards through the South Doorway, sooner than I expected him, and so he was the first to find – that *thing*.' He gripped his hands together to stop them trembling. 'I swear, I don't know how anyone could have got in here so fast.'

'They must have been concealed somewhere in the cathedral when the guards cleared it,' I said. 'God knows there are enough places to hide. They knocked over the statue to distract you, and slipped in here while the gate was open. The footsteps you heard – which direction were they heading?'

The man flailed his hands helplessly. 'I couldn't say – the sound echoes around the vaults and bounces off the pillars, it confuses the senses.'

'But if you had to hazard a guess,' I said through gritted teeth, fighting the urge to slap him again.

'Let's see – I was in here when I heard the crash. I hurried down the north aisle, and the footsteps appeared to be running away from me, towards the South Doorway.' He ran out of breath and finished with an extravagant shrug.

'But if the Emperor and his guards were entering by the South Door, they would have seen anyone leaving that way. The soldiers are still posted outside. And you say the West Door was locked?' The priest nodded. I turned to Hajek. 'Then . . . ?'

He motioned to Rudolf with his head and gave me a curt nod. We understood one another; he knew I had been about to speculate that the person must still be inside the building, and did not want me to alarm the Emperor. I slipped out and looked around the nave. It was vast; there were any number of side chapels, oratories and private vaults where someone who knew the basilica well might closet himself, and that was without considering the network of hidden staircases and passageways that must riddle a place like this. The Emperor's two bodyguards stood to attention outside the Wenceslas Chapel.

'You,' I said, pointing to one, 'help me. We're looking for an intruder who might still be in the building. And you' – I turned to his partner – 'make sure no one gets into that chapel.' Both nodded, seemingly too shaken to question orders from a complete stranger with no obvious authority. I hesitated to leave only one guard defending the Emperor, but I sensed that whoever had left the dog's tongue had no intention of attacking him directly – at least not yet. He liked to operate in the shadows, sowing fear. Besides, I recalled the way Hajek had made flames leap from his fingertips; he was well able to fight if the need arose, I guessed.

The guard I had told to accompany me – who, though he was thickly muscled, could have been no older than Besler, with his wispy ginger moustache and pimples – looked expectant, awaiting his next instruction.

'That way,' I hissed, gesturing towards the apse. 'Try anywhere a man might hide himself.' He nodded and took off, one hand on the hilt of his sword, surprisingly quiet on his feet for a man of his size.

I turned in the opposite direction, west along the aisle, pausing to listen. I could sense no movement anywhere, only the muffled noise of the crowd outside the South Door. I paced the transept to the crossing to look up and down the nave, when I caught a faint sound at my back. It appeared to come from the Royal Mausoleum, an ugly marble construction topped with effigies of long-dead Hapsburg forebears. I paced slowly around the perimeter of the tomb to see a flight of steps at the side leading down to a lattice-work iron gate barring the entrance to what I guessed must be a crypt. I paused at the top, straining to hear, and was certain I heard it again; a soft scuffling that might have been no more than rats. I took the stairs as quietly as I could and tried the latch of the iron gate to find it unlocked, though it opened with a protesting groan that would have given anyone hiding underground plenty of warning. I cursed and waited in case my quarry had been put to flight, but the crypt gave back nothing but silence. I stepped into the dark and found myself enveloped by the mineral smell of damp stone.

I pressed close to the wall and made my way along by touch until my eyes began to adjust. I had no tinder-box with me and would not have dared to light it, but in the gloom I could make out the shapes of low arches and the vast bases of the cathedral's supporting pillars. I guessed that I must be among the foundations of the basilica, though it was impossible to see without a light how well preserved this underground space might be. I drew my dagger and moved further in with the blade held out before me, trying not to think about the crumbling wall under my hand and the weight of stone above. A more superstitious man might have been troubled by the thought of the bones mouldering in the sarcophagi under the cracked flagstones; I was not afraid of the dead, but I had a deep dislike of enclosed spaces, and the further I progressed into the bowels of the church, the more I had to work to steady my breathing, repeating silent reassurances to myself as the air grew close. Sweat prickled between my shoulder blades, despite the chill. I was almost on the point of retracing my steps when I heard, unmistakably, the rattle of a stone dislodged somewhere up ahead, as if kicked. I quickened my pace towards the source of the sound, suppressing a yelp as I stubbed my toe on a lump of fallen masonry, and thought I glimpsed a movement disappearing into a thicket of shadow behind a plinth. I lunged after it with my knife thrust forward, and felt a sharp pain up my arm as a heavy object collided with my wrist, sending the dagger flying from my hand and clattering to the floor. Before I had a chance to recover, another blow landed, this time on the back of my neck. My vision blurred, my legs folded under me, and as I collapsed, clutching at the wall, a fleet figure pushed past, shoving me hard as he disappeared into the dark, weaving through the rubble as if he knew the way with his eyes closed. I tried to push myself upright but my arms would not obey. I heard the distinct metallic clank of a key turning. Had he locked me in? Snatching shallow breaths, I searched the floor with frantic fingertips until I found the knife, but before I could grasp it I was dimly aware of another sound: the grating of stone on stone, somewhere behind me. It echoed around my bruised skull as my eyes closed, despite my best efforts.

FOURTEEN

'Bruno?'

I opened my eyes to a powerful smell of alcohol and herbs and the recognition of a throbbing cold at the base of my skull. When I could focus, I made out Hajek's face inches from mine in the wavering light of a candle. He set down the smelling salts and peered into my eyes, holding the flame close until I blinked and pulled away.

'You're still with us, then,' he said, and I heard in his voice the quiver of relief. 'Don't move too fast, I need to see where you're hurt.'

'I'm fine,' I said irritably, attempting to sit as a wave of nausea rippled through me. An icy trickle slid down the back of my neck and I reached up to find a freezing cloth bundled against my nape.

'Ice pack,' Hajek said briskly. 'To bring down the swelling. Someone fetched you a nasty blow there, you were lucky it wasn't worse. Here, keep it on. I found a candlestick by the door, taken from one of the altars. He must have used that.'

I pressed the cloth to my head, wincing as it touched the bruise. 'I thought he locked me in?'

'He did. The priest had the key. Evidently someone else does too.'

'How did you find me?'

186

'You didn't come back. The guard returned, said he'd checked all the towers and found no one. Eventually we reasoned you must have gone below ground.'

'Didn't you see him come out? The man who attacked me?'

'No. He couldn't have come through the cathedral. There were guards on every entrance.'

'I heard a noise . . .' I let my arm fall to my side and closed my eyes; Hajek took over the pressure with the ice pack, which was beginning to melt down my collar. 'Before I passed out. The scraping of stone . . .'

He nodded. 'There's a network of secret passages running under the castle. We'll make a proper search when you're recovered. For now, if you can move, we should get you somewhere more comfortable.'

'Don't worry about me. We need to find him . . .' I tried to lever myself up with my right arm and cried out as my damaged wrist buckled under the pressure. I was embarrassed that this was the second time Hajek had been obliged to nurse me as if I were as helpless as Rudolf. The thought jerked me upright. 'You haven't left the Emperor alone?'

'Of course not.' He smiled. 'I sent your boy Besler to fetch Ottavio Strada – he and the guards took His Majesty discreetly back to his chambers.'

'And Besler found him? Then, Ottavio—' I shook my head. I had wondered if Strada might have been my attacker – he knew the castle complex intimately – though surely he could not have slipped through a secret passage in time to be back for a summons to escort the Emperor? I supposed it would depend on the underground passage and how long Hajek had waited after my disappearance to send for him.

I saw the doctor's teeth gleam in the dim light as he smiled. 'I know what you're thinking. But what possible reason would young Strada have for leaving the Emperor threatening messages? You can't suppose he's connected with the murder of Bartos?'

'I don't know. Something to do with his sister? He was the

one who took Rudolf the first casket, after all.' I recalled Ottavio saying that when the Emperor sank into his moods of melancholy, Katherina was the only one who could comfort him. Even if he were not responsible for the brutal murder of Bartos – which, admittedly, I found hard to imagine – might it be in his interest to push Rudolf into such a state by frightening him with the Scriptures and severed body parts, in order to further his family's influence? I decided not to say this to Hajek; it sounded far-fetched, even to me.

'True. But he was in the library when Besler looked for him, and said he had been engaged in a complex task of cataloguing new arrivals all evening with his assistant – he was not pleased to be interrupted. I think it unlikely that he could have been haring through secret passages moments before.' He sighed. 'This business grows ever darker, Bruno. I wish you had not become caught up in it. You could have been killed down here. I intend to speak to the Emperor when he is less shaken, suggest that he reconsider what he has asked of you. It is too great a burden to lay on a stranger.'

I pushed determinedly to my feet with only a slight wobble, steadying myself against the wall and hoping he hadn't noticed. 'The blow was not struck with much force,' I said with more conviction than I felt. 'He could easily have cracked me across the skull if he wanted to inflict real damage, but he did not. I think he only wanted to incapacitate me so that I didn't catch him. Where is Besler now?'

'Waiting for you in the cathedral.' He nodded at the ceiling. 'He will take you back to the House of the Green Mound so you can rest.'

'I don't want to rest. I need to . . .' I faltered. What did I need to do? My thoughts were scrambled; I had lost all sense of time. I needed to return to Golden Lane and search Sukie's house; I needed to talk to David Maier. I wanted to confide in Hajek everything I had learned this afternoon, but I was uncertain now about trusting him; here he was again, keen to deter me from the investigation.

'Bruno.' He laid a hand on my arm, firmly enough to let me know he was in earnest. 'Your physician orders you home. It's late, and you will be no use to anyone without rest. I will give you something to help you sleep, in case the pain disturbs. I would accompany you, but I must settle His Majesty before I can leave. Here – you dropped this.' He handed me my dagger; I concentrated on sheathing it so that I didn't have to meet his eye, ashamed that once again I had failed to defend myself.

In the circumstances I lacked the strength to defy him, though I was determined not to take whatever medicine he offered; I recalled what Katherina had said about Jacopo fearing Hajek was trying to dull his wits.

'Did you know about Bartos and the curse?' I asked, holding on to the wall as he ushered me up the stairs from the crypt.

'No. But it doesn't surprise me. His Majesty is obsessed with the idea that his brother means him harm, but he can't move against him without evidence, not when Matthias is the favourite of Rome and Spain. Cursing him from a distance is just the kind of impotent gesture that would make Rudolf feel better, without actually doing anything. I'm disappointed to learn that Bartos lowered himself to such a charlatan's performance.'

'It sounds as if Bartos was prepared to do anything for money,' I said. 'Someone knew, though. That can't be coincidence, the fact that his tongue was cut out. I have wondered why he was mutilated like that, if it was merely to intensify the fear of a vengeful Golem. But now it seems more specific. Someone knew the Emperor would see the significance in the severed tongue and interpret it as a punishment for putting a curse on his brother. Who could Bartos have told?'

'No idea. He did not have confidants, as far as I knew. The other alchemists found him hostile – he didn't drink with them, for fear they were out to steal his work. And something so potentially damning as a commission from the Emperor to curse his brother – I can't see him sharing that willingly.'

'Unless he was paid for the information,' I said, thinking of

Montalcino and San Clemente. They would have been interested to know that Rudolf was so afraid of his brother that he had resorted to the tricks of the Old Town Square hustlers.

But the doctor was wrong, I thought, as Besler rushed forward to fuss over me and I waved his attentions away. Bartos *had* been close to someone – Sukie Moller. I wondered if she knew about the curse, and who she might have told.

I was woken by shafts of cold light filtering through the shutters. As I blinked away the confusion of tangled dreams, I became aware of two things: a persistent dull ache at the back of my head and a low growling sound coming from somewhere beneath me. When I propped myself on one elbow to peer through the bed curtains, I saw that Besler had pulled a pallet into my room and was sprawled on the floor, long limbs flung out, snoring gently. I smiled, unexpectedly touched; evidently he had felt a protective urge to sleep at my side in case I needed him in the night. I would have to put a stop to that; it undermined my status to have him feeling he needed to take care of me. Although, I reflected, the best way to prevent that would be for me to avoid being ambushed by people who wished me harm.

I slid out of bed and crossed the room to use the chamber pot as silently as I could manage, trying not to wake him. I wanted a few moments to myself to think. My head and my wrist still hurt, though not as badly as I had feared, and I considered again my encounter with the stranger in the crypt. He had had the advantage of me; I remained convinced that, if he had wished, he could have struck me harder, even killed me, but that had apparently not been his intention. He was clearly someone who knew the layout of the castle, its most secret passages, and had also obtained a key to the crypt. Not Strada, if he had been occupied in the library all evening, though Hajek would have to verify that. The priest should be questioned too, and the messenger who had instructed him that the Emperor wanted to hear Mass: whoever had left that dog's tongue needed to have known when Rudolf would be on his way to the cathedral. Perhaps the priest had been persuaded to let someone make a copy of his key – and who might command a priest's obedience, if not a man with greater spiritual authority – an emissary of the Pope, for example?

I tucked the pot under the bed and dressed quickly. Despite my various bruises, I felt surprisingly well rested – so much so that I wondered if I had been slipped some kind of sleeping draught, though the only thing I had accepted last night on arriving back in Bethlehem Square was a bowl of warm milk from Greta. I eyed Besler as he slept, untroubled as a child with his flushed, open face; might Hajek have persuaded him to give me some remedy, knowing I would not touch the small vial he had pressed into my hand as we left the castle? I exhaled sharply, impatient with myself; if I started mistrusting even Besler, I would drive myself mad. At the threshold, I paused and surveyed the room. I had been too tired and dazed to notice the night before, but I had an unsettling sense that things were slightly off-kilter; nothing obvious, only the strong suspicion that someone had been through the room in my absence.

The bells across the square had only just tolled seven, but David Maier struck me as the kind of man who would rise early. I wanted to talk further with him, and thought I could lean on him with the threat of telling Rabbi Loew what I had witnessed the night before. I crept down the stairs and along the entrance hall with my boots in my hand in the hope of slipping out unnoticed, but found the front door locked. Perhaps Hajek was simply cautious on account of his valuables, but the absence of a key made me uneasy; it gave the impression of being imprisoned.

As if reading my mind, Greta appeared in the doorway to the kitchen, wiping her hands on her apron.

'Robbers,' she said, jerking her head at the door. 'You can't be too careful. Come. Eat. The doctor says you need strength.'

'Where is he?'

She shook her head. 'Didn't come home. I presume he stayed

191

at the castle, as he does when the Emperor has need of him. Come.'

The scent of toasting bread reached me; despite the urge to leave, I found myself salivating.

'Thank you, Greta, that's kind,' I said, following her into the kitchen. She made a tutting noise designed to convey that she had her instructions and was not doing this simply from the goodness of her heart. Even so, I thought, I could perhaps turn it to my advantage.

It was only when she set down a plate of good wheat bread, browned over the fire and dripping with melted butter that I realised how ravenous I was. I inhaled four slices with honey before I paused to draw enough breath to speak.

'I hope Besler is making himself useful to you,' I said, leaning back in my chair.

She sniffed. 'He's a good boy. Better manners than some.'

I laughed. 'I can only apologise. I got my manners at a Dominican convent.' I thought a swipe at the Church might appeal to her Protestant roots, and I could have sworn she almost smiled.

'That explains much,' she said. 'But I did not mean you. I was thinking of our last house guest.' Her mouth tightened at the memory, as if she had tasted something sour.

'Doctor Dee?' I recalled Xena von Rozmberk wrinkling her pretty nose at the thought of John spitting food as he talked. 'Yes, you are not the first to object to his table manners.'

'I don't care how a man eats,' she said with unexpected force. 'Besides, he is English, what do you expect? I do mind being spoken to as if I am an ignorant peasant girl, no more than a slave to fetch and carry. Six months he lived in this house, and still he mistook my name.' She set a fresh bowl of milk in front of me so emphatically that the contents sloshed over the rim.

'Ah.' I nodded. This was a lesson I had been taught by Sir Francis Walsingham – not that I had ever received anything approaching a formal training in espionage, once he had satisfied himself that I had a facility for cryptography and dissembling. But he had given me this advice, with uncharacteristic earnestness, one evening by the fire in his book-lined study at the house in Barn Elms, while mist whitened the windows outside.

'Always make people feel they matter, Bruno. That is the way into their confidence. Especially with people of the humbler sort, who are too often overlooked by those of superior status and learning, as if they are not also created in God's image, with their own joys and sorrows. Remember servants' names, remember which of their children is sick or starting an apprenticeship – show them, in other words, that you regard them as real, as fully real as you are. I have heard great men speak to their dogs with more affection and interest than they do their servants, and that is no way to earn loyalty. You have a formidable memory – I assure you, in our line of work, it will prove as valuable to commit these details to mind as all the reams of Scripture and philosophy you carry in there.' He had tapped the side of his head with a forefinger, then levelled it at me. 'But be warned,' he had added, with a twitch of a smile, 'you cannot dissemble in this. People will smell insincerity a mile off. If you ask your cook how her daughter's new baby does, you must also be prepared to listen to the answer, God help you. Your reward will be that you do not know what else she might tell you in addition.'

I had laughed, mainly at the idea that I might ever be in a position to have a cook, but I had done my best to heed his words. I had watched Walsingham closely, though, and realised that with him it was never merely a means to an end. He was genuinely interested in people from all walks of life; he listened when they talked and I had seen the way they responded to his attention.

I looked at Greta now with as much sympathy as I could muster. 'John is often distracted by his work,' I said. Her expression told me what she thought of this as an excuse. 'But he is kind underneath,' I persisted. 'He doesn't mean to slight people – it's only that often they are less immediate to him than all the ideas jostling for space inside his head. He forgets his own children's names sometimes.'

She looked partially mollified. 'I told Dr Hajek that man would bring trouble to our door, and I was right,' she said with evident satisfaction. 'Communing with the dead at all hours. I've seen some things in this house, believe me' – she turned back to the range – 'but the doctor's father would have been spinning in his grave at that kind of going on.'

'Angels,' I said, draining the milk and wiping my mouth. 'John Dee believed he was communicating with angels, not the dead.'

Greta gave an eloquent snort. 'Why would the Lord of all Creation send His angels to speak to an Englishman?'

'It's a fair point,' I agreed. 'But you don't believe John capable of murder, surely? You shared a home with him for six months – you must have seen that he is not a violent man?'

She faced me again and folded her arms. 'He is an ambitious man, and that is as bad, in my experience.' I caught a note of regret in her voice and wondered who she was thinking of; her dead husband? 'This city has an alchemy of its own. It changes people,' she continued softly. 'It makes them greedy for gold and power. In pursuit of those, they find themselves doing things they would never have imagined before Prague worked her subtle magic.' She was no longer looking at me but inward, at some distant memory. 'Well.' She shook herself out of it and picked up my empty bowl. 'I must get on. You want hot water to wash, I suppose?' She had returned to her old, semi-hostile tone; I saw that I would get no more out of her today. Still, I felt I had made a tentative start.

'If it's not too much trouble. Oh – I met your sister yesterday,' I added, mopping up a spilled drop of honey with the tip of my finger. 'At least, I guessed she was your sister.'

Instantly her face closed up; she dropped the bowl into the sink with a clatter. 'What do you know of my sister?'

'The sign of the Winged Horse? The tap-woman looked very

194

like you, and Besler mentioned that your father had owned a tavern in the Lesser Town, so I put two and two together. Was I right?'

'Why did you go there?'

'I was near the castle, and someone recommended the food.'

A little of the tension eased from her shoulders. 'Magda is a fine cook,' she conceded. 'Our mother taught us well. When we were children, you could not get a seat at the Horse at dinner time – every visitor to Prague wanted to eat there, my mother's food was so famous. People would queue for hours at the door. But Magda can't do justice to her recipes because Jan Boodt cuts corners with the ingredients.' A shadow passed across her face. 'I haven't eaten there for a long time, and neither should you. It attracts the wrong sort of people now.'

'Who is Jan Boodt?' I asked.

'My brother-in-law.' She took a cloth and swiped it across the table in front of me, scattering crumbs with a ferocity that seemed aimed at this Jan Boodt. 'Now – I have so much to do it would make your head spin, so you'll excuse me.'

'I'll send Besler down to help,' I said.

She straightened and glared at me. 'If I needed a boy to help me manage this house, I would hire one, and one who has at least set foot in a kitchen in his life. I don't have time for your lad tripping at my heels with his foolish questions. He'll wheedle no more out of me, so I suggest he goes along with you.' She rested her fists on her hips and waited for me to deny it. 'Don't take me for a fool, Dr Bruno.'

'Greta,' I said, 'I wouldn't dare. Thank you for the breakfast.'

She gave me a long look that told me she was not taken in by me, and returned to her work. I wondered why she was so keen for me to stay away from the Winged Horse.

FIFTEEN

'What is the name of this book you want?'

'I don't know yet.'

'Then how do you know he has it?'

'I don't know what he has. That's why we're going to look.'

'But surely, if you don't know whether—'

'Besler.' I stopped in the middle of the street, so abruptly that a man with a handcart was forced to swerve around us, muttering something in Czech that even I could tell was less than complimentary about my mother. 'I need to talk to David Maier. The book is an excuse. When we get there, you stay in the background and don't interrupt.'

'I can't understand a word you say anyway.' His lower lip jutted.

'So look at the books. You might learn something.'

'Not if they're all in Hebrew.' He kicked a stone. We were both in a bad humour: Besler at being dragged from sleep and denied a leisurely breakfast, and I at the enforced delay while I waited for him to dress and make himself ready. I had considered slipping away alone, but Greta was clearly wise to the fact that Besler's helpful gestures were a ruse in pursuit of information, and I feared that if he woke and found me gone, he would decide to act on his own initiative. There was no knowing where that might lead, with a murderer in the streets and the Catholics as good as threatening his life to keep me in their control; I wanted him where I could see him. He pulled a hunk of bread from the pouch at his belt and gnawed on it as we walked.

'They may not all be in Hebrew,' I said, pulling my collar against the wind. Bohemia was still resisting spring; a chilly greyness enveloped the city, adding to the sense of enclosure. 'You can make yourself useful, see if there is anything – I don't know, folk tales or fables – that would make a suitable gift for a girl.'

'A girl, Maestro?' He nudged me, and his face broke into the first smile of the morning; he could never maintain a sulk for long.

'A *child*,' I said. 'But one who is sharp-tongued in three languages, so we had better find something to her liking.'

We reached the familiar pointed gables of the Old-New Synagogue and found the street behind it as David had described, though I had not been prepared to see a crowd gathered outside so early in the morning. I slowed my pace; even before we were close enough to pick up murmurs of conversation, even before I could see which shop they were focused on, I knew in my gut that something was badly wrong. Some of the faces that turned to us registered suspicion, though most were too preoccupied to notice. They spoke among themselves in Yiddish, in low, urgent tones; I motioned to Besler to stay back as I followed their attention to see a bookbinder's shop with all its windows smashed. A reprisal attack, as Rabbi Loew had predicted?

'Is this David Maier's place?' I asked the woman nearest me. She showed a flicker of surprise at my formal Hebrew, but her eyes were dull with distress as she nodded. A quick glance up and down the street told me that no other properties had suffered the same violence. This attack had been specifically directed at David. I recalled his conversation of the previous night with the man in the cloak, David's attempt to disengage himself from whatever he was involved in. It was no great stretch to think that someone wanted to make clear to David the consequences of walking away.

Besler nudged me, and I noticed in the centre of the little group a heavily pregnant woman in her thirties, crying softly, with two whimpering children clinging to her skirts and an infant that could not be more than a year in her arms. A tall, slender woman in a headscarf stood with an arm around the mother's shoulders, murmuring words of comfort. As I stepped closer, she half-turned and caught my eye and I found myself disconcerted once again by Esther Loew's beauty.

'Dr Bruno,' she said, assessing me with a small frown. 'What are you doing here?'

'I was hoping to browse some books,' I said, indicating the shop. 'David—' I broke off; I did not want to say anything that would hint at my encounter with David the night before. 'I'm so sorry to see there has been another attack,' I finished. 'When did this happen?'

'In the early hours, Sarah says.' She nodded at the crying woman.

'And no one saw anything?' I gestured to the houses all around. 'You can't smash that much glass without waking the neighbours – there must have been witnesses, someone fleeing the scene. Surely people raised the alarm. Did David not think to give chase?'

Esther watched me for a moment, then handed Sarah into the care of another bystander and drew me aside. Besler followed us at a distance.

'David did not come home last night. Sarah was alone in the apartment above the shop with the children when she heard someone downstairs, followed by the sound of breaking glass. They were terrified and hid under the beds. I can only presume you have had the good fortune never to experience anything like this. Otherwise you would know that the sensible course is to stay silent and hope it's only your property that suffers violence.'

'Forgive me,' I said, chastened. 'But how do you mean, he didn't come home? Is that usual?'

'No, of course not,' she said with a trace of impatience. 'David is often out in the evenings on business, Sarah doesn't ask where or with whom. But this is the first time he has not come back. Naturally, with this attack' – she gestured to the shop – 'she is worried sick.'

'Has anyone examined the shop?'

'Not yet. Sarah's eldest boy went to fetch my father, I thought it best to wait for him.'

She was keeping her composure admirably, but I caught the tremor in her voice.

'Would you mind if I take a look? Perhaps you could help me.'

She hesitated before giving me a brisk nod. I heard her exchange a few words with Sarah, who shrugged miserably, as if it hardly mattered; her baby had begun to cry and she was distractedly shushing it. I followed Esther to the door, motioning for Besler to come with us. There was a flurry of indignation as we passed through the little crowd, but Esther possessed a calm authority that meant their muttering quickly subsided as she ushered me to the threshold, our feet crunching over shards of glass on the step.

The door closed behind us and I took in the surroundings. There was some disarray – books pulled off shelves, papers scattered – though not the wanton destruction I had seen at Ziggi Bartos's lodging. Esther's gaze drifted around the room with a vagueness that I put down to shock, her fingertips trailing across the edge of a shelf.

'This must be very distressing for you,' I said, wanting to offer comfort and feeling I could say nothing useful.

'What? Oh – yes, of course,' she said, wrenching her attention back to me. 'But it is not as if we haven't seen such things before, unfortunately.'

'Were any other properties targeted last night?'

'Not that I know of.'

'Then why David, I wonder?' I looked at her. 'His wife is quite sure he is missing? He couldn't be, I don't know, visiting a friend overnight?'

She returned my look with scepticism. 'Where would he go? David doesn't have friends outside the community, only business contacts, and he is diligent when it comes to his family – he would never have gone away without telling Sarah. And with all this—' she indicated the windows and shook her head.

'Those casements are too small for a grown man to climb through, and the door has not been forced. Would Sarah have left it unlocked last night, if she was waiting for her husband to come home?'

'You would have to ask her,' Esther said, 'but I would think it unlikely – some of these books are very valuable.'

'Then . . .' I met her gaze and saw her eyes dart away from mine; I hardly needed to state the obvious. If the door was not left unlocked, whoever did this had entered with a key.

I crouched to pick up a book from the floor – a commentary on the Talmud – and brushed it down. She was right; it was a beautifully bound edition; it was fortunate that it had not been damaged in the looting of the shop. A thought struck me; I glanced down at another volume lying at my feet and saw that it had landed face up, almost as if it had been placed there. A quick glance around showed the same for the rest of the books that had apparently been hurled from the shelves: not a single one had landed as you would expect a book flung in a hasty search might, with its pages splayed or torn. Whoever had been through the shop had clearly had too much respect for that. Esther stooped to retrieve another volume, dusting it down as I had. I wondered if she had made the same observation, but she said nothing as she replaced the book carefully on the shelf.

The shop was formed of one main room; at the back, a door ajar gave a glimpse of another chamber. I pushed it open and found myself in a small room that was evidently used as an office, just wide enough for a desk and chair. In one corner a set of narrow stairs led to the family's quarters above, and in the alcove beneath, a row of iron-bound chests lined the wall. I motioned for Esther to join me; Besler pricked up his ears and moved towards us, but I held up a hand to forestall him.

'Besler, I need you to search the shop thoroughly,' I said. 'See if whoever turned it over has left any trace of himself.'

'Like what?' The petulant look was back; he was afraid of being excluded.

'I don't know – a button from his coat, a ring, a kerchief – anything he might have dropped in his haste. And if you find nothing, see if there's a book that would do for the girl.'

I closed the door on his scowl; Esther looked at me expectantly.

'There is something I must tell you,' I said, lowering my voice. 'I saw David last night, in the Lesser Town. I think he may be in trouble.' I was not sure why I was confiding in her and not the rabbi, except that I sensed she would have the correct instinct about what to do. It was also gratifying to have her undivided attention, though I told myself that was not my principal motivation.

'What do you mean?' Her eyes widened.

I told her in brief what I had witnessed at the sign of the Winged Horse and David's nervous response.

'Your father mentioned that he thought there were spies among you,' I said. 'From what I overheard last night, the obvious conclusion is that David has been trading information and something – I would guess the murder of Ziggi Bartos, with its deliberate reference to the Golem – made him rethink his position. He wanted to end the arrangement, and now you tell me he has not been seen since, and his shop has been turned over. That doesn't seem like a coincidence. Though what secrets he was selling and to whom, I have no idea.'

Esther had grown pale during my story; she leaned against the desk for support. 'Oh, our enemies are always interested in what we are up to, even the most mundane details.' She spoke casually, but something in her tone made me frown.

'Which enemies, though? The Catholics?'

'I don't know. You're the one who saw this man in the cloak.'

'Not really. I know only that he was fairly tall and that they were speaking in Hebrew. Which tells us that he was an educated man, but little more. I thought the Maharal should know. Especially now that David is missing.'

'Certainly. Although you may find there's not much goes on in this city that my father doesn't know about.'

I looked at her, but she didn't elaborate. I wondered if Rabbi Loew had spirited David away somewhere safe for his own protection, just as I suspected he may have done with John Dee. But if that were the case, would he not have told David's wife? And why had the shop been attacked?

I squeezed past the desk, noting that its drawers had been opened and searched. Squatting in the alcove, I examined the chests under the stairs to see that all the locks were intact. I lifted one – it was heavier than I expected – and heard the muffled slide of money bags packed tightly together. Whoever had been through the shop did not care about coins, it seemed.

'What puzzles me is *why* David would betray his community? From the short exchanges I've had with him, he struck me as a devout man.'

'Well, perhaps that is your answer,' Esther said evenly. 'Maybe he believed that whatever he was doing would prevent a greater harm to our people. Knowing David, I would think that quite likely.'

I glanced up in time to catch that fleeting expression of sorrow I had glimpsed on her face the day before; it was there and gone in the space between heartbeats.

'Esther – I feel I am missing part of the picture,' I said softly. 'If there is anything you can add that might help me to see it more clearly, I urge you to tell me. It is all connected somehow, I'm certain – Bartos, the Golem, John Dee, David – but I – I can't understand how.' I stood and looked at her until she met my gaze, and I was startled to see the shine of tears in her eyes.

'No,' she said, barely audible. 'You can't.'

'Then – help me? What harm do you mean? What does David know?'

She watched me and I saw her making calculations, weighing

up how much to say. After a long moment she seemed about to speak, when the door burst open and Besler's face appeared in the gap. Rarely had I been so irritated to see him.

'The Maharal is here,' he announced grandly. 'And I have something to show you, Maestro.'

Esther blinked away all trace of emotion, so that I almost fancied I had imagined it; her eyes flicked to Besler with interest, but before he could explain, the figure of Rabbi Loew filled the doorway behind him. The rabbi put his hands on the boy's shoulders and gently moved him out of the way. He looked tired, and the smile he offered me was strained; a glance passed between him and Esther that I could not read.

'Go and attend to Sarah, my dear,' he said to her, 'she needs you.' Esther nodded and slipped past him, giving me one last look over her shoulder as she left.

'You are kind to be concerned, Dr Bruno,' Loew said, 'but you can leave this with me now.'

'Then – you know where David is?'

'Not yet.'

'But you knew he was betraying your community?'

There was a long silence. Loew looked at me, pulling at his beard. 'Regrettably,' he admitted. 'Though I'm sure he was doing what he thought was right.'

'You spoke to him about it?'

'I didn't get the chance. I only recently learned of the situation.'

But Esther knew, I thought. She had not appeared shocked when I told her of David's treachery.

'I warned him to be careful in the streets last night,' I said with sudden anger at myself. 'I meant it as a jibe, to let him know I'd seen the full purse he had taken. But I never really thought he was in danger, otherwise I would have followed him. I should have, in any case – I could at least have found out who he'd been talking to, and we would have a better idea—'

Loew laid a hand on my arm. 'It was not your responsibility, Bruno. In any case, we don't know that David has come to harm. Do not concern yourself unduly. There are people out looking for him – I pray he'll be found safe and well.'

I wondered if he really believed that, but he could make his face as inscrutable as Walsingham when he chose; his mild expression gave nothing away. Perhaps that was the essence of leadership, I thought. It was clear that I was being dismissed, and I resented it.

'How can I not be concerned?' I said stubbornly. 'That letter John wrote to you – he warned of danger to your people. He knew there was a threat, and I'm certain it is all connected. What am I missing?'

'You are seeing connections because you wish to make sense of this, understandably,' he said with the same infuriating calm. 'It's still early – go home and get some rest. Or I can ask Esther to make you something to eat, if you're hungry?'

'Yes please,' Besler said from behind the rabbi. I glared at him.

'John mentioned danger to B,' I persisted. 'If B is Benjamin, then perhaps he knew of David's betrayal. Maybe he tried to intervene in some way. And John found out, and realised he was in danger—' I stopped and looked around. 'Where is Benjamin?'

'Looking for David, I presume. Go home, Dr Bruno. This is a matter for us now.' He was still smiling gently, but in his voice I heard a steely resolve that was not to be contradicted. I hesitated, weighing up the advantages of arguing further, and decided there were none for now. I would do better to speak to Benjamin directly.

'Give you good day,' I said, bobbing a brisk bow to the rabbi. 'Come on, Besler.'

'Maestro—'

'Outside,' I hissed as I pushed past him in the doorway. 'Let me know if there's anything I can do,' I called to Rabbi Loew as we left. He was stooped over, examining the drawers of David's desk.

'You could pray for him,' he said without looking up.

'I'll leave that to you,' I said, casting a last glance around the dingy shop. 'I'm not sure my credit is good with the Almighty these days.' Besides, I had more practical steps in mind.

The little crowd in the street had dispersed, evidently reassured by the arrival of Rabbi Loew, though a couple of women remained at a distance, speaking in subdued tones. I turned to Besler, who was hopping up and down beside me like a puppy.

'What did you find then?'

'Two things of note,' he said, eager for praise. 'The first – see, here.' He pointed to the ground outside the shop. 'Most of the broken glass is on the outside. That's curious, no? If someone had smashed the windows to break in, it would have fallen through to the floor of the shop.'

'Very good,' I said. 'So what do you conclude?'

'That whoever did it was already inside. Perhaps they wanted to make it look like a break-in.' He frowned. 'But why?'

'I think that, despite what Rabbi Loew says, someone around here knows what David was doing, and why. You're right, this wasn't a real robbery – they didn't touch the money, and it wasn't a warning either. Nothing was damaged except the windows – they couldn't even bring themselves to throw the books around. I'd guess whoever did it was looking for any papers that might show what information David was selling, or to whom. Maybe David even did it himself, to cover his disappearance. Good work – what else did you come up with?'

'I found this, caught on one of the broken panes.'

He held up a scrap of something between finger and thumb. I took it from him and saw that it was a fragment of faded crimson wool.

'Ah. Well, at least that's confirmed who we need to speak to,' I said, tucking it into my sleeve. 'A pity the rabbi arrived before I had time to look at the books – though I don't suppose there was anything suitable for the child.'

'Not unless your child is interested in Talmudic commentary and rabbinical ethics,' said a female voice behind me.

I jumped and turned to see Esther by the shop door; she

must have followed us out. I wondered if she had overheard my theories about the break-in. She attempted a smile, but the way she twisted her hands together betrayed her anxiety; I felt a sudden desire to take her in my arms and reassure her. I cleared my throat to cover my embarrassment.

'Why do you want a child's book anyway?'

'I've made the acquaintance of a young lady of eleven years, whose life has little colour in it except for stories,' I said as she fell into step beside us. 'I promised to find her something new. Though I suspect David Maier was not the person to ask.'

'You're right there. I suppose this child knows something pertinent to your investigation, and you want to bribe her with a book?'

'You wound me, Esther.' I laid a hand flat across my chest. 'Is it beyond the bounds of possibility that I might want to help the girl out of the goodness of my heart?'

She gave me a wry look from the tail of her eye. 'From the little I have been told about you, I think you are a man who knows how to calculate his own advantage in any situation.'

So she had asked about me. Could that mean something? 'An inevitable corollary of life in exile,' I said. 'All I can say in my defence is that I hope you will come to know me well enough to weigh my good qualities alongside my instinct for survival.' I left a pause to see how she would respond to this tentative overture; when she pointedly ignored it, I hurried on: 'I think this girl might be in danger. I need to persuade her to trust me – I hoped a book might help.'

She walked in silence for a while longer and I feared I had given offence by expressing a wish to know her better. But eventually she raised her head and looked at me.

'I might have a book that would serve,' she said. 'My mother used to read it to me and my sisters when we were little. So I am told – I don't remember much, she died when I was five. My sisters have passed it around their children – perhaps it might do?'

'That's very generous,' I said. 'What manner of book?'

'Oh, stories of virtuous Jewish women. Ruth, Judith, Deborah, Rahab and the rest. It's more exciting than it sounds – Judith is positively bloodthirsty. She decapitates an enemy general, if you recall. I don't know if that would be suitable for your young friend?'

'It sounds ideal.'

'Come back with me to the house now if you like, you can take it with you.'

'Thank you, sincerely. Is it in Hebrew though?'

'German. My father commissioned the printing of a translation when my eldest sister was born. He thought there might be a market for it, to counter the popular Christian view of Jewish women, but he was over-optimistic in that, as in most things.'

'And what is the popular view?'

'Surely you know?' She pressed her lips together as she looked to see if I was toying with her. 'That we are all lascivious temptresses, bent on seducing unwitting Christian men.'

'I have heard this said,' Besler remarked, nodding earnestly. I sent him a silencing glare; he was too far away for me to kick him.

'There you are, then.' Esther gave a brittle laugh. 'It's one of the reasons they make us wear a badge or a yellow hat in some cities – so we don't lure you in without your knowing. I suppose we should at least be thankful that Prague does not force such indignities on us. Though that could all change on the Emperor's whim.'

'No sign of Benjamin this morning?' I asked, hoping to steer the conversation back to safer ground.

'He's looking for David. Why?'

'Just that I would be interested in talking further with him. He seemed an intelligent young man.'

'He is. And there are few enough of those about.'

'You've known him a long time?'

Her face softened. 'Since childhood. His father was my father's closest friend. He is like one of the family.' She paused as if she had been about to disclose more, but fell abruptly silent.

I stole a sidelong glance at her, but she gave nothing away. I had seen the way Benjamin looked at her, and it was far from brotherly.

'His profession must keep him busy.'

'It does. Between you and me, although he is highly valued in the community for his skill as a physician, really he dreams of being a writer.'

I smiled. 'Tell him to be careful what he wishes for. It's a lonely life.' I had not intended to say the last part aloud; Esther turned to me, curious.

'I suppose it must be,' she said. 'Is that why you have come to Prague chasing adventure?'

I was about to deny the charge when I caught the smile hovering at her lips; she was teasing me. I smiled back and felt a lurch under my ribs. God, but she was beautiful. Do not, I told myself sternly, get any ideas about Esther Loew. But I could do nothing about the charge that shot through me as we reached her door and she laid her hand on my arm.

'Wait here, I'll fetch the book,' she said, showing us into the small parlour where we had met the rabbi on our previous visit. 'Be patient, it's a question of remembering where my nieces and nephews might have put it.'

Besler settled himself in a chair by the fire; I listened to Esther's footsteps climbing the stairs and an idea occurred.

'Stay there,' I whispered to Besler. 'If she comes back, say I have gone to use the privy.' I slipped out of the room and tried the handle of the closed door across the hallway.

It opened on to a room that was obviously Rabbi Loew's study. If I felt a small pang of guilt at abusing Esther's generosity, it was quelled by my conviction that her father was not telling the whole truth about John Dee's disappearance, or David Maier's, or the murder of Bartos, and that whatever he knew could help us. Somewhere among his papers I might find crucial evidence of what he was keeping back.

It was a comfortable room, the kind I imagined for myself in idle moments when I indulged the fantasy of a home and family: teetering piles of books and papers on every surface, though I suspected there was an idiosyncratic system to the homely clutter, and that the rabbi would be immediately aware of any disturbance. I would have to tread carefully.

I skimmed the papers on his desk, but found only notes for a sermon, pages of household accounts, and a child's drawing of a smiling figure with a bushy beard, the words 'Grandfather, love from Eli' written beneath in smudged letters. Tucked under the base of a candlestick I found the charcoal rubbing I had brought of Dee's last letter to the rabbi. A wide drawer was built into the underside of the desk; I expected to find it locked, but instead it opened smoothly and inside there was a small wooden casket, bound with iron hoops and decorated with brass inlay, almost identical to those sent to the Emperor containing the eyeballs and tongue and the Bible verses. I stared at it, momentarily disconcerted; surely the rabbi could not be behind such tricks? I dismissed the idea immediately as impossible; he was hale for his age, but he was not up to sprinting around the cathedral and lurking in underground passages. Then perhaps whoever had been sending those malicious messages to the Emperor had also targeted him? I flipped the clasp, bracing myself for some gruesome spectacle, but found, to my surprise, a curved dagger on a bed of blue velvet.

I lifted it out and examined the blade. I knew a little about weaponry; my father had been a mercenary soldier who taught me the basics of how to handle swords and daggers in my youth, and I had spent enough time around nobles who admired expert craftsmanship to know that I was looking at a fine – and highly valuable – example of an Ottoman knife. The hilt was crusted with turquoise and rubies, the blade gleaming steel with intricate patterns chased into the surface and damascened with gold. An ornamental rather than a functional weapon, it seemed, but even so, not what I would have expected to find in the desk of a respected Jewish intellectual. Rabbi Loew was full of surprises. Tucked under the casket's velvet inlay I noticed a piece of paper. Unfolding it, I read, in neat Hebrew script:

A token of my esteem, and of the future bond between us that cannot be sundered by any steel nor by the hand of man.

I stared at the words, willing them to give up a hidden meaning. A gift, then; at first glance, nothing so unusual. But something was niggling at me. I glanced at the papers on the desk. The writing; that was it. The note with the dagger was written with care, the characters formal and laboriously printed, a contrast to the fluent sloping lines on the papers I assumed were written by the Maharal. As if the note in the box was written by someone unused to writing in Hebrew. In fact . . . I snatched up the ghost of Dee's letter and compared the two. It was difficult to say for sure – some of the words in the charcoal rubbing were so faint – but the formation of certain characters was almost identical. Had *John* given Rabbi Loew the dagger? It was a peculiar choice of present between two scholars, but perhaps it held some significance only they knew. Where would John have acquired such an item? And what *future* bond? Did they not have a bond already? I wished I could ask the rabbi, but there was no way to do so without revealing that I had trespassed on his privacy. As if to remind me of my breach of hospitality, a board creaked overhead; I slammed the knife back into the drawer and scurried across the hall in time to fling myself on the settle beside Besler and adopt a casual pose as I heard Esther's footsteps on the stairs.

He shot me a quizzical look, but I only shook my head as she opened the door, a battered old volume in her hands.

'Here it is. It has no great value in itself, but it means a lot to my family,' she said, caressing the cover with her palm as if reluctant to hand it over. 'If you're sure this girl will take care of it?'

'I will return it to you safe and sound with her undying thanks,' I said, tucking the book into my bag. 'And mine, for your kindness. I hope the search for David brings good news.' But as I spoke the words I had a horrible sense of foreboding.

'Please tell your father again, he knows where to find me if there is anything I can do to help.'

'I'll remind him,' she said, showing us to the door.

'Oh – one other thing.' I paused on the front step. 'Where would I find Benjamin, if I wanted to speak to him?'

'You're very eager to see him today.' She spoke lightly, but the implicit question was serious.

I touched my fingers to the back of my skull. 'I hit my head yesterday and the swelling is still bad – I thought I might ask him to examine it.'

'You're living with a doctor of physick.'

'Always good to get a second opinion.'

She gave me a long look then, one familiar to any man who has tried to lie to a woman sharper than him, starting with his mother; it was a look that said, Do you think I was born yesterday?

'I see you've injured your wrist too,' she observed, nodding at the bandage. 'You seem quite accident-prone, Dr Bruno – you should take better care of yourself. Well, if you must see Benjamin, you'll find him at the hospital. It's next to the cemetery. But if you want my advice, you'll take your medical consultations elsewhere.'

'Why? He's not a good doctor?'

'Oh no, he's a very good doctor. But he may insist that you read his play script by way of payment.'

I laughed. 'I consider myself warned. Thank you again for the book.'

From the churches beyond the Jewish Town a peal of bells rang out to mark the hour of nine.

'We should go,' I said with a brief bow. 'We have a long walk. This city could do with more than one bridge.'

'You are not the first to say so,' Esther said. 'Where are you headed?'

'To the castle.'

She nodded. 'Then you should take a boat. The street behind the Old-New Synagogue leads down to the river, by the saltpetre

211

works. There's a jetty there, you can usually find boatmen to take you across, then it's a short walk to the Old Castle Stairs. Don't let them charge you more than a thaler – they'll always fleece foreigners if they can.'

I thanked her again; as we reached the corner, she called after me.

'Dr Bruno? I mean it – take care of yourself. Prague can be dangerous and you—' She stopped, as if she feared saying too much.

'I what?'

'You ask too many questions,' she finished, more quietly, as she closed the door.

I had to pull Besler by the sleeve into the next street; he was staring after her with a dazed smile, reminding me of a bear I had seen once in London, drugged to keep it docile while its keepers transported it.

'Here's what we'll do,' I said, snapping my fingers to bring his attention back to me.

'She must like you, Maestro,' he said with a sudden grin. 'Esther, I mean. She seemed very concerned for your welfare.'

'I suspect her concern is more about the questions I'm asking. I'd like to know why. Besides, I get the impression that she has some kind of understanding with Benjamin.'

'Benjamin?' He looked scornful. 'What could he offer her that you can't?'

'Aside from being the right religion, close to her family and ten years younger with an established profession? You're right, Besler – he has nothing in his favour. The girl's a fool.'

'You always say that the goal of your philosophy is to transcend religious difference,' he pointed out.

'I'm not sure that would wash with the daughter of a rabbi.'

'You *do* like her.' He elbowed me in the ribs with a sly smile.

'I find her interesting,' I said as casually as I could manage. 'Listen – I do want to speak to Benjamin, but I also need to take this book up to Golden Lane and see if I can buy the child Sukie's cooperation with it. If she can be persuaded to part with the potion Bartos gave her, I can try some experiments and we might at least understand what it is, and if it sheds any light on why he was murdered. You go to the hospital and look for Benjamin – invite him to have dinner with us. And impress upon him that it's important.'

Besler's face brightened at the mention of dinner. 'When are we eating?'

'God's blood, boy, we've only just had breakfast. Where do you put it? Let's say midday, at the sign of the Winged Horse.'

'Some of us didn't get a proper breakfast,' Besler muttered as he walked away.

SIXTEEN

The wind sharpened as I approached the river, its breath damp with the promise of rain, and I quickened my pace to warm myself, trying not to dwell on thoughts of Esther's dark eyes, that brief flash of unspoken emotion I had seen in them when she told me I could not understand David's betrayal. I passed the saltpetre works along the shore, breathing through my mouth to avoid their unmistakable stench, and realised that the gated walls that separated the Jewish quarter from the Old Town were largely symbolic; on this side the Vltava formed a natural boundary, so that anyone coming in by boat could pass from one side of the city to the other without being checked by the guards on the Stone Bridge. I shielded my eyes with my hand and looked across the river at the castle brooding on its high ridge, wondering if David had crossed by boat after he left me last night, and what might have happened to him on the way.

Wooden jetties stuck out from the shoreline at intervals in front of the mounds of earth dug from the pits; some were substantial, built on thick wooden piles driven deep into the silt, with heavy cranes and winches at the ends for hauling the saltpetre on to barges for transportation. I found a smaller jetty with a low craft tied to the end, where a man in a patched jacket and wool cap sat chewing at the stem of a clay pipe. He squinted up at me as I approached, his expression neither hostile nor especially welcoming.

'How much to cross?' I asked in German, hoping I could make myself understood.

He sized me up, registering my clothes and my accent. 'Five thalers,' he said without removing the pipe.

'I was told one.'

'Who told you that?' He checked up and down the river as if to identify which of his competitors might have undercut him.

'A local.'

'Well, it's gone up. Bad weather.'

I cast a sceptical eye at the sky and made as if to walk away.

'All right, four,' he called after me.

I turned back. 'Two. Final offer.'

He weighed this up and eventually tapped his pipe out on the side of the boat and tucked it away with a grudging nod. I climbed into the boat and settled myself on a piece of sacking that covered the small bench in the prow. The boatman cast off and took up the oars, hauling against the current to turn us.

'Busy today?' I asked, to make conversation.

He grunted. 'It's early yet. 'Course, the best money's at night, but I'm not made for sitting around idle. And the wife just finds me jobs to do around the house if I stay there. Rather be freezing my bollocks off out here.' He grinned. 'You married?'

'No.'

'Sensible man.'

'Why is it better at night?'

He looked at me as if his assessment of my good sense might have been premature. 'I can see you're new to town. Because, my friend, there's plenty of people who like to come and go without declaring their business to the guards on the Stone Bridge and will pay for the convenience, that's why.'

'Business here?' I jerked my thumb back at the Jewish Town receding behind me on the far bank.

'Oh yes. You'd be surprised how much gets done at night.

The fine folk from the Lesser Town' – he nodded towards the far bank – 'do not want to be seen visiting moneylenders. Whatever would the neighbours say?' He affected a cultured accent and cackled. ''Course, if they only knew, the neighbours have been over the night before doing the same thing. Everyone with their secrets. This is the way to get in without going through town. Nice and discreet. Although . . .' He grimaced. 'It's noticeably quieter since this murder. People are afraid it might be stalking the streets.'

'What might?'

'Jesus, where have you been, mate? The *Golem*.' He peered closer at me. 'You're not Jewish, are you?'

'Would it matter?' I said stiffly.

''Course not. Live and let live, I say. I get good business from them too. I've seen it, you know,' he added with a nonchalant sniff.

''You've seen the *Golem*?' I leaned forward. The wind had grown fiercer as we moved into open water; I thought I must have misheard.

'That's right. One night, couple of months ago, I was over the other side tying up, I looked across and I saw this shadow of a figure, all black, outlined against a wall that was sort of glowing with a strange light. Ten feet tall, he must have been. Like a man, but misshapen somehow. It kind of wavered as I looked at it, and then it disappeared.' He shook his head in wonder. 'Never seen it since. They say he keeps it in the attic of the synagogue, but it must have got out.'

I stared at him. He appeared to be entirely serious.

'And what had you been drinking that night?'

'Yeah, yeah – that's what the wife said, but I know what I saw. I asked him about it once and he just laughed and said it was quite harmless. Not so harmless now though, eh.' He made a face.

'Wait – you asked who?' I had to shout to make myself heard.

'The rabbi.'

'Rabbi Loew?'

'That's right. Old fella, big white beard. You know him?'

'Yes. I have business with him.'

'You're not the only one. He's a night-time regular.'

'You ferry *Rabbi Loew* over the river at night?' It seemed so unlikely that I wondered if my German was at fault.

'Yeah. Anyway, I told him I'd seen his Golem and he laughed and said I'd better keep it to myself or everyone would want a look. Then he said they'd all see it when the moment came.'

'What did he mean by that?'

'How should I know? The man speaks in riddles at the best of times.' He looked over his shoulder, concentrating on pulling against the current so we didn't drift too far downriver from the opposite jetty. The tendons in his neck stood out like cords with the effort; by his face I guessed he had ten years on me, but he was strong as a bull.

I squinted across at the castle, considering his words. David Maier had clearly said that Rabbi Loew made those who sought his wisdom go to him, that he did not visit Gentiles. There was only one person on the west side of the river with the power to demand the Maharal make the journey at his convenience. We sat in silence as I considered the implications.

'Where does he go at night then?' I asked the boatman after a while.

'No idea. I take him across and I wait to bring him back, and he pays me well, and that's the end of it. What he does in between is none of my business. Nor yours,' he added with a stern look. 'One thing I do know – he always has a great bag of books with him.'

'Does he go alone?'

'Sometimes with a younger man. More often with his daughter lately. Now she's a beauty, for all she sits there in silence with a face on her like she's been made to drink vinegar. Ah, if I were twenty-five again, and not stuck with a scold.' He adopted an expression midway between wistful and lascivious, until a wave caught us side-on and the cold spray jolted him out of his reverie.

'She doesn't enjoy these night-time outings, then?' I asked.

'Not by the look of her.' He bent his head to wipe his face on his jacket. 'I'd say she accompanies the old man under duress. He chats away – well, you'll know what he's like, if you've met him – but she never says a word.'

Interesting, I thought. 'He's brave, for an old fellow. I wouldn't like to be walking around these streets in the dark at his age with only a girl at my side.' I rubbed my shoulder, remembering the ambush by the Spaniards.

The boatman laughed. 'Who'd be fool enough to attack a man with a monster at his command? Besides,' he added as we pulled up alongside the jetty, 'there's always someone waiting for them on this side. Never see him properly, he stands well away from the lanterns and wears his hood up, but one time he turned and I saw he had a long sword under his cloak. So I reckon the rabbi's well looked after. Still, you're right to be wary, sir – it can be dangerous out here after dark, even if you know how to fight.'

'Yes, I've learned that the hard way,' I said, touching the bandage on my wrist. A thought occurred. 'Talking of danger – were you working last night?'

'For my sins,' the boatman said, throwing the rope with a deft flick of his wrist over a post at the end of the jetty. 'Why, what danger?'

'A friend of mine from the Jewish Town was up by the castle last night, but he didn't get home and his wife has been worrying. I wondered if you'd seen him coming back across? Plump, fortyish.' I described David Maier as the boatman pulled us in and tied up.

'The bookseller? Yeah, I know him,' he said. 'He's a regular too. I didn't bring him back yesterday, but I can ask around, see if any of the lads remember. Might need a bit of help to jog their memories though.' He lifted one eyebrow and looked at my purse.

I sighed and passed him another thaler; he bit it and grinned.

'That'll do, mate. Mind you, there's plenty of reasons a man

218

might choose not to go home at night.' He winked. 'Maybe he just wanted to avoid the wife.'

I was beginning to sense a theme in his conversation. 'I don't think that's David's way. If any of your friends saw him, we'd at least know which side of the river he went missing. His family would be grateful.'

'I'll see what I can do. You'll find me down here, or over there—' he jerked a thumb towards the opposite bank – 'or taking my supper at the Winged Horse. Ask for Martin Novak.' He extended a callused hand.

'Bruno,' I said, shaking it.

I set off towards the Old Castle Stairs, trying to process everything the boatman had told me. So Rabbi Loew crossed the river regularly at night with a bag of books, in the reluctant company of Esther, to be met by an armed escort. It was not hard to guess his destination; he must be visiting the Emperor. But why? Rudolf was interested in mysticism; perhaps he had come to believe that the key to the mysteries of the universe could be found in the Jewish Cabala. That would account for the clandestine meetings: there was already consternation among the Catholic authorities about the degree of lassitude Rudolf allowed the Jews in Prague, it was not hard to predict how the Pope and Philip of Spain would react if they thought the Emperor was studying Jewish lore with the most influential rabbi in Bohemia. Suppose he were tempted to convert? That was too outlandish, surely, even for Rudolf. But it would be an easy rumour for the likes of San Clemente and Montalcino to spread through the town and back to Rome; a disgruntled populace who already felt the Jews had excessive power would readily believe it. What might then follow? Escalated attacks on the Jewish quarter, wider civil unrest, a perfect excuse for Philip and the Pope to step in and demand the imperial crown pass to Matthias, whose Catholic faith was never in doubt.

I paused halfway up to catch my breath; it was a steep climb from the river to the castle, and I had begun to feel the effects of the two attacks I had suffered since arriving in Prague.

Cursing my injuries and those who had inflicted them, I marvelled at Rabbi Loew's stamina; these stairs would be a challenge for a man nearing seventy. He must feel his visits to the Emperor were worth the effort, for the good of his community. I leaned against the wall, my right hand hovering near my dagger just in case, and thought again of Dee's letter to the rabbi. *I fear our enemies suspect, if not all, then part . . .* Dee must have been in Loew's confidence about his secret meetings with Rudolf. Perhaps he had even brokered them. And somehow Dee had found out that their mutual enemies – the Catholics – guessed at it too, putting him and the rabbi in danger. Was that the answer? And what was David's role? David did not approve of sharing Jewish learning with non-Jews, but would he go so far as betraying Rabbi Loew? And to whom – the Catholic authorities? Surely he would be aware of the possible consequences for the rabbi and his people. Since Paul IV, a succession of Popes had made it clear that it was a Christian ruler's duty to show the Jews the error of their ways and bring them to baptism, not the other way around. I knew that in Italy, within my lifetime, Jews had been publicly burned for the crime of 'Judaising'; Bohemia may not be so harsh, but if Rabbi Loew were to be accused of attempting to convert the Holy Roman Emperor, he was certain to face severe punishment. Would David really have risked that, and taken money for it? Esther had said that David believed he was preventing a greater harm; that made a grim kind of sense now. If Rudolf was forced out and a more dogmatic Emperor came to the throne, who knew what measures he might impose to keep the Jews in their place?

Then there was Benjamin. I had no doubt that it was he who had been through David's shop and created the illusion of a break-in. I had suspected it even before Besler had found a scrap of Benjamin's scarf on the broken window; he must have wrapped it around his fist to protect his hand when he shattered the glass. I had to assume, then, that Benjamin knew what David had been doing and wanted to remove any evidence –

presumably in the form of correspondence, given the way the desk drawers had been plundered. Did that mean that Benjamin also knew what had happened to David?

At the top of the Old Castle Stairs, I paused to tuck my knife into my boot before passing through the Eastern Gate, though I knew that hiding it would arouse more suspicion if I was searched. But I was fortunate; the guards were caught up in an argument with a man trying to bring in a handcart loaded with bottles – one had been broken in the course of the inspection and he was loudly demanding compensation – and gave only a cursory glance at my empty sheath before waving me on my way. I passed under the shadow of the Daliborka Tower and into Golden Lane.

It was busier than on my previous visit, though no one appeared much interested in me; mostly they hurried up the street with purpose, heads down, hands tucked inside their coats as if they had something to conceal. I recalled what Hajek had told me about the alchemists of Golden Lane choosing to look away from other people's business, and surmised that he had never met Goodwife Huss. I had to hope that she was out, especially if I needed to force the lock.

I knocked softly at the door of Sukie's house, not wanting to attract attention. When there was no reply, I tried the latch and, to my surprise, the door opened.

'Hello?' I called into the gap, still keeping my voice low. 'Sukie?'

Again, silence. I glanced up and down the street and, taking advantage of a moment with no passers-by, slipped inside.

I found myself in a low-ceilinged room much like Bartos's lodging opposite, though where his place had been crowded with objects, at least on my first visit, the Mollers owned painfully few possessions. There was a kitchen area with a small stove and a table at the back, and two rickety wooden chairs by the hearth. Efforts had clearly been made to keep the place neat, and I felt a pang to see that the walls were washed and cobweb-free up to a certain height, presumably the extent of

Sukie's reach. The air was somehow stuffy and freezing at once; beside the grate stood an empty basket with a few splinters of firewood at the bottom, but there was no sign that a fire had been lit recently. A straw mattress was rolled up in one corner, and over the back of a chair hung a man's shirt, a needle and thread tucked into the sleeve where the frayed cuffs were in the process of being mended.

I made my way to the ladder that led to the attic room and called up softly, though I was fairly sure by now that the house was empty.

'Sukie? It's Bruno, the Italian. I've brought the book I promised.'

After a moment, I climbed up and squeezed through the hatch to find myself in the space under the eaves. Here, some attempt had been made to make the place cosy; once-colourful woollen blankets covered the pallet that served as a bed and a raggedy cloth doll reclined on the pillow, but my eye was caught by the ceiling. The roof sloped sharply on either side, so that I had to crouch even in the centre, but the plaster had been whitewashed and on it someone had painted an impressively accurate map of the constellations, with as much care and precision as any nautical chart, so that from her bed Sukie could memorise the patterns of the stars. I wondered if her father had done this for her, when he had still held some optimism about their new life in Prague; if so, he was clearly a talented draughtsman. The small casement above the bed gave a good view over the lane and Bartos's house opposite.

I cast around in search of any possible hiding place for whatever the alchemist had entrusted to her. The bed yielded nothing and I turned to the wooden blanket box at its foot. At first it appeared to contain only clothes, but when I lifted out the few heavily patched garments – a couple of rough woollen dresses, some breeches and undershirts – I found a bundle of notebooks and papers. Curious, I opened one to find meticulous designs for bridges, siege machines, arquebuses that could fire repeated rounds, and equipment for the refinement of saltpetre and gunpowder, all rendered in a steady hand. Though I couldn't

222

understand the notes in Danish, it was clear that Erik Moller was an engineer of significant skill; I wondered how he had failed to capture the Emperor's interest. I emptied the chest completely and checked it for a false bottom, but found no sign of any alchemical writings nor any potions or powders. I tapped my way around the ceiling, seeking out cavities in the rafters, and then around the low walls. Finally, I pulled out the bed and here I had better luck; I rapped my knuckles against the wooden panelling of the wall that divided the Mollers' house from the Huss's next door and heard a hollow echo. The panel was closely fitted, but a little careful probing allowed me to find an almost invisible gap to insert my fingertips and prise it away from the wall, revealing a narrow crawl space behind, barely big enough for a child.

I knelt and peered in. Without a lantern I could not make out how far the passage extended, but I lay on my belly and wriggled my head and shoulders in far enough to see that it opened out into a cavity between Sukie's attic and the next, where the wind whistled through gaps in the roof tiles that also allowed a little light to filter through. Squeezing in another few inches, I found a bunched-up blanket, the stub of a candle, a package wrapped in oilskin, and a rind of cheese. I sniffed the cheese; it was dry but not yet mouldy, suggesting that Sukie had been hiding out up here until recently. I called her name again, and heard a scuttling ahead that could have been rats. When no further response came, I propped myself on my elbows like a Sphinx and unwrapped the package. Inside I found a copy of Anders Sørensen Vedel's *Den Danske Krønicke* – evidently one of the books Sukie had managed to hide from her father. I flicked through the pages without much hope, but a leaf fluttered loose and I drew it out, suppressing a gasp of surprise. It was covered in notes written in a spiky hand I recognised immediately as belonging to Ziggi Bartos. From the way it was laid out, I guessed it to be some kind of recipe. It was too dim to read properly, and in any case the notes were mainly in Czech, though I made out one word even in the poor light: *aurum*. Shifting to one side, I managed awkwardly to tuck the paper into the lining of my doublet.

As I did so, a firm hand seized my ankle and dragged me backwards into the attic room.

I flailed, cursing, splinters lodging in my palms as I fought to resist, but my assailant's grip was strong; before I could turn I found myself pinned prostrate with a knee in my back and a powerful breath of stale wine in my ear. A fist curled into my hair and lifted my head up, poised to slam my face into the floor; instinctively I shouted,

'Erik, wait!'

He was sufficiently disconcerted at being addressed by name that he hesitated, long enough for me to jerk my head back hard and catch him on the chin; he yelped and loosened his grip as I twisted sideways, sending him off-balance momentarily. He was still half-straddling me; he pulled his fist back to land a punch, but he'd failed to throw the force of his weight behind it; I caught his hand and bent it sharply back, he howled and I brought my other elbow up fast to connect with the soft flesh under his jaw. He sprawled backwards and landed against the small bed; before he could rally I drew my knife from my boot and pointed it at him.

'Listen,' I said in German, between snatched breaths, 'I'm not here to harm you or your daughter.'

He glared at me as he probed inside his mouth with two fingers and examined them for blood, his chest heaving with the sudden exertion. Then his eyes strayed to the blade and all the fight slumped out of him.

'I'll put this away if you promise not to hit me,' I said, holding up my hands before lowering the knife. He nodded mutely, and I took the risk of believing him. Though he was a big man, tall and broad-chested, he had a pathetic air; his fair hair thinning, what must once have been muscle now running to fat. I guessed he was not yet forty, but he wore his troubles heavily on his face; his eyes were red-rimmed and bleary, with deep shadows etched beneath. 'I want to help you find Sukie. I think she has something in her possession that might put her in danger, and we need to recover it before she does anything foolish.'

He sat straighter against the bed and worked his jaw from side to side.

'Made me bite my tongue, you fucker.' He spat blood on the floor and pointed at the spilled contents of the blanket box. 'Trying to steal my designs, are you?'

'Check if you like – all your papers are still there. I was looking for something else. Besides, I can't read Danish.'

'Wouldn't do you any good if you could. You may as well help yourself, you'll get nothing for them. I was promised payment two years ago and I'm still waiting.'

'*Dio mio*,' I muttered, pulling a splinter from my thumb, and his gaze sharpened.

'You're the man who paid my tab at the Winged Horse.' It sounded more like an accusation than an expression of gratitude. Despite the strong smell of alcohol coming off him, he was not slurring; I guessed he had been drinking the night before and I hoped I might have caught him before he started afresh.

'That's right.'

'Why?'

'Because I wanted information.' I pointed a finger at him. 'And because your child needed to eat. She's running around half-starved without a coat, begging bread from the neighbours, while you're stacking up a bill you can't pay to drink yourself into this state.'

His face filled with fury and for a moment I thought he might attack me again, but instead he crumpled, burying his head in his hands.

'I don't know how we came to this,' he mumbled through his fingers. 'My method was sound, I'm sure of it. I should have made good money by now, but all I do is wait, and while I wait, someone else will no doubt come up with something better and cheaper. And Jan Boodt gave me credit and said I could pay it off if I won, but of course I lose every time and that has only made things worse.'

'If you won what?' I asked, growing impatient.

He let out a bitter laugh, his face still covered as if he couldn't bear to be seen. 'Cards, dice, fighting dogs, you name it. He runs gambling nights in the cellar to cover his own debts, and he fixes the odds so you can't win. And now I am in worse straits than before, so what is there to do but drink to forget about it?' He lowered his hands and looked at me. 'I suppose I should thank you, but I no longer trust anyone in this town to act from charity. You must want something in return.'

I tucked away this piece of information about the notorious Jan Boodt to consider later.

'I want you to sober up and help me find your daughter,' I said sternly. I had had enough of his self-pity. 'Ziggi Bartos left something with her for safekeeping, and I need to know what it was. Did she tell you about it?'

He heaved in a ragged breath that juddered through him. 'She wouldn't. She had a gold locket that belonged to her mother – I took it while Sukie was sleeping and sold it. So, she doesn't trust me any more. She hides things.'

I didn't blame her. 'Did you see her at all last night?'

He shook his head. 'I was out with colleagues in the Old Town, I lost track of the time.' He darted a quick defensive glance at me; I returned it stony-faced – I was not going to absolve him for his failures as a father – and he hurried on: 'Sukie wasn't in bed when I came home, so I went to that old busybody next door – the girl has been known to fall asleep in front of her fire sometimes. The Huss woman told me Sukie had gone out for food with a Spaniard but given him the slip. So I tried the Winged Horse, because Jan Boodt always has those Spaniards hanging about—'

'Spaniards?' I echoed stupidly.

'Yes, two of them, often around his gaming table.'

'Does one have a scar by his right eye?'

He looked surprised. 'That's him. Battle scar, so he claims. Vicious bastards, the pair of them. Anyway, Magda stopped me before I could reach the back room. She said a man of your description had bought Sukie dinner and paid off my tab, and I should go before Jan found out or he would pull me back into debt again. She said very few people get the chance for a clean slate and I shouldn't squander it.' His gaze flickered guiltily to me again.

'What time was this?'

'I don't know. Past midnight.'

'And you've seen nothing of Sukie since?'

'No. I've been out half the night searching for her. Ah, God.' He reached for the child's rag doll and pressed it against his forehead. 'If my Emilie is looking down on me now, she must be so ashamed.'

'No,' I said, more gently. 'If your Emilie is where Sukie gets her determination and resourcefulness – and God knows it can't be from you – she would tell you to pull yourself together and find your daughter. Now think – where might Sukie have gone? Who does she know in Prague?'

He lowered the doll and sat up, chastened by my words. 'Magda Boodt has a soft spot for her,' he said. 'She feeds her sometimes, though I don't like Sukie going to that place. I would have said Bartos too, but obviously now – hold on.' His eyes narrowed. 'You said Sukie has something belonging to him. Is it valuable?'

I hesitated; if Erik thought there was money to be made, he would likely try to find Sukie on his own. I was glad I had managed to tuck Bartos's paper inside my doublet before he dragged me out of her hiding place.

'I don't know. But I think it's the reason he was killed. That's what I need to investigate, anyway.'

'Why? Who are you?'

'My name is Bruno. I work for the Emperor. And I'm Italian. Not Spanish.'

He looked me up and down as if taking me in for the first time. 'You all look alike to me.'

'I could say the same about you Norsemen, but you would not like to be mistaken for a Swede, I think?'

He smiled faintly for the first time. 'God forbid. I'm sorry I hit you – I didn't know you worked for the Emperor. You'd hit a man if he was in your daughter's bedroom.'

I agreed that I would. 'The woman next door said you didn't get on with Bartos.'

His expression darkened. 'I was neighbourly enough when he first arrived. Invited him for a beer, a game of cards. But he wasn't the friendly type – at least not in any good way. Too busy looking out for himself. I told Sukie to stay away from him, but she was fascinated by his experiments.'

'Perhaps he made her feel useful,' I said pointedly. 'How do you mean, he wasn't friendly in a good way? Was he improperly friendly towards Sukie?'

'Oh no, not like that. I mean he was the sort to attach himself to people in order to use them. As far as the other thing goes, I think he was a sodomite.'

'Really? You think, or you know?' It struck me as odd that, in all the rumours I had heard about Ziggi Bartos, there had been no mention of this.

'Well, I never saw him *at it*,' he said with a curl of his lip. 'But there was a man who often came to visit him in the dead of night, he always looked over his shoulder as he entered the house, and they would keep the shutters closed.'

'Surely, in Golden Lane of all places, that could mean anything? They might have been sharing secret experiments.'

He looked doubtful. 'I suppose. But once I was coming home late as this man was leaving. He and Bartos were standing on the threshold, clasping hands, but they let go as if they'd been burned when they heard me coming.'

'Did you get a look at the visitor?'

'I wasn't really paying attention. It was raining and I was in a hurry to get indoors.'

'You mean, you weren't in a state to focus properly. You must have had an impression, though – tall, short, strong, stooped?'

He shrugged. 'Average height, to the best of my recall. But he wore a hooded cloak – I never saw his face.'

'So you can't even be certain it *was* a man?' I sighed. 'You said he visited often – the same person every time?'

'No idea. Same cloak, anyway, or one very like it.'

Winter in northern Europe: one dark hooded cloak looked much like another, and everyone wore them. I bit down my frustration; a drunk was the world's least helpful witness. I wondered if Sukie knew any more about this visitor; she would not have missed a detail if she did. What Erik saw through wine-blurred eyes as two men holding hands might equally have been a man and a tall woman, or two conspirators passing something hidden between them. But it was a useful piece of information, nonetheless. Hajek was wrong: Bartos evidently did have a collaborator, someone he did not want to associate with publicly.

'All right, listen,' I said. 'The priority is to find Sukie. I'll keep making enquiries, and you do the same. If you discover her, I charge you on pain of the most severe consequences not to touch any items Bartos entrusted to her, but to bring them immediately to Dr Thaddeus Hajek. You know him, I presume?'

Erik gave a dry laugh. 'Oh yes, I know Dr Hajek. I've been trying to get an audience with him for months to see if there's news about my payment, but he always seems to be busy.'

'Well, send word that you have information about Bartos – that should bring him running. And if I find Sukie first, I will bring her directly here.'

'Thank you,' he said, meeting my eye almost for the first time. 'And for settling my debt – I will find a way to repay you, I swear, once I'm paid what I'm owed.'

'Repay me by finding Sukie,' I said, picking up the bag containing Esther's book; I was not about to trust Erik with it. Halfway down the ladder an idea struck me. 'Oh – there is something else you can do for me,' I said, poking my head back through the hatch.

Erik was still clutching Sukie's doll; he looked like a carnival giant in the girl's tiny room. 'What?'

'Take me to one of Jan Boodt's gaming nights.'

He raised an eyebrow. 'Seriously? You must have money to burn.'

'I'm good at cards.'

'Ha. That's what they all think. Whatever skill you have will avail you nothing. I told you – he cheats. You'll lose, and go on losing, and then he'll threaten to break your legs. But I'll take you tonight, if you're sure?'

'I'm sure,' I said. I had a feeling there was something useful to be learned at Jan Boodt's, if I could keep my purse and my legs intact.

SEVENTEEN

The great cathedral bell tolled the half-hour as I hurried up Golden Lane. I asked a guard how to find the Powder Tower and followed his directions along the north side of the basilica, where I discovered it was impossible to miss: a squat drum of a tower built into the castle walls, overshadowed by the vast bulk of St Vitus's. It rose three storeys above the courtyard on this side, but extended down several more on the outer wall, with its foundations at the foot of the Stag Moat escarpment beyond. It must have been constructed as part of the castle's original fortifications; small windows spaced at intervals around each floor were designed for firing ordnance. I tilted my head to see black smoke belching from ventilation shafts set into the red-tiled conical roof.

This, then, was the domain of the alchemists, the focus of all Rudolf's ambition and investment. I watched the entrance as men with soot-smudged faces and stained aprons bustled in and out; a guard at the door occasionally stopped someone to check credentials – I saw one show a metal token – while others were waved through with a nod of recognition. When I saw a lull in the traffic, I announced myself and explained that I was there to see Dr Hajek.

'Tell him it's urgent,' I said; then, seeing the guard didn't look convinced, I added, 'Tell him it's about Ziggi Bartos.'

This caught the attention of a bald man waiting behind me; he offered to find Hajek, looking me up and down with frank curiosity as he headed into the tower, and I regretted having used the dead man's name so freely. After a few moments, the doctor appeared in his shirtsleeves, wearing leather gloves and apron and trailing an acrid smell. He greeted me with a smile, though I caught a wariness in his eyes.

'Bruno! Do you have news?'

'I need you to look at something.'

'Intriguing. Let's find a little more privacy. But first, come – it's high time you saw what I have built here, under the Emperor's aegis. Follow me.'

He led me up a curving staircase which emerged into a cylindrical chamber that filled the first floor of the tower. I stopped at the top of the steps, awed by the sight before me. All around the room, alcoves were set into the thick walls and in each, one or two men toiled at a workbench crowded with flasks, alembics and bottles of all shapes and sizes. Some of these were set on iron tripods over oil burners and linked with glass tubes, as different coloured liquids simmered and bubbled, escaping in wreaths of steam. A stout athanor burned in the centre of the chamber, emitting a coil of smoke that rose up to hang below the soot-blackened vaults of the ceiling. The soup of vapours in the air caught in my throat, making me cough; the commingled smells – mineral and vegetal, sulphuric and scorched – assaulted my nostrils. There was something infernal about the noise, the heat, the sweating faces and tormented expressions of the men who frowned in concentration over their pelicans, retorts and crucibles; it brought back fond memories of John Dee's laboratory in Mortlake, but on a far greater scale. I was delighted and amazed to see the evidence of their industry; here were the alchemical arts, condemned as necromancy and driven into the shadows in so many places, celebrated and pursued openly in the heart of the royal palace.

Hajek noted my response and I saw that it pleased him.

'On this floor, they are engaged in distillation techniques,' he informed me. 'Above, I have men essaying the properties of minerals and gemstones, and on the floor below us, metallurgy and optics. In the basement, they're experimenting with new methods to manufacture gunpowder and saltpetre.'

I glanced at the furnace in the centre and the naked flames on the tables, and thought of Greta's late husband. 'Is that . . . safe?'

Hajek spread his hands and grinned. 'Nothing of value is without risk, Bruno. You know that. What do you think?'

'It's extraordinary,' I said with appropriate reverence.

'Isn't it? I believe there is nothing like this in all of Christendom. A dedicated laboratory pushing the frontiers of alchemical and scientific knowledge on every possible front. His Majesty is rightly proud of it – he drops by most days and often participates in experiments. What did you want to show me?'

'Can we go somewhere quieter?'

He nodded, and led me up to another floor. Where the previous room was filled with sounds that seemed almost human in origin – gurgling, bubbling, belching, spitting – this chamber was filled with a mechanical din: the repetitive grinding of metal on glass and the scraping of whetstones, though I noticed that the men paused in their tasks to stare at me as we entered. One flight more, and we found relative peace: a low-ceilinged room under the tower roof, where bunches of plants hung drying along the beams and the men at the workbenches were engaged in quiet and precise tasks of chopping, dissecting, weighing, preserving, bottling. Hajek approached a thin, grey-haired man with prominent eyes who was bent over a table examining a sprig of orange berries through a magnifying lens; they exchanged a few words in low voices, before the man clapped his hands, barked something in Czech, then he and the other workers promptly disappeared into the stairwell, leaving us alone. I breathed in; the room smelled pleasantly of herbs after the bizarre concoctions of the distillation chamber, though the heat rising from the lower floors hung heavy in the air. Sweat gathered inside my collar. I drew the paper I had found in Sukie's hiding place from my doublet and passed it to Hajek.

'I thought you might make more sense of this than I can.'

He ran his eyes over the writing and snapped his head up to look at me. 'Good God. Where did you get this?'

'Not important for now,' I said. I did not want Sukie brought in for interrogation. 'But it's Bartos's hand, I think?'

'No question.' He looked again at the paper, all the levity gone from his expression.

'What is it – some kind of recipe?'

'*Sebevražedný strom.*' He pointed at the words. 'Do you understand this?'

'*Strom* is tree, I believe? The first word, I have no idea.'

'It means "suicide tree". God's blood. Surely he couldn't—' His gaze shot to an alcove opposite the stairs barred with an iron gate. Behind this a tall wooden cupboard had been built into the wall. He rushed over to it, but the gate was firmly locked and the cupboard door secured by a thick iron chain and a padlock. 'Impossible,' he muttered to himself, tugging at the handle. He turned back to me, his face pale. 'Those scraps in the fireplace at Bartos's house, you asked me to see if there was anything legible, remember? There was nothing that struck me as significant then, so I forgot about them. But on one, I now recall, there was a word that could have been "kernel".'

'And?'

'The Suicide Tree. Do you know of it? *Cerbera odollam.* Native to the Orient. Some months ago a merchant came through with rare plants he had traded with the Turks. I'd heard of the effects of this fruit and paid handsomely for several specimens – I wanted to experiment with its properties and in fact I'm trying to grow a tree from seed in the glasshouse. But Bartos couldn't possibly—' He broke off and rattled the cupboard doors again.

'I deduce from the name that it's a poison,' I prompted.

'One of the deadliest,' Hajek said. 'But very difficult to detect. It appears to act on the heart, though I wanted to discover more about precisely how. I'd planned to feed some to a dog and then dissect it. We keep a supply of dogs to use in experimentation – there's a boy who rounds up strays for the purpose. Don't look so squeamish, they'd only die in the street otherwise, and I can hardly test the effects of toxins on people, can I?' He looked back at the paper in his hand. 'It's said that, in the East, the suicide tree is the most common way for husbands to murder their wives, and vice versa, because although the taste is bitter, it's also mild and easily disguised with spices. The kernel of one fruit is sufficient to kill a healthy adult within a day.'

'Could it be dissolved in a liquid?'

He gave me a curious look. 'I had only heard of its use as a dried powder added to food, though I suppose in theory an infusion would be even more fast-acting, if one could be made that was palatable. In fact, this appears to be exactly what Bartos was attempting to create here.' He flicked the paper. 'But he could not have succeeded. It's impossible.'

'Why?'

'Because all toxic substances are kept in this cupboard and only two of us have the keys, myself and the master herbalist.'

'And you trust him?'

'Implicitly.' A flicker of doubt passed across his face. 'Wait there.' He crossed to the stairs, bellowed orders to the room below and returned to me. 'You have some theory about this,' he said, almost accusingly.

I shook my head. 'Nothing that will hold together, as yet. I believe Bartos was working on a version of *aurum potabile*. This would appear to be his recipe, which you've confirmed includes a potent toxin. He had received a quantity of Spanish gold shortly before his murder – he exchanged it in the Jewish Town. Put all that together, and it points to one conclusion.'

Hajek tapped his nail against his teeth. 'You think he took Spanish money to poison Rudolf under the pretence of giving him *aurum potabile*.' He looked doubtful. 'It's plausible up to a point, I suppose, but he could never have carried it out. I don't see how he could have had access to the poison. And even if he got that far by some means – do you think the Emperor simply knocks back a draught of whatever is put in front of him?'

'I wondered about that,' I said. 'You have people to test the elixirs, then?' An undesirable job; I imagined as many were felled by incompetence as by malice.

'Of course. All edible or potable substances must first be tested extensively in the laboratory on rats and then different sizes of dogs, in recorded experiments performed in the presence of colleagues,' he said. 'Once an alchemist is sufficiently sure of his product, he is then required to demonstrate its manufacture and safety to me. By the time we get as far as presenting it to Rudolf, I will have to be satisfied by multiple proofs that it poses no harm to humans or animals. Finally – and very few make it to this stage – he must drink his own potion in front of the Emperor. If he is still fit and well forty-eight hours later, His Majesty will consider trying the product.'

'Has this ever happened?'

'No,' Hajek said shortly. 'The closest we came was last year – an Italian claimed to have created a tonic that would guarantee a cockstand for five or more hours, even in old men. Naturally, the Emperor was curious.'

'And did it work?' I was curious too, from a purely scientific perspective.

'Sadly, no. The young man he brought with him to demonstrate the efficacy of his invention was in fact suffering from a severe and extremely painful case of priapism caused by a fistula, nothing to do with the Italian's potion. In fact, I cured him by draining the blood from his rod via a tube inserted through the—'

'I see,' I cut in quickly, wincing. 'So you're saying that even if Bartos had perfected this toxic elixir, there is no way he could have given it to Rudolf without first being obliged to drink it himself before witnesses?'

'Exactly. Ah, Klaus.' He nodded over my shoulder; I turned to see the thin, grey man appear from the stairwell, his eyes bulging further with alarm.

He wiped his hands nervously on his apron. 'Thaddeus?'

'This is Klaus Berengar, our master herbalist,' Hajek said to me. 'Klaus, take a look at this.' He handed the man Bartos's recipe and gave him a brief outline of my theory.

'Impossible,' the herbalist said at once, with the same certainty as Hajek. 'I keep detailed records of exactly who has requested ingredients from the restricted supplies and whether the request was approved or denied. Bartos never submitted a request for the *cerbera odollam*. I would have remembered that.'

'He couldn't have broken in and taken it when your back was turned?' I asked. 'I was told the laboratories here operate around the clock – surely you can't always be supervising?'

Berengar gave me a withering look. 'No, he could not. If I am not here, my assistant supervises, but he does not have my keys. Only Dr Hajek or I can approve requests for dangerous substances, and as you see, there are two locks to get past. If they had been tampered with, we would have noticed right away.'

'Nevertheless, we ought to check,' Hajek said, nodding to the cupboard.

Grim-faced, the herbalist opened first the iron gate and then, with a different key, loosed the chain securing the cupboard doors. Inside was a poisoner's paradise: shelves of jars and bottles lined up neatly with labels pasted beneath in some code that prevented the substances being readily identified. Through the vessels' clouded glass I saw twisted roots, dried berries, powders, gnarled objects that might have been fruits or tubers; others contained preserved scorpions, snakes, lizards, insects and frogs, in garish and strange colours.

'Here,' Berengar said, lifting out a jar as I tried to guess what some of the more bizarre venoms might be. He held it up to the light; inside I could make out what looked like small wooden balls.

The herbalist set down a board on a nearby table and pulled on a pair of leather gloves.

'We bought six of the dried kernels, if you recall, Thaddeus,' he said, unstoppering the jar. 'You took one to cultivate, which leaves us with five. And indeed—' he paused to check – 'here are five. So whatever Ziggi Bartos had written there, it existed only in his imagination.' The satisfaction in his voice was tinged with a palpable relief; his professionalism was not in doubt.

But Hajek was frowning at the jar.

'Tip them out,' he said. Berengar let the kernels roll onto the board and I peered closer. They had a nondescript appearance for such deadly objects: brown and egg-shaped, with a ridged shell; indeed, looking for all the world like large—

'God's death,' Hajek cried, lunging forward and grabbing one. 'This is a *walnut*, Klaus. A fucking walnut! And so is that.' He pointed to another that was markedly smaller than the rest.

The herbalist stared at him, all colour drained from his face. He picked up the offending walnut and squinted at it, as if willing it to transform before his eyes. 'But the other three . . .' he faltered.

'Yes, well done, three are still genuine.' Hajek's voice was strangled with fury. 'But two kernels of one of the deadliest fruits known to man are missing, replaced with fucking *walnuts*. And you hadn't noticed. So we have no way of knowing how long they've been out there, in someone's possession, or where they might be now. Jesus Christ and all His saints.' He hurled the walnut with impressive force at the far wall, where it cracked and rolled sheepishly across the brick floor. 'How in God's name could this have happened?'

'I – I don't know, Thaddeus.' Berengar looked genuinely terrified; I did not believe he could have played any part in the theft. 'My keys are never out of my sight. The locks have not been forced in any way, as you see.' He allowed a slight pause before dropping his gaze to his feet. 'And you're sure you have your keys?'

'Of course,' Hajek snapped, drawing a large bunch from a

ring at his belt. He worked two free and laid them on the table. 'Truth be told, I rarely use them.'

'Well, that is what I was thinking,' Berengar said, not meeting his eye. 'Perhaps, given that you don't use them on a day-to-day basis, you might not have noticed if someone borrowed them?'

'What are you talking about? How would anyone borrow them? I keep them on my belt.'

'I merely thought – since you and I have the only keys, and I can assure you no one has taken mine—'

'Don't try and cast the blame on me for your failures,' Hajek said. 'The lock must have been picked, then. Bruno here can do it in a matter of minutes, perhaps there are others with his dubious skills. Perhaps *you* took them, Klaus. After all, a trained herbalist who keeps a close eye on his most potent ingredients, as he is supposed to, would surely notice the difference between *odollam* and a fucking walnut. Did someone pay you?'

Berengar drew himself up and regarded Hajek coldly. 'If I had wished to profit from the illicit sale of my herbs, I could have taken the money and retired by now. You have known me near twenty years, Thaddeus, and I have never given you cause to suspect me – that you should accuse me of such base actions—'

'Dr Hajek,' I cut in, picking up one of the keys he had set on the table. 'He could be right. Look, here.' I laid it flat on my palm. Between the teeth was lodged a tiny fragment of red wax.

'Ha!' Berengar seized on it and examined the other key. 'Yes, and the same with this one. Someone has evidently taken an impression of your keys in wax, for the purpose of making a copy.'

It was Hajek's turn to look stricken. 'But how could that be? They are on my person at all times, except when I sleep, and even then they are in my bedchamber.'

'Then I fear you are going to have some difficult conversations with your servants,' the herbalist said with an unseemly glee at his own vindication. Hajek caught my eye and I glimpsed the depths of his hurt; he could not have looked more betrayed if he had found his wife with another man. I felt sorry for him, though it confirmed my suspicions that Greta was not to be trusted. He pulled himself together and held out his hand for the keys.

'Very well,' he said briskly. 'The question of *how* this occurred you can leave with me. We must limit the damage as best we can. The most pressing problem is that someone has access to this cupboard, and we don't know how long he has been at liberty to help himself, nor which other substances might now be in circulation. Klaus, find your assistant, question him, and if you are satisfied with his integrity, proceed to take a thorough inventory of the contents. Note anything missing or substituted, down to the last scruple. Test every ingredient if you must, to verify that it corresponds with the label. Then fetch a locksmith to fit new locks on the gate and the cupboard. There's no time to waste.'

'I'm still waiting for an apology,' Berengar said, drumming his fingers on the bench with a wounded dignity.

I thought Hajek might lose his temper again, but he took a deep breath and bowed his head. 'Forgive me, my friend. The fault is mine. I would not have believed it possible, but trust me, I will get to the bottom of it.'

'Do not blame yourself,' the herbalist said, mollified. 'It's a rare master who has not been deceived by his servants, one time or another.'

Hajek shook his head. 'I never would have imagined . . .' he began. 'Well, no matter. There is much to do. Bruno, come with me.'

I nodded farewell to the herbalist, who had turned to survey the shelves of bottles and flasks with a daunted expression. In the stairwell, Hajek gripped my sleeve and pulled me aside.

'You must tell me how you came by that paper, Bruno. Does this potion exist? We found no sign in his lodging – did Bartos entrust it to someone? We must recover it before anyone attempts to use it.'

I hesitated. 'Do you know a Danish engineer named Erik Moller?'

Hajek frowned in surprise. 'Moller? He's a drunk and a debtor. Why on earth would Bartos confide in him?'

'Not Erik. His daughter. She's eleven.'

'Good God.' He pressed his curled fist against his forehead. 'You're telling me this poison is in the hands of a *child*? Does she know what she has?'

'I think he impressed upon her that it was dangerous. Unfortunately he also made clear that it was valuable. She's absconded with whatever Bartos had made – I imagine she'll try to sell it at some point. She thinks she can clear her father's debts. He's out looking for her.'

'Worse. If Moller gets hold of that potion, it will disappear into the hands of people with no conscience and God knows what uses it may be put to.' He banged the side of his fist against the wall. 'If you knew this child had it, how did you let her disappear with it?'

'How did you let Greta steal your keys?'

He recoiled as if I had struck him. 'That is a hard blow, Bruno, believe me. I have always considered myself a shrewd judge of character – it's crucial to my work here. And I've known Greta for decades – I still cannot think her culpable.'

'I suppose we don't know that it was her,' I said. 'You have other servants.'

He shook his head. 'None that have access to my bedchamber.' Then, catching my look, he smiled wearily. 'Not like that, though you are not the first to speculate. Not Greta – there has never been a flicker of anything between us. She is like a sister to me. And,' he added, in a sterner tone, '*not* because I prefer the company of men, as Jacopo Strada has tried to insinuate over the years.'

'It would be nothing to me if you did,' I said mildly. 'There are worse sins.'

'Oh, I agree. And I have my peccadillos, Bruno, as we all do, but that is not among them.'

'Was it said of Bartos?'

He frowned. 'That he preferred men? Not that I ever heard, and there's precious little that escapes notice in this Tower, especially if it might be used to discredit someone who was not widely liked. Why, has it been suggested?'

'I was trying to build a picture of his connections.'

He looked at me a moment longer and nodded. 'Well, I suppose I must speak to Greta. Your job is to find this child.'

'I intend to. But while I am here – can I look again at Bartos's body?'

'He's in the ground, Bruno. I had him taken away before dawn this morning. What did you want to examine?'

I paused. I had hoped to satisfy my curiosity on this matter without alerting anyone else to my suspicions, but in the absence of Bartos himself, Hajek was the only one who could answer. 'The wound in his side,' I said. 'Could it have been made by a curved blade?'

He let go of my sleeve and stared at me, eyes wide. 'How on earth did you know that?'

'I was thinking about the appearance of the incision,' I said, hoping he would not press me further.

He quirked an eyebrow. 'John Dee did not exaggerate your powers of recall. I came to the same conclusion. The shape of the wound, the angle of the puncture to the heart, all suggest a curved dagger in the Ottoman style.'

'Are those common in Prague?'

'I wouldn't say so. The Emperor has a collection in the *Kunstkammer*, presented to him and his father by various emissaries over the years. He displays the finest in a locked cabinet – some are extremely valuable. But it's not a weapon used by regular citizens. Apart from anything, it takes practice to handle an Ottoman blade with accuracy. That's why I thought initially of a professional soldier.'

'Does the Emperor give his collection away as gifts?'

'Possibly. He has a tendency to bestow treasures on a whim, and lament it afterwards. Jacopo would know, he keeps the inventory – although I suppose that has fallen to Ottavio now. Why do you ask?'

'Only that it would narrow the search if we knew we were looking for a man who owns an Ottoman knife and knows how to use it.'

'And who also has a grudge against the Jews and wanted to be rid of Ziggi Bartos.' He grimaced. 'You're thinking of San Clemente.'

In fact, I was not, though now that I considered it, he fit all the criteria. 'I heard he fought in the Ottoman wars,' I said. I recalled that the Spaniard with the scarred face who attacked me on the first night had carried a curved blade. Perhaps he had also fought the Turk.

'Yes, the War of Cyprus,' Hajek said. 'That had occurred to me too. God's blood – if San Clemente is involved, you have no hope of pursuing this to any official conclusion. Rudolf will not endanger his relationship with Spain over the killing of an alchemist with no name or family.'

'He might if he knew the alchemist had been hired by Spain to poison him.'

'For the moment that is only speculation. We have no proof without Bartos's *aurum potabile* – and even if you find this girl and the potion, I doubt we could conclusively tie it to the ambassador. I see now why Bartos's place was turned over so quickly.'

'Perhaps Greta's testimony will incriminate San Clemente?' I said. 'She must have acted at someone's behest.'

Hajek gave a mirthless laugh. 'I would say her brother-in-law, in the first instance. He has his fingers in all manner of pies. But she'll be unwilling to testify against him, and you may be sure that if San Clemente or the nuncio are ultimately behind it, their hand will be invisible. Find the Moller girl, Bruno, before she harms herself or someone else.'

He hurried away down the stairs, muttering 'fucking walnuts' incredulously to himself as he went. Descending after him through the lower floors of the Powder Tower, I was aware of the stares that followed me, the hushed conversations in multiple languages that fell silent and started up more urgently as I passed, the name 'Bartos' hissing around the blackened circular walls in my wake. Hajek was right: nothing stayed secret in here for long. The irony was not lost on me. I wondered which of the men watching me with hostile eyes might have been Bartos's mysterious midnight visitor, his potential collaborator – or lover, though that seemed increasingly fanciful on Erik's part. Perhaps none. Certainly no one the dead man had trusted as much as an eleven-year-old girl, who was now in significant danger.

EIGHTEEN

The bells of St Vitus tolled eleven as I hurried back across the courtyard, past the convent of St George towards the East Gate. A thin rain had begun to fall, chased by the wind into shifting veils that lent the castle a melancholy aspect. I cursed again my complacency the night before in leaving Sukie alone in the tavern; the thoughtless decision of a moment that I would give anything to undo. I trusted – as Bartos obviously had – that she possessed enough sense not to try the elixir for herself, but sooner or later she would attempt to sell it, and that would attract the attention of unscrupulous people, if it hadn't already.

I made my way to the Winged Horse to find it busy, though it was too early yet for the midday dinner rush. I took a seat in the same nook by the fire where I had eaten with Sukie, my back to the wall so that I had a good view of the tap-room, though none of its occupants seemed at all interested in my presence. From my visit to the Powder Tower I could confidently identify the majority of them as alchemists – not the individuals, but the type. Stained smocks, smudged faces and fingers, the smell of smoke and sulphur that clung to their hair and clothes. After a few minutes Magda appeared, glaring down at me.

'You again,' she said, tight-lipped. But I was too alarmed by her appearance to question her hostility; a livid bruise bloomed along her right cheek. 'Stable door blew open in my face,' she said flatly, before I could ask.

I ordered a mug of beer; she paused, head tilted, as if considering whether she could comply with such an outlandish request. 'Is there a problem?' I said.

She glanced towards the kitchen and leaned one hand on the table. 'Look, I'm not in the habit of turning away customers,' she said in a low voice, 'but if you know what's good for you, you'll find your food and drink elsewhere.'

'And why is that?'

'Because there are people in this town who are taking a good deal of interest in you and your questions. People you don't want to cross, trust me.'

'I see. And what if I don't know what's good for me?'

She shrugged. 'Then you can't say you weren't warned.'

'Will a stable door hit me in the face?'

Her jaw tightened. 'That'll be the least of it.'

She turned to go and I caught her by the sleeve. 'Listen, Magda. Sukie is in danger. Her father is driving himself mad with worry.'

She let out a bitter laugh. 'That's rich. Do you know how many times I've given that child a hot meal from my own pot because Erik Moller never worried about her enough to shift his arse out of whichever shithole he'd passed out in?'

'Well, exactly,' I said. 'You care about her, I know you do. Erik says that, apart from Ziggi Bartos, you're the only person she would confide in. So if you know where she is, for God's sake tell me before she's found by someone who doesn't care.'

She brushed my hand away, but not before I had seen the expression of guilt and fear that flashed across her face.

'And your sister is suspected of theft,' I added, pressing my advantage. 'Did you and your husband put her up to that? Will you compensate her if she loses her position?' I had no idea how Hajek would deal with Greta over the keys, but I could see that my words had struck Magda's conscience. 'I mention it because whatever you're mixed up in is your business, except that it's beginning to have consequences for other people. Greta, Sukie – people I don't think you want to see hurt. If you help me, I can help you.'

A number of emotions wrestled for control of Magda's face; eventually she settled on fury. She perched on the edge of the stool opposite and jammed her elbows on the table, leaning across until her face was inches from mine. Even then, she spoke so quietly I had to strain to hear her.

'*You* listen. My husband has sunk this tavern so deep in debt we're on the edge of losing everything. So I will do whatever I must to survive. My sister understands that. Thaddeus Hajek won't throw her out – I know him.'

'Did someone offer you money to get those keys? Is that why Greta agreed to it? Who was it?'

She pointed a finger in my face. 'There's nothing you can do to help me, Dr Bruno, except to stay out of my business. Oh yes, I know who you are – Greta's told me all about you. I'm sure you mean well, but you're a stranger and you don't know the kind of people you're dealing with here.'

'Actually, I think I do,' I said. I gestured to her cheek. 'And what about Sukie? Are you going to let your husband do that to her as well?'

With the speed of a snake striking prey, she slapped me across the face before I had a chance to dodge. 'Get out of my tavern,' she hissed through her teeth. 'I can't tell you where Sukie is, but I can promise I would *never* let anyone touch a hair of her head. You'll have to believe me.'

'All right, I'll go.' I fought the urge to rub my smarting face, for the sake of my pride. 'But listen to me. Sukie has something with her, she wants to sell it. If you know where she is, and if it's not too late, I beg you, don't let her touch it. Nor anyone else. Get it to Dr Hajek as soon as possible – I'm sure he'll reward you.'

She raised an eyebrow. 'Dangerous, is it?'

'In the wrong hands, yes.'

'Hmm. I suppose *the wrong hands* is all a matter of perspective,' she murmured, and I could see her calculating. I regretted having spoken; she was already picturing the silver thalers dancing in her mind's eye. Her expression changed in an instant as a shadow fell across the table. I saw her flinch, and looked up to see a large man with a stubbled jaw and a face like a boiled ham standing over me.

He barked something at Magda in Czech and she jumped up so fast she knocked her stool over, fumbled to right it and finally stood, smoothing her skirts repeatedly in a nervous gesture.

'I was just saying to my wife,' the man said pleasantly, turning to me and speaking in German, 'how well we must be doing, that she has the leisure to sit gossiping with customers.'

So this was the famous Jan Boodt. His hair was a fading red and his gut strained at his jerkin; though he was determinedly smiling at me, there was a wild light in his eyes that suggested he was just waiting for me to give him an excuse to pin me against the wall with his arm across my throat.

'Please – the fault was mine,' I said, forcing myself to match his friendly tone. 'I asked about the history of the tavern.' It was the first thing that came into my head, and it sounded as unconvincing to my ears as it evidently did to his.

'History, is it?' He grinned, showing several missing teeth. 'Well, you've come to the right place – my wife's so old, she's like a walking chronicle.' He chuckled at his own joke, then peered closer at me as understanding dawned. 'Wait a moment – is this Erik Moller's guardian angel?' When Magda nodded, he reached out a meaty hand and clasped mine, harder than necessary, to demonstrate the strength of his grip. 'Good to meet you, friend. You must be a wealthy man, as well as a stupid one. Fast as you reach for your purse, he'll run up another debt twice as big. You going to keep bailing him out, are you?'

'I'm hoping he's learned his lesson,' I said evenly.

Jan Boodt threw his head back and laughed from his belly as if this was the funniest thing he'd ever heard. 'You *are* a fool then,' he said. 'Men like him never learn. *Weak*, that's what he is.' The laughter stopped abruptly; his lip curled with contempt. 'Despite the evidence of all his senses, he goes on believing the winning card will turn up in the next hand. And yet somehow Lady Luck never smiles on Erik Moller, fickle whore that she is.' He adopted an exaggerated expression of regret.

'That's because it's not a matter of luck, but strategy,' I said.

He looked at me with renewed interest. 'Oh yes? Card player yourself, are you?'

'When the mood takes me.'

'Huh. Well, if the mood takes you later, we can always fit one more at our table.' He jerked his head towards the yard door. 'Starts after midnight. Come in through the back and you can show us your strategies. Bring a full purse, mind – I don't give credit to strangers.'

'I might take you up on that,' I said.

'Good man. It'll be a pleasure bleeding you dry.' He cuffed me on the shoulder so hard I almost fell off the stool.

'Jan,' Magda said in a warning tone.

'Shut your mouth, woman. Figure of speech. I'd have thought you'd be pleased to see his pretty face here again, eh? You didn't mention he was handsome. She likes the dark ones,' he said to me, as if in a theatrical aside. 'Got a taste for Spaniards, haven't you, my love? Not that he'd look at a dry old bitch like you,' he added to his wife. 'Don't you have pies need putting in the oven, or are we not expecting any customers today?'

Magda bobbed her head, sent me a meaningful glance, and disappeared in the direction of the kitchen.

I pushed my stool back, my jaw clenched tight. I have always reserved an especial contempt for men who use their fists on women and children. Every sinew in my body burned with the urge to punch Jan Boodt in the face, but I was not at my fittest after my tussle with Erik earlier and though Boodt must be well into his fifties, he was at least six feet tall and looked like the kind who would fight dirty. I was familiar with his sort: a bully with a small amount of power in his limited domain, which he threw about to mask his fear of his own weakness. I had encountered plenty of Jan Boodts in the Dominican order; they were no different, though they did their bullying in Latin. Montalcino was one. It took all my self-discipline to maintain a detached expression. For now I needed Boodt to think I was biddable.

'Not staying for dinner then?' he said as I gathered up my bag.

'I have pressing business elsewhere, I'm afraid.'

'I'm sure you do,' he said with that wolfish smile. 'You're a busy man, from what I hear. Give your mate Erik my regards, won't you. Tell me, did he ever find his daughter?'

I turned with a sharp look, but his broad red face was all innocence.

'Why, have you seen her?'

'Me? No. Magda mentioned she'd run off again, poor mite. Can't blame her, really. I'll keep an eye out, though. See you later. Don't forget – full purse.' He tapped his belt with a grin, but he kept his eyes trained on me all the way to the back door.

I relieved myself in the yard, looking up to survey the blank windows of the guest chambers that surrounded it on three sides. I had an uneasy feeling that both Sukie and the poison were somewhere on the premises, but I knew I wouldn't get far if I attempted to search the place with Jan Boodt watching me. I would come back this evening and let him take a few thalers off me at cards; he would be less guarded if he thought he had the upper hand. It occurred to me that, even if Greta had mentioned my assistant to her sister, neither Magda nor Jan had, to my knowledge, set eyes on Besler. While Jan was presiding over his game in the cellar and Magda busy with customers in the tap-room, I could send the boy to comb the rest of the inn; if anyone challenged him, he could put on his best guileless expression and claim he was lost.

250

For this to work, I then realised, I could not be seen eating with Besler at the Winged Horse; it was fortunate that I had arrived early. I would have to intercept him and Benjamin before the Boodts could connect them with me. As I headed across the yard to the gate, I passed the stable lad wiping down the flanks of a sweating horse that had clearly ridden up the hill at a clip. The boy greeted me and I nodded to him in return, then I stopped abruptly and turned back.

'What's that?' I pointed to the cloth in his hand.

He looked at it, shrugged, and went back to wiping the animal, whose breath steamed from its flaring nostrils as it danced on the spot.

'Can I see?' I persisted, and before he could argue, I snatched the rag from him and held it up by the corners. I knew immediately where I had seen it before, and my stomach lurched. It was a striped woollen shawl.

'Where did you get this?' I demanded, taking a step towards him and causing the horse to throw its head back in alarm.

He pulled at the bridle to steady the animal and frowned at me. 'I found it.'

'Where?'

He gestured to the stable block. 'In one of the stalls, earlier today. The mistress sometimes throws out old things that can't be mended to use for the horses. Why?' Then his face fell. 'Oh God, does it belong to one of the guests?'

'I think so,' I said, trying to keep calm. 'Best if you let me return it.'

'They must have dropped it. I just assumed – oh well, I'm done with it anyway. Rough old thing – can't think why they'd want it back. Come on, girl, let's get you fed.' He slapped the horse's neck and led it away, while I folded the shawl into a small square and considered what to do.

I was certain it was Sukie's. It suggested that my instinct had been correct; the girl had come here seeking Magda's help. Was she still here? As well as the guest rooms there were all the outbuildings, attics and storerooms: any number of places

251

to hide a child, with or without her consent. I glanced over my shoulder and saw Jan Boodt watching me from the window of the tap-room. I tucked the shawl into my belt and hurried out through the gate, hoping he hadn't seen.

Why had he made that insinuating comment about Sukie's disappearance? Did he know something, or was he merely toying with me, wanting me to think he did? If Magda had hidden the girl and the elixir without Jan's knowledge, I could ruin everything by blundering in. I believed Magda was sincere when she swore she wouldn't let anyone harm Sukie, but since she clearly couldn't even protect herself from Jan's fists, I wasn't sure how much that assurance was worth.

I needed to speak to Magda, but for now there was no way to do so privately. I would have to keep to my original plan of asking Besler to search the inn later; it was all I could come up with, though midnight was more than twelve hours away. I had to hope Sukie would be safe until then.

As if I had summoned him by my thoughts, I emerged into the square and immediately collided with Besler on the corner. He was flushed and panting; apparently he had run all the way from the river. I grabbed him by the shoulders, turned him around and marched him smartly away from the tavern before he could even muster the breath to speak.

'What's going on?' he asked, when we had turned a corner and he could manage words.

'You can't go in there for now,' I said. 'I'll explain later. Where's Benjamin?'

'Still looking for David. He said he can't spare the time to eat with us. But that's not why I ran up the stairs.'

'No? Why, then?'

'There's a boatman down at the river says he's got news for you. They think they've found something.'

I stared at him. 'A body?'

'He wouldn't tell me. But he said to hurry.'

'It must be David,' I said. 'Come on.'

NINETEEN

'How did this boatman know to give you a message for me?' I asked as we hurried down the Old Castle Stairs. 'Have you been shouting our business all over town again?'

'No.' Besler looked indignant. 'But he was very chatty. He asked what I was doing in Prague, I said I was here with my master, a famous Italian writer, and he mentioned he'd brought you over earlier. Then he told me one of his fellows had seen something last night that might interest you, and you should come quickly.'

I felt a lurch of relief as we approached the riverbank; if Martin Novak had found a body, surely he would have alerted the authorities. This sounded more like he had turned up a witness, which could be useful, though I had no doubt he intended to squeeze me as much as he could in return for information that might well turn out to be nothing. But when I reached the jetty and saw the look on Novak's face – all the salty good humour drained from it – I revised that view. Whatever he had found, it was not good news. Beside him was a younger man with large ears, dressed in boatman's garb, whose expression was even more stricken; he was twisting a shapeless dark object between his hands and glancing over his shoulder as if he expected to be arrested at any moment.

'What news, then?' I asked, lowering my voice.

Novak leaned in, but before he could speak, the younger man launched into a monologue in Czech, gesticulating frantically in the direction of the Stone Bridge. Though I couldn't understand his words, it was clear from his tone that he was on the defensive. I saw Besler's eyes widen in response. Novak held his hand up for silence and eventually the young man subsided and dropped his gaze to his boots.

'This *idiot*,' Novak said with emphasis, 'was supposed to be working the river last night. But he thought it was a good idea to tie up his boat and nip off into the trees for half an hour.' The young man attempted to speak; Novak stopped him with a look. 'As he was coming back to the jetty, he saw two men getting into his boat. He shouted after them, but they set off upriver.' He nodded towards the bridge. 'As they pulled away, the one who wasn't rowing tried to stand up in the boat and was pointing back this way, like he was protesting. Lude here thinks it was your friend, the Jew.'

'David,' I said.

'Him. The one who's missing. He's taken him over at night before, right, Lude?' He spoke rapidly to the young man and Lude nodded eagerly, though he still looked terrified.

'So – did he follow them?'

'He ran along the bank as far as he could – they weren't going too fast because it's against the current, though he says the man rowing was strong. But there's a point before the bridge where the tow path runs behind houses, and he lost sight of them there.'

'He didn't recognise the rower?'

'No. Lude says he had a cloak and a scarf around his face.'

'Of course he did.' I did not even have the energy to curse at this. 'So what did Lude do?'

'Crossed on to the bridge to see if there was any sign of them, but it was too dark. All he could see were a few bobbing lanterns on the water. So he comes back here to the jetty and waits like a turnip, praying to St Anthony of Padua, and after about an hour, miracle of miracles, what should come drifting

254

back down, no one in it, but Lude's boat? All in one piece, except a few scratches where it had struck the bank. Both oars laid neatly inside.'

'And it was completely empty?'

'Not completely.' Novak exchanged a few words with Lude and the boy held out to me the object he'd been wringing between his hands. I recognised it immediately: David's rabbit fur hat, the one he had been wearing the night before.

'Only this in the boat?' I asked. Lude glanced at Novak and the older man grimaced.

'That and some blood.'

'*Madonna*.' I had tried to stay hopeful for David, but deep down I had feared the worst. Poor Sarah. 'How much blood? A lot? A little? Spattered all over, or pooled in one spot?'

Novak relayed this and Lude held up his thumb and fore-finger an inch apart.

'One small stain in the bottom of the boat,' Besler translated.

Then perhaps the wound was not significant, I thought; there might still be a chance of finding him. Although if this was the same person who had killed Ziggi Bartos, he was clever enough to avoid covering himself in his victim's gore. A man with experience of killing, Hajek had said. Or of anatomy. A soldier or a doctor.

'Can I see the blood?' I asked.

Lude shook his head vehemently.

'He's washed the boat out,' Novak said.

'Why?'

'He didn't want to be blamed, of course.'

'And did he report it? The theft of the boat, what he saw?'

The two men exchanged a glance and Novak sighed. 'No, he didn't. Because he's a fucking idiot, that's why, before you ask. He's married to my wife's niece, who's waiting for him at home, seven months pregnant, and instead of earning money to provide for his first child, he takes a half-hour off to tup a cheap whore in the bushes, and that's how he came to leave his boat unattended where anyone could steal it, and he doesn't want any of that coming out, you can see why. His wife's got two brothers who would knock his teeth through the back of his idiot head if they knew.' He glared at Lude, who looked as if he might cry.

'So no one knows except you two?' I turned and squinted upriver, where the outline of the Stone Bridge was just visible through the drizzle. 'What's up there? Why would you go that way if you wanted to dump a body?'

Novak shrugged. 'There's the islands, I suppose.'

Lude muttered something and crossed himself.

'What's that?'

'He said "Devil's Channel",' Besler explained.

'It's a canal that runs round the back of Kampa Island, by the old watermills,' Novak said. 'It's all overgrown – hard to get a boat through.'

'Take us there,' I said.

'You've got to be joking.'

'Take us now, unless you want me to go back to the castle and inform the authorities that your nephew or whatever he is failed to report the abduction of an important witness in a murder enquiry.'

I must have sounded more convincingly authoritative than I felt, because Novak, with much tutting and swearing under his breath, nodded us towards his boat and didn't even demand extra money.

He had to work hard to haul against the current. I observed the tendons standing out on his forearms and reasoned that whoever had taken David in the boat must have been strong and fit, just like whoever slung Bartos over the bridge. Was it the same man? David could not have recognised the boat thief, or suspected any danger from him, or he would never have embarked, just as Bartos had not anticipated the killing blow from his attacker. Gusts of rain blew into my face; as the Stone Bridge loomed ahead, I tried to keep my thoughts steady and piece it together. David had been meeting someone regularly in the yard of the Winged Horse to sell information about the

Jewish community; I didn't know what, but I sensed that Esther had an idea. Was it connected with Rabbi Loew's visits to the castle? Whatever the reason, last night David had tried to end the arrangement. The only person, other than me, who knew of his movements was the man in the cloak, the one who had paid him in the yard. He would have had time, while David and I spoke, to make his way down to the river and wait, knowing David was on his way home, though it would have been an extraordinary piece of luck on his part to time it with the half-hour window when Lude abandoned his boat. Did the man in the cloak want to silence David because he was afraid David would reveal their dealings? Surely David was the one who had more to lose from doing that.

There was an alternative explanation. Benjamin Katz knew that David was betraying their community. He may even have known the specific secrets David had been selling, given that he had made straight for David's house and gone through his papers. And why, I wondered, had Benjamin felt the sudden need to remove evidence of David's activities last night, of all nights, just when David had decided to end the association? Had he feared David was about to be exposed? Or did he know David wouldn't be coming home last night? If so, it could only mean one of two things. Either Benjamin had followed David, witnessed the man in the cloak take him upstream and assumed the worst, so raced back to make sure nothing incriminating could be found at David's house (but if he'd thought David was in danger, surely he would have tried to help, or at least raised the alarm?). Or else it meant that Benjamin *was* the man in the cloak.

I was so entangled in weighing the likelihood and potential ramifications of all these possibilities, particularly the last one, that I hadn't realised Besler was speaking to me until he shook my arm.

'What?'

'I said – if his body was dumped in the water, why has he not drifted back downriver like the boat did?'

'Might have weighted him down with something,' Novak said with a sniff. 'If that's the case, it'll take a couple of days for him to bob to the surface. You have to wait till the corpse bloats up and fills with gases. We see it a lot,' he added, catching Besler's look of horror. 'Accidents, murders, jumpers. You'd be surprised how many bodies we fish out in a year. Mate of mine found one a couple of days ago, washed up by the saltpetre works. Young lad. Sad business – no one cared, because it was the same day they found that alchemist hanging off the bridge and all anyone could talk of was Golems. No drama in a drowned corpse, they're two a penny.'

'Really? The same day?' That seemed like a remarkable coincidence. I wondered that no one had mentioned it. 'Who was he? Was there an investigation?'

Novak gave a dry laugh. 'For a lad with no family, who catches stray dogs for a living? They wouldn't waste their time. They reckoned he lost his footing and slipped into the water. It happens. Too many people don't know how to swim.' He shook his head. 'Poor bastard. Couldn't have been more than sixteen. He'll be in a pauper's grave now, I suppose.'

'Stray dogs?' Something about this story was pricking at my instincts, though I couldn't think why. Hajek had mentioned using dogs for experiments. 'At the castle?'

'That's right. Who knows what they do with them, up there. But the lad who drowned – I don't even know his name, God rest him – he worked up there. 'Course, he was a bit slow. Didn't speak much. I guess the dogs understood him, though. Here we are then – Devil's Channel.'

He jammed his oar into the water and the boat lurched to the right, into a small opening in the bank where high walls on either side cut out the little light from the sky. I put aside thoughts of the drowned dog-catcher as we entered a narrow canal that passed under the arches of the Stone Bridge and curved around in a semicircle. Here the water was unmoving; immediately an eerie silence fell, the rhythmic splashing of Novak's oars the only sound.

'The Knights Templar built this, so they say,' he informed us. 'To move goods in and out from the old watermills further up. And for other secret dealings, according to the legends, hence the name. They owned all the land and the properties on both sides – this is going back a couple of hundred years. When the new mills were built across the river, this fell out of use, as you see. No one comes here now – least, not for any good purpose.'

I looked around as we progressed. I had the sense that he was talking to dispel the quiet; despite his bluster, Novak was clearly uneasy. I suspected he was only obliging me out of a sense of guilt on Lude's behalf. I could see why he disliked the place. It smelled of stagnant water and rotting vegetation; an oily scum floated on the surface, broken only by unidentifiable refuse poking through here and there. The buildings on both sides had a neglected air; streaks of green slime covered the walls and weeds grew through cracks in the brickwork.

'How deep is the water?' I asked.

He shrugged. 'Ten, twelve feet, maybe. Enough for a body to sink, anyway.'

I instructed Besler to watch the water on his side for any unusual object; I did the same on mine, though I was rapidly losing faith that we would find any trace of David. As we progressed, the walls on the left gave way to overhanging trees, their branches reaching tangled and untended over the channel, until we came to a place where a tree had fallen across at an angle, tipped sideways by storms or subsidence, and it became impossible to take the boat any further.

'That's as far as I go,' Novak said, lifting the blades out of the water. I could see he was impatient to turn around and be gone. 'If you want to climb up on to the bank here, you could walk along a bit further, you might see down into the channel through the trees on the other side, but I doubt you'll find anything. If your mate's here, he's at the bottom.'

I stood precariously in the prow and peered into the thicket ahead as the small craft tipped with every movement. The trees

259

and high walls blocked the light so much that in the depths of the channel it felt more like dusk than midday. Even so, I could clearly see a trail where the tips of branches had been recently snapped and a piece of dark cloth fluttered from a broken twig; someone had forced their way through beneath the tilted trunk.

'Good luck to them, I'm not risking my boat,' Novak said, when I pointed this out. 'You want to get past this, you'll have to walk or swim.'

I hesitated for a moment, before grabbing on to one of the branches and hauling myself on to the bank. I scrambled up and pushed through the tangle of exposed roots until I could see clear to the channel on the other side of the obstruction. Here I found one of the abandoned mills Novak had mentioned, its great wheel motionless. Coots had built their scrappy nests between the broken slats, but there was no sign even of birdlife now; the only movement came from needles of rain stippling the dark surface of the water. I sighed; this was fruitless. I moved to go back and quickly turned again, my eye caught by something opposite. A ledge ran along by the mill wheel, and a few feet to the right there was a small door set into the wall for loading and unloading. In this alcove, on the ledge just above the waterline, I could see what appeared to be a heap of rags or sacks. I slid down the bank to the edge of the channel for a better view, and in the low light I thought I could make out a pale starfish shape amid the jumble of dark sacking. A sudden movement made me start, but it was only a rat, scurrying along the ledge to sniff with interest at the object. It was then that I realised the white shape was a hand.

With only the briefest hesitation, I pulled off my doublet and boots and jumped into the freezing water, gasping and spitting as I resurfaced with weed clinging to my face. The channel was no more than twenty feet wide and I crossed it in a few strokes, trying not to swallow the water or think about what my legs were brushing against beneath the surface. The rat vanished into a crack in the door as I levered myself up on the stone ledge beside the body and drew back the wet cloth.

It was David. His eyes were closed, his face crusted with dried blood. There was just enough space in the alcove to roll him on to his back and part the cloak wrapping him to see a dark sticky mass covering the lower half of his jacket, though I could not make out the exact site of the wound that had killed him. 'Ah, God, I'm sorry,' I whispered, as I tried to work out how best to move his body back to the boat; in some indefinable way, I felt that I should have been able to prevent this. If I could swim with him across the channel, Novak could help me carry him around the obstruction. I was mustering the strength to attempt this when I realised something strange; I could feel warmth against my fingers where I had touched his clothes. I looked down to see a trickle of fresh blood on his stomach, as if—

Dio mio – was he still *alive*? Corpses didn't bleed, except in legends. I ripped open his doublet and saw that moving him had reopened the wound. I tore off my wet shirt and pressed it against the place where fresh blood bubbled up; at the pressure, the ghost of a groan escaped his lips. I tried to wipe the mess from his face with a corner of his cloak. His skin was freezing and grey-green beneath the gore.

'David? Stay with me, I'm going to get you to safety.' I had no idea if he was conscious, but I kept talking to him while I manoeuvred my hands under his armpits. As I lifted his head, I thought I heard a sound; I leaned my ear to his mouth and caught the laboured rattle of a breath.

'David?'

His eyelids flickered and opened a fraction, though I doubted he could focus or had any idea who I was. Another rattling sound came from deep in his throat; I felt his fingers flutter against my sleeve and realised he was trying to speak.

'Tell me,' I said, and this time I heard the word clearly: '*Esther.*'

'What about her?'

261

'She—' His breathing sounded as if fluid was trapped in his chest. 'The book of—'

'Which book? A book of Esther's?'

'*Esther*,' he repeated, more urgently, grasping at my wrist – 'my doing—'

With that, he seemed to collapse in on himself, as if the effort of dredging up those words had taken his last reserves. I realised I didn't have much time. The wound appeared to be low down in his stomach; evidently it had missed vital organs, or he would have been dead long before, but I had no way of knowing if he was bleeding internally or if there was any chance of saving him. I could see that trying to heave him up the opposite bank would be impossible, while the shock of cold water might staunch the flow of blood. I tied my shirt around his waist and eased him into the canal, holding him face up with his head above the murky water while I swam behind him, kicking hard to keep us both afloat as I struggled through the branches of the fallen tree, calling out to Novak and Besler. It was slow progress and several times I feared he would slip from my grasp or that we would both be submerged, but somehow by sheer force of will I persisted, until I felt Novak's strong hands on my arms and David and I were both landed inelegantly like a pair of fish in the bottom of the boat. The boatman laid David out in the prow and covered him with his cloak, while Besler threw his coat around my shoulders; I was shivering so violently I feared I would bite my tongue in half.

'Jesus,' Novak said, starting back from the injured man. 'What's that on his head?'

I leaned around him to look and immediately understood what he meant. The water had washed the dried blood from David's face. I had assumed it had come from a head injury where he had been hit to knock him out, but I now saw that the source was quite different. Carved into his forehead was a sign. I glanced up at Besler, who had turned pale at the sight. He recognised it, even if the boatman did not.

'That's the alchemical symbol for Death,' I said.

TWENTY

Everything happened in blurred fragments after that. Novak rowed us back to the Jewish Town, where Besler ran on ahead to Rabbi Loew's house to fetch help, while Novak and I lifted the wounded man and tried to carry him between us, though I was so numb with cold by that time that it was painful to walk and I could barely feel my hands; I was relieved when Benjamin appeared with another man to take my share of the load. The last I saw of David was his head lolling backwards, eyes closed, that ominous mark on his forehead livid red against the grey skin. There had been no repetition of his attempt to speak; I might have believed him dead already, were it not for the slow oozing of warm blood from his stomach.

I found myself in Rabbi Loew's parlour, dressed in unfamiliar dry clothes loaned by one of the brothers-in-law, with a woollen blanket wrapped around my shoulders and a cup of hot wine clasped between my hands. I had sent Besler back to the Old Town to fetch Hajek – I thought the doctor ought to see the body – and now I shivered on the settle by the fire, conscious that the dank smell of the Devil's Channel still clung to my skin, as the feeling returned painfully to my limbs. Esther paced behind me; her face, when I glimpsed it, was a tight mask of anxiety. Now and again she paused as if she were about to speak, but thought better of it and resumed her agitated movement. I hardly knew what to say to her; I was struggling to make sense of David's last words. Was he telling me that Esther was involved? That he had been killed by her, or because of her? Or because of a book? How was it *his doing*? I thought of that dagger in her father's desk drawer, and hoped she might leave me alone long enough for me to see if it was still there.

'Will he live?' she blurted suddenly, coming to a halt above me. I looked up and met her angry gaze.

'I don't know. Perhaps if he has good medical attention . . .' It was unlikely, but I guessed she already knew that.

'Benjamin is with him,' she murmured. I didn't reply; I still could not entirely discount the possibility that Benjamin knew exactly what had happened to his cousin. Had he ransacked the shop in search of the book David mentioned?

'Was he lying there all night?' she asked. 'I can't bear to think of it. How could he have survived?'

'I didn't have a chance to examine him properly, but he appears to have been stabbed in the stomach,' I said. 'If the knife perforated the bowel, he would be bleeding internally but not enough to kill him right away. Not like a blow to the heart or lungs.' Not, in fact, like the blow that killed Ziggi Bartos. Which meant what? It could not be the same killer? Or that the killer, with his apparent knowledge of anatomy, had deliberately chosen to inflict a cruel and lingering death on David? That argued against Benjamin, who couldn't even bring himself to deface his cousin's books. But if it was not the same killer, it was certainly someone wanting to make David's murder appear connected with that of Bartos. This was why I had sent Besler for Hajek; he would be able to tell if the same kind of curved dagger had been used – assuming the family allowed him to examine the body.

'That awful mark on his head,' Esther said, as if she had been following my thoughts. 'He was meant to be found, don't you think? Otherwise, why maim him like that? Unless it was a kind of punishment.'

'I think you're right,' I said, privately feeling it was a relief that David had not suffered worse mutilations, the way Bartos had. 'If he was stabbed in the boat, the killer could have thrown him overboard and he would have drowned. Instead, he was left on an exposed ledge where he could easily be seen as soon as people started looking.'

'Did they mean to leave him alive?' she asked quietly.

I shook my head. 'I couldn't say. It might simply have been that the attacker didn't know what he was doing.' Or wanted it to look that way.

'So.' She came to a halt by the fireplace and stared into the flames, the light catching the curve of her cheek as she frowned, ordering her thoughts. 'We have an alchemist murdered, with the Hebrew word for Death cut into his face. And now, the attempted murder of a Jew, marked with the alchemists' sign for Death in the same way. So how are we supposed to read it? Was David attacked as *revenge*? Was this a message to us from the alchemists?' She was largely speaking to herself, so I didn't interrupt. 'But that makes no sense – the alchemists are not our enemies. If anything, they are better disposed to us than the good Christian citizens of Prague – we share the same approbation from society. Then why would someone wish to make it seem that we are attacking each other?'

'Esther,' I said softly. She turned, startled out of her speculation, as if she had forgotten I was there. 'This morning, before we were interrupted, you almost shared with me what you knew about David's betrayal. Does it have something to do with your father's secret visits to the Emperor?'

She stared at me, astonished. 'How did you—?'

'Not important. But they were not as secret as you imagined. My guess is that David chose to pass on that information to someone at court, someone he believed might be in a position to intervene – to have a quiet word with the Emperor before it became common knowledge that he was fraternising with the rabbi and a more formal denunciation was required, with all the potential ramifications for your community. Am I right?'

She continued to watch me, her face impassive.

'But then Ziggi Bartos was murdered,' I persisted, 'and for some reason – perhaps because the manner of his death was so obviously intended to stir fear of the Jews – that alarmed David enough to end his arrangement. An hour or so later, someone tried to kill him. It's reasonable to suppose they wanted to silence him about the nature of that arrangement. Don't you want them caught?' When she still didn't speak, I shrugged. 'Well, guard your secrets if you must. But it's David's wife and children who are paying the price for them.'

It was unnecessarily cruel, but effective; she collapsed as if I had kicked her in the back of the knees, slumping on to the settle beside me with her face in her hands. I reached out and took her right hand, turning it palm upwards between mine. Most unexpectedly, she leaned in until her forehead was touching my shoulder.

'It's not your fault,' I said, stroking her palm with my thumb. 'David made his choice – he must have known there was risk involved.'

She shook her head. 'It *is* my fault. You don't understand.'

'You keep saying that. Then help me. Who was paying David? Was it the Catholic faction – San Clemente or Montalcino, or one of their emissaries? Did they fear your father was trying to convert the Emperor? Were you the one who told David about the secret visits to the castle, is that what you mean?'

She mumbled into the wool of the blanket, so that I had to strain to listen. 'None of this would have happened if I had only—'

'If you had what? Esther?'

I squeezed her hand gently; a hot tear fell from her eye and splashed on to our clasped fingers. It seemed to jolt her out of her distress; she jerked her head up, snatched her hand back and stared at me as if I had taken liberties.

'Stop all these questions, I can't bear it,' she cried, rising to her feet and smearing the tears away with her knuckles. 'I should be with Sarah now, not stuck here with you, being interrogated.'

'You're welcome to go,' I said mildly. 'I can wait here – I don't need a nursemaid.'

'My father said not to leave you alone.' She shot me a resentful glare, and I felt a lurch of anxiety; I wondered if Rabbi Loew had realised someone had been through his desk. One thing was certain; in that brief moment of intimacy, I had ascertained that Esther had no blisters or calluses on her hands. She had not rowed a boat upriver at speed the night before; the idea was absurd. But could she have been present when David was abducted and stabbed? Waiting on the bank somewhere? Why had he spoken her name with such urgency? I had not yet told anyone of David's last words to me; I had no idea who I might trust with them.

'We could go together,' I suggested. 'I would be glad to hear news of David's condition. Since I found him,' I added, sensing that she was about to object.

'Very well,' she said with obvious reluctance. 'You had better borrow a coat or you will take a chill again. My father has a spare. Wait here.'

I watched her through the open door of the parlour as she crossed the hall to her father's study, where she took a key from a pouch at her girdle and fitted it to the lock. It appeared I was right; Loew knew his sanctuary had been breached, and he must have been able to guess at the intruder. What secrets did he want to protect?

Bundled into the rabbi's heavy coat, my teeth still chattering, I followed Esther to the hospital beside the cemetery. A small crowd had gathered outside and I recognised some of the faces from David's shop that morning, though now they were blank with shock and grief. People held one another's arms or clasped hands; no one spoke, and they parted wordlessly as Esther led me through to the door. It was an impressive two-storey building, recently constructed and smelling of new stone. We waited in an entrance hall and after a moment the inner door was opened by Rabbi Loew in his shirtsleeves, all the brightness drained from his face. He ushered us into the ward. We passed a line of beds, their occupants following us warily with their eyes as we walked to the end and stopped in front of another door.

Esther touched her father's arm. 'Is he—?'

'He's breathing, barely.' The rabbi nodded to the closed door. 'Benjamin is doing all he can, but—' He spread his hands wide in a gesture of helplessness.

'Has he spoken at all?' I asked.

He gave me a curious look. 'No. He's not conscious. Why do you ask – did he speak to you?'

'He tried, I think. But I could not make out the words.'

I did not miss the glance he exchanged with Esther. 'Well, we are grateful to you, Dr Bruno. If you had not sought him, he might have been missing for days. At least his family have had the chance to say goodbye.'

'Where is Sarah?' Esther asked.

'Your sisters took her home. Her distress was so extreme – understandably – that it was impeding Benjamin's efforts. He gave them a draught to calm her. You should go to her, my dear – they will want help with the children.'

Esther looked mutinous for a moment, then nodded, giving me a last look before she left, though I could not work out what she meant to convey.

Loew laid a hand on my shoulder. 'You should go too, my friend. Get some rest. I'm sure Dr Hajek will take good care of you.'

'Hajek is on his way here,' I said. 'I thought he should see David.'

He gave me a sharp look. 'That was not your decision. This has nothing to do with him.'

'You know that's not true, Rabbi. Look at the manner of the attack – the parallels with the murder of Bartos are obvious.'

'This was a crime against our community, meant as revenge for our supposed part in the alchemist's death.'

I could not contain my incredulity. 'Is that really what you're telling yourself? That it was a random attack by some passer-by with a grudge against the Jews, that it could have happened to any Jew who found himself in the wrong place?' I shook my head. 'You don't believe that and neither do I. This occurred as a direct result of your secret meetings with the Emperor and David's attempts to stop them.'

The rabbi closed his eyes slowly and lowered his head. 'How did you know about those meetings?'

'Doesn't matter. David talked to someone about your visits because he didn't approve of them.'

'That's true, he didn't. He tried to talk me out of it. I told him I knew what I was doing. And now here we are – five children about to lose a father through my stubbornness. I do not need you to remonstrate with me, Dr Bruno. I already have God to answer to.' He dragged his hands over his beard.

'So what *were* you doing at the castle all those nights? What did Rudolf want from you?'

He blinked. 'I thought you knew?'

'Not everything. But it would help if you filled in the gaps.'

Loew looked at me for a long moment, then let out a heavy sigh. 'He is, as you must know by now, a man with an insatiable appetite for the forbidden. And with the power to make our lives more comfortable, or a great deal more difficult. So if he demands of me something that is within my power to give, I would be a fool to refuse.'

I frowned, trying to fathom this cryptic response. 'Do you mean the Cabala? He asked you to teach him?' I wondered if the book David had tried to speak of was a cabalistic work. A book belonging to Esther? I had no idea if women studied the Cabala, but if any did, it would be her.

'That was among the subjects we discussed, yes.'

'And David thought you should not be teaching a Gentile, even if he is a sovereign? Or was he afraid you would be accused of Judaising and those around you would suffer the consequences?'

Loew hesitated. 'More the latter, I think. But I was trapped, you see. If I had refused to do what the Emperor asked of me, he could have chosen to punish my community out of pure pique. And if I agreed, there was always the chance that at some point I would be accused of trying to convert him, he would find himself under combined pressure from Rome and Spain to renounce us publicly, and the community would be sanctioned as a result anyway. It's a card the Emperor always has up his sleeve – an easy way to buy the Pope's approval if he faces criticism over his faith. Just punish the Jews to prove his loyalty. Do you know what it is to live like that, Dr Bruno? To know that you and your family, your friends, your neighbours, could be uprooted and banished at the stroke of a pen? To always keep a bag by the door, in case you need to leave in a hurry?'

I shook my head. The part about the bag I understood; I knew all too well what it was to be rootless, for my home to depend on the whims of princes, but not how it felt to carry the weight of an entire community's security on my shoulders.

'It was a gamble I could not expect to win, in the long run,' he continued. 'I thought the best course was to humour Rudolf, keep the visits secret and hope his interest would fade in time. He is a man whose passions are notoriously intense and short-lived.'

'But David disagreed with that course,' I said. 'He wanted to act, so he took the secret to someone he thought could intervene. Someone sufficiently interested to pay him for information about your midnight visits. Who?'

Loew held out his hands, palms up. 'I don't know. I only learned of David's betrayal last night.'

'But if you had to hazard a guess?'

He let out a weary breath and placed both hands on my shoulders, fixing me with a serious look. 'Dr Bruno. A dear friend lies dying in there – for now, that must be my priority.'

'And I want to find the person who did this to him,' I said. 'Don't you?'

'Well, of course. But—' He stopped, his brow creased with doubt, and I understood his dilemma.

'But you don't want your visits to the castle coming to light,' I said.

'Precisely. It will have to be reported to the authorities as he was found in the Lesser Town, but I can't see that a clumsy investigation would do any good. Let them think it a crime of hate, as I said, or a robbery. We have governance over our own affairs here – no need to have the whole of Prague whispering about alchemical signs or Golems, nor for David's family to bear any shame over his informing.'

'Then tell me what else you know,' I pleaded. 'I am already looking into the alchemist's murder – it's clear they're connected. We can find this killer if we pool our knowledge, I'm sure of it.'

The look he gave me was almost pitying. 'And if he turns out to be someone powerful, do you think he will be held to account? For the murder of a Jew and an alchemist?'

'So you *do* know something.'

'I know Prague, Bruno, as you do not.' He shook me gently by the shoulders: a paternal gesture. 'Go home. Have a hot bath.'

Before I could protest, the door to the back room opened and Benjamin appeared, wiping his hands on a cloth. His face was leached of all colour and his eyes raw.

'*Rav*, I think you had better send for Sarah,' he said quietly.

Loew nodded, understanding. 'I will go myself. Goodbye, Dr Bruno,' he said with a nod to me, in a tone that was a clear reiteration of his instruction to leave.

After the door had closed behind him, Benjamin raised his head as if noticing me for the first time.

'We owe you our thanks for finding him,' he said, his voice flat, as if he were too weary for more emotion. 'How did you know where to look?'

'He was seen last night in a boat rowing upriver, with a man in a cloak. The boatmen suggested the channel.'

If Benjamin knew anything about the second man, he gave no sign of it.

271

'May I assist you?' I offered. 'I have some medical knowledge.'

He cast an eye over me. 'Not in the rabbi's best coat you can't. Besides,' he added, as I laid the coat on a chair and pushed up my sleeves, 'there's nothing to assist. All I can do now is make him comfortable.'

I held the door open and followed him into the back room. It was comfortably warm here; a fire was stoked in the hearth with a pan of water simmering over it on a tripod. Benjamin crossed to the fireplace and, using the cloth to cover the handle, lifted the pot of hot water from its stand.

Two windows overlooked the trees that fringed the grave-yard. Against the rear wall, David lay unmoving on a narrow bed, eyes closed, his skin covered with a sheen of feverish sweat, only his chest rising and falling with shallow breaths. Benjamin had removed his wet clothes and a blanket covered him from the waist down. A poultice had been laid over the site of the wound on his abdomen; I moved to examine it.

'Wash your hands before you touch him,' Benjamin snapped, pouring hot water into a basin. I did as I was told, then lifted the dressing. The cut beneath was no more than an inch and a half across, still weeping blood and fluids, and giving off a faecal odour. I pressed the poultice back; it smelled of astrin-gent herbs.

'I've cleaned it, but the wound is too deep to suture,' Benjamin said, coming to stand at my side, his hands resting on the bed frame. I glanced down and noticed that his knuckles were criss-crossed with tiny cuts and his right thumb was bandaged.

'What manner of weapon made it, would you say?'

He glanced at me. 'A dagger, I'd guess.'

'What kind?'

'I couldn't tell you, I'm no expert. Small, though. A narrow blade, four inches long, perhaps. I could close the entry wound, but the point has punctured the bowel, there's no remedy. I've given him a tincture of dwale to dull the pain.'

'Did he speak to you?'

'I think he is far beyond speech now.'

He is if you've given him dwale, I thought, and wondered if Benjamin had decided it was in his interest for David not to wake.

'What language did David usually speak?' I asked.

'He knew several. Yiddish, Hebrew, of course. But also German, Czech, Latin and Greek. A little French and Italian, enough to read the books that passed through his shop. Why do you ask?' Before I could answer, I saw the light of under-standing reach his eyes. 'Did he say something to you when you found him?'

'He tried to speak. I couldn't understand the words. I wondered which language would come most naturally to him in a half-conscious state.'

'He spoke Yiddish among his family and friends,' Benjamin said. 'That would have been his instinctive tongue, I imagine. You really didn't understand a word?' There was apprehension in his voice.

I shook my head. 'Talking of books,' I said, 'did you find the one you were looking for last night, in David's shop?'

There was a crash as the enamel bowl in his hands fell to the floor; he swore under his breath as he knelt to mop up the spilled water. 'What book?' he said, not looking at me.

'Come on, Benjamin, I know it was you. I can see your hands. You left shreds of your scarf where you broke the window. It didn't even look like a convincing break-in. You did it as cover for removing something you feared would incriminate David – am I right? Something that would link him to the person he'd been selling information to.'

He raised his eyes and I saw in his expression that I had hit the mark. I decided to push my advantage.

'A book, was it? A book of Esther's?'

He stood, brushing himself down, and frowned, guilt briefly overtaken by confusion. 'What on earth are you talking about?'

Evidently he was not ready to acknowledge all the details, so I tried a different tack. 'How did you know that David was informing? Did you follow him?'

273

He let out a tense breath and set the bowl down on a bench. 'Yes. About a fortnight ago, perhaps. He was angry about—' He stopped, as if fearing to say too much.

'About the Maharal making secret visits to the Emperor,' I finished for him. Novak had mentioned a young man accompanying the rabbi at times; I supposed it had been Benjamin.

He stared at me in astonishment. 'You *know*?'

'That he was teaching Rudolf the Cabala? I guessed.'

'The—?' I saw that same twitch of puzzlement cross his face, before he nodded. 'Cabala, yes. So. David wanted to confront the rabbi about it. He felt the potential consequences for our community when the visits and their purpose were discovered by Rudolf's advisers, as they inevitably would be, were not worth the risk. We argued – I told him it was not his place to contradict the Maharal's judgement. David was furious. He said that if the Maharal was so blind to our interests, he would take matters into his own hands.' He paused to look at the man on the bed. 'This worried me, so I kept a close watch on him. When I saw him going over the river at night, I followed.'

'Then – you saw who he was meeting?'

'No. I know they met in the yard of the Winged Horse, but I couldn't get close enough without revealing myself. The other man kept his face covered.' He turned back to David and fussed with the blanket, drawing it up to cover him, checking his temperature. He was not telling the whole truth.

'But you must have some idea of David's contacts – you went through his shop.'

'I don't know,' he said curtly. 'And now, as you see, there's nothing more you can do here—'

'Did you follow David to the tavern last night?'

'No.' He began arranging the cleaned instruments on a shelf. 'But I guessed where he was – I went to the shop late to see him, about eleven, and Sarah said he had gone out to deliver some books. So I decided to wait for him to come back – I meant to tell him I knew what he was doing, that he had to stop. Three hours I must have waited, in the street by the jetty so that I could intercept him on his return, but he didn't come. So I went to his house again.'

'You weren't worried, after three hours?'

'Not at first. I was too angry with him for breaking a confidence – I felt his actions could only make things worse.'

'*Your* confidence?'

He hesitated. 'Yes. I was the one who told him about the rabbi's visits, you see. That's why I didn't want him confronting Rabbi Loew – because the rabbi would know it came from me, and he had sworn me to secrecy. I meant to wait for David at the shop – I know where he keeps the spare key. Sarah and the children were in bed, so there was less fear of a scene in front of them. And I thought I could take advantage of his absence to search for anything that might show who he had been talking to, and therefore what danger that might pose to the Maharal. David was a meticulous keeper of records – if he had received money, he would have noted it somewhere, and that might give me an idea.'

I highly doubted that, however scrupulous an accountant, David would have written 'received for selling secrets' and the name of his contact in one of his ledgers. I suspected Benjamin was trying to give me a false scent.

'I was searching through his papers,' he continued, 'when Sarah called out from upstairs – "David, is that you?" I didn't want her to come down and catch me, it would have required too much explanation. I panicked and punched a hole through the window. She screamed, but I knew she would stay up there with the children if she thought it was an attack. So I broke some more panes, scattered a few books on the floor and ran.' He moved back to the bed and looked down at his cousin. 'It wasn't until early this morning that I learned David hadn't come home at all. That was when I feared some harm had come to him, and went to tell the rabbi what I knew.'

'And did you find what you were looking for in David's accounts?' I asked. 'Anything that might suggest the identity of his attacker?'

'No,' he said, but I caught the breath of a hesitation. 'If I knew that I would not keep it to myself, I swear.'

But he did know more than he was willing to tell me, I was certain of it. I was on the verge of asking him again about David's mention of a book, and why he might have said Esther's name, but at that moment David's breathing stuttered and quickened. Benjamin rushed to prop up his head with one hand, feeling for his pulse with the other, as a woman's cry split the air from the next room and the door crashed open to admit David's wife, leaning heavily on Rabbi Loew. I moved away from the dying man's bedside, certain now that the words I had heard from his lips were the last he would ever speak, and that it was up to me to decipher his meaning.

TWENTY-ONE

'What now?' Besler asked.

'Now,' I said, stretching out a hand, 'I need you to pass me that cloth. And for the love of God, go and look out of the window or something, Besler – I feel like an exhibit in a travelling show.'

He handed me a clean linen and obediently loped across to survey the yard with his back to me; from the hunch of his shoulders and the way he hung his head, I could tell he was as affected as I was by David's death. I stood up in the tub as water streamed off me and pooled on the flagstones. After a vigorous rub of my hair, I wrapped the cloth around my waist and reached for a fresh shirt.

Hajek had ordered us back to the House of the Green Mound as soon as he arrived in the Jewish Town; there had been a stand-off between him and Rabbi Loew about his right to examine David, and I had been only too ready to retreat, unwilling to impose on their grief any longer. There was no sign of Greta at Hajek's house, so I had put water on to heat and filled a tub in the laundry room behind the kitchen, where I washed the filth of the Devil's Channel off my skin while Besler sat disconcertingly close on a stool and peppered me with questions until he was up to date with everything I had learned that morning.

'But I am still no clearer,' he said now, gazing out at the rain with his arms folded as I pulled on clean hose and breeches. 'Has Greta been dismissed?'

'I don't know.' I cast around for my boots, grateful that Besler had retrieved them and my doublet from the riverbank while Novak and I had settled David in the boat. 'Let's concentrate on what we do know.'

'Can we eat something while we do?'

I conceded that for once he was right; we had not eaten since breaking our fast that morning, so we moved through to the kitchen, where I stoked the fire and Besler rummaged in the cold store for bread and cheese. The place felt oddly desolate without Greta's grudging but homely presence.

'Well, then,' I said, when we were seated at the table. 'Here is what we know so far.'

'Should I take notes?' He jumped up, poised to run for a quill and ink.

'No. Better not to have any record of our hypotheses. Keep the notes in your head – that's why you've been studying the art of memory.'

He nodded fervently and took his seat again. I began counting the points on my fingers.

'Ziggi Bartos had been working on some kind of elixir, for which he expected to be well paid. We know he had taken Spanish money – that could have been for publicly slandering John Dee, but it's not far-fetched to suppose that there was Spanish gold behind the promise of reward for the elixir too. At the same time, Greta was somehow persuaded to make a copy of Hajek's keys to the poisons cupboard in the Powder Tower. What's the one bond that would trump her loyalty to her master?'

'Family,' Besler said through a mouthful of bread.

'Exactly. That was Hajek's guess. Jan Boodt is a man with heavy debts who beats his wife. Suppose he is offered money to get hold of those keys. Magda asks her sister – Greta agrees, knowing that Magda will be the one to suffer if she refuses.'

'But then, who paid Boodt for the keys?'

'That's a missing link in our chain. But Erik Moller said

there are two Spaniards who hang around the gaming nights at the Winged Horse, one with a scar. I'm guessing they're the same men who attacked me on our first night looking for letters, in which case we can assume they work for the Catholic faction at court. San Clemente and Montalcino.'

'Who claim to know nothing of Bartos's murder.'

'Yes. Though that could be a bluff, so that they can monitor how close I'm getting to the truth. Let's suppose the Catholics offered Bartos money to make an elixir for the Emperor. *Aurum potabile*, the promise of making the flesh incorruptible. Rudolf would not be able to resist. But the elixir would contain a deadly poison, obtained by Bartos with the copied keys. Heart failure within a day – goodbye Rudolf, long live the Emperor Matthias. The dawn of a new era for conservative religion – that would be worth a great deal to King Philip and the Pope. I wonder how much they offered Bartos? It must have been a princely sum, to run that kind of risk. Unless they had some other hold over him.'

'But he would have to take the potion first, in front of the Emperor, if there was to be any hope of Rudolf drinking it,' Besler pointed out. 'And then he'd be dead, so why would he agree to that? It's not like he had dependants who could use the money after he'd gone.'

'True. That is a major flaw in the theory. Could he have worked out some kind of substitution trick?' I shook my head; we were straying into the realm of fantasy. 'Whatever the eventual plan, someone guessed at it, or else he confided in them.'

'The mysterious midnight visitor,' Besler suggested.

'Possibly. Either way, Bartos believed he had reason to fear betrayal, so he gave the elixir to Sukie Moller for safekeeping.'

'And now she has disappeared.' Besler helped himself to another hunk of cheese. 'He was right to fear, because he was murdered. Do you think it was the Catholics, then? Those Spaniards?'

'It's the most obvious answer. Bartos may have had a fit of conscience or cowardice and decided he wasn't willing to risk his own life. In that instance, his paymasters would have been worried about him talking. Imagine if he'd taken his knowledge of a Catholic poison plot, with all the details, to someone with influence at court?'

'Someone like Hajek,' Besler said, absently pulling his bread apart.

'Why do you say that?'

'Because he oversees the alchemists, and he is close to the Emperor. If I were Bartos and I wanted to speak to someone in authority, I'd go to him first.'

I considered this. 'True, though surely Hajek would have mentioned that? But if the Catholics thought there was even the possibility that Bartos might confess, that's reason enough to get rid of him.'

'Then why make his death so public, and risk people looking into what he'd been up to?'

'Because of the Jews,' I said, the answers falling into place as I spoke. 'If David had taken his knowledge about the rabbi's secret lessons with Rudolf to the Catholics, they might have reasoned they could kill two birds with one stone. Silence Bartos and rouse public feeling against the Jews, as a warning to Rudolf. David understood that – so he tried to bring the arrangement to an end, and they silenced him too.'

We both fell quiet for a moment, remembering that final, desperate scramble to carry the dying man from the river.

Besler leaned against the window ledge, his brow still furrowed.

'But those caskets sent to the Emperor, with the eyes and tongue and the words from Scripture in Bartos's hand – what was the purpose of that?'

'To frighten Rudolf. Anyone who knew of his volatile disposition could calculate that such tricks would pitch him into a state of fear and distress. If the Catholics had lost their opportunity to poison him, they could still do their best to upset the balance of his mind, and argue he was unfit to rule.'

'Then it seems you have solved it, Maestro. The only difficulty is that we don't have any proof.'

'I know.' I pushed my damp hair back from my face. 'That's the frustration. I wish I knew what Benjamin had taken from David's house – that must be evidence of some sort. If we only had a name.' I wondered how feasible it would be to search Benjamin's place without being caught. 'If Hajek concludes that David was also killed with a curved blade, that would suggest the same assassin. San Clemente fought against the Turks as a young man – he'd have the skill to use an Ottoman knife, and probably owns one.'

Besler looked doubtful. 'Would the ambassador carry out a murder with his own hands, when he has hired thugs at his command?'

'It sounds unlikely, but Hajek thinks Bartos did not expect violence from his killer. He was undefended. I don't suppose San Clemente would have any moral qualms.'

'You said Rabbi Loew also has an Ottoman knife,' Besler pointed out after a pregnant pause. 'Suppose he knew about the poison plot. Bartos was changing all that money in the Jewish Town, people must have wondered. The rabbi would have a vested interest in stopping someone who wanted to assassinate Rudolf, a friend to the Jews, and replace him with Matthias, who is not.'

'And what of David?'

'David was informing on him, putting him in danger. That must have angered him.'

I shook my head. 'No. Rabbi Loew is not a killer, I would stake my life on it. But he is hiding something.' I counted off another finger. 'Then there's John Dee. If he had suspected what Bartos was planning, that would make sense of his urgent dispatch to England, and Walsingham's reply telling him to do whatever was necessary to prevent it. It would also explain why the Catholics wanted to discredit John, so that he would not be believed.'

'But you said John could not have killed Bartos – he was not even in Prague at the time.'

'True. Unless his disappearance is an elaborate bluff, and someone in the city is sheltering him. I can't help thinking there is more to his letter than I've understood – the one he wrote to Loew before he disappeared. He said their enemies suspected – I'm sure that referred to the rabbi's secret meetings with the Emperor – and that there was danger to B. Loew thought that was Benjamin, but what has he to do with any of this? Could it be connected to this book he was searching for in David's shop?'

Besler stood and disappeared again into the cold store. 'You're grasping at straws in the wind now. Your first theory is the more plausible – that the Catholics are behind both murders. All you need to do is find a way of proving it.'

'That's all, eh?' I grimaced. 'The Spanish ambassador and the Papal nuncio? Hajek is right – we don't have a hope of incriminating them. Look at the way Bartos's lodgings were cleaned out before his body was even cold. They'll have taken care to cover any trace of their involvement.'

'Then how do we proceed?'

I leaned my elbows on the table and pressed the heels of my hands into my eyes. 'Damned if I know, Besler. The priority is to find Sukie and the elixir, but I don't think there's much we can do about that until tonight.'

'I have been thinking, Maestro,' Besler said. He was leaning in the doorway to the cold store with a seed cake, which he was methodically pulling apart and eating.

'Careful.'

'Yes – about that person who knocked you out in the cathedral crypt.'

'What about them?'

'Well – how did they know the Emperor was on his way to hear Mass in the cathedral?'

'The priest said a messenger was sent from the palace, and the guard came to clear the building. Why?'

'So . . .' He took a bite while he worked out his theory. 'This person just happened to be hanging around the cathedral with a freshly severed dog's tongue at the moment the Emperor decides to hear Mass. That's quite a coincidence.'

'You mean, they must have had advance warning?' I nodded. 'You're right. The priest could have told someone as soon as he got the message.'

'Or someone at the palace knew the Emperor's plans,' he said through cake. 'The messenger should be questioned.'

'I'm sure Hajek has thought of that, but I'll check. How long would it take to secure the cathedral? Half an hour or so, I would guess. Not that long, but long enough, I suppose.'

'To find a dog, chop its tongue out, put it in a box with the verse, hide in the cathedral, push over a statue and slip into the chapel without being seen by the soldiers?' Besler looked unconvinced. 'Still cutting it fine.'

'If they used the underground passage that leads to the crypt, perhaps it could be done.' I pushed my chair back and stood. So much had happened since the attack that the figure in the crypt had been pushed to the back of my mind. 'We should have looked into that – worked out where that passageway leads and who might have a key.' I would have done so if Hajek hadn't insisted on sending me home, I thought. 'Well, there's your answer to what we do next,' I said. 'Find the stable boy, tell him to make the horses ready.'

Besler slipped out to the yard, taking the seed cake with him, presumably in case he got hungry on the ride to the castle. A few moments later his face appeared again around the kitchen door.

'The boy asks if you got the message?'

'What message?'

'He says a man came while we were out with a note for you, Greta took it. Then Hajek came back and started shouting at her, she was crying, and the boy took fright and hid in the stables. When he came out, Greta was gone.'

'Right. Get your riding cloak while I see if I can find this note.' I wondered who would be writing to me at Hajek's house; it was a mark of how mistrustful I had become in Prague that I assumed it could not bring good news. There had been no sign of a note in my room when I fetched my clean clothes.

Could Greta be trusted to pass on a message, or might she merely have forgotten about it in the turmoil of Hajek's accusations about the keys? I wandered into the front parlour and noticed a folded paper on the mantel, above the empty fireplace. The room was chilly; already the house was feeling Greta's absence. The note bore my name on the outside in an elegant hand; I turned it over to find it unsealed. Impatiently, I unfolded it and my heart sank.

Dear Dr Bruno
It was my great pleasure to make your acquaintance yesterday, and I would be honoured if you and your young assistant would do us the honour of dining at the Rozmberk Palace this evening. I keep a Venetian cook, so I hope you will feel at home. If that does not tempt, then perhaps the information I have to share might. Come for supper at seven and we will have music after.
Yours
Xena, Countess von Rozmberk

'*Merda,*' I muttered, folding the paper. I had no great desire to spend the evening indulging a pouting, flirty girl who was frantic for male attention, nor to keep Besler from doing anything that might result in his being called out by her husband, but she certainly knew how to intrigue. What information was she promising? It could be no more than a ruse, but she did appear to have the run of the palace; who knew what a sharp young woman with little to occupy her might observe or overhear? On a second reading, that 'us' was more reassuring – perhaps the count had returned. He was a man whose acquaintance I was interested in making, and he knew John Dee. I had to smile at the idea that a Venetian cook would make me feel at home; she must think the Italian states one great, homogenous mass where we all spoke and ate the same. I couldn't help wondering how much use a Venetian – whose skills were presumably fish-based – might be in a landlocked country. But the prospect of a good meal was tempting, and it would be unwise to give offence to the highest noble family in Bohemia. Besides, it would pass the time until Jan Boodt's gaming session.

'*Merda* what?' Besler asked, from the doorway.

'We're dining with the Count and Countess von Rozmberk this evening.' I pointed a finger at him. 'Best behaviour.'

He rolled his eyes. 'You sound like my father. You don't seem very happy about the invitation,' he added as we headed out to collect the horses.

'I don't know, Besler.' I pulled my cap down over my damp hair. 'I'm finding it harder and harder to believe that anyone in Prague wishes us good.'

His eyes widened. 'You think it's a trap?'

'I think we would be clever to keep our wits about us. Don't drink too much. And no matter how much encouragement she gives, you behave to her as if you were a monk.'

He grinned. 'Some of the stories I have heard about monks, Maestro—'

'Yes, all right, that was a bad example. You respond like someone who does not want to find himself on the wrong end of a duelling sword. Understood?'

'Yes, Maestro.' He lowered his eyes.

'Good. Let's take a look at this crypt first.'

TWENTY-TWO

It was gone three in the afternoon by the time we reached the castle and handed the horses to the care of a groom. The cathedral was sinking into shadow as the daylight faded, but we found it filled with the fluting voices of boy choristers rehearsing with their music master, a sound that pricked me with memories of my youth in the Dominican order. Hearing those pure, clear notes rising to the vaulted roof prompted a moment of melancholy; though I had fought to escape the strictures of religious life, there were times when I felt the loss of its community. Something of this must have shown in my expression, because I caught Besler looking at me with concern and quickly smiled encouragement.

The priest stood at the High Altar preparing for the office of Vespers. He flinched at the sight of me, as if my presence could only herald further disaster. I sympathised.

'Father, I am investigating the terrible threat to His Majesty yesterday and I want to examine the crypt,' I said. 'I will need your key.'

His fingers strayed to his belt. 'Do you have some written authorisation? Only, I am not supposed to open the crypt unless His Majesty requests it.'

'You were not supposed to let anyone within touching distance of the Emperor while he was at prayer either,' I said pointedly. 'I can go back for a letter if you insist, but I can't imagine His Majesty will be pleased to hear that, having allowed his assailant into the chapel, you are now attempting to hinder efforts to catch them.'

The priest blanched, and began working a key loose from the ring.

'Thank you,' I said as he passed it over. 'I will make sure he knows how helpful you've been. We'll need lights too. Tell me about the secret passages.'

'I have never seen them,' he said, fussing over which candles to take from a nearby stand. 'But the foundations of the original rotunda are more than six hundred years old, and the castle has been a fortress since the time of St Wenceslas, so it's hardly surprising that there's a labyrinth of tunnels beneath our feet. People would have built them for escape, I suppose. But to the best of my knowledge, most of them were blocked up long ago. I couldn't tell you how to find them, nor whether they are safe.'

'Well, it appears that one leads to and from the crypt, and someone knows how to access it,' I said, snatching the candle from his hand as I tried to contain my impatience; I wanted directions, not a history lesson. 'You really have no idea where the entrance might be?'

'I assure you, sir,' he stammered, and in his frightened rabbit face I read sincerity; he was so anxious, I was certain he would have blurted out any secrets if he thought it would save him from further blame. 'I have been dean here for four years, and sub-dean before that, and I have not met a cleric who has spoken of a secret entrance, nor have I ever seen such a passage marked on any recent plans.'

'Plans?' I stared at him as if he were an unpromising child who had unexpectedly said something clever.

'Yes – you may have more luck with older drawings, but those are not in the cathedral archive. I only keep a record of the most recent works.'

'Then where are the older plans?'

'In the imperial library, of course.'

Of course. I exchanged a glance with Besler. It seemed my first instinct had been correct: who would have better opportunity to study ancient maps of the castle and its grounds than the librarian? A spot of hot wax dropped on to my hand from the candle; I swore aloud, then immediately apologised to the priest. He gave me a look of forbearance which seemed to imply that he had forgiven me worse. I felt a little bad about slapping him the day before.

'We should go before we waste these candles,' I said.

'Take a tinder, in case the light is snuffed out.' The priest retrieved one from somewhere beneath the altar cloth. 'There are strange draughts in that crypt.'

I thanked him; that sounded promising. Where there was a draught, there was a connection with the outside. I could not now turn up at the library and ask to look at old plans of the cathedral without arousing Ottavio Strada's suspicions; we would have to discover the tunnel for ourselves.

The priest walked with us as far as the mausoleum; at the top of the stairs to the crypt, he let out a high nervous laugh.

'Foolish of me even to say this, I know, but – you won't open any tombs, will you?'

I hesitated, unwilling to rule out the possibility. My thoughts flashed back to a time in Canterbury, four years earlier, when I had been obliged to open a grave in pursuit of a killer. I blinked hard to dispel the memory; it was not one I cared to revisit.

'Not if I can help it.'

'Only – there's a curse.'

'Naturally,' I said, persisting with my forced humour, because I could see the alarm on Besler's face. 'What self-respecting crypt doesn't have a curse?'

The priest lowered his voice. 'It's why His Majesty won't set foot in there. In case he disturbs the bones of Boleslaus the Cruel.'

I looked at him; he was evidently waiting for me to ask. 'Go on,' I said, feeling the wax running down the sides of my candle. 'The short version.'

'He was a notorious fratricide. He killed his elder brother, Wenceslas the Good, to become Duke of Bohemia.'

'Ah.' No wonder Rudolf didn't like the story. 'Well, we'll try not to bother him. Come, Besler.' I took the boy by the sleeve; he appeared rooted to the spot.

'You should not make light of such things,' the priest called as we descended. 'If there is any city in Christendom that has given the powers of darkness free rein, it is this one. As should be abundantly clear from the events of the past few days, but it seems we will not heed the warning.'

'Cheerful soul,' I muttered as I unlocked the iron gate and closed it behind us. 'Well, we can guess where he stands on matters of religious tolerance.' I wondered if the priest was Rudolf's confessor, the one who had been instructed to omit the phrase about papal authority from the Mass. A priest of conservative leanings, who feared his sovereign was turning away from the influence of the Holy Mother Church, might easily ally himself with the likes of San Clemente and Montalcino. I could almost suspect him of leaving the dog's tongue on the altar himself as a warning to Rudolf, if it weren't for the fact that he could not have been the person who attacked me in the crypt.

I took a few steps forward. The light from our candles seemed very small in the darkness, serving only to make the shadows beyond its reach appear denser. The silence had an unnerving, expectant quality, like held breath.

'Do you think the curse is real?' Besler said, uncomfortably close to my ear.

'No, but if you creep up on me like that again, you'll wish it was only old Boleslaus after you. Go and look over there, we can cover more ground. But keep my candle in sight.'

'What are we looking for?' he asked, moving all of five paces away.

'Anything that might conceal the entrance to a passage. It's likely to be well-disguised as part of the wall or floor. But someone came in and out yesterday, so there should be marks of fresh use – fingerprints in the dust, signs of stones being moved.' I held up the light to examine the wall in front of me. With no idea how far the crypt extended under the cathedral, I realised we could be searching for hours. I began to wish I had insisted the priest accompany us; I did not entirely trust him, and it would be easy for him to alert someone to the fact that we were down here alone.

'How simple things were in bygone times,' Besler remarked from somewhere to my right. 'When people were known by only one character trait. Boleslaus the Cruel – you'd know what you were dealing with before you met him.'

'Besler the Annoying,' I said, animated for a moment by a visible line where one kind of stonework met another, older section. I pressed my fingers along the join but nothing yielded.

'Bruno the Miserable,' he retorted. His candle had vanished behind a column. 'Here, come and look at this.'

'I'm not miserable,' I said, affronted, as I followed his voice. I rounded a corner and saw him standing in front of an arched recess framed by two fractured pillars, looking down at two plain stone sarcophagi. Between them, a slab the size of a gravestone had been set into the floor.

'Do you think that's him?' Besler whispered, as if anxious not to disturb the dead.

I crouched to step under the arch and held up the light, but the inscription on the slab had been rendered illegible by time. Instead, something else caught my eye. 'Told you,' I said, pointing out the faint trace of fingermarks at the top edge of the slab. 'I think you've done it, Besler. Let's try moving this.'

He knelt across from me and we tried every means to prise the slab from the floor, with no result except broken fingernails.

'*Dio porco.*' I sat back on my haunches, sucking a bleeding finger. 'I distinctly heard the scraping of stone yesterday before I passed out – it has to move somehow.'

'There must be a mechanism,' Besler said, running his hands around the raised edge of the slab, though we had already checked it for any hidden hand-holds. Suddenly, he shrieked and dropped his candle, falling backwards on his arse against the tomb.

'What?' I brought my light closer to see if he was hurt; he looked up at me with wild eyes.

'Something touched my foot.' He pointed with a shaking hand to the sarcophagus behind him. 'It came from there.' And then, good Protestant that he was, he crossed himself, muttering to Jesus to protect him.

I held up a hand for silence and caught the patter of claws skittering away.

'That was a rat, Besler, not Boleslaus reaching out of his grave to grab you. Let's see where it came from.' I knelt to look; each stone coffin was raised up on feet carved like lion's paws, raising them six inches or so off the plinth beneath. Gingerly, I reached into the gap and felt around until my hand encountered a space between the stones. I slid my fingers in and they closed around a metal rod, almost like—

'I think it's a lever,' I said, pulling it up with some effort; I heard a grinding of metal and a solid thunk as something turned beneath the slab.

'It moved,' Besler exclaimed, the ghost of Boleslaus forgotten as he pushed down on the top end of the stone and watched as the other half swung upwards.

'A basic pivot,' I said with admiration. 'I've seen a device like this in a great house in England, where it concealed a hiding place for priests beneath the floor. But this must be hundreds of years older. Come, relight your candle.'

The slab only lifted to an angle of forty-five degrees; I had to lie on my back to wriggle into the gap, feeling my way with my feet – there was no knowing how far the drop might be. But I made contact with a flight of steps and eased my way in as Besler held the heavy stone to prevent it falling.

I counted eight steps before I found myself standing in a narrow corridor hewn out of the rock below the cathedral's foundations, high enough for me to stand. I held up the light but could only see a few feet ahead.

'We should find something to prop that slab open,' I said, shuffling forward into the darkness as I heard Besler shunting himself through the gap behind me. 'We don't know how the mechanism works from this—'

Before I could finish speaking, there came a crash of such force it sent small rocks and dust scattering down from the roof of the tunnel; the echo reverberated through the foundations loud enough to wake all the dead kings of Bohemia. The draught from the sudden movement of the stone blew out both candles and I heard Besler bumping down the steps behind me.

'Are you all right?'

'I couldn't hold it,' he said, and I caught the quiver in his voice. 'It became too heavy for me and I slipped.'

'Do you think someone pushed on it?' I thought of the priest again.

'I don't know. I'm sorry, Maestro. Are we trapped?'

'Well,' I said, reaching for the tinder-box and striking it so that he could see my resolute smile, 'we know it must come out somewhere. Nothing for it but to go forward, Besler. *Andiamo.*'

It must come out somewhere, I told myself repeatedly as we progressed between walls of black rock slick with damp, although it felt as if we were burrowing into the heart of the castle's bedrock. I concentrated on steadying my breathing, reasoning that the tunnel had been built strong enough to have survived for six hundred years so ought to last a little longer. I would not have endured five minutes as a secret priest in England, I reflected, if my survival had depended on hiding for hours in a hole barely big enough to stand up in; I had a grudging admiration for the courage of those who saw that as their mission, even though I had helped to send more than one of them to the executioner at Tyburn. With these thoughts I distracted myself from the very real possibility that whoever had last used this route had locked the exit behind him, and that we might be forced to return to the crypt, only to find the stone slab shut fast too. No one except the priest knew we were down here, and it might be in his interest not to mention it. Besler had stopped his usual prattling, and I could feel him holding the sleeve of my doublet between his thumb and forefinger like a child afraid of being separated from his mother in a crowd. I pretended I hadn't noticed, and wished again that I had persuaded him to return to Wittenberg.

At length we came upon a pile of rubble where the roof had crumbled so badly that the way appeared blocked.

'Are we trapped?' Besler said in a high, strangled voice, bumping into me as I stopped to examine it.

'Someone came through here,' I said with forced determination. 'So there must be a way. Hold up the light.'

I could feel a draught from beyond the rockfall; on closer examination, I saw a gap wide enough to squeeze through.

'Follow me,' I said, fighting my rising panic as I climbed over the fallen stones, praying I wouldn't dislodge anything that would bring the rest of the roof crashing down. On the other side, I found that a half-hearted attempt had been made to board up the tunnel with planks, though the wood was now rotten with damp. I moved one of the broken slats aside and emerged into a place where the tunnel forked. It seemed to me that the air from the right-hand branch was colder, though it was hard to be certain. I paused as Besler scrambled through behind me.

'Our friend in the crypt must be very familiar with these passages,' I said, 'to know that there was a way through that rockfall.'

'Skinny too,' Besler said, rubbing his elbow. 'Which way now?'

At that moment, like an omen, another rat darted past from the left-hand passage, squealing indignantly at the disturbance. He must have got in somehow, I reasoned.

'Here,' I announced, pointing with more confidence than I felt.

The passageway began to slope noticeably upwards, which seemed a good sign, but the further we progressed, the more it began to smell of decaying flesh, which did not. The odour

293

was faint at first, but grew stronger with each step, until it was thick in my nose and I found myself slowing in dread of what we might find ahead. The last fool who thought he could escape this way? Or some as yet unknown victim? Behind me, Besler made a choking sound.

'What *is* that?' he said through his sleeve.

'Nothing good.' I could feel my dinner rising in my stomach. 'Stay behind me.'

I walked on a few more paces and sensed movement; at the furthest reach of the candle's glow I made out a mound wedged into a crevice in the side wall. It appeared to be writhing repulsively.

'Brace yourself,' I said, 'this won't be pleasant.' I picked up a loose rock and hurled it with force at the seething mass; a crowd of rats fled, shrieking, scuttling over our boots as we pressed ourselves against the rock face while they passed. I knew they wouldn't be deterred for long; reluctantly, I moved closer and crouched to see what they were feasting on. The relief I felt when I realised made my legs buckle and I had to steady myself against the wall.

'Poor fellow,' Besler said, looking down at the mauled lump of fur and flesh that was just about recognisable as canine.

'I feared worse,' I said, taking a kerchief from my doublet and lifting the creature's bloodied jaw. 'No tongue. So that part of the mystery is solved, anyway. I'd guess the other branch of this tunnel leads out to the Stag Moat, somewhere near the kennels where they keep the strays for experiments.' Thinking of the kennels brought to mind the boy Novak had mentioned, the dog-catcher who had been fished out of the river on the same day Bartos was found hanging from the bridge. It was too much of a coincidence for my liking; I must speak to Hajek about it. I let the unfortunate animal's head drop as Besler squeezed past behind me.

'Look, I think it's the way out,' he said, suddenly animated. I followed him to see a faint glimmer of light ahead. The tunnel ended abruptly in another flight of steps cut into the rock; at the top there was a hatch of latticed metal like a drain cover. I took a deep breath; if this was locked, we were stuck down here.

'Now would be a good time to pray, if you were so inclined,' I said, passing him my candle and setting my foot on the first step. At the top I leaned back and pushed with both hands on the grille. It didn't move, but when Besler held the light up I saw that it was fastened by a simple latch; once undone, this allowed the hatch to swing down on smoothly oiled hinges. I laughed aloud, giddy with relief.

Climbing out, I saw that we were in an empty room where the dank smell of underground and decay persisted. Besler followed me up and looked around.

'It stinks of death in here too,' he observed in a whisper.

'Wait, I know where we are,' I said, taking in the trestle table pushed into one corner, and the drainage channel cut into the floor. This was the room below the palace where Hajek had shown me Bartos's body that first night. So the doctor's anatomising chamber held the entrance to a passage that connected directly with the cathedral crypt, and presumably at least one other exit. Useful for anyone who needed to move about the castle grounds unseen.

'But it couldn't have been Hajek hiding in the cathedral,' I said, closing the hatch behind us. 'He was with Rudolf the whole time.'

'Anyway, why would Hajek want to terrorise the Emperor with severed body parts?' Besler said.

'You're right, he's the last person who would want to do that.' I recalled Hajek's words to Ottavio Strada: *If we lose His Majesty, we are all dead men.* 'Hajek is invested in keeping Rudolf sound in mind and body.' But then so is Ottavio, I thought. Someone else has access to this passage. I would have to confide our discovery to Hajek, to see if he had shared the secret with anyone.

The room had only one door; I had expected to find it locked, but Besler turned the handle and it opened. Before I could stop him, he had stepped out into the corridor.

'Which way?'

I pointed. Torches were burning low in brackets along the wall. Now we had only the problem of how to explain our presence in the bowels of the royal palace if we should be caught. We passed a door I recognised as Hajek's laboratory and continued in the direction of the stairs, Besler hurrying in front despite my entreaties to progress cautiously. I could not blame him; I was also keen to be above ground again. We had almost reached the staircase when the corridor bent at a right angle and Besler collided with someone coming the other way, causing him to drop an armful of books.

'Herr Besler? What in God's name—'

'We were looking for Dr Hajek,' I said quickly, stepping into the light to see Ottavio Strada rubbing his elbow and looking at us with consternation.

'How did you get in? This part of the castle is open only to the royal household.'

'Hajek must have given my name to the guards,' I said, before Besler could blurt anything about tunnels. I crouched to help the librarian gather the books. 'They let us through.'

'They should not have done.' He pursed his lips in disapproval, and I could see him eyeing the dust and cobwebs on our clothes. 'I will have to speak to Hajek about that – especially now, with concerns about those dreadful packages sent to His Majesty. I have not seen the doctor today – would you like me to pass on a message if I do?'

'Thank you, but it can wait.' I smiled, laying the final book on top of the pile in his arms. 'Do you work down here too?'

Strada wrinkled his nose. 'Not if I can help it. The place smells like a charnel house, thanks to Hajek's experiments. But there are storage chambers here where I keep books that need repair, or which are no longer wanted, before we sell them on. I was taking these down in case they can be salvaged.'

'You repair them yourself?'

'No. I can mend superficial damage, but I don't really have the skills for anything more demanding. Fortunately there is a book dealer in the Jewish Town who is also an excellent book-binder – I make use of his services.'

'Really? Some of my books are the worse for wear after so much travelling – perhaps I should pay him a visit. What's his name?'

'Maier. David Maier.'

'And you recommend him?' I said, keeping my expression neutral and willing Besler not to speak. 'Have you known him a long time?'

'Oh, some years.' Strada shifted the pile in his arms to stop the books slipping. 'He's not cheap, but there is no better craftsman in Prague for restoring books. You might find a few interesting items in his shop while you wait. In fact' – his face brightened – 'since you are here, why don't you come up to the library and see a recent treasure I acquired from him – I think it will interest you.'

'I'd be delighted,' I said, genuinely eager to see the library, but also curious to speak further with Strada on the subject of David Maier. So the librarian had direct dealings with David; that would make him an obvious candidate for the bookseller's contact at the castle. But if they had legitimate reason for doing business, why would they need to skulk about meeting secretly in the yard of the Winged Horse? There was also the fact that Strada appeared to have no idea that David was dead – unless he was highly skilled at feigning, which was entirely possible with a Mantuan.

'Wait here while I put these away,' he said, and disappeared around the corner with his books.

'Don't say a word about David,' I hissed to Besler, when the librarian was out of sight. 'I want to see if he lets anything slip.'

'I'm not an idiot,' he said, ruffled, 'even if I am annoying.'

I laughed. 'I was annoying at your age, too.'

'Still are,' he murmured.

'Am I really miserable?' I said, after a pause. 'Is that how you see me?'

He considered the question. 'Well, you don't seem especially happy, Maestro. In Wittenburg, I mean. Sometimes I glimpse you around the university and you're always solitary. I get the feeling you don't much like your life there. Perhaps it is too small for you. You're different since we came to Prague – more . . .' he twirled his fingers as if he might pluck the right word out of the air. 'Inspired,' he said, eventually, looking at me as if he feared reprimand for his bluntness.

I nodded. It was a fair assessment. I had allowed myself to become reclusive after the disappointments of leaving England, and it had grown harder to shake myself out of my brooding. 'It does not bode well if I can only find inspiration in the face of violent death,' I said.

Besler gave me a sly grin. 'Or perhaps it is meeting Esther Loew that has revitalised you.'

I did not have the chance to refute this, because Strada appeared from the other end of the corridor, briskly clapping his hands.

'Come, then,' he said, 'and I will show you a most rare and secret book that I had from the Jewish bookseller.'

I could hardly climb the stairs fast enough; could this be the book David had spoken of with his dying breath?

TWENTY-THREE

I had seen many great libraries across the courts of Europe in the course of my travels, but the imperial library stopped my breath. Strada flung open the doors and ushered us in, spreading his arms wide to show off his domain with as much pride as if he had built the place with his own hands. We found ourselves in a long room lined with polished oak shelves and panels, the floor tiled with geometric patterns in black and white, the vaulted ceiling painted with allegorical frescoes. A mezzanine gallery ran around the upper shelves, accessed by two curving spiral staircases in the same gleaming wood. At the far end, opposite the door, an archway revealed another, similar room beyond. There were writing desks set into the window alcoves, and stands displaying larger, chained manuscripts, their gilt illuminations glowing in the warm light of candles in glass lanterns. And on all sides, books bound in finely tooled calfskin crammed the shelves from floor to ceiling. I gazed around in wonder, breathing in the scent of leather, paper, wood and beeswax, feeling instantly at home.

Strada seemed gratified by my response.

'I recognise a fellow bibliophile when I see one,' he said, smiling. 'What do you think?'

'Extraordinary,' I said. 'How many volumes?'

'More than twenty thousand. Though much of the imperial

library collected by His Majesty's late father remains in Vienna. Follow me – there is something I'd like you to see.'

He led us through the first room and into the second, while I trailed in his wake, trying to catch the titles as we passed: I saw works by Copernicus and Roger Bacon, Marsilio Ficino and Paracelsus; the Antwerp edition of della Porta's *Magia Naturalis*; Ramon Lull's *De Secretis Naturae*; Schylender's *Medicina Astrologica*, and countless more works on astrology, chiromancy, Neoplatonism, Zoroastreanism, Cabala and cryptography. It was a treasure trove of every imaginable volume on the Holy Office's Index of Forbidden Books, titles I had dreamed of reading as a young friar; I could have lost myself in the stacks for weeks.

'Look at this,' Ottavio said, approaching a hatch set into the wall at chest height. I had taken it for a cupboard, but when he opened it, I saw a dark cavity behind, with two taut ropes stretched vertically in the void. 'Watch.'

He pulled on one of the ropes and I heard the turning of a pulley above; after a moment, an empty wooden container rose to fill the space. 'It's a contraption of my own devising,' he said modestly. 'I mentioned that I was interested in mechanics. This shaft is a disused chimney breast – with a basic system of weights and pulleys, I can load a crate of books here and lower them to storeroom level without having to carry them down the stairs.'

'Very clever,' I said, admiring, and he blushed at the praise.

'But come – this is not what I brought you to see.'

At the far end of the next room, he opened a door in the corner that led to a panelled reading room lined with more books. Here he climbed a small ladder to the upper shelves and withdrew a bound manuscript which he laid on a table. I moved closer to examine it and he held up a hand to forestall me, pulling out a silk kerchief from his sleeve and passing it over with a wrinkle of his nose.

'Would you mind wiping your hands before you touch the book? You're very . . . dusty. Both of you. What have you been doing?'

'We helped Dr Hajek's servant move some furniture down to his cellar this morning,' Besler said as I searched for a reasonable explanation. I glanced at him, impressed by his quick thinking.

'Hm. I would advise you in future to change your clothes after manual labour before you present yourself at the palace.' Strada turned to me and gestured to the book. 'You know what this is?'

'*Dio mio.*' I wiped my hands on the kerchief and opened the cover to find parchment pages covered in small, neat Hebrew writing, carefully etched in browning ink. 'The *Sefer Yetzirah.* How old is this?'

'At least a hundred years, by my estimate,' he said, gazing fondly at the book as if it were his own newborn child. 'You've read it?'

'I read the first printed edition.' Gingerly, I turned another leaf. There was none of the ostentatious decoration that characterised the gospels of this period; the pages were plain and austere, the words alone sufficient.

'Ah – Mantua, 1562,' Strada said. 'Of course. Well, this manuscript contains marginal commentary from a Jewish mystic which is, I believe, unique. It's a remarkable treasure.'

'Where did you find it?'

'From this book dealer I mentioned, Maier. The book belonged to the Chief Rabbi of Prague – he took some persuading to part with it. But His Majesty was determined to have it, and he is hard to refuse when he has set his heart on something.' He smiled, and I recalled Rabbi Loew saying the same.

'Do you visit this Maier's shop often?' I asked. 'It sounds as if it would be worth a trip, if he has other such treasures on offer.'

Strada chuckled at my naïveté. 'Oh, he doesn't keep things like this on the shelves. But he is good at tracking down rare items if he knows what you want. Always for a price, of course – you know what they're like.' He curled his lip in distaste.

301

'But in answer to your question, I rarely set foot in the Jewish Town. Maier comes to me when he has something he thinks would interest the Emperor.'

I nodded. 'So he brought this manuscript here himself?'

'In fact, no, not on this occasion. He entrusted it to his cousin, a young doctor, who turned out to have an ulterior motive – he fancies himself as a writer and producer of plays, and offered his services to His Majesty to put on theatrical entertainments at court, if you can imagine such audacity.'

'It's not without precedent,' I said. 'In Mantua, twenty years ago, the Jew Leone di Somma was in charge of the Gonzaga family's court entertainments. I heard he had great influence.'

'But this is not Mantua,' said a rasping voice behind me.

I started, as did Strada; we turned to see Jacopo and Katherina Strada sitting together at a table in an alcove between the stacks, engaged in writing letters.

'Papà,' Ottavio said, smoothing over his surprise. 'I did not know you were up?'

'I am having one of my better days, as you see.' He addressed this to me. 'I am inundated with correspondence, Dr Bruno, and my hand is no longer steady enough to hold the quill. Fortunately, I have a skilled amanuensis – my daughter can emulate my writing well enough, and in this way we deceive our agents and suppliers in foreign parts, who might be inclined to drive a harder bargain if they thought my powers were failing. My son is not sufficiently ruthless to negotiate in my stead.'

'Why are you in here?' Ottavio asked.

'To renew my acquaintance with the collections,' Jacopo said, giving his son a look that hinted at a hidden meaning. 'Katherina thought the walk would do me good.'

Katherina glanced up modestly from under her lashes and met my eye.

'How are you today, signorina?' I asked, with a small bow.

'Quite well, thank you,' she said, though her face was as wan and strained as her father's.

302

'What about you, Dr Bruno?' Jacopo asked, as if she had not spoken. 'Are you ruthless when the situation calls for it?'

'I prefer to think of it as determined.'

'Call it what you will, we are talking of the same quality.'

'No. Determination has limits.'

'Then it is not true determination, is it?' The old man smiled like a fox. 'Your delicacy doesn't fool me. I never met a Neapolitan who didn't have a seam of ruthlessness running through his core. Cut your throat as soon as look at you, most of them.'

'Well, I hope—'

'You've done things you'll have to account for when you face your Maker, Giordano Bruno, I recognise it in your eyes. Even if you salve your conscience by telling yourself you're always on the side of progress.' He leaned his elbow on the table and pointed a bony finger at me. 'You could teach my son a thing or two. He gives way too easily. Too afraid of causing offence, aren't you, boy? If I didn't know his mother to have been pure as the lily, I would wonder if any blood of mine flows in his veins.'

'I'm doing my best to learn from you, Papà,' Ottavio said with a dry smile, though I could see his colour rising.

'So the young doctor had no success with his petition to put on plays, then?' I asked, to steer the conversation away from these simmering family resentments.

Jacopo snorted. 'I sent them on their way with a few stern words. Books for the Emperor's private collection are one thing, but allowing them to tell their stories before the whole court? Outrageous presumption.' He shook his head.

'You said you sent *them* on their way – he was with someone?'

'Yes, the Jewish boy brought his betrothed with him when he delivered the book, perhaps he thought her charms might help to advance his cause. It didn't work. Can't abide a man who hides behind a woman.'

'I thought their ideas were interesting,' Ottavio said mildly.

'Well, we all know you are easily swayed by a pretty face,'

Jacopo said with a sneer, and the librarian turned away to hide his embarrassment. Though I had not especially warmed to Ottavio, I had had enough of watching him belittled by his father, and was about to take my leave when the door to the private room slammed open, juddering on its hinges, and on the threshold stood the Holy Roman Emperor between two guards, dressed in a sable-trimmed robe, his face agitated. I saw his eyes narrow with suspicion as they raked the company and his gaze fell on the open book on the table. Katherina rose instantly from her chair and helped her father haul himself to his feet; Ottavio and I dropped to one knee.

'What are you all doing with my *Sefer Yetzirah*?' Rudolf said peevishly.

'I was showing your magnificent collection to Dr Bruno, Majesty, so that he could admire your discernment in acquisitions,' Ottavio said to the floor.

'Huh. Taking the credit yourself, no doubt. Get up. Where is Hajek? He's not in the Powder Tower.'

'I have not seen him. How may *we* serve, Majesty?' Jacopo said, easing his way out from behind the desk and bowing unsteadily before his sovereign. I did not miss the fact that he had seamlessly slid a book over the paper his daughter had been copying the instant the door opened.

'Jacopo. I did not expect to see you.' Rudolf frowned, sizing him up. He didn't look especially pleased about it.

'Not on my deathbed yet, Majesty.' The old man produced a phlegmy chuckle. 'Is there something troubling you?'

'Yes, as it happens. It seems the Golem has struck again, and I have to find this out through servants' gossip. Should I not be the first to know, if my subjects are being slaughtered in the streets by some ungodly monster?'

'You mean another murder, Majesty?' Jacopo's eyebrows lurched upwards in shock.

'Apparently. These fellows' – he gestured to his bodyguards – 'heard it from a soldier on the gate, who heard it from the brewer when he made his delivery, who heard it – well, doesn't

304

matter. It's on good authority. A waterman fished up a body this morning, killed in the same manner, and it seems this time the Golem has turned on one of its own.' He paused for effect, watching our reactions.

'You mean, the victim is a Jew?' Ottavio stared at him.

'So they are saying. What does it signify?'

'Perhaps it is a warning,' Jacopo said softly.

Rudolf turned a sharp gaze on him. 'Of what?'

The old man shrugged one shoulder, as if to suggest this hardly needed explanation. 'That however much you give them, they will always want more. That they cannot be controlled, like this creature. If it has no loyalty even to its own people, how would you expect it to show loyalty to you?'

'Oh, for goodness' sake,' Besler blurted out in exasperation, 'he was killed by an *alchemist*. It's nothing to do with the Golem. Rabbi Loew would never do such a thing. He's a good man.' He folded his arms and glared at Jacopo. I bit down a smile, impressed; he had been browsing the shelves so quietly while I spoke with the Stradas in Italian that I had almost forgotten he was there.

Rudolf peered at him, frowning. 'Who are you?'

I stepped forward. 'This is my assistant, Hieronymus Besler, Your Majesty.'

The Emperor seemed to notice me properly for the first time since his arrival. 'And *you*. You knew about this murder?'

'Yes, Majesty. Since this morning.' I lowered my gaze in a show of deference, but not before I caught Ottavio's sharp look from the corner of my eye.

'And you didn't think to bring me the news immediately? You assured me you could find this killer.'

'I said I would try, Majesty. I am trying. Unfortunately I was too late to prevent him claiming another victim.'

'Walk with me,' he said, turning suddenly on his heel. 'I want to talk to you.'

'Why not speak here, Your Majesty?' Jacopo said, gesturing around the library with a conciliatory smile. 'We can put our heads together. We are all united in our desire to catch whoever is responsible for these dreadful crimes and ensure the safety of your kingdom and your person.'

'It's not a subject for women,' Rudolf said crisply. It was the first time he had acknowledged Katherina's presence, though he still didn't look at her.

'She can leave,' Jacopo said, as if she were not standing beside him.

'There are matters I wish to discuss with Dr Bruno in private.' Rudolf turned his back pointedly on the Stradas. 'You should rest, Jacopo,' he added over his shoulder. 'You don't look good.'

'I will take care of him, Your Majesty,' Katherina said softly, but the Emperor walked away without a word, snapping his fingers for me to follow.

TWENTY-FOUR

He led us back to the *Kunstkammer* and told the guards to wait outside. The lamps had not yet been lit, and in the fading afternoon light, the curiosities in their dusty cases had lost some of their lustre. The stuffed bear in the window embrasure looked melancholic, as if his dull glass eyes were fixed longingly on distant forests.

'Why did you say the Jew was killed by an alchemist?' Rudolf demanded, pointing at Besler, who was craning his neck to look open-mouthed at the creatures suspended from the ceiling, like a child watching his first snowfall.

'The mark on his head, Your Majesty,' Besler said, reluctantly pulling his gaze back to the Emperor.

I explained briefly how we had come to discover David's body, leaving out the part about seeing him at the Winged Horse. Rudolf ran his thumbnail along his teeth, his expression growing perturbed as he listened.

'So it's a reprisal?'

'Or it was supposed to look like one,' I said. 'An alchemist is murdered and mutilated with Jewish letters. Then a Jew is found dead marked with an alchemical symbol in the same way. If the first murder seemed intended to stoke fears of a Golem, this one seems almost meant to quell them by making it appear a feud between the Jews and the alchemists.'

'An eye for an eye,' Rudolf said, nodding. 'Except you say the killer left his eyes alone this time. Can it be the same person?'

'I think the killings are linked, certainly. But I don't believe it's to do with a quarrel between Jews and alchemists. The two victims were murdered because of their connection to you, Your Majesty.'

'Me?' He looked alarmed. 'But I never met this Maier in my life.'

I hesitated. 'No, but he supplied the *Sefer Yetzirah* that brought Rabbi Loew to your door. And he regretted his part in that transaction.'

The effect of this on the Emperor was remarkable. His face drained of all colour, his eyes bulged in shock and he grasped at my sleeve as if he feared collapse.

'How could you know of my business with the rabbi? I suppose John Dee told you? I should never have trusted him with my secrets.'

'Dee told me nothing, Your Majesty. You must realise the rabbi is quite recognisable when he crosses the river at night. The rest I guessed at.'

Again he looked faint. 'The *rest*?'

I took a deep breath. 'Yes. I know that he visits you in private to teach you the secrets of the Cabala.'

A long pause unfolded. Rudolf cocked his head and looked at me oddly. '*And . . . ?*'

'And, David Maier feared the association would antagonise the Catholic authorities, which would make things worse for the Jews in the long run. So he tried to interfere by telling someone at court about the rabbi's visits, in the hope that this person would use his influence to dissuade you from continuing.'

'Who? No one has approached me.'

'I don't know, but I think that person killed him, or arranged his death. I had thought the most obvious choice for Maier would be San Clemente or Montalcino, they would be the most

308

eager to use that information against you, but . . .' I let the sentence fall away. But I have just learned that David had a ready-made contact at the court in the person of Ottavio Strada, I could have said. Hajek had told me how the Stradas were jealous of anyone coming close to the Emperor for fear it would displace them: witness Jacopo's attempts to spread the rumour that Hajek was a sodomite. If David had told Ottavio that Rabbi Loew had secretly become Rudolf's mentor, that would not have sat well with Jacopo and his prejudices.

Rudolf considered this. 'So you suspect the Spanish? I would not put it past them. And you think the alchemist, Bartos, was also killed because of me? How so?' As he spoke, an expression of appalled understanding dawned on his face. 'Because of the curse I put on my brother?'

I met his eye and kept my expression steady. 'I have not clarified all the details yet, Your Majesty, but I don't believe it was connected with the curse.' Hajek would not forgive me if I mentioned the theft of the poison and alarmed the Emperor with news of how close an assassination plot had come to succeeding. Hajek could explain that in his own time.

'Then what? His discoveries?'

'It's possible.'

Rudolf nodded slowly. He released his grip on my sleeve and crossed to the window, where he rested a hand companionably on the bear's shoulder and looked out at the dusk falling over the courtyard.

'He was my favourite at one time, you know,' he said, half to himself. 'I had high hopes for Bartos. Such promises he made me! A handsome boy, too – face like a Botticelli angel.'

'Not when I saw it.'

'No. Well.' He grimaced. 'Perhaps my attentions made others resentful of him. Is that what you meant?'

'Something like that,' I said carefully. 'Your Majesty, did you pay him to curse Matthias?'

Rudolf gave a dry laugh. 'No, I did not. I said I would reward him once I saw how effective it was, or not. He did not ask for coin, anyway. What he wanted in return was the guarantee of an audience for his work in progress. He told me he was close to success in creating *aurum potabile*. I have been disappointed often enough to be sceptical, but strangely I did not doubt his boast. If anyone could have achieved that, it was Bartos. He had more talent than Dee or even Hajek, in my view.' He let out a long sigh. 'I suppose we will never know now how near he came. Thaddeus tells me no such elixir was found when the boy's house was searched.'

'Then we must assume it existed only in his imagination,' I said firmly. I did not want him to get wind of the idea that Bartos's potion was out there somewhere.

'Pity,' Rudolf murmured. He spread out his hands before his face and looked at the backs of them with distaste. 'The incorruptibility of the flesh. Is there any greater prize? I fear it more than anything, more than death itself. When I look at an old man like Jacopo, wasting from within, it repulses me to the core. I cannot bear the stink of disease, the creeping decay of the body.'

'But did not Paracelsus say that decay is the midwife of great things?' I said.

He gave me a scathing glance. 'Can you look at a dying old man and truly believe that? It's not even immortality I crave – I would be content with my three score-and-ten, if I could live them without losing the youth and vigour of your boy here.' He gazed at Besler with a mixture of envy and avarice. 'I would give my kingdom for that – wouldn't you, if you had one? I think perhaps that is the goal of all my striving here, all the work in the Powder Tower - to stave off the failing of this mortal envelope. Sentimental wisdom says we defy the ravages of Time by passing the torch to the next generation, but that has always seemed to me a poor consolation.' He turned with a curious look. 'Tell me, Bruno – you and I are of an age, I think. Did you never feel the urge to get children, pass on your name?'

'It has not been possible, Your Majesty,' I said, a little stiffly.

I never liked speaking intimately about such things, especially with strangers.

'Ah.' He cast a sympathetic glance in the direction of my breeches. 'You are afflicted in some way?'

I heard Besler snigger.

'Oh – no. *No*. Not in that sense. I am afflicted by a lack of means. Without dependable patronage, I could not think of raising a family.' No harm in dropping a hint, I thought.

'I see.' Rudolf's attention drifted back to the window. 'It is my *raison d'être*, as far as the world is concerned. The sole purpose of my existence is to get a legitimate heir, so that he can get one in his turn, and so on.' He leaned against the bear. 'I suppose that's why I have been so consumed with the desire to find some other purpose for myself. To be remembered for more than simply continuing the line. Imagine it' – his eyes shone – 'to be the sovereign who championed the discovery of a new star, or the means of turning base metal to gold, or reversing the decline of the body. To commission an invention that will change the course of history, so that in a hundred years people will say, Ah yes, that happened in the Emperor Rudolf's reign, God be praised for his foresight. Something more meaningful, anyway, than merely planting my seed in some woman who is no better than a brood mare. Any fool can do that.' He paused, revising. 'Well – apart from the Count von Rozmberk.'

'Your Majesty does not wish to marry?'

He made a dismissive noise. 'Women do not much interest me.'

I looked at him. I thought of his remark about Ziggi Bartos's beauty, and Erik Moller's story of the man who visited Bartos at night. Good God. My throat tightened. Could it possibly be—

'I mean to say, they interest me in the usual way,' Rudolf added hastily, seeing my expression. 'But once the act is over, I never before met one who could command my attention for long.' He rested his palm against the glass and regarded his

311

reflection with a wistful expression. 'In my youth I would listen to songs and poems of love and think perhaps there was something missing in me, that I had never experienced such flights of feeling. You remember how Petrarch says "Love discovered me all weaponless, and opened the way to the heart through the eyes". Have *you* known something of this? To love someone so intensely that thinking of them becomes an exquisite torment, that you believed you would die if you were denied them?'

'In a manner of speaking,' I said. I had no desire to elaborate, but wanted to keep him in this confessional vein. 'Although some would say that love is not necessary in a dynastic marriage.'

'Oh, there are plenty who would say it, not least my mother, and my uncle Philip of Spain, who are both determined I should marry his daughter, my cousin.' He traced a line through the condensation of his breath on the window. 'San Clemente importunes me on the subject every time I see him. I have taken to burning his letters unread.'

'You do not like the match?'

He lifted a shoulder. 'The Infanta is a pleasant enough young woman, I believe. But I will not die without her, and it would be cruel to shackle her to a man who does not love her ardently.'

'Perhaps you might learn to love her, in time, Your Majesty?'

His face hardened. 'Have you not listened? I do not want the kind of love that must be learned. A dutiful, worthy sentiment, of polite congress and chilly sheets. No' – he thumped his fist against his breast – 'love must strike like a thunderbolt or it is not worth the name. If you have felt anything of the kind, you will know this to be true.'

'So you will not marry unless you find a woman you would die without?'

A small, private smile curved his lips as he looked back to the window. 'In a manner of speaking.'

There followed a long silence, in which I fancied I could hear the dust motes swirling in the still air. Rudolf seemed lost in his thoughts. I stood awkwardly, unsure whether the audience was at an end. Besler had wandered away to look at the cabinets. After a few moments I cleared my throat and the Emperor wrenched his attention back to me.

'Well, this has been interesting,' he said in a brisker tone. 'In future, I want to hear any news about this business directly from you, not via court rumour. If there is a murderer out there killing people connected with me, I cannot be the last to learn of it. Here—' He reached inside his robe and removed one of the pendants he wore around his neck, pressing it into my hand. I looked down to see a silver medal engraved with the alchemical symbols for the four elements.

'Show it at the gate and they will let you through to my private apartments,' he said. 'Come every day, if need be, but I must know everything you have discovered. I do not want to be left in the dark. Those grotesque offerings of the eyes and tongue – this killer is trying to send a message to me. The Jews and the alchemists – both groups I have promoted and favoured, in defiance of the Church and public opinion. So what does he want – to frighten me off? Force me to withdraw my support for both?'

'That would be my guess, Majesty.'

'Well, find him before there are any more deaths. Because I will not be intimidated. Do you hear?'

I bowed and waited to be dismissed.

'Did you know there are things missing here?' Besler piped up from across the gallery.

Rudolf snapped his head around to look.

'What do you mean?'

'Well, it's small things, Your Majesty. Here, for example.' Besler tapped the glass case with his forefinger. 'It says "five tail feathers from a phoenix", but there are only four. And elsewhere, it's not even so obvious. Just the sense of a gap, but things have been moved around to cover it, do you know what I mean?'

'The *sense* of a gap?' I said, sceptical, but Rudolf had crossed the room with surprising speed.

'I *knew* it,' he said. 'Show me.'

Besler pointed out the places where he supposedly intuited missing items. I joined them to look over his shoulder, still unconvinced; the *Kunstkammer* was so overstuffed with objects displayed with no apparent order or taxonomy, some labelled, others left to guesswork, that I couldn't see how anyone could claim to know what should or should not be there, particularly Besler, who had never seen anything like it in his life. The phoenix feathers looked remarkably like those of a golden pheasant. But the Emperor seemed animated by Besler's observations.

'Strada is stealing from me,' he declared, after examining a few more cases. 'I suspected so for some time, but if I mention that I think something is missing, he tells me I have imagined it, or that I gave it away some months ago and must have forgotten.' He pressed a hand to the side of his head. 'He makes me doubt my memory and the evidence of my eyes.'

'You mean Ottavio?' I said.

'*Jacopo*. I do not think he is as ill as he pretends. Or else his strength comes and goes at his convenience.' Rudolf twisted his mouth to one side. 'Your boy is observant,' he said, patting Besler's arm.

'Surely there is an inventory,' I said. 'You could check . . .' Even as I said it, my gaze roamed around the gallery and I realised what a Sisyphean task it would be. Even if such an inventory existed, you could spend years going through every last coin, crystal and pinned butterfly.

Rudolf gave a curt laugh. 'That is the problem,' he said. 'There is an inventory, but it was compiled by Jacopo, in some arcane cipher only he understands, going back decades to my father's reign. Even if I were to demand it and had all the time in the world at my disposal, I could not say for certain if the collection tallies. It's in Italian, for a start, but no dialect I can fathom. Perhaps you'd have better luck.' He looked at me with sudden inspiration. 'In fact, that's an idea. I'll tell Jacopo you are to have access to the inventory. He won't like that if he's hiding something.'

'Why would he steal from you?' I asked, regretting the suggestion. 'Is he short of money?'

Rudolf's face darkened. 'He thinks I owe him.' He began to pace the length of the gallery, peering into each cabinet as he passed. Besler and I followed at his side. Shadows had started to creep in from the corners, but Rudolf made no move to light the lamps.

'There is a child,' he said vaguely, after a pause.

'Katherina's child?' I prompted.

'Yes. She says it is mine. Jacopo saw in him a chance to cement his family's status,' he continued. 'He has petitioned me relentlessly to make a formal settlement on the boy. At present I am not inclined to do so. I think he is not right in the head.'

I recalled the bestial noise I had heard in the Stradas' apartments. 'He is very young yet, Your Majesty, as I understand.'

Rudolf grunted. 'I provide for him, I do not contest that he is my son, but really – give him a title? Confer on him the right to sit one day on a council of nobles, growling like a dog? I think not.'

'He may grow out of that,' I said.

'Let us hope. I prefer to wait for evidence before I commit. And so because I will not dance to his tune, Jacopo is taking from under my nose what he sees as his grandson's due. I guessed at it, but if I mention anything, they tell me I am misremembering, or my mind is troubled by the cares of state. Now your boy here has confirmed it.'

I thought of Jacopo and Katherina huddled together in the library, the old man's boast that she could copy his hand, the way he had hidden the paper when the Emperor entered.

'I don't know if Besler's hunches count as proof, but if proof exists, it can be found,' I said carefully.

'Good. Then find it for me.' Seeing my hesitation, he turned to look at me. 'You speak of patronage. That's why you came to Prague, is it not? In the hope of obtaining from me what you could not get from Elizabeth of England or Henri of France

315

– a royal imprimatur for your books?' A sly smile appeared at the corner of his mouth. 'You see, I know all about you, Giordano Bruno. I have read your work. I admire your boldness. I will undertake to endorse your next one if you can do these small favours for me.'

'Find a murderer, and bring evidence that your trusted adviser is cheating you?'

'Exactly.' He tucked his hands inside the sleeves of his robe as if the deal was now agreed. I noticed that he had stopped, frowning, in front of a cabinet of ornamental daggers in jewel-encrusted scabbards. Following his gaze, I saw the discrepancy immediately.

'One's missing,' I said, indicating. To the right of the display, between a slim knife with a green ivory hilt, and a more ostentatious Ottoman weapon with interlaced arabesques in gold down the blade, there was an empty space on the purple velvet cloth, where dust showed the ghost of an outline. Another of Jacopo's pilferings?

Rudolf followed the direction of my finger. 'No,' he said firmly. 'That I do remember – I gave that one away. It was a gift to me from the Venetian ambassador two years ago. I thought it ugly. Worth a bit, though.'

'Who did you give it to?' I asked.

His eyes narrowed. 'How is that your business?'

'Hajek thinks a curved blade was used to kill Ziggi Bartos.'

He studied me for a moment, then shook his head. 'If so, it was not that one.'

'How can you be sure?'

'Because it would be impossible. You will have to take my word for that.' He reached for the amulets around his neck, rubbing them between his fingers as if seeking confirmation. 'You can go now,' he said abruptly. 'You have much to do. If you should find Hajek, tell him I want to see him. And send my guards in to me on your way out.'

I bowed, though he had already turned his back and begun walking away. As Besler and I reached the double doors at the other end of the *Kunstkammer*, a mournful tolling of bells across the city announced the hour of four.

'What now?' Besler asked. I leaned my forehead against the closed door. My shoulder and head were throbbing from the blows of the day before and I would have liked more than anything to sleep for a couple of hours, or to lose myself in the library until we were obliged to have dinner with the Countess von Rozmberk, which I was looking forward to as much as a visit to the tooth-puller. But I did not want to loiter around the castle; I half-feared the Emperor would return with a copy of Jacopo's inventory and set me to work cataloguing his collection. I also felt it would be wise to avoid the Stradas; I had seen the naked resentment on Jacopo's face when Rudolf took me aside to share his confidences. I did not wish to make an enemy there, even if their worst crime was only stealing from the Emperor.

'Now,' I said, in a whisper, in case the guards were lurking close to the door, 'I want you to go to Golden Lane and find Erik Moller, see if he has any news of Sukie. Try to stop him drinking, if he hasn't started already – he needs to be sharp for this gaming night later.' Moller, drunk and angry, would be a liability at a time when I would need to tread carefully to get information from Jan Boodt. If he blundered in and made threats, it could wreck my plans.

Besler looked doubtful. 'In my experience, a man who has set his mind on getting drunk does not enjoy being hindered.'

'Well, remind him about his dead wife,' I said. 'Impress upon him that his daughter's safety depends on his clear head. I'll meet you at seven at the Rozmberk Palace.'

'And what will you be doing in the meantime, while I play nursemaid to a drunk alchemist?'

'Don't call him an alchemist, you'll upset him. I want to look at that tunnel again, see where the other branch comes out,' I said, dropping my voice still further. 'Then I'm going back to the Jewish Town to find whatever it was that Benjamin had to take from David's shop so urgently. It must be significant.'

317

'What will you do – break into Benjamin's house?'

'If I have to. I need to know what he's not telling us.'

'That won't leave much time to wash and change for dinner. Ottavio was right, we are filthy from that passageway. You still have cobwebs in your hair.'

I looked down at my doublet and breeches. 'Nothing a good brush won't fix. I had a bath earlier.'

'But, Maestro – we are dining with a beautiful countess. We ought to make an effort.'

'She'll have to take us as we are – I haven't got the time to spare. Besides, Besler – women don't like it when you try too hard.'

His brow creased. 'Really?'

'Oh yes. A bit of dirt and sweat – you'll look like you've been doing something manly.' It was too easy to tease him; I almost felt bad. 'In any case, you should not be trying at all – her husband will likely be there.'

Ignoring his obvious disappointment, I opened the door to see Ottavio Strada hovering in the antechamber; immediately I knew there was no prospect of returning to the tunnel.

'What did he want from you?' he asked when the guards had left.

'To hear what I knew about the murder,' I said. 'His Majesty is greatly disturbed by the news.'

'Naturally,' Ottavio murmured. 'We are all curious to hear what you know of the business, Dr Bruno. I must say I find it odd that we had a conversation about David Maier in the library and you didn't think to mention that he had been murdered.' He arched an eyebrow; his tone was light but his expression held some accusation.

'His death is not yet common knowledge,' I said. 'For the sake of the family, I thought it best to let people hear officially.'

'From soldiers' gossip, you mean?' He gave me a narrow look. 'Or perhaps you wanted to see if I would mention it.'

'That too,' I said evenly.

'Because you think I might know something?'

'Why on earth would I think that?'

He stared me down a moment longer, then shook his head as if to dispel his thoughts. 'Forgive me – I am on edge. I'm always in an ill humour when my father has been berating me.'

'My father could be a bully at times,' I said as we walked side by side down the corridor. 'He was a soldier. He risked his life to earn enough for my education, then resented me for it. He never missed a chance to let me know that books and scholarship were less than manly.'

Ottavio gave a mirthless laugh. 'My father has the same complaint, but not over scholarship. He thinks a man should be without scruple if he wants to get on. It's as if he believes honest dealing is a sign of weakness. Tiziano called him a charlatan.'

'Really? I had the impression there was a great mutual admiration.'

'That is what Jacopo would like people to think. You know they had a profitable enterprise together at one time, defrauding the Emperor's father? Tiziano would have studio copies made of his paintings and my father would authenticate them as genuine for Maximillian. They made a good deal of money that way, until my father tried to cheat Tiziano as well, which is when they fell out. You have to admire the audacity, I suppose.'

'Does your father have military experience?'

He looked surprised. 'No – he trained as a goldsmith and later an architect. Although in his youth he travelled a good deal in the service of two successive popes, I'm not sure in what capacity. He is close-lipped about it, so I suspect intelligencing. Why do you ask?'

'He has a military bearing,' I said vaguely. We had reached the top of the staircase leading down to the courtyard.

'He would be flattered to hear that you think so. Listen – if you have nothing more pressing, please come back and explore the library further,' he said as I made to take my leave. 'We were interrupted before – you barely had a chance to scratch

319

the surface. I will leave you in peace to roam the collections, if you would like? If not, I will see you to the gate.'

He seemed determined to keep close to me. Either way, I could not betray my knowledge of the secret tunnel; that would have to wait for another opportunity, and the prospect of a couple of hours in a warm library was tempting. But I needed to know what Benjamin Katz was hiding, so with genuine regret I declined Strada's offer, saying I would be pleased to return the next day.

Outside, torches had been lit in the courtyard, though they sputtered in the damp air. The rain had eased off, and the clouds drifted apart enough to show a silver crescent moon. I shivered as I bade Besler farewell and watched him hurry away, huddled in his cloak, in the direction of the cathedral and Golden Lane. Strada caught my arm as soon as he was out of earshot.

'Bruno, I must ask – did you see David Maier before he died?' There was a note of urgency in his voice.

'Yes. I was the one who found him. He was barely alive though.'

'But did he speak at all?'

'A few sounds only. Nothing intelligible.'

'You're sure? Nothing about . . .' he hesitated, chewing at his lip. 'About books?'

I worked to keep my face expressionless. 'Not that I recall. Would you expect him to?'

'Oh, I had asked him to find me a couple of volumes that His Majesty was interested in,' he said, sliding his glance away to the gate. 'I suppose it was not uppermost in his mind when he'd been stabbed.'

'How did you know he'd been stabbed?'

He blinked.

'The Emperor's guards told me. I was talking to them while you were in the *Kunstkammer*.'

'I see. I'm afraid I know nothing of any books. You could try his shop – I imagine someone will be taking over the business eventually.'

'I will do that,' he said, his eyes still darting everywhere but at me. We had reached the gatehouse. 'Well, please come back and visit the library whenever you have time. I would like to show you more of the collections. And I apologise again for my father's brusqueness.'

I waved a hand. 'No need. We don't choose our fathers.'

He gave a half-smile, but he seemed preoccupied. 'True. And they do not know us as well as they think.' Then he dipped his head in a brisk bow and turned on his heel.

I watched him walk away with quick, light steps, hunched into his jacket against the cold. He was lying, that much was obvious, but about which part? Why was he so concerned that David might have spoken of a book? And what did that have to do with Esther?

I decided that, if I could find nothing of use at Benjamin's house, I would have to confront her directly and appeal to her conscience. She was protective of her friends and her community, understandably, and resented my questions because she saw me as an outsider, but perhaps I might persuade her to trust me. If I was honest with myself, I was also looking for an excuse to talk to her again; the thought caused my pulse to quicken. I had not met a woman who fascinated me so much since Sophia, the woman I had left behind in England. Esther reminded me of her in some ways; I saw in her the same impatient intelligence, the same apparent lack of awareness of her own exceptional beauty and its effect on men. But I could hardly try courting her now, I reprimanded myself; not merely for all the reasons I had outlined to Besler, but because she was also in mourning. Perhaps, if I were to secure the Emperor's patronage and stay a while in Prague, and if I was mistaken about her understanding with Benjamin, I might hope for a chance to know her better, especially if I distinguished myself as the man who brought David's killer to justice.

I retrieved my dagger from the guards at the gatehouse and was sheathing it as I stepped out into the street, entangled in these thoughts, when I felt a presence at my shoulder.

'*Ven conmigo, por favor,*' said a soft voice in my ear. I turned slowly to see the smaller of the two Spaniards who had attacked me the night Hajek rode to my rescue, the one with the scar. He was not wearing the kerchief around his face, and he was smiling with disconcerting charm, despite holding a blade to my ribs under his cloak.

TWENTY-FIVE

He had remarkably good teeth, I noticed, straight and very white against a dark, close-cropped beard. He wore gold rings in both ears. A vain man, despite the scar. I was too tired to feel anything beyond irritation at being accosted.

'*Qué quieres?*' I said, as if he were a pestering child.

'Forgive the interruption.' He gestured up the street with a tilt of his head. 'He wants a quick word, that's all. Won't take long.'

I looked at him, weighing up the possible outcomes of trying to run or fight. We were close to the castle gatehouse; if I shouted, the guards would surely come out, but we might both be arrested for public brawling. The Spaniard looked fit; I was not convinced I could outrun him. In the end, I nodded acquiescence and he steered me up the hill, away from the river, into a series of winding cobbled lanes behind the castle walls.

'You can put that away,' I said, feeling the point of his knife. 'We both know you're not going to kill me in the street.'

'*How* do you know?' he said conversationally.

'Because your master wants information. He'd gut you if you silenced me before he's heard it.'

He cocked his head as if to agree that this was a fair point, and lowered the weapon, though he held it by his thigh instead of sheathing it. I glanced down to check and had to look again, muting my reaction: the knife in his hand had a curved blade.

'Interesting dagger,' I remarked as we turned into a narrow alley with a row of small limewashed houses on one side and a high stone wall on the other.

'I took it from a Turk after I cut him open from his gizzard to his balls,' he said. 'He gave me this to remember him.' He indicated his scar.

'A Turk? You were a soldier, then?'

'Sailor. I fought under my lord San Clemente at Lepanto.'

He stopped in front of a house and rapped sharply three times on the door before opening it and ushering me inside.

The door closed behind me and I found myself alone in a low room, sparely furnished, with a fire blazing in the grate. Despite my apprehension, I was moving towards its warmth when the door at the back opened and Fra Agostino da Montalcino appeared, unsmiling, a slim book tucked under his arm. I was momentarily wrongfooted – I had expected San Clemente – but I inclined my head to greet him in a manner I knew he would find provoking.

'*Pax vobiscum, Frater,*' I said, determined not to give him the advantage. 'I had thought the nuncio's residence would be grander somehow.'

'This is a place San Clemente keeps to do business. It's discreet. I think he brings his mistresses here, but we need not dwell on that.'

'And where is your Spanish *inamorato* today? I had thought you went everywhere together.'

He almost smiled. 'The ambassador is a useful ally, up to a point, but we differ in outlook. For him, the Catholic faith is purely a question of politics and his own strategic advantage – much like your old abbot in Naples. I do not say San Clemente's faith is insincere – only that it is largely concerned with earthly matters.'

'Whereas you take genuine pleasure in torturing people for Jesus,' I said.

'Whereas I have one eye on eternity. I see clearly the Devil and his legions at work in the heresies gaining ground across Europe, propagated by men like you who seek to remake the heavens, and I believe it is the solemn duty of the Church to stamp them out and save those souls from perdition, by whatever means necessary. I wonder if you ever think about your soul, Bruno.'

I watched his eyes glinting in the firelight and did not doubt that he believed his own rhetoric.

'I try not to. I can't imagine what state it's in by now.'

'Quite. That has always been at the heart of your intellectual arrogance – you never consider that one day you will have to stand before the Judgement Seat.'

'*Historia vero testis temporum*,' I said with a shrug designed to irritate him. In his presence part of me reverted to my twenty-year-old self. 'I prefer to think history will judge me.'

'You see? Proving my point. I could almost admire your self-belief, if it weren't so grievously misplaced. History will forget your name before the ashes of your inevitable pyre are cold, and quoting Cicero won't save you. I pray I live long enough to see you humbled as you deserve.'

'Well, long life to us both. But I presume you didn't bring me here to discuss my damnation, so come to the point, Brother, I've got things to do.'

'Yes, you've been very busy today. Back and forth to the Jewish Town, and yet you haven't made time to update us on your findings, as you promised.'

'Because I have found very little.' I was not surprised to hear he had had me followed, though I was annoyed with myself for failing to notice.

'Nevertheless, I would like to hear what little you do know, starting with the murder of the bookseller.' When he moved his head, the folds of stubbled flesh under his chin bulged over his collar.

I sighed. I presumed he was putting me through this charade in order to remind me that he was in control. Grudgingly, I repeated the story of tracing David's movements and finding the body, leaving out the part about seeing him the night before at the Winged Horse, or any mention of Rabbi Loew. If it was

Montalcino or one of his agents that David had been meeting, the nuncio might give himself away; if not, I was not going to hand him that information.

He paced back and forth as I gave my brief account, one finger absently stroking the bristles on his mole, always treading on the same squeaking board until the sound made my teeth hurt and it took ferocious restraint not to shout at him to stand still. When I had finished, he stopped abruptly and fixed me with his inquisitor's glare.

'You say he was marked with the sign of death, in the same manner as Bartos?'

I nodded. 'But unlike Bartos, not mutilated further.'

He frowned. 'Then – you think it could be the same killer? Why, though – how is the bookseller connected?'

By now my patience had worn thin. 'Why are you asking me this? You know full well who killed Bartos – your Spanish friend out there, with the scar and the Turkish dagger. I don't know why, exactly – I assume Bartos no longer served your purpose and you had to silence him because he knew too much.' I jerked a thumb at the street door. 'So go and ask the Spaniard if he killed the bookseller, and why, and stop playing these games with me.'

He looked at me for a long time, his face empty of expression, though I could see his mind at work in the minute twitching of his mouth. I had forgotten how good he was at this: how he gave nothing away beneath that veneer of calm, allowing the poor wretch under interrogation to gibber and bluster until he had condemned himself with his denials. Twenty years ago I had fallen for it, but I was wiser now, and better practised myself at dissembling. I returned his stare, neither of us breaking eye contact, until eventually he glanced down at the book in his hands.

'And that is your conclusion, is it, after all your investigations? That *I* arranged the murder of the alchemist because he was a pawn in some plot of my devising?'

'You or San Clemente, or both of you. It hardly matters – you're in it together.'

'What if I were to tell you that you are not as clever as you think?'

'You told me that twenty years ago and I refused to believe you.'

At this, he did allow the faintest curve of a smile. 'Think how much trouble you might have spared yourself if you had. And what, then – I left an animal's body parts on the altar to frighten the Emperor? Does that sound to you like something that I, the emissary of His Holiness, would do?'

Admittedly it did not, but he was not beyond a double bluff. 'I think it would certainly be in your interests to tip the balance of the Emperor's mind – after all, if you cannot kill him, the next best thing would be to have him declared unfit to rule, so that his brother can take over.'

'*Kill* him?' Montalcino looked at me with concern. 'I fear it is the balance of your mind that is disturbed, Bruno. I hope you have not repeated such a slanderous accusation to anyone else or I would be obliged to respond. After all, I presume you have no proof to back up your wild theories?'

I remained silent. Let him worry that he had left some loose end to unravel.

'Where is the child?' he said abruptly. Another interrogator's trick: to switch tack without warning.

'Which child?'

He clicked his tongue. 'The Danish girl. The one you have taken a great deal of interest in lately.'

'Why do you care?'

'I believe she is in possession of something that does not belong to her.'

'And what would that be?'

'Now you are playing games, Bruno. What the alchemist gave her for safekeeping.'

'Ah. You're talking about Bartos's *aurum potabile*, I assume. Who does it belong to, then? To you? Because you paid him for it?'

'*If* Bartos had succeeded in making such a substance, it

327

would rightly belong to the Emperor, would it not? The alchemist was under his patronage, after all. I imagine Rudolf would move heaven and earth to find it, if he knew it existed.' He examined his fingernails.

'But that is the last thing you want. If it came into the Emperor's hands, it would be tested extensively and discovered to contain a deadly toxin, which would raise questions about why Bartos would have made such a concoction, and who put him up to it. It's widely known that he was exchanging sums of money in Spanish escudos shortly before he died.'

'Plenty of foreigners deal in escudos, it's a strong currency.' His nonchalance was a front and I waited it out. After a moment, he relented. 'If you know where that elixir is, you could prevent a lot of unpleasantness by bringing it to me.'

I laughed. 'Unpleasantness? This diplomatic mincing of words doesn't suit you, Fra Agostino.'

He nodded towards the street door. 'That Spaniard out there, San Clemente's man – he and his compadre are charged with looking for the girl. I don't think they're sentimental about children. It would be better for her health if you find her first and persuade her to part with it willingly. Is that blunt enough for you?'

I saw in his face that he was in earnest; the novelty of toying with me had worn off, and I had no doubt that the man with the scar would not show mercy if he tracked Sukie down and she refused to hand over the potion.

'For God's sake, Montalcino,' I said wearily. 'She's eleven. Even you must have some shreds of conscience. Tell him to hold off, I'm trying to find her.'

'Then try harder. I'm afraid I have no authority over those Spaniards, they answer to San Clemente. I hear they can be somewhat uncouth.'

'Yes – I saw what he did to Bartos's house.'

'What?' I did not miss the flicker of apprehension in his eyes; I understood him well enough to recognise it as the fear that some piece of information had escaped him.

'He tore the place apart. Then he, or someone else, came back later to clean it out. On your orders, I would guess.'

'How do you know this?'

'Because I was there after his first visit.'

'Looking for the elixir?'

'Looking for anything that would shed light on the murder. It was as if a hurricane had ripped through the room. I suppose that was the point – to remove any evidence of your association with Bartos, and create so much chaos that anyone who came to search could have no idea what may or may not have been there.'

He looked away to the fire, stroking his mole and calculating.

'That is not what happened,' he said eventually, in a quieter voice. 'You are correct that San Clemente's men were sent to search Bartos's lodgings to remove anything potentially compromising.'

'Like the *aurum potabile*.'

He held up a hand to stop me. 'I do not say that the rest of your theory is correct. But it is true that we had dealings with Bartos over certain matters – like a whore, he was for sale to the highest bidder. After news of his murder spread, it was clear that questions would be asked about him, and we thought it wise to ensure that there was no evidence of any association. But when San Clemente's people arrived, the house was as you described. The door unlocked and everything as if in the wake of a violent storm.'

'The door *un*locked? You're sure?'

'Quite sure. Naturally, we have concerns about what this person might have removed. Or perhaps you found something of interest? Hence our wish for you to share your discoveries with us before you take them to the Emperor.'

I searched his face for some hint of falsehood, trying to understand what he was saying. He was an accomplished liar, God knows, but if he was admitting to having Bartos's lodgings searched once, why would he lie about the first time? It only made sense if he was telling the truth.

'The door was locked when I got there,' I said. 'I picked the lock and found the place turned upside down, but I didn't have time to lock it again behind me. That means your people arrived after me, and whoever went through it first had a key.'

'Which they must have taken from Bartos's body,' Montalcino said. 'It therefore follows that the person who ripped his house apart was his murderer. Their identity as much a mystery to me as to you.' There was a hint of triumph about the way he looked at me as he said this.

I hardly knew what to make of it. The most obvious explanation all along had been that San Clemente and Montalcino were responsible for the alchemist's murder, and the sight of the Spanish sailor's curved dagger had all but convinced me; I had believed their pretence of not knowing who killed him was merely bluffing, so that they could monitor how close I came to finding proof of their involvement. But what if I was wrong? Not about the poison plot: the nuncio's urgent desire to recover Bartos's elixir told me I was on the right track with that. But about the motive for killing him. What if there was not one searcher, sent by the Catholics, who tore the house apart and came back later to clean it up, but two separate groups? Looking for different things, or the same thing? I pinched the bridge of my nose, processing what this meant: if Montalcino was telling the truth, then there was someone else who had wanted Bartos dead, for reasons as yet unknown. I was as good as back where I started.

'You honestly didn't order his murder?' I said, letting my hand fall to my side. I don't know what I was hoping for at this stage; that he would suddenly confess to the killing after all? 'You would swear to me that San Clemente's men didn't do it?'

I saw a twitch of impatience at the corner of his mouth. 'Think logically, Bruno. Let us suppose, for a moment, that it was in my interests to silence Bartos about any business I may have had with him. As I explained to you at our last meeting, it is not difficult to make someone disappear in this city, especially with experienced men like those Spaniards at one's disposal. Ask yourself, then – what could I or my associates possibly gain from hanging the man off the bridge in such a garish display, that would draw the whole city's attention to his activities?'

'To turn public opinion against the Jews?' I heard how feeble it sounded.

'Any advantage to that would be greatly outweighed by the disadvantage of the whole town speculating about motives for his death, as is currently the case,' he said. 'Besides, I have no particular argument with the Jews of Prague at present. They have too much power, granted, but that has been true since Maximillian's time. It is not an immediate priority for the Vatican.'

It might be if they knew that the Holy Roman Emperor was taking secret lessons in Jewish mysticism from the Chief Rabbi, I thought – which must mean Montalcino did not know about Loew's nocturnal visits to the palace, which in turn argued against him or San Clemente being David's contacts.

'*Merda*,' I said forcefully, shaking my head. I needed to rethink everything.

Montalcino was clearly enjoying my discomfort. 'I'm sorry, have I spoiled your hypothesis? You were determined to prove me a murderer, weren't you? You've always resented me because I was one of the few who refused to mistake your wilfulness for brilliance.'

'No, they are legion, believe me,' I said. 'Anyway, you are a murderer. Perhaps not in the case of Bartos, but could you even count how many people died at your hands during your years as inquisitor? Dozens? Hundreds?'

'None. My job was to examine them and pass them over to the secular arm for sentencing. My hands and my conscience are clean.' He held the former out to demonstrate: pale and soft, long fingers studded with gold rings, oddly feminine except for the coarse hairs sprouting from his sleeve. 'Besides, heresy is punishable by law, and just punishment cannot be called murder. You should rather ask how many souls I saved by purging their bodies in the flames.' He gave a self-satisfied little smile; he couldn't help himself. 'Still, I'm glad to have persuaded you that I had nothing to do with the alchemist's death.'

'It means someone else had reason to kill him and ransack his rooms,' I said, feeling bleak at the prospect. His mysterious midnight visitor? 'Did you or San Clemente ever visit his lodgings at night?'

He looked surprised. 'I can't speak for the ambassador, but I only met Bartos once, and that was here. All our dealings with him were through San Clemente's men – they befriended him at a tavern, I believe. Whether they went to his house, I have no idea.'

'Find out,' I said, and paused when I saw his gloating expression. 'What?'

'You see? We both have the same goal, Bruno – we want to discover who killed Bartos and what they took from his rooms. It would be more efficient if we worked together, as I told you before. I propose a bargain.'

'Go on, then.' I knew whatever he suggested would be to his advantage, but my agreement might be the price of Sukie's safety.

'You bring me whatever that child has in her possession. Potions, writings, anything Bartos gave her. And you do not voice your theories about poisons to another soul.'

'I feel it would be negligent of me not to at least mention to the Emperor that the papal nuncio and the Spanish ambassador entertained plans to assassinate him,' I said, mainly to see how he would respond.

'You really want to cause a diplomatic incident with no supporting evidence?' He raised an eyebrow. 'I think you know how that would play out. Our reputations are a good deal more robust than yours.'

'We don't know what evidence there is yet,' I said. 'Perhaps the killer found something.'

'Then, once you have discovered who he is, you will remove

it before it reaches the authorities or the Emperor. Oh, come, Bruno,' he said, seeing me hesitate. 'You said yourself – Bartos's killer had another motive altogether. What would you gain by alarming Rudolf over fantasies of assassination plots? Do you think he will reward you doubly?'

'No. I think he would be on his guard against you in future, though, which might prolong his life. It's not about rewards.'

He let out a scathing laugh. 'Of course it is. Don't pretend you're doing this from some high-minded ideal of justice for a man you never met. What's Rudolf promised you? Patronage, I suppose? Don't count on it – he is even more unreliable in that regard than Queen Elizabeth or King Henri.'

I decided not to rise to that. 'So if I make no mention of Bartos's association with you, what do I get in return?'

'Cooperation. Ensure that our names are kept out of your investigation and I will guarantee that San Clemente's thugs spare the girl. And anything we learn that might point to the killer, I will share with you, and you can take the credit with the Emperor. After all, we want this person caught so that Prague can stop thinking about Ziggi Bartos.'

I weighed this up and nodded. 'Very well. But you must swear that those Spaniards will not lay a finger on the child.' The priority was keeping Sukie safe; I could always revise the terms of the agreement if I found conclusive evidence tying him to a plot against the Emperor. It was no more than Montalcino would do if it suited him.

'You have my word, Brother,' he said, meeting my eye with a beneficent smile. We both knew how little that was worth, but for now it would have to do.

'Am I free to go?'

'Please.' He gestured to the door. I hesitated, waiting for the catch, then nodded curtly and crossed the room. As I reached it, he said, 'Oh, there was one other thing.'

Of course there was. I stopped, my hand on the latch. 'Yes?'

'Do you recognise this?'

I turned; he was holding out the book. I'd guessed he had

333

not been carrying it by chance, but I was not prepared for what I saw when I took it from him and opened it.

It was a notebook, a journal of sorts, the pages covered with tiny handwriting and meticulous diagrams: of alchemical symbols, astrological charts and cabalistic numerical equations, hastily scribbled marginalia and Hebrew characters heavily underlined. I would have known John Dee's hand anywhere. I flicked over a few pages and read the following entry:

The Angel of the Lord hath appeared to me, and rebuketh you for your sins . . .

My heart sank. I read on:

Hell itself is weary of Earth . . . The Son of Darkness cometh now to challenge his right, and seeing all prepared and provided, desires to establish himself a Kingdom.

'How did you get hold of this?'

'The question is rather what should be done with it.'

'Where is John?'

He widened his eyes, all innocence. 'I don't know, as I told you.'

'John would only have been parted from this book by force. He even sleeps with it.'

'Fortunate, then, that he is a heavy sleeper. Or unfortunate, for him.'

Greta. Rabbi Loew said John feared his notebook had been stolen at Hajek's house.

'I've already agreed to your bargain,' I said, biting down my anger. 'How many threats do you need to make?'

'This is a separate problem,' Montalcino said. 'John Dee, before he disappeared, had conceived the same fanciful notions as you about poison plots. It seems he'd been watching Bartos closely out of professional envy, and saw enough to form ideas.'

'How do you know that?' I asked, and in the same breath realised the answer. 'Oh. You saw his letters.' The housekeeper had a lot to answer for. For a brief moment, I found myself hoping that Hajek had thrown her out on the street.

'In fact, we didn't see them. But we know Dee was sending reports back to England. What we don't know is how much detail he gave.'

'I've no idea. He'd disappeared before I arrived in Prague.'

'But you met the merchant Overton at the Spider as soon as you got here. Were you sent to Prague by Francis Walsingham?'

'I came at John Dee's invitation, as I told you.'

He narrowed his eyes. 'I wish I could believe you, Bruno, but you do have a tendency to skirt the truth. I don't think it would take much to coax an honest answer out of that assistant of yours.'

I didn't flinch. 'Leave the boy alone. Do you think if I had come on secret business I would have told him anything about it?'

He gave me a long look, then made an impatient noise.

'Hm. At a certain point, Dee suspected his correspondence was not secure at Hajek's house. We believe he entrusted it to Rabbi Loew. Get it back.'

I shook my head. 'John took it from the rabbi before he vanished. Wherever he is, his letters and papers are with him. But maybe you know that already.'

'I assure you, Bruno – if I had John Dee in my keeping, I would have had that information from him by now and I would not need to ask you. Consider that the rabbi may not have told you the whole truth. If he has copies of Dee's correspondence, I want you to find them. And decipher them – you know the codes the English use.'

'Or what?'

He lifted the notebook out of my hands and held it at arm's length as if it were contaminated. 'There's enough in here to see John Dee condemned for necromancy. And given Rudolf's close association with him, it would look very bad for both of

335

TWENTY-SIX

The scarred man was no longer outside the house, which only made me more concerned; I wondered how long it would take for Montalcino to convey the message, via San Clemente, that he was not to harm Sukie. He could be searching for her even now.

I hurried down the hill towards the Winged Horse, fuelled by anger and fear, before I gradually slowed my steps, reminding myself to stay calm. I had to speak to Magda alone. She knew where Sukie was, I was sure, and I needed to warn her that the girl was in danger. Even if Magda had managed to hide Sukie at the tavern without Jan's knowledge, it could only be a matter of time before he discovered her, and if he knew that the Spaniards were looking for her and the elixir, he would not hesitate to exploit that for his own gain. Whether Magda could help me to spirit Sukie away without being caught was another matter. And where could Sukie go? Not back to her own house; the Spaniards were certain to be watching it. I could take her back to Hajek's but they were likely watching me as well; the only way to ensure her safety was by taking Bartos's elixir to Montalcino. Even then, I had doubts about whether he would keep his word once he had it in his hands; he may fear that the child knew too much.

I pulled up the hood of my cloak when the sign of the

338

Winged Horse came in sight, lit by two guttering torches either side of the main door, and slipped down the alley that led to the yard entrance. Here I loitered in the shadow of the outbuildings, watching to see who came and went from the back entrance. It was mostly men coming out to relieve themselves in the piles of straw behind the stables; the stench of piss carried across the courtyard and I pressed my sleeve to my mouth. The chill began to bite through my clothes; I wrapped my arms around my chest, shivering and cursing my lack of a plan. I could be standing here all night without catching sight of Magda. But after a few moments a shorter, stocky figure appeared with a large basket and headed towards the woodpile in one corner; I recognised her as one of the serving girls from the tap-room. I approached her as she was loading up firewood.

'Excuse me.'

She yelped and backed away, dropping her armful of logs; I bent to pick them up.

'My apologies – I didn't mean to scare you. Will you do something for me? Ask your mistress to come out and see me. Alone.' I offered a coin and what I hoped was a winning smile.

She looked at the money as if waiting for the catch, then shook her head. I wondered if she didn't understand German.

'Please? I need to give a message to Magda. It's very important.'

'I can't,' she whispered, picking up her basket and backing away with an anxious glance at the tap-room door. I wondered if she feared the wrath of Jan Boodt.

'It's nothing bad,' I said, holding out the coin on my palm as if coaxing a skittish horse with an apple. 'You won't get into trouble if you keep it between you and your mistress.'

'No, I mean – I *can't* speak to her. Mistress has been taken ill with one of her headaches and she's in her room, not to be disturbed, he says. If I disobeyed, I'd lose my job. Sorry.' She made to leave, the log basket only half-full.

'Don't worry. You can keep this if you don't mention to anyone that I was looking for her. Especially not your master.'

She took the coin with a quick smile and it disappeared into her apron. 'I don't tell *him* anything. You could try again tomorrow, she might be better.'

Tomorrow might be too late, I thought.

My diversion with Montalcino meant that there was no time for me to get to the Jewish Town and back before the dinner, which I was now dreading even more after the nuncio's warning. I might have looked for an excuse to avoid it if he hadn't thrown out that hint about the Count von Rozmberk taking an interest in John Dee. As I passed a shop window I caught a glimpse of my reflection and decided that if I wanted the countess's cooperation, it would be an idea to tidy myself up before presenting myself at her table, so I wandered down to the Lesser Town and found a barber. Fortunately, he appeared to speak only Czech, so I was left alone in his chair with my thoughts while he gave me a shave.

I found myself in the unusual and unwelcome position of having to trust Montalcino, and despite long experience of his talent for wearing many faces, I began to feel that I believed him on the matter of Bartos's murder. Who else, then, could have wanted the alchemist dead? A sense of despair settled over me as the barber whetted his razor and applied it to my throat; instinctively I flinched at the pressure of the blade. It could be anyone. Some rival alchemist he had provoked, someone calling in an unpaid debt. The only remotely useful lead was the midnight visitor, but since Erik Moller in his cups was the sole witness, it was hardly reliable, and seemed more than likely to have been one of San Clemente's Spaniards handing over payment.

I stood and the barber brushed the dirt from my clothes, then handed me a looking glass. I considered my newly smooth face from various angles. Younger, certainly, without the grey in my beard that Besler had delighted in pointing out, though the past couple of days in Prague had left a stamp of exhaustion in the shadows under my eyes. It would have to do; in any case, it was probably a good thing if the young countess did not find me too appealing. There was a knowingness in the way she looked at me that made me think the evening would be testing.

I did not want to arrive at the Rozmberk Palace too early and my mind would not settle, so I wandered through the Lesser Town and found myself in a park that sloped steeply towards the castle. I kept walking, along winding paths that led through copses of leafless trees, with no sense of destination except a general upward motion. Gradually my stride took on a steady rhythm and I stopped noticing the damp beading on my hair and clothes as I tried to order all the whirling questions in my head. I could not shake the feeling that I was missing something vital, some piece of the picture that would cause everything around it to fall into place. The question of David's murder troubled me greatly. Was it possible that, despite appearances, the two deaths were unconnected? Was I looking for *two* killers?

TWENTY-SEVEN

Shortly before seven, I entered the narrow street called Jirska behind the basilica of Saint George to find Besler already waiting at the portico to the Rozmberk Palace. I could see immediately from his face that all was not well.

'Is it Erik?' I said. 'Is he in a state?'

'I don't know, he wasn't there. But the house has been turned over.'

'What?'

'The lock was splintered when I got there, everything inside pulled apart. I looked in the upper room in case Erik had been hurt, but there was no one, only the mattress ripped open and papers scattered everywhere.' He paused to catch his breath. 'Then the old neighbour came in and started screaming at me, threatening to call the watch – it took a couple of thalers to persuade her I wasn't with the men who'd done it.'

'Did she see them?'

He nodded. 'Spanish. One small with a scar, one big with his head shaved. She said she tried to stop them but the small one said if she didn't go home and close the door he'd come back in the night and slit her throat. She didn't know where Erik was, but she suggested a few taverns where I might find him. I tried all of them except the Winged Horse, but no luck. Then I looked for you, but you'd vanished.'

I swore softly. So the Spaniards had already searched Sukie's house and would know the elixir was not there. I wondered where they would look next, and had to pray that Erik was still out searching for his daughter. I couldn't see what they would gain from harming him, unless they thought they could use him as leverage. I hoped to God that Montalcino would find them quickly and tell them to leave the elixir to me.

'Listen, don't drink too much tonight, understand?' I said in a low voice as I raised the large lion's head knocker on the palace door. 'You'll need your wits about you for the Winged Horse later. And no matter how the countess behaves to you, your manner must be polite but respectful. Do not under any circumstances attempt to flirt with her.'

'Says the man who's had a shave especially,' he murmured, from the side of his mouth, as the great door swung open and a steward in Rozmberk livery ushered us inside.

We crossed an inner courtyard with a fountain in the centre and an arcade like a cloister on three sides, and were shown into a high entrance hall with sweet-scented rushes on the floor and beeswax candles burning in sconces on all sides. A wide stone staircase curved up to a gallery on the first floor, and on the wall above the stairs hung a vast portrait of a handsome blond man with elaborately curled moustaches. He was tall and broad-shouldered, at least in the estimate of the artist, and wore ornamental military dress, one hand resting casually on the pommel of a sword at his side, his severe blue gaze fixed straight ahead, as if to demand of the onlooker what right they had to be standing there in his hallway.

'Good-looking fellow,' I observed to Besler as the servant took our cloaks.

'That portrait is at least thirty years old,' said a woman's voice at our backs. I turned to see Xena von Rozmberk watching us with a pert smile. Her blonde hair was piled in a complicated arrangement on top of her head and twined with pearls; she coiled one loose strand around her finger. She was wearing a gown of rose silk cut low in the bodice, her small breasts pushed up by a corset so rigid it deserved a place in Montalcino's arsenal of torture implements. Besler's eyes locked on to her cleavage as if pulled by magnetic force. I sighed inwardly. It was going to be a long night.

'My lady,' I said, bowing. 'I hope we will have the pleasure of meeting the count in person?'

She smiled and held her hand out for me to kiss. 'Please, you must call me Xena. I can't bear all that formality, it's so stuffy. The count is still away in the country, I'm afraid – I hope my company will not be too dull for you.'

'Never,' Besler said with excessive gallantry, completely ignoring my warning look. So that 'we' in her invitation had been deliberately misleading; perhaps she had guessed that I would not have accepted if I'd known of the count's absence. My unease was increasing by the minute.

She led us through a chilly grand hall with painted ceilings and on into a smaller, more welcoming salon bright with candlelight, where a fire blazed in the grate and a table had been set in the window alcove with three places. Until that moment I had persisted with the belief that we must be joining a dinner party; now it was clear that this was to be an intimate supper for the three of us. I caught the steward's eye as he bowed and retreated; his small, private smile seemed to be saying, good luck.

We were not alone, though; on the far side of the room, a quartet of singers – two young men and two boys – stood with their hands clasped, and at an invisible signal from their leader, broke into an intricate tapestry of song, their voices rising intertwined to the rafters.

'Palestrina,' I said softly, after we had listened for a while.

'Yes, but the madrigals – I didn't think we'd want to hear anything religious over dinner,' Xena said, laying her hand on my wrist. 'I adore all things Italian, you know. My husband has promised to take me there one day. Come, let's have some wine and you can tell me all about – where is it you are from?'

'The Kingdom of Naples,' I said.

'Of course. I suppose you don't have winters like this, that last forever. Tell me what it's like to swim in the warm sea and feel the sun on your skin.' She smiled up at me, without removing her hand. The singers reached a crescendo. I reminded myself that I was a Dominican friar for over ten years, I knew how to steel myself against the charms of women. It was Besler I had to watch.

Not that Xena von Rozmberk was the kind of woman who presented any real danger to me; she was pretty and lively, no question, but somewhere along the way she must have been advised by some matron that men liked girls to giggle and agree with them rather than voice an opinion of their own. No doubt there were men who found that appealing, and it was clear that Xena was not lacking in wit, but hers was an intelligence that was calculating rather than thoughtful, the main focus of her interest being herself. There was none of the quiet watchfulness that I saw in Esther Loew's dark eyes, that hinted at a mind given to deeper reflections. (Stop thinking about Esther, I cautioned myself again, to no avail.)

Xena had grown up around Hradcany, the castle district, she told us; her father had been the Emperor's chancellor and a political ally of the Count von Rozmberk. Their marriage, she said with an airy lack of discretion, was a piece of dynastic bargaining intended to remedy the count's failure to produce an heir in all his previous unions. To steer the conversation away from such uninvited intimacies, I told her stories of my life in Naples and my travels of recent years, leaving out the parts about murder and concentrating more on the entertainments and fashions of the English and French courts (I did not know much about clothes, but I had learned that women appear to be insatiably interested in what other women wear).

The Venetian cook brought in plates of pasta with anchovy sauce, herbed polenta, salt cod in cream, grilled liver and sweet dishes of rice and almond custard, and with each course Xena asked me if I was feeling at home; I didn't have the heart to tell her that Venice was no more my home than Paris or London, so I smiled and praised her good taste, which seemed to satisfy her.

The music was sublime, the food excellent, but I couldn't relax. I sipped at my wine, only half-present, my mind preoccupied by thoughts of Sukie, Magda Boodt and Erik Moller. The serving girl's report that Magda was indisposed troubled me; I suspected that Jan was the cause of her headache, and Magda was my only hope of an honest explanation of how Sukie's shawl came to be in the stables at the tavern. Without her, all I had was guesswork. As for Erik, I would know he was in trouble if he failed to turn up at the gaming night. I grew restless to be away; I had to make an effort to stop my leg jiggling under the table.

'Maestro?' Besler said in a strangled voice. I wrenched my attention back to the conversation and saw panic in his eyes; his face had flushed scarlet. 'I said, perhaps you know the answer?'

'Forgive me – what?'

Xena leaned forward, giving me a view down the front of her dress. 'I was just asking Besler here, since he is training to be a doctor of physick, if there is any truth in the theory that for a child to be conceived during the act of love, the woman must achieve her pleasure before the man takes his?' A knowing little smile hovered around her lips; she was enjoying the game of trying to discomfit me.

I blinked. 'I'm not sure the medical schools have reached a definitive conclusion on that question,' I said.

'Oh.' She toyed with the stray lock of hair. 'Only, you see, the count has been assured that he will have a son, but I fear that if that is the prerequisite, he is going to be disappointed. Which would make two of us.'

'Assured by whom?' I said, returning her bold gaze.

'Angels.' She let out a scoffing laugh, then clapped her hand to her mouth. 'I should not have said that.'

'Wait,' I said, 'your husband speaks with angels? Or—?'

She glanced nervously at the singers and lowered her voice. 'Dr Dee sees them in his magic mirror.'

I nodded; I had seen that mirror many times in Dee's London house: a solid disc of obsidian about a foot in diameter, in which he said the spirits appeared to him.

'My lady – Xena – does your husband know where John is? I would be grateful for any reassurance that he is safe.'

'The night before the count left, he had invited John Dee to do his scrying. I listened at the door. I should not have, I know, but since they always discussed me and my womb, I thought I had a right to hear what they were saying.' She tipped her chin defiantly. 'I heard John Dee declare that a great and marvellous change was coming to Prague, which would bring low the pride of Rome and guide all of Christendom towards a universal religion.'

That sounded like one of John's grandiose ideas – dangerous stuff, if typically short on detail. 'What else?'

She bit her lip. 'He said that he, John, had been instrumental in bringing this about, but now his enemies had poisoned the Emperor's ear against him. Then he said he suspected a terrible harm aimed at their great enterprise, but without proof he could not make Rudolf listen, and in the meantime he feared for his life.'

'Whose life – Rudolf's?'

'His own. "I fear they will destroy me," is what he said.'

'How did the count respond?'

She waved a hand. 'Oh, John Dee always thought someone was out to get him. My husband was used to his complaints. The count was more interested in what the angels had to say about getting a son. Apparently they said that if he gave refuge to God's messenger, by which I presume John meant himself, he would have his desire. Then the next morning, my husband was gone, so I don't know how he expects that part to come true.'

'When was this?'

'Almost a month ago. He left at dawn, before I was awake – he didn't say goodbye. Later he sent a messenger to inform me that he had important business at his estates in Trebon. He

347

has written a couple of times to say he expects to be back any day, but' – she gestured around the room to indicate his continued absence. Her rosebud mouth was pinched in an expression of petulance, but I could see the loneliness that underlay her need for male attention. In that moment she looked very young.

'Do you know if John went with him?'

She shrugged. 'I only know that I didn't sleep well that night, there was a lot of disturbance. Comings and goings in the courtyard, messengers and horses being dispatched. Nor do I care, really. John Dee is a selfish old fool who attaches himself to men of influence to advance his own interests.'

I smiled at her ferocity. 'I fear the same might be said of me, my lady.' I paused. 'Or you.'

She looked briefly outraged, before she burst into a peal of laughter. 'You are not wrong,' she said, 'although I am not an old fool. And neither are you.' She glanced coyly from under her lashes. 'Come, this conversation grows too solemn for my liking. Let's have some dancing.' She clapped her hands and the viol players struck up a vigorous tune. I was wondering how to extricate myself from this horror when I was saved by the arrival of the steward, his face perturbed. He leaned down to Xena and whispered in her ear. She looked at me with disapproval.

'Dr Bruno, apparently there is a woman at the door in a state of distress, who insists on seeing you.'

Esther. My thoughts immediately flew to her; what could have happened? I pushed my chair back; it was clear that Xena was not pleased to be upstaged by some other woman's demands, but I ignored her expression and bobbed a quick bow, excusing myself.

But when I followed the steward through the courtyard, it was Greta I found cowering in the portico, shaking so that she could barely speak. Her face was bone-white.

'He found out that Magda hid the girl,' she said, clutching at my sleeve. 'I think he's killed her.'

TWENTY-EIGHT

I told the steward to convey my apologies and rushed after Greta to the door, not waiting for my cloak.

She took my arm – I felt how heavily she leaned on me for support – and we headed through the cathedral courtyard to the castle gate.

'What did he do to her?' I asked through clenched teeth. The Venetian food was roiling in my stomach; all I could think was that I could have prevented this if I had gone straight to the tavern.

'He cracked her head off a beam and she fell to the floor like a rag doll,' Greta said between heaving breaths. 'I didn't know who else to turn to – I knew you'd be here because I took the note this morning.'

'Someone needs to find her father,' I muttered, and Greta stopped, her face creased in confusion.

'Her *father*? Oh, no – you misunderstand. It's *Magda*. She tried to stop him getting to the child and he threw her across the room. I would have asked Dr Hajek, but it's too far over the river, and he is so angry with me . . .' Her voice tailed off into a hiccupping sob.

'Then – Sukie is unharmed?'

'She was when I left. He's fetched her a few slaps, poor mite – she wouldn't give him her precious bundle, but it's just bruises.

I'm terrified of what he might do next, though. Oh God, my poor sister. I knew he'd be the death of her one day. I told her so.'

We were halfway down the steps to the Winged Horse when I remembered that I had left my dagger at the gatehouse on entering the castle precincts – I had not expected to need it at the countess's dinner. No matter: I would kill Jan Boodt with my bare hands if I had to.

'Did he get the girl's bundle in the end?' I asked.

Greta nodded miserably. 'She fought him like a little wildcat – she's a brave one – but he forced her to give it up. Now he's locked her and Magda in the tower room and put one of his boys on the stairs, there's no way I can get to them. I'm afraid Magda will die in there, if she's not dead already.'

'Which boys?'

'The bully boys he pays to keep an eye on things at his gaming nights, make sure there's no trouble. Persuade people to pay up if they try to talk their way out of it.'

Hired thugs, then. Bad news on both counts: Boodt had the poisoned elixir and Greta was apparently expecting me to fight my way past this boy on the stairs. I wondered if the thugs were armed.

'There are windows in the tower,' Greta whispered as we approached the inn. 'They're small, but you could fit through, if you could get on to the roof.'

'Even if I could, I can't bring an injured woman and a little girl out on to the roof.' I leaned against the wall in the shadows and considered. 'There's a serving girl who works in the tap-room. I don't think she has any great affection for your brother-in-law. If I can get on to the roof, ask her to distract this boy on the stairs, tell him his master has sent for him or something. That might give us enough time to get the women out, assuming I can pick the lock – though how I'll manage that without my dagger, I have no idea.'

'Would this help?' She reached into the pockets of her smock and brought out a thin-bladed knife, of the kind used for paring fruit.

'Were you planning to stab someone?' I had an alarming vision of Greta taking it upon herself to deal with Jan Boodt.

'I was preparing the vegetables this morning when Dr Hajek came thundering in, shouting fit to wake the dead. He'd found out that I'd taken something—'

'His keys.'

She hung her head. 'Yes. He told me to get out of his house – didn't even give me a chance to get my things. I just ran out with this and a parsnip still in my hand.'

'Well – better than nothing. You can throw the parsnip at Jan if all else fails.'

She attempted a shaky smile. The knife was too small for the sheath at my belt so I slipped it inside my boot.

We picked our way down the side alley to reach the entrance to the yard. As we entered, keeping to the shadows, I saw another figure loitering by one of the outbuildings, watching the main door; I motioned to Greta to keep out of sight. The clouds had thinned enough to allow slivers of moonlight through, and on looking more closely I realised there was something familiar about the man's bulk and his hunched shoulders.

'Erik,' I hissed. He turned, startled, and I saw his hand move inside his jacket. I stepped forward to forestall him. 'It's me. What are you doing here?'

He grimaced. 'Some fucker's been through my house. I still think Magda Boodt knows where Sukie is – I'm waiting for her to come out so I can talk to her. I don't want to run into Jan.'

'You'll be waiting a while.' I stopped. He looked different. 'Are you *sober*?'

'Of course.' He sounded almost offended. 'I have to find my daughter.'

'All right, listen. We're going to do just that. But you have to promise to do exactly what I say.'

When I had finished explaining my plan to both of them, I watched Greta head for the tap-room and Erik disappear into the shadows behind the woodshed. The Winged Horse was built on three sides of a rectangle, with the main tavern on the ground floor of the short front section and most of the guest rooms on the two wings either side, balconies running along the first two storeys. The tower Greta had mentioned was an odd protuberance jutting into the courtyard beside the tap-room, and housing the spiral staircase that led to the upper floors. At the top was a small, hexagonal room with a conical roof and windows on each of the six sides. A doorway at the foot of the tower opened directly on to the staircase; I presumed that the guard was lurking somewhere inside.

I waited until the yard was empty before climbing on to an upturned barrel and hauling myself to the roof of the stable block and on to the first-floor balcony. Here I paused, trying to ignore the throbbing in my bruised shoulder, while I waited to see if anyone in the rooms had noticed me. When it seemed that there was no movement, I pulled myself up to the next balcony and, with the help of gaps and irregularities in the brickwork, from there to the roof of the guest wing. The day's rain had made the tiles slippery, my hands were freezing, and more than once I feared I would lose my grip as I shinned to the apex. Reaching the highest point, I sat astride the roof, keeping my body pressed low, while I steadied my breath and shunted myself along until I was close to the tower room, watching for the signal.

After a few minutes, I saw the serving girl emerge from the tap-room door and cross to the staircase entrance at the foot of the tower. I waited, straining to see in the light of the few torches that guttered around the yard, and shortly after she appeared again, followed by a thick-necked youth. It was hard to see from my vantage point, but he appeared to have a cudgel hanging from his belt. They vanished into the tap-room and almost immediately Erik Moller slipped out of his hiding place and into the staircase. I would have to work fast.

I pulled myself around a chimney stack and on to the short span of roof that abutted the tower room. Leaning down, I peered through one of the arched windows, one hand shielding my face against the glass, and felt my stomach lurch; I could see the prone body of a woman slumped against the wall, Sukie lying beside her. Neither of them seemed to be moving.

I tapped on the pane and Sukie jerked her head up; her eyes bulged with astonishment at the sight of me, and she would have cried out, if not for the dirty rag tied around her mouth. I tried to beckon her across to open the window, but she held up her hands and I saw that her wrists were bound as well. There was no other remedy; I took a deep breath, leaned back and stamped my heel with as much force as I could muster against the window. It took a couple of kicks for the glass to shatter; I froze as shards tumbled down to the courtyard below with a musical tinkle, but apart from some excited whinnying from the horses, no one seemed to have noticed. I pulled my sleeves over my hands and grasped the window frame, hauling myself through, feeling my hose and breeches tear on jagged splinters stuck in the frame. I dropped into the room, landing on a floor of herringbone brick. I pressed a finger to my lips as Sukie flung herself into my arms.

'Listen, I need you to be very brave and keep quiet,' I said when she had calmed a little, taking out Greta's kitchen knife and cutting through the strips of cloth that held the girl's hands before removing the gag from her face.

'He stole it,' she whispered tearfully, rubbing her wrists. 'Ziggi's elixir. I couldn't stop him.' In the half-light I could see that she had a cut on her lip, but she seemed otherwise unharmed. I knelt by Magda and turned her on to her back. She lay unmoving, eyes closed, her skin cold. The hair at her left temple was matted with blood. I touched two fingers to the side of her neck and felt the faintest fluttering of a pulse.

'Thank God,' I breathed. 'Keep talking to her, Sukie, while I get this door open. Your father is outside, but you can't go with him just yet.'

'Why not?'

'He needs to take Magda to safety. And . . .' I hesitated. 'There are men looking for you. They know where you live. It would be better if you stay safe somewhere else until I deal with them.'

She nodded, as if nothing could surprise her now, and I heard her whispering determinedly to Magda in Czech as I bent to tackle the door. It took longer than I would have liked, with freezing fingers and only a fruit knife; my hands shook and I had to keep pausing to listen – any moment I expected Erik to be ambushed by the youth with the cudgel, furious that he had been lured from his post. But eventually the lock clicked, I turned the handle and Erik almost knocked me over as he bowled into the room and swept his daughter into his arms, weeping copiously and murmuring in his own language.

'I'm pleased to see you too, Far, but there's no time to waste,' she said when he finally set her down. She spoke so sternly that I almost laughed. 'You must look after Magda.'

'She's right, Erik,' I said. 'That lad will be back at any moment, we could do without a fight.'

He lifted Magda as easily and carefully as if she were Sukie's size, and settled her over his shoulder. I winced; it was not going to do her head injury any good, but the only alternative was leaving her there, which would surely kill her. I closed the door behind me and followed him down the stairs, taking Sukie by the hand, with a reluctant glance back at the room. I would have preferred to try to lock it again, but that would take too long. With luck, by the time Jan realised that the women had escaped, they would be safely away from the inn.

Greta was waiting by the stable block with a handcart she had lined with fresh straw. When she saw her sister's limp body hanging down Erik's back, she clasped both hands to her mouth, but rallied quickly.

'Jan uses this to make deliveries, he won't notice it missing tonight,' she said. It had been an inspired idea on her part: a man pushing a cart is less likely to be stopped by the watch than one carrying an unconscious woman over his shoulder. Erik laid Magda gently in the straw and Greta settled her head on a linen cloth, then moved to cover her with sacking, stroking her sister's hair away from her face as she did so. At this, Magda's eyes fluttered; Greta gasped and knelt beside her, clutching at her hand. Magda seemed to be whispering something; tearfully, Greta murmured reassurance. Magda's eyes closed again and Greta stood, laying the last piece of sacking over her face. She straightened up and turned to me.

'Bruno, she said they're going to kill you tonight.'

'Who?'

'Jan and the Spaniards.'

'Useful to know,' I said brightly, aware that Sukie was still clinging to my hand. She turned her face up to me, her bruised lip trembling. 'Don't worry about me, I can look after myself.'

So all Montalcino's attempts at persuasion had been empty posturing, I thought; perhaps he had only wanted to ascertain how much I knew about their arrangement with Bartos, and decided it was too much to let me go. Or perhaps, now that Jan Boodt had the elixir and would no doubt sell it to the Spaniards, the Catholics had decided I was dispensable. Apparently Montalcino was even prepared to forgo the pleasure of seeing me tried and burned by the Inquisition, a fate he had been predicting for me since the first time I contradicted him twenty years ago. That also meant that any promise he had made to keep Sukie safe was likely to be equally empty.

I hurried the strange little rescue party to the gate, wanting to get Magda and Sukie away as quickly as possible, but Erik hesitated in the archway, his eyes on his daughter.

'Let me take my girl,' he said, giving me a pleading look. 'I can't rest if she's out of my sight.'

'We talked about this,' I reminded him. 'Those men who searched your house will be back. Greta's going to hide her somewhere they won't look for her, and you're going to take Magda to your neighbour. There isn't much time, Erik. Please.'

He kissed Sukie and picked up the handles of the cart, negotiating it over the cobbles; I hoped Magda's head was well-padded. I took out the Emperor's silver medal and pressed it into Greta's hand.

'You know what you have to do?'

She nodded, and smiled at Sukie. At that moment, the tap-room door opened again and the broad figure of Jan Boodt thundered into the yard. I grabbed Sukie and pulled her into the nearest stall, crouching down behind the door. Fortunately, the horse was docile; it nosed my head inquisitively as I prayed that Jan would not step on any broken glass and think to look up at the tower.

I heard him bellow something in Czech, and Greta's defiant reply; there was a brusque exchange that I did not understand, followed by the sound of a man pissing copiously. After a couple of minutes, Greta's face appeared over the stable door.

'What was that about?' I whispered.

She glanced back at the door. 'He's complaining that they're short-staffed in the tavern without Magda and he's got his card game later.' Her face darkened. 'He's still maintaining the lie that she's sick in bed. He said I can only stay here tonight if I work for my keep, so I told him I just needed to run an errand first. I'll be back as soon as I can to keep an eye on you.'

'Thank you,' I said. She appeared to be serious. I lowered my voice. 'And take care on the way – those men are out there searching.'

She gave me a reproving look. 'I've known every alleyway and staircase between this inn and the castle blindfold since I was smaller than she is now. They won't see us, I promise.'

I watched Sukie put her hand trustingly into Greta's and the two of them disappeared through the archway. I had to hope I had made the right decision. I turned, straightened my doublet and headed towards the tap-room to face my murderers, with only a fruit knife and a middle-aged widow for protection.

TWENTY-NINE

The main room was crowded, the air thick with woodsmoke from the fire. As soon as I set foot inside a hand grabbed my arm and I started, braced to fight, but it was only the plump serving girl with a triumphal expression on her face.

'Greta said you would give me money,' she prompted. 'For getting rid of that boy.'

'Getting *rid* of him?' I looked at her in alarm.

'Yes. I locked him in a storeroom. I said I was scared to go to the beer cellar alone, and I would let him put his hand inside my dress if he came down with me. He's so stupid he agreed. Then I pushed him inside and locked the door.' She held out her open palm, pleased with her own ingenuity.

I laughed, impressed. No wonder the lad hadn't come after us. 'That's worth double.' I slipped the coins into her hand. 'What's your name?'

'Irenka. Let me know if you need any more help.' She grinned, and weaved her way back through the throng to the serving hatch.

I moved towards the hearth, where Jan Boodt was holding court, surrounded by a group of men drinking beer and smoking clay pipes. To judge by their clothes, they covered the gamut of Prague society; a couple in worn leather jerkins, others in good quality woollen doublets and expensive riding boots.

There was no sign of the Spaniards. The conversation petered out as I approached and Jan spread his hands wide.

'Here he is, lads, the man who likes to throw his money away! What have you done to yourself, you been attacked by wolves or something?'

I looked down at my torn clothes. 'That was when your wife tried to rip my breeches off with her teeth,' I said.

One of the men beside him let out a low whistle; there was a taut silence while his mates waited to see how he would respond to this. He stared me out for a long moment, then let rip a roar of laughter and slapped his leg.

'Wouldn't put it past her. I'd believe you, too, if she wasn't laid up in bed. Here, sit down. Fuck off, Jiri, let my new friend have a seat,' he said, cheerily elbowing his neighbour off his stool and offering it to me. I sat gingerly, waiting to see what would happen next. 'You need a beer,' he said, looking around and snapping his fingers when he saw Irenka. 'Another pitcher, girl, and a cup for my guest, and hurry up about it.'

I waited until I had watched the others drink beer from the same jug before tasting it. Jan Boodt was now in possession of Bartos's poison, I reminded myself; I had to watch his every move, while giving the impression that I was at ease in this kind of raucous male gathering. That had never been the case, but I had learned during my time in Naples how to play along, and I joined in the crude jokes and good-natured insults until, another pitcher in, the two Spaniards appeared, looking breathless and disgruntled and muttering an apology to Jan. I studied them with apprehension, but could see no sign of blood on their hands or clothes. The one with the scar met my eye with a brief nod of acknowledgement.

It appeared that their arrival was the signal for the men to depart for the cellar. On the way down the stairs, I caught Jan by the arm and asked if I could have a quiet word. He hung back, his curiosity piqued, and let the others go on ahead.

'I asked you this morning if you'd seen Moller's daughter,' I said, keeping my voice low.

358

'And I told you I haven't.' He lifted his chin, daring me to argue.

'Yes. But I didn't explain the reason for my interest.' I paused; he motioned for me to continue. 'She has something in her possession that would be worth a lot of money to me. I wondered if you might know anything about it.'

A knowing smile curved across his face. 'Ah. So that's why you're chucking money at Moller, is it? You're hoping to get your hands on this thing the girl's hiding?'

I made a non-committal gesture and he nodded; I had the impression that he respected me more now that he thought my motives were not purely altruistic, as if he didn't trust a man who wasn't out for himself.

'Let's suppose I did have some idea what you're talking about,' he said, leaning back against the wall and folding his arms. 'When you say a lot of money – how much are we talking?'

'A hundred thalers,' I said. It was reckless: I didn't have a hundred thalers, in fact, I was burning through the money Overton had left for me at an alarming rate, and he had not given any indication as to what I was expected to do once it ran out.

Boodt chewed his lip as if considering the offer, and eventually shook his head.

'No, I don't think so,' he said, levering himself off the wall.

'Wait. How much, then? Name your price.'

He looked at me keenly, still smiling. 'It's not for sale. I've promised it to someone else.'

'Those Spaniards? Whatever sum you've agreed, I'll add ten per cent.'

He cocked an eyebrow. 'You're well informed, aren't you? Tell you what we'll do—' he clapped me on the shoulder – 'you can both try and win it off me.'

I had pictured the cellar as a dingy basement crowded with barrels and boxes, but Jan's gaming room was a civilised affair:

a brick-lined space with iron wheels to hold candles suspended by chains from the arched ceiling and a brazier burning cheerfully at either end. There were wooden shelves built into the wall opposite the door holding an array of bottles, tankards and glasses, and in the centre of the room, a large round table. Six of us pulled up stools around it, the company eyeing me with varying degrees of greed or wariness while Jan shuffled his cards with great ceremony. Irenka came in with a pitcher of beer in each hand and filled everyone's cups; again, I watched to make sure the others drank with no ill effects, and kept a close eye on my own mug while the cards were dealt. I had made sure to sit on the other side of the table from Jan Boodt, to minimise his opportunities of slipping something into my drink or stabbing me under the table, but to my alarm the small Spaniard pulled up the stool next to me.

'*Hola. Soy Diego*,' the man with the scar said, jabbing a thumb at his chest, as if it had been remiss of him not to introduce himself earlier. He raised his tankard to clink against mine.

'Bruno.'

'They call him Osito,' he added, nodding to his large, shaven-headed friend who sat across from us, scowling.

'*Osito?*' I laughed. The nickname meant 'little bear'; it was hard to think of anything less appropriate.

Diego shrugged. 'It's what his mother called him.'

Jan Boodt called for silence, and turned to the player on his left, who was about to lay the first card, when the door burst open and Erik Moller tumbled through it, apologising profusely for his lateness. I noticed the sly glances exchanged among the other men; Erik was clearly a joke among them. He pulled up a stool and caught my eye for the space of a heartbeat; long enough to give an almost invisible nod, which I took to mean that Magda was now in the care of Goodwife Huss. I had not been able to think of anywhere else to take her; the goodwife had struck me as a practical woman, and her unfavourable opinion of men in general made her more likely to sympathise with the victim of one.

Jan rapped his knuckles on the table and called, 'Vada'. The game was Primero – 'Italian rules, in honour of our guest,' Jan declared, to the disgruntlement of the company – with a five-thaler stake. I lost the first two hands without even trying, which helped to lessen suspicion of me, but as the game progressed, I began to get the measure of the players: the earnest, grey-bearded man in the finely cut doublet, who studied his cards as if for a university examination; the younger, chubby fellow in workman's clothes to Jan's right, who huffed and rolled his eyes at every new card he picked up, only to lay down a chorus or a fluxus with a shrug, as if he couldn't think how it had got there. Jan thought he was a good bluffer, but his tell was quickly obvious; he pulled at his left earlobe when he knew he had a winner and chewed the skin by his thumbnail when his cards were bad. The conversation was all in German; the Spaniards appeared to speak no tongue except their own, but made themselves perfectly understood through gestures and eloquent curses that transcended language barriers. Diego was particularly sharp and took several hands; he could make his face entirely unreadable and seemed to have remarkable powers of memory. I watched closely for any sign that the game was rigged, but could see none; perhaps that would come later, once the players had relaxed.

After an hour, when I had won two hands – more by luck than strategy – and lost several more, the door opened and Greta appeared bearing a tray with another pitcher of beer.

'Time for something stronger, I think,' Jan said, rubbing his hands. 'Get the schnapps, woman, and seven glasses.'

Greta bobbed a curtsy and busied herself at the shelves with her back to us; a couple of minutes later she brought the tray over and made a circuit of the table, setting a glass with a large measure of clearish liquid in front of each of us. Jan ostentatiously shuffled the deck with one hand while he picked his glass up and knocked it back in one, before slamming it on the table and motioning for Greta to refill it. I sniffed cautiously; it was some kind of aqua vitae, flavoured with herbs. I watched the other men down theirs and did the same, although I snapped my wrist back so fast that no one noticed most of it went down my chin.

'Leave the bottle,' Jan said. 'And you can empty that, woman, while you're here, and bring back some bread and pickled eggs,' he added as Greta was about to go. He pointed to the piss pot in the corner, which was on the brink of overflowing. Silently, Greta did as she was told. She did not look at me once, but I thought she seemed unusually self-possessed, given how distressed she must be about her sister.

'Right.' Jan looked around the table with a glint in his eye. 'Now we raise the stakes, my friends.'

The stake became ten thalers, and one by one the players bowed out, shaking their heads at their losses, until only Jan, Diego and I were still in. I was certain he must have manipulated the cards to bring about that result, but the trick had eluded me.

'Private game now, boys,' Jan said, grinning at me. The others took this as a dismissal and trooped out; Erik shot me an anxious glance as he left and I tried my best to look reassuring. Finally the three of us were alone, apart from Osito, who moved away from the table and settled himself on a stool in front of the door, glowering with his arms folded. It occurred to me that I should begin to feel afraid at this point; there were three of them, all practised fighters, and there was no way I could reach the stairs if they decided to stop me. But my fear was tempered by curiosity as Jan reached into his jacket and brought out an unusual silver flask, about eight inches high with a cork stopper, engraved on both sides with a delicate pattern of vines and flowers. He shook it and we heard the liquid sloshing about inside.

'Well, then. This is the prize.' He paused to pull a dirty kerchief from his sleeve and wipe his brow.

'May I?' I asked, holding out my hand; I wanted to examine the bottle.

'Ah, no.' He lifted it out of my reach, the way you might

tease a dog to make it jump. 'We can't have it tampered with, can we? Supposedly this is very valuable to both of you. So what is it?'

I couldn't tell if Diego had understood; his face remained impassive, so I translated, but he merely shrugged, as if to say he neither knew nor cared.

'*Aurum potabile*,' I told Jan. 'Liquid gold. It's something Ziggi Bartos was working on before he was killed.'

Jan nodded. He seemed to be sweating heavily. 'What does it do?'

'The alchemists believe it makes the body incorruptible.'

'What, eternal life?' He laughed, and it turned into a sputtering cough.

'Not necessarily. But proof against disease and ageing.'

'Does it work?'

'He evidently believed so, since he went to such trouble to hide it.'

'Huh.' Boodt turned the flask in his hand, squinting at it. 'All right. You can play each other for the right to buy it from me. Best of seven games.'

I presumed this was purely for his amusement, since he already had a deal with the Spaniards and knew they were planning to dispose of me. He set the flask down and shuffled the cards, dropping them twice and cursing. It looked as if his hands were shaking.

Diego moved so that we sat opposite one another. His dark eyes were expressionless, though the droop of the right caused by his scar lent him a melancholy look.

He took the first two hands; I won the next. From the tail of my eye I could see Jan tugging at his collar; several times he poured himself another mug of beer and drank it off as if he had a raging thirst. Was he drunk, or merely nervous about my imminent murder on his property?

I won the next hand with a Supremus – two aces and a six and seven of clubs – and the Spaniard's eyes narrowed. My mouth had dried and I was finding it hard to concentrate, though the outcome of the game hardly mattered if they did not intend to let me leave. I glanced at the door, wondering how much damage I could do to Osito with Greta's fruit knife in order to get past.

Jan dealt two cards to each of us and shuffled again, ready to deal the next two, when suddenly the deck fell from his hands, scattering over the floor as he clutched at his throat. He hauled himself unsteadily to his feet, knocking over his stool, and staggered to lean one hand on the wall, where he vomited forcefully. When he had voided his stomach, he wheeled around, struggling for breath, his eyes wild and unfocused. He clawed at the air with his right hand. Diego shot me a questioning look; I shook my head, baffled.

Jan lurched past the table, making for the shelves at the end of the room. He reached out as if desperately grasping for something – water, perhaps? – but collapsed dramatically before he got there, grabbing on to a shelf and bringing the whole lot crashing down in a cascade of broken glass and spilled liquids. At the sound, the cellar door flew open, knocking Osito out of the way, and Greta barrelled through, hands pressed to her face, shrieking in horror at the sight.

'Quick, he needs a doctor,' she cried, grabbing at my hand as she passed; I felt the Emperor's medal slide into my palm. She knelt by Jan, feeling for his pulse.

'I'll go,' I said, seeing my chance. I jumped up and ran for the door before the Spaniards could react.

Greta pointed at Osito. '*You* – help me, we need to take him upstairs and make him comfortable. Hold him under the shoulders,' she said, in perfect Spanish; her tone of urgency and command didn't brook contradiction, and the Little Bear did as he was told, seemingly too stunned to argue.

I turned back at the foot of the stairs in time to see Diego slip the silver flask inside his doublet. Greta, lifting Jan's feet, glanced up, caught my eye and gave me an unmistakable wink.

THIRTY

A lamp burned low in the kitchen at the House of the Green Mound when I arrived in the stable yard; through the window I saw Hajek sitting alone at the table in the dim light with a sad supper of bread and cheese. I banged on the glass and he leapt up to open the door; I fell through it, doubled over with my hands on my thighs, snatching ragged breaths.

Hajek peered out into the night before slamming and bolting the door.

'Christ, what happened? Is someone chasing you?'

I shook my head, still unable to speak.

'Take your time,' he said, pulling out a chair for me. 'I'd offer you hot wine, but I can't get this range to light. It's temperamental – Greta's the only one who knows how to persuade it.' He snorted. 'Spend my days surrounded by furnaces and I can't even light my own bloody stove.'

The room was freezing. I sensed his gruffness was covering more complicated feelings.

'Perhaps I was too hasty with her this morning,' he mused.

'She just saved my life,' I managed, when I could gasp out words. 'And I think Jan Boodt is dead.'

I sat and relayed the evening's events. I had run all the way from the Winged Horse, terrified the Spaniards would catch up with me, but it seemed they had chosen to cut their losses and disappear with their prize. That did not mean that Montalcino's order to dispatch me would not keep for another day. When I came to the part about finding Magda, and what Jan had done to her, Hajek flung his chair back as if he were about to charge out of the door.

'And where is she now?'

'In the care of a woman called Huss in Golden Lane. I thought Jan wouldn't look there. That was before I knew Jan wouldn't be looking anywhere.'

'And the Danish girl?'

'Safe.'

'I must see how Magda is. She'll need medical attention.'

'Keep away from the Winged Horse, then,' I said. 'People will be asking questions.'

He drummed his fingertips on the table, thinking. 'Actually, that might be a good reason for me to look in. Offer a professional opinion on Jan's death. The man was overweight and drank too much – bound to put a strain on the heart. No need for anyone to suspect foul play. None of the others who drank the schnapps were affected?'

'No – although most of them had left by the time Jan was taken ill, so I can't be certain. But I don't think so. I drank a little and I feel fine. Apart from all the running and climbing on roofs.'

'Then it was not in the bottle, whatever she gave him.'

'The schnapps was the only thing she poured for us in separate glasses. She must have put it directly in his. I'd be willing to bet that whatever the Spaniards took away in that silver flask is not Bartos's elixir.'

'You think Greta substituted it?' His eyes widened.

'More likely Magda. She'd have had the opportunity when Sukie first came to her, knowing Jan would have the flask from the child by force eventually. I told her the potion was dangerous.'

An odd look passed across his face. 'She always was sharp as a needle. That brute knew she was cleverer than him and hated her for it.' His fists clenched at his sides and I realised with a sudden jolt: *he loves her*.

'Thaddeus,' I said, looking him in the eye. 'Forgive me, but do you care for Magda?'

He smiled sadly. 'Since I was twenty-eight. But my father was a gentleman and would not countenance his son marrying a taverner's daughter, so that was that. And Greta had already disappointed her parents by running off with an alchemist – my father's apprentice – so it was Magda's duty to take on the Winged Horse. Which she did, and ran it very successfully by herself for a couple of years after her father died, though she was only in her twenties, until that bastard Jan Boodt, who was the brewer's lad, won her over. He's been making her life hell ever since.'

'And you never married?'

'Never met another woman like Magda,' he murmured, looking at the floor, with a shyness I had not seen in him before.

'You should go to her,' I said gently. 'I don't know how badly she was hurt, there wasn't time to examine her, but . . .' I did not need to make the rest explicit.

'Magda is a survivor,' he said, as if he could make it true by force of will. 'Will you be all right here?'

'I'll be sleeping the sleep of the just,' I said, pushing myself up from the table. 'I feel I have earned it. How was David's family? And the rabbi?' *And Esther*, I wanted to add, but stopped myself.

He made a grim face. 'As you'd expect. Awful business. One interesting thing, though. Benjamin allowed me to examine the body eventually.'

'And?'

'Not the same weapon. A long, straight blade this time. Narrow, too.'

'A different killer, then?'

He spread his hands wide. 'I couldn't say. You're the one piecing this together. I must fetch my bag.'

'Oh,' I said as he reached the door, 'what time did Besler come back?'

Hajek frowned. 'Besler? He didn't. I assumed he was with you.'
We looked at one another.

'*Merda*,' I said with feeling.

He was not back when I awoke the following morning. In the grey dawn, the elation of the previous night – my rooftop rescue of Magda and Sukie, Greta's astonishing extrajudicial punishment of Jan Boodt, my escape from the Spaniards – had ebbed, to be replaced by a bleaker outlook. I was no nearer to finding out who killed Bartos and David, Montalcino still wanted me dead, he was bound to discover at some point that he had been cheated out of the poisoned elixir, I didn't know if Sukie was out of danger and, for all I knew, Magda might have died in the night and Jan survived. That would be the worst of all outcomes: if by some chance he pulled through, he would know exactly what had been done to him and Greta would face a charge of attempted murder, for which she would surely be condemned to death.

Then there was Besler. I had considered going to fetch him last night, but it was gone two when I arrived at Hajek's and the prospect of crossing the bridge again with those Spaniards out there deterred me. Besides, I doubted I would have been in time to prevent the inevitable. I thought of Count Vilem's portrait hanging in the hall: he was tall, blond and blue-eyed, just like Besler. As Xena had pointed out, she was no fool; if you were looking for a young, healthy man to do what your husband could not, it made sense to find one who resembled him. I almost laughed at my own vanity: it was not my reputation that had stirred her interest, but Besler's colouring. She must have set her sights on him the moment she noticed him. I feared that she may not be as clever as she thought, though; she had failed to take into account the fact that servants have sharp eyes, and those in the Rozmberk household would have served her husband for years before she arrived. Their first loyalty would be to their master, and they may not like to see him cuckolded. Or perhaps they would be so invested in the continuation of the dynasty and their own employment that they would turn a blind eye if it resulted in an heir. I had to hope it wouldn't result in Besler on the wrong end of a duelling sword.

I put the book Esther had given me for Sukie into my bag and set off for the castle again. The sky was clearing and a pale sun hung low over the spires, though I felt the wind's keen edge. As I crossed the Stone Bridge, I glanced over the parapet at the entrance to the Devil's Channel and shivered. After I had checked on Sukie and Magda, I would go back to the Jewish Town and see if I could offer any support, by which I meant see Esther. I still wanted to find out what Benjamin was hiding, and what he had taken so urgently from David's house.

Almost without intending it, I found myself climbing the street that led to the Winged Horse, though my steps slowed as I approached. Perhaps it was unwise to be seen here, but I couldn't go the rest of the day without putting my mind at ease about Jan.

As I rounded the curve of the street, I saw Irenka outside sweeping the front step. She raised a hand in greeting.

'Morning,' she said cheerfully, leaning on her broom. She looked considerably fresher than I did after the night's adventures. 'We're closed today, but I can do you some breakfast if you want?'

'Closed?'

'Yes. As a mark of *respect*.' She couldn't have made the word sound more risible. 'You didn't hear? The master died last night. He was taken ill very suddenly – the mistress's sister found him. Perhaps you'd gone by then?'

'I must have. Do they know what happened?'

'Well, the doctor turned up and he said the master's heart had given out. It's common, apparently, at his age, if you're a drinker. Terrible shock. So we're all in mourning today.'

'My condolences.'

She grinned; I returned it, complicit.

'I hope you let that boy out of the storeroom.'

She pressed a hand to her mouth with a giggle. 'Oops. Completely forgot, in all the excitement. Oh well. Won't do him any harm to reflect on his sins a while longer. He'll be out of a job now. Do you want to see the mistress?'

I stared at her. 'She's better already?'

'Oh – no, I meant the new mistress. Her sister. She's looking after the place for now. We'll be open again tomorrow. There's only so much mourning you can do when people need to eat.'

'And Magda?'

The girl's face grew sombre. 'I haven't heard anything. Mistress Greta might – should I fetch her?'

'No, it's all right, I'll come back later. Just give her my good wishes.'

'I will, sir. Give you good day.' She bobbed a curtsy and returned to her sweeping, whistling a merry tune. She might need to work on her performance of grief, I thought.

I continued on to the castle with one weight off my mind, while trying to convince myself that no news must be good news as far as Magda was concerned. I showed the Emperor's token to various guards and was eventually admitted to the private wing, until I arrived at the door of the Strada's apartments.

A nervous-looking maid answered my knock, and ran quickly to announce me. A moment later, Ottavio appeared from the corridor looking peevish, for which I couldn't blame him.

'Bruno. I do think you might check first before dumping distraught children on us in the middle of the night. This isn't an orphanage.'

'Oh,' I said, glancing anxiously over my shoulder at the stairs. 'That's awkward – I have four more waiting outside.'

He relented and gave a brief smile. 'You'd better come in.'

'I apologise,' I said as he closed the door. 'It was an emergency – I had to find a place the child would be safe, with someone who was kind, and I thought of your sister.'

'Ah. There I was thinking you were going to say me. Safe from what?'

'Some unscrupulous men were looking for her. She needed to be somewhere they couldn't reach her.'

'Why, what has she done? Is she a thief?' He looked alarmed.

I hesitated, then reasoned that he had done me a favour and I didn't want him to suspect Sukie of wrongdoing. 'No. She was close to Ziggi Bartos,' I said, lowering my voice.

'Really?' He frowned. 'She's just a child.'

'I know. But Bartos trusted her. I don't think he had many people he could confide in. These men know he gave her something to look after before he was killed.'

'Really? An alchemical discovery, you mean? What was it?'

'Doesn't matter. The point is, she doesn't have it any more, but these men may still wish to silence her. Can she stay here until she's out of danger?'

Ottavio looked worried, but eventually he nodded. 'I suppose so. As long as it doesn't put my family at risk. My sister is charmed by her, but of course Kat does love to look after people. Come.'

I wondered if that was true, or if it was what he told himself in order to avoid his share of emptying their father's bedpan.

He pushed open the door to a small salon, where Sukie sat cross-legged on a floor cushion, reading a book aloud to a small boy who leaned his head against her arm and sucked his thumb, docile as a kitten.

When she saw me, she jumped up, her face contorted with distress; it pained me that she now associated me with bad news.

'Can I go home?' she said, clutching at my sleeve. Her wild hair had been brushed and neatly braided, and the cut on her lip dressed with a salve.

'Not yet, I'm afraid. I need you to be patient and stay here a little longer.'

'Is my father all right?'

'He's fine. He was a hero last night,' I added. 'I could not have saved you and Magda without him.'

She smiled uncertainly; I sensed she was not quite ready to believe in her father's heroism yet. Her face grew sombre again. 'Magda – is she . . . ?'

'I don't know yet,' I admitted. 'But Jan Boodt is dead.'

'Good,' she said emphatically. No pretence of mourning for her.

'I've brought you the book I promised,' I said, holding out the bag.

'Thank you. But I have lots of books here – Katherina has been very kind and let me look at hers.' She said this a little too loudly; I gave her a questioning look and she glanced past me at Ottavio, who was standing in the doorway, before dropping her voice. 'Bruno, I need to speak to you. In private.'

I nodded, and turned to Ottavio. 'We're just going to take a walk in the courtyard. She needs fresh air.'

His eyes narrowed. 'I can open a window?'

'And exercise,' I said. After a beat, he smiled and stepped aside for us to pass, but I could see the suspicion in his face. It was understandable; I had, as he said, dumped the girl on his family and only now let him know that murderous thugs were looking for her. He must wonder what else I hadn't told him. As Sukie left the room, the little boy erupted into one of those unnerving, bestial screams that seemed to endure long past the lung capacity of any human.

'Oh good God,' Ottavio said, casting around frantically for someone to deal with it.

Sukie clung to my arm, her elfin face tight with worry. When we reached a quiet corner of the courtyard, she pulled me into the shadow of a doorway.

'It's Katherina,' she said solemnly. My heart lurched.

'Has she mistreated you?'

'Oh – no, she's been very kind. She braided my hair, then she let me sit in her chamber and look at her books.'

'What, then?'

She reached into the pocket of her dress and drew out a piece of paper. 'I found this tucked inside one of them.'

I unfolded it and my eyes widened at the sight of neat, spiky writing that was almost as familiar to me by now as my own. It was all in Latin. I read the first few lines:

I burn for you like an athenor.

Our love is the conjoining of Sol and Luna, it is the chymical wedding that brings about the great transmutation. I am Sulfur, you are Mercury. In the fire of our union we become purified, and what is generated when our bodies and souls conjoin is the most noble substance of all. There will come a day when we need no longer hide in the shadows. You are my Lux Major, I walked in darkness until I stepped into your light.

There was a good deal more of this, replete with alchemical imagery and bad poetry, but I did not need to read on to get the gist.

'Holy God. Did you understand this?' I asked.

Sukie gave me her best eye-roll. 'Most of it. I told you, I can read Latin. It's a love letter.' She paused to see if I had understood. 'It's Ziggi's writing.'

'I know. In Katherina's book, you said?'

She nodded. 'Do you think they were sweethearts?'

I folded the paper again and handed it back to her. 'He certainly sounds very ardent, but we don't know that she returned his feelings. For God's sake, don't ask her. Put this back before she sees it's missing.'

'I'm not stupid.' She squirrelled the paper away again. 'But if they were – does that have anything to do with his murder?'

I blew out air through pursed lips. 'It's possible. I need to think. You did the right thing to show me. Have you found any more like this?'

'No, but I could.' Her eyes brightened at the prospect. 'I can be an espial for you.'

I hesitated. 'You promise me you won't get caught? We don't want anyone else with a grudge against you. And the Stradas are doing you a favour, at my request – if Katherina catches you snooping through her things, they'll throw you out, and they

373

won't trust either of us again, which would make life difficult. Don't give any hint that you've seen that letter. But if there are more like it, I would be interested to know what they say.'

'I'm very good at passing unnoticed, actually,' Sukie said with an assertive little roll of her shoulders, as if I had insulted her professionalism. I suspected that meant she had sometimes been forced to steal food, but I didn't ask.

'When Jan threw Magda against the wall and I heard her head crack, I thought he would do the same to me,' she said quietly as we crossed the courtyard. 'That's why I let him take the flask. Did you get it back?'

'Not yet. But I will.'

'I promised Ziggi I would take care of it. I've let him down.' She kicked a stone, her hands tucked under her arms. 'It was valuable, you see. He had it made especially by a silversmith.'

I stopped. 'Why was it so valuable?'

'Because it was magic.'

'Right.'

'Don't say *right* in that voice, like I'm a baby. I mean, it was a magic trick. It could pour two different liquids out of the same spout. He showed me once.'

'Of course.' I turned to her, delighted. 'That's how he planned to – how did it work? Did he explain it to you?'

'It had two chambers inside, and there were pipes. If you knew how to put your fingers over the little holes on the outside, you could change the pressure and it would push out liquid from the second chamber instead of the main one.'

'Brilliant,' I said, half to myself. That at least solved the mystery of how Bartos had intended to drink the elixir in front of the Emperor without also being poisoned, though it was a high-risk strategy. 'Did he design it himself?'

'He said a friend gave him the idea, but he perfected it. So you have to find it.'

Outside the Stradas' apartments, I handed her Esther's book. 'This belongs to a friend of mine, and it's very precious to her. They're stories of brave women – I thought you might like it.'

Sukie nodded earnestly as she tucked it under her arm. 'I'll take great care of it. Please thank her.'

I had intended to leave, but the door was opened by Katherina this time, holding her son awkwardly on her hip. He appeared to have screamed himself to sleep and looked almost cherubic with his head on her shoulder.

'Come in,' she said to me. 'My father wants to speak to you.'

I followed her along the corridor, thinking about the letter Sukie had shown me. All the flowery talk of conjoining could have been allegorical, I supposed, but Bartos had certainly made it sound as if a union of bodies had occurred. Was *Katherina* his midnight visitor? She was relatively tall for a woman; it was not impossible that a bleary-eyed drunk would mistake her, in the dark and wrapped in a heavy cloak, for a man. And if they had been lovers, did it then follow that the child she was now carrying was not fathered by Rudolf, but by *Bartos*? *Dio porco*, that put a different slant on things. The Holy Roman Emperor, King of Bohemia and Hungary, cuckolded by a low-born alchemist? Perhaps that had been part of the attraction for Bartos.

Only the night before, I had despaired of finding anyone with a motive as persuasive as Montalcino's for wanting the alchemist dead; now a whole new prospect had been revealed. If Bartos was in love with Katherina, that would explain why he was so easily persuaded into the Catholics' plot – he would have a reason besides money to profit from the Emperor's death. Was that what he had meant when he said the day was coming when they would no longer have to walk in the shadows? As for Katherina, she was her family's passport to influence at court and proximity to the Emperor. They still hoped that her son would be ennobled; perhaps, given Rudolf's reluctance to marry, they even dared hope that he would one day make Katherina his wife and her children legitimate heirs. It was one thing for the Emperor to tire of her and look elsewhere, quite another for her to do the same. If her father and brother had found out about Bartos, they may have feared that the liaison would prove catastrophic for their family's fortunes, particularly if they knew she was pregnant by him. That was more than enough reason to want the alchemist out of the way.

But there was another possibility. What if the Emperor himself had discovered Katherina's infidelity? The magnitude of this made my head spin so that I stopped in my tracks. Katherina turned and looked at me with concern.

'Are you all right, Dr Bruno? Is it your head?'

I touched my fingertips to the bruise at the base of my skull. 'I was late to bed, I'm afraid.'

'I sympathise. My father had a bad night, and when that happens, I don't sleep either.'

'Then I'm sorry to have added to your burden by asking you to take care of Sukie. I can pay you for your trouble.'

'It's no trouble. She's a sweet girl – very bright. I gave her a bath this morning, she was sorely in need of it. I think she has lacked a mother's attentions.'

And a father's, I thought, though I hoped that might change. 'Well, thank you for all your kindness. She'll have read her way through the imperial library by this time tomorrow,' I said.

She smiled. 'I like to see a girl hungry for knowledge. My father may have his faults, but he always insisted that I should learn as well as Ottavio.'

We paused outside the door to her father's chamber.

'And how are you?' I asked, with a meaningful glance at her stomach.

'Well enough. But, please . . .' She hoisted the child on her hip and pressed a finger to her lips. 'My father and brother still have no idea.'

I wouldn't be so sure about that, I thought, as she knocked and opened the door for me.

Jacopo Strada was propped up on his pillows, a book open on his lap, his face grey. 'Here he is,' he said as I entered, in a tone that implied nothing good could come of my appearance.

'Signor Strada.' I crossed the room and bowed. 'I'm sorry to see that you are unwell today.'

'You're not sorry, you Neapolitan snake,' he said, pushing himself upright.

'Papà,' Katherina said in a warning tone.

'Pardon?' I said.

'You heard me. You are my compatriot – does fellow-feeling count for nothing with you?'

'I don't know what—'

'His Majesty says you want to look at my inventory.'

'Ah.'

'Yes, *ah*. You've told him I'm stealing from him, is that it?'

'His Majesty did not need me to put that idea in his head. He notices things missing.'

'Of course things are missing – he gives them away on a whim. You've seen his state of mind – he doesn't remember from one day to the next. I have the devil's own job trying to keep track of his sudden fits of generosity. But if you're determined to prove me a liar, be my guest.' He gestured to a large chest under the window. 'Go on, help yourself.'

I hesitated, then crossed the room to lift the lid, feeling his sharp eyes on my back. Inside I found dozens upon dozens of ledgers. I took one from the top and opened it. The pages were crammed with lines of spidery handwriting, all initials and abbreviations, some of which were clearly dates, the rest a meaningless jumble that looked like one of Walsingham's ciphers. There was no hope of making sense of any of it.

Jacopo watched me with his fox-like smile. 'Feel free to read through them all and check them against the collections, won't you,' he said. 'Although I'll be long in my grave by the time you've finished.' He let out a wheezing laugh.

'I don't think that will be necessary,' I said, straightening. 'Do you remember an Ottoman dagger, gold handle set with turquoise and rubies? A gift from the Venetian ambassador?'

He sat up, frowning. 'Of course I remember that. Very fine workmanship. It disappeared about a month ago – at least, that's when I noticed. How do you know about it?'

'Did he give it to John Dee?'

'He wouldn't say who he'd given it to. What would John Dee want with a dagger? He'd only use it for opening letters. Unless he feared the Catholics were going to slit his throat one dark night.' He laughed again and fell into a coughing fit, clutching at his chest and gesturing frantically for his enamel bowl. I looked around; Katherina had taken a seat by the fire with the boy in her lap, so I had no choice but to leap forward and hold the dish under the old man's chin while he spat out a lump of phlegm.

'Talking of murder,' he said when he had recovered, 'are you any nearer to discovering who killed the alchemist?' His face gave nothing away.

'I am continuing my enquiries,' I said evenly. 'It's a question of finding someone with a compelling enough reason to want him dead. If you have any suggestions, I would be glad to hear them.'

'I hear there's been another death. A Jewish bookseller. Connected?'

'Possibly.'

'Well, then. If you want my advice, I think you should be looking across the river.'

I'm sure you do, I thought. 'Why is that?'

'Sounds like a case of an eye for an eye. A deal that went wrong.'

'How?'

'The bookseller was crooked. Ask my son – he did business with him. The Jew was forever trying to palm off books that were bad copies, or overcharging. Suppose he tried to cheat the alchemist, and Bartos threatened to report him or expose his corruption? Next thing you know, the alchemist is dead, with all the marks of a Golem on him.'

'You're saying the Golem killed Ziggi Bartos?' I gave him a sceptical look and folded my arms.

'No, you fool.' He paused for another cough, pressing his hand to his heart. 'I'm saying the Jews killed him and made it look like the work of a Golem, to sow terror in the city and emphasise their power.'

I didn't bother to point out the obvious flaws in this argument. 'Then who killed the bookseller?'

'The alchemist's friends, probably.'

'He didn't have any.'

'Except Sukie,' Katherina said quietly.

'What's that?' Jacopo leaned forward, a hand cupped to his ear.

'The little girl who's staying with us. She was friends with Bartos, the alchemist. She told me.'

I watched her closely for any sign of emotion when she spoke his name, but she kept her tone entirely flat.

'Well, I doubt she stabbed the bookseller and threw him in the river,' Jacopo said dismissively. 'No – this is a dispute between the Jews and the alchemists, you mark my words. I need to rest now. Listen to me, Dr Bruno. You and I understand one another, I think?'

'In what sense?'

'We are both Italians, men of letters, who – despite our native abilities – are obliged to depend on the favours of men who are our intellectual inferiors.'

'Papà!' Katherina stood, as if she might stop him speaking.

'Quiet, girl. Bruno knows I am right. We have both learned to shift for ourselves. So I need you to impress upon His Majesty that I am not cheating him. Say you have looked through the ledgers and you are satisfied that he has no cause for concern.'

'That will not go well for me if he discovers that I have lied to him.'

'It is not a lie.' He fixed a level gaze on me, giving nothing away.

'And what will you do for me in return?'

'Ha! Spoken like a Neapolitan. I will tell him that it would be a jewel in the crown of his reputation to keep a man of your abilities at his court to produce your books under his patronage.' He paused, waiting to see my response. 'And of course we will continue to keep that girl safe here.'

After a moment, I nodded.

'Good.' He fell back on his pillows, as if all this politicking had exhausted him. 'Katherina will see you out.'

'*Is* he stealing from the Emperor?' I asked her, when she had closed the door behind us.

'You don't really expect me to answer that?' She adjusted her son's weight in her arms and glanced at me from the tail of her eye. 'For as long as my father remains in charge of the collections, he sees it as his responsibility to maintain them in the best possible state. Sometimes that necessitates selling certain pieces in order to purchase others. But always for the Emperor's glory and profit.'

'And you forge letters for him to make these sales?'

'It's not forgery,' she said, defensive. 'He dictates them, I write them down. As he said, his hands are shaky now.'

'But you write them down in his handwriting?'

She looked at her feet. 'My father is a proud man. He doesn't want the people he corresponds with to know how ill he is. Besides, his writing carries more authority. I have a good eye for copying – even Ottavio can't tell the difference. You know, now that I think of it, I remember those knives you mentioned,' she said, changing the subject.

'*Knives?*'

'Yes, they were a pair. The Ottoman daggers, very beautiful. Why would he give one to John Dee?'

'Perhaps it was a reward for something. If they were a pair, where is the other? It's not in the *Kunstkammer.*'

She shook her head. 'I don't know. Maybe he gave it to someone else. Or sometimes he takes things that please him to his own private quarters to look at. Like a magpie. Why are you asking, anyway?' Her eyes widened as she spoke, as if she had already found the answer. 'Oh – you think it was used in the murder? Then – is John Dee involved? My father suspected he might be.'

'I thought your father suspected the Jews?'

'He suspects everyone. He has a somewhat jaundiced view of people.'

'He is a Mantuan through and through, then,' I said.

She laughed. 'I'm sure he would say you are a Neapolitan through and through. I've always thought that absurd – the idea that people are all alike depending on their birthplace, or their family name, or the sign they were born under. As if we don't all have to make our own choices.'

'How do you see yourself, then, Katherina?' I asked at the door.

Her face grew serious; her brown eyes met mine for a moment and slid away. 'I'm a mother,' she said, stroking the boy's back as he began to stir. 'That comes before everything.'

I reflected on her words as I hurried down the stairs. It was as if I had spent the last couple of days playing a complex game of chess, found myself in a stalemate, and suddenly Sukie's discovery of the letter had thrown all the pieces into the air; I still had no idea where they might land. So there were two Ottoman daggers: one had been given by Rudolf to John Dee, who – for reasons unknown – had passed it on to Rabbi Loew. The other was missing, but presumably must be in the possession of someone who had access to the imperial collections, meaning the Emperor or a member of the Strada family.

Could *Rudolf* have killed Bartos? There was a horrible kind of logic to it. He discovers the woman he takes for granted has fallen in love with another man; perhaps she even wants a conventional marriage and family with Bartos. The Emperor is incensed; he summons his rival to a private audience and stabs him. Rudolf may not have been a soldier, but he was well-versed in anatomy and would have had tuition in fencing and swordplay as a boy, like all young nobles; he would have a good idea how to inflict a fatal blow to the heart. What he definitely would not have done with his own hands was to mutilate the body and sling it over the bridge; for that he would have required the services of someone close to him, whom he trusted. Not Jacopo, clearly. Ottavio Strada? He might have been only too pleased to help dispose of the man who threatened his family's position. Or – here my throat tightened – Hajek?

There were two obvious flaws in this theory, I thought as I stepped out into the courtyard. It was Rudolf who had tasked me with finding the killer. Unless it was a test, to see if I had the ingenuity to work out who was responsible and the loyalty to relinquish the idea of justice when I discovered the truth. What had he said to me, that first night in the *Kunstkammer*? 'Who do you think killed him?' But if he had intended it as a riddle, nothing about his subsequent behaviour suggested that kind of cool detachment. I had seen him in the wake of the two grisly caskets with their cryptic messages from Bartos; he had been terrified. An attack of guilt? I found it hard to believe that a man whose boldest response to the brother who threatened his throne was to have someone else curse him at a distance could be capable of stabbing a man while looking him in the eye from a foot away.

I passed the vast flank of the cathedral with a glance at the door. Where was Katherina in all this, I wondered. She was a woman who had clearly learned to hide her feelings and turn them inward; even so, if Bartos had been her lover – if he was the father of her unborn child – she must be suffering unbearable grief, compounded by the suspicion that either her father, her brother or the Emperor were responsible. How could she endure it? And then it struck me: *the messages from Bartos*. Only five minutes ago, Katherina had told me of her gift for copying her father's writing, so that even her brother could not distinguish the forgery; could she also have mimicked Bartos's distinctive hand from his letters to her? She had asked specifically about my head. Only Hajek and Besler knew I had a head injury – apart from the person who had hit me in the crypt, of course. And that person would have needed access to the underground passage and advance warning that the Emperor was on his way to hear Mass, which could only have been someone inside the palace complex. It seemed highly likely, now that I thought about it, that Katherina was behind the macabre messages. But what had she hoped to achieve by them? To prick the Emperor's conscience? To frighten him by implying that his guilt was known? Had she cut that poor dog up herself?

Only Katherina could answer those questions, and I knew she would never admit any of it to me; the Stradas would close ranks if my enquiries came too close to them. I had to hope that Sukie would turn up something more conclusive that I could use to persuade them.

I presented myself at the door of the Rozmberk Palace and was met by the taciturn steward, who regarded me with even greater disdain, if that were possible.

'I left my cloak behind,' I said.

'Not all you left behind,' he muttered, showing me into the courtyard. 'Wait there.'

After a few minutes, he returned to announce that the countess would see me briefly, but she was very busy. I was led through the entrance hall, avoiding the gimlet eye of the count's portrait, and into a small parlour. Everywhere there was a bustle of servants, an air of panicked activity. Xena sat pensively in a window seat, her hair tucked under a plain hood, a white rabbit fur cape around her shoulders. Without the cosmetics of the night before, she looked very young.

'I came to present my apologies, my lady, and thank you for your hospitality.'

She regarded me coolly. 'I consider it most ill-mannered of you to disappear like that, Bruno. Who is this woman who has you at her beck and call? My steward said she was old.' She wrinkled her nose as if she had caught an unpleasant smell.

'My host's housekeeper. It was an emergency – she brought news of a friend who had been badly injured.'

'I see. You might have explained before you left. Still, we managed to amuse ourselves in your absence.'

'I'm sure. Where is he?'

'Your assistant?' She turned back to the window as if the subject held little interest. 'I sent him on his way. You find us in a state of busyness – a fast rider came this morning from Trebon to say that my husband is coming home. We expect him tonight or tomorrow.'

'No more dinner parties for a while, then.'

She smiled serenely. 'I'm sure the count will wish to make your acquaintance when he arrives.'

That gave me an idea. 'May I borrow paper and ink? I would like to leave a message for him.'

Her eyes narrowed. 'Saying what?'

'Actually, it's a message for John Dee, which I hope your husband might be in a position to convey to him.'

'Nothing about me?'

'No, my lady.' You are not as interesting as you imagine, I added silently.

'Very well.' She called the steward and sent him for writing materials. 'Was your friend all right?' she said, while we waited. 'The one who was injured.'

'I think she will live.'

'*She?*' Xena raised an eyebrow. 'There I was thinking you were a stranger in Prague, but you seem to know a host of women.'

'I make friends quickly. Though not as quickly as you, perhaps,' I added, because I wanted her to know that I was angry about the way she had used Besler.

'Don't presume to judge me, Bruno,' she said in a low voice. 'You told me yourself – those of us who depend on the favour of powerful men must adapt to circumstances in order to survive.'

'That's not quite what I said.'

'I'm sure you yourself are not unfamiliar with bending the rules.'

I did not reply, because at that point the steward returned with paper, quill and inkwell, and I leaned on an ornamental table to compose my note, which I wrote in English, knowing she would attempt to read it the moment I was gone. She was right, I thought; who was I to judge what stratagems a woman needed to employ to secure her future. Theirs was not an easy lot; even a woman like Xena, with all the advantages of beauty

384

and a good family, could find herself jettisoned if she failed to fulfil the one task demanded of her.

'You mentioned that you sometimes spend time in the Emperor's *Kunstkammer*,' I said as I scattered fine sand over the letter to blot the ink. 'Have you ever noticed anything strange while you were there?'

She looked intrigued. 'Like what?'

'People behaving suspiciously. The Stradas, for example.'

She threw her head back and let out a frank laugh that was very different from the artificial giggles she had employed the night before. 'The Stradas are always behaving suspiciously.' She laid a hand on my sleeve. 'I will tell you something about the Stradas. A few years ago, when my father was still alive, Jacopo Strada became determined that I should be married to his son. He thought it would be a good alliance between our families. My father was not convinced – the Stradas are not of noble blood, after all. But they have a certain position at court, and my father agreed to formal introductions. I didn't mind – I thought he was handsome. Well.' She leaned closer. 'We were permitted to walk together in the castle gardens with his sister as chaperone. She's a cold fish.' She gave a little shudder and pulled her cape tighter. 'Anyway, I managed to shake her off and when we were alone, I told him he could kiss me.'

'And?'

'I've never seen anyone disappear so fast. You'd think I'd offered to castrate him. So what does that tell you?'

'He was shy?'

'He was *thirty-two*,' she said scathingly. 'I was seventeen. It tells me he has an aversion to women. You notice he is still not married. Anyway, I have the count now, who is much better stock.'

She made it sound like purchasing horses for breeding; perhaps among families like hers there was little difference. There was something almost admirable about her self-belief.

'And Katherina? I take it you don't like her?'

'It's more that she doesn't like me – she couldn't have made that more obvious. And I'm a Pernstein by birth – I would have been a *very* good match for her brother. But she's one of those women who thinks everyone is a rival. She's terrified of losing the Emperor's affections. I honestly think she entertains hopes that he will marry her one day, poor cow.' She laughed with all the casual cruelty of youth and beauty.

'Really? You don't think she might tire of waiting and fall for someone else?'

'Katherina? You've *met* her, I presume?' She shook her head. 'That woman is devoted to her father and the Emperor to the point of obsession. And in any case, do you think Jacopo Strada would allow her to marry another man? Not while her cunny is still a valid currency with Rudolf. Though she's getting on now, so who knows how long that will last.' She stood and smoothed out her skirts. 'Well, I thank you for your gracious apology, Bruno. Consider yourself forgiven. I will pass your letter to my husband – I'm sure he will want to see you.' She paused and darted a furtive look at me. 'Perhaps best if you don't bring your assistant, though.' It was the closest I had heard her come to an admission of shame.

I walked towards Golden Lane, glad to have my cloak again, sunk deep in my thoughts. I hoped Besler had gone straight home to Bethlem Square – he would surely need a rest after his busy night – but I was unhappy about the thought of him wandering the city alone. I wondered how long it would take Montalcino and San Clemente to discover that Bartos's silver flask contained a substitute and not the poisoned elixir; when they did, they would redouble their efforts to find Sukie and me. Montalcino had threatened Besler at our first meeting; if his thugs couldn't now get to Sukie, might he revert to that plan as a way to make me do his bidding? I doubted he would be placated even if I did produce the letters from John Dee that he had demanded. I had no intention of handing anything over, but I would try asking Rabbi Loew again if John had left any correspondence with him. There was clearly something more than the rabbi had told me between him and John – the 'bond' symbolised by the gift of the dagger, whatever 'our enemies suspect' – and I hoped I could persuade the rabbi to confide in me.

I called at Goodwife Huss's to see if Hajek was there, and how Magda was doing. The goodwife had risen to the occasion and the house smelled of simmering herbs as she brewed up tonics to nurse her patient back to health. Magda was lying on a bed by the fire, looking alarmingly like an effigy on a tomb, her face as white as the cloth that bound her head. She drifted in and out of consciousness, the goodwife informed me, though the doctor had sat by her side all night and only left about an hour ago, promising to come back as soon as he could.

'She'll live.' She leaned across with a proprietorial air and brushed a stray lock of hair from Magda's forehead as she said it. 'It's a question of how much damage has been done. I've seen people lose the power of speech from a blow to the head. We won't know until she wakes fully – if she does. I tell you, if I got my hands on the brute that did this, I'd string him up by his balls.'

'You don't need to, he's dead.'

'Good,' she said, sounding like Sukie. 'Hope he roasts in Hell. That's one less, at least.'

I was not sure if she meant brutes or men in general, so I changed the subject hastily. 'And Erik?' I had glanced through the Mollers' window on my way but the house appeared empty.

'Erik Moller,' said Goodwife Huss, in a tone of disbelief, 'got up and went to work this morning in the Powder Tower, shaved and wearing a clean shirt, with no smell of drink on him. Is that your influence?'

'Sukie's really,' I said. 'He just needed to be jolted out of his self-pity.'

I asked her to tell Hajek that I needed to speak to him, and set off to the end of Golden Lane, where I descended a flight of steps cut into the wall in the shadow of the prison tower, and followed the slope of the ravine down into the Stag Moat.

I had not yet explored the castle gardens, but it had occurred to me that if Bartos was killed because of his relationship with Katherina Strada, either by the Emperor or by one of the Strada men, it was likely that he was stabbed within the castle complex. He had no defensive wounds, Hajek had said; he was not expecting violence from his killer, and he would surely have been on his guard if he had been lured to a meeting somewhere out of the ordinary. So he must have gone willingly to a place that was familiar to him, not suspecting anything amiss until that curved blade slipped between his ribs at close quarters. If that had happened in the palace, how had they moved the body? I guessed that those underground tunnels had played a part and I wanted to see where the other branch emerged.

The Stag Moat was a deep ravine, with steep wooded slopes on both sides tapering down to the dried bed of a stream that ran along the bottom. I half-slid, half-climbed down and became aware of a great cacophony of birdsong to my right. Looking up, I saw that on the south-facing slope, opposite the castle walls, trees had been cleared to make way for an elaborate wooden structure with a high roof and large arched windows; through the glass, I could see foliage and dozens of tiny colourful shapes flitting back and forth. This must be Rudolf's famous heated aviary, where he kept birds brought back from the tropics. I would have liked to take a closer look, but I pressed on along the path between the high banks. The deer grazing among the trees raised their heads to give me a speculative glance as I passed, but otherwise there was no one about. Despite the cold wind, sunlight pierced the thin gauze of cloud; tight buds were beginning to appear on branches and the air held a breath of spring, but there was something baleful about the sheer dark walls of the castle rising above me to my left. I had the sudden uneasy sense that I was not alone after all, and paused to look around, but I could see no sign of anyone following. I quickened my pace nonetheless.

As I walked on, the sweet trilling of the aviary faded, to be replaced by a frenzied chorus of yapping. The squat round shape of the Powder Tower loomed ahead, and in its lee, at the bottom of the slope, I saw a row of kennels with a fenced enclosure at the side. A dozen dogs leapt against the pales of the fence, jostling for attention from a skinny boy in his mid-teens who was throwing them scraps from a bucket. Suddenly, I remembered Novak's story of the lad who had drowned the same day Bartos was found. Perhaps his successor could tell me more.

I wandered over, noticing how scrawny most of the dogs appeared. Several of them were afflicted with mange or scabs. One feisty little mutt who might once have been white stuck his snout through the fence and whined softly as I approached; I reached out to pet him and the boy called out a warning in Czech. I shook my head and he repeated it in German.

'I said, they might seem friendly but they'll take your finger off if you give them a chance.'

I withdrew my hand hastily. 'They don't look too well.'

He shrugged and jerked his head towards the Powder Tower. 'Hardly matters. Most of them will end up in there having mercury or God knows what pumped into them, poor fuckers.'

I grimaced and looked back at the dogs. The small white one – some kind of terrier mongrel, I thought – was standing on his hind legs, peering at me through the fence with knowing brown eyes. I understood Hajek's argument for the necessity of it, but I had never felt comfortable with the degree of detachment it required.

'They'd only starve on the streets otherwise,' the boy said, as if he divined my sentimental tendencies. 'I bring them in and they get a bit of feeding up if they're lucky.'

'Have you been doing the job long?' I asked, careful to keep my voice neutral.

'Two days. I've always had dogs at home, though – I'm good with them.' He sounded defensive, as if I was questioning his credentials.

'I can see that. But I thought there was another boy who looked after the kennels?'

He made a sombre face. 'Yeah. My mate Pepa. He died.'

'I'm sorry. What happened?'

'Drowned. Fell in the river, they reckoned. He always was clumsy, on account of his size. My dad – he's a night-soil man – heard one of his friends say he saw Pepa down on the bank with a woman, so he probably went with a whore. He used to do that – he couldn't get a girl any other way. He was nice, but a bit soft in the head, you know.' He tapped his temple. 'Sad, though – he loved these mutts. Even used to sleep here with them sometimes. But then it worked out lucky for me, didn't it, getting his job? I'd better get on and feed this lot.'

'What do you feed them?' I asked, to prolong the conversation. An idea had begun to take shape in my mind, but it was too inchoate yet to make sense.

'Kitchen scraps, mainly.' The boy showed me his bucket of offal; it looked revolting and smelled worse. 'No point treating them like royalty. Although I suppose the scraps are from the Emperor's table, so in a sense . . . They'll eat anything, though, this lot. The other day I was cleaning out the run and I swear to God, I found an eyeball.'

'A *what*?'

'I know. Turned my stomach, I can tell you.'

'A *human* eyeball?'

He gave me an odd look. 'Wouldn't have thought so. I assumed it had come out of the butcher's bucket. Probably from a sheep's head or something – you should see the stuff that's in there sometimes. How would a human eyeball get in there?'

The boy clearly didn't pay much attention to the news on the streets. 'Maybe someone threw it in,' I said. 'You didn't find anything else? A tongue, perhaps?'

He made a face. 'Don't remember seeing one, but like I said, you could chuck anything in there and they'd gobble it up before you'd blinked. The eyeball only escaped because it rolled under a corner of the kennel where they couldn't reach it.'

'How do you get the dogs in and out of the castle?' I asked. 'You don't bring the corpses out through the public courtyards?'

''Course not. People are funny enough about what goes on in the Powder Tower as it is. There's a secret entrance.' He pointed to the rocky outcrop behind us, where the tower rose imposingly from its foundations. 'For getting things in and out of the laboratories discreetly,' he added.

Like bodies, I thought. I thanked him and gave him a thaler. 'If you find any more body parts, I'd be interested to know. You can give the information to Dr Hajek in the Powder Tower.' I tried to ignore the voice in my head that said, what if Hajek already knows?

He tossed the coin in the air with a grin, but as he caught it, his face grew sombre. 'Wait – you don't think it was that alchemist that was murdered, do you? Because he was killed down at the bridge, I thought. How would his eyeball end up here?'

'Good question,' I said. 'Probably was a sheep.'

A sharp bark made me turn back; the little white dog had slipped a paw between the pales of the fence and was mauling the air as if he wanted my attention.

'He likes you,' the boy said cheerfully.

Well, there's one name to add to the list next time I see Montalcino, I thought. Except the dog didn't have a name. Any day now he would be taken to the Powder Tower, dosed with mercury or arsenic and cut open to see how his organs reacted. I shook myself and walked away before I did anything rash.

THIRTY-ONE

The secret entrance to the tunnel was concealed behind laurel bushes, though a trail of flattened grass and broken twigs marked the path to it. It looked dank and forbidding, much like the mouth of an underground water conduit, except that it was barred by an iron gate which proved locked. Evidently only authorised people had access to this means of entry. I tried peering in but no light penetrated the rocky depths. The boy had said it led to the Powder Tower; it must also link up with the passage that ran from the cathedral crypt to the cellars beneath the private apartments, where Hajek had his laboratory and Ottavio his storeroom.

A severed eyeball in the dogs' pen; a big lad, perhaps a little slow-witted, who often spent the night right outside the entrance to this tunnel, found dead in the river the morning after Bartos's body was hung from the bridge; none of this was conclusive in itself, but it was enough to suggest connections. If Bartos had been killed either in the Powder Tower or the palace, his body could have been brought out under cover of darkness through this tunnel, his eyes and tongue flung over the fence for the dogs on the way. I thought of Erik carrying Magda through the streets in a handcart last night; it would be possible to bring a cart down here into the moat, if you could enlist a strong boy to help move the corpse to the bridge and make sure he couldn't talk about it afterwards. But the poor unfortunate Pepa had been seen at the waterside with a woman. *Katherina?* I couldn't see her colluding willingly in the disposal of her lover's body, especially if her father or brother were responsible.

I rubbed my eyes; all this was nothing but speculation, and yet I was sure I was edging in the right direction; I just needed one solid piece of evidence that would tie it all together. I was considering how to proceed when I heard the crack of a twig somewhere behind me. I whipped around, alert for any sign of movement, but there was only the wind through the branches and the occasional guttural noise from the wild animals in the enclosure on the opposite bank.

I pushed my way out through the bushes, holding Greta's fruit knife point-first and regretting that I had still not retrieved my own dagger from the gatehouse. Now that I remembered, I had not collected my horse either. I stood on the path at the foot of the tower, scanning every inch of the slopes on either side, but again I saw no one. I couldn't shake the feeling that I had been followed, so I scrambled quickly up the bank by the Powder Bridge and was admitted into the castle courtyard by the stables. I had sent a boy to fetch my horse when I was distracted by a hammering on one of the windows above; I glanced up and saw Sukie frantically gesturing to me. What had she found now? She pointed down and then disappeared; after a couple of minutes she emerged breathlessly into the yard and ran over to me, holding out Esther's book.

'Did you find something?' I whispered.

'I have to give this back,' she said.

'Why – don't you like it?'

'I do, but Katherina wanted me to get rid of it.'

'Did she say why?' I took the book from her, puzzled. Inside the cover, Esther Loew had written her name in Hebrew letters.

'She says it's not suitable for a good Christian girl. She seemed quite angry about it.'

'Really? That's . . .' I was surprised to hear that Katherina had reacted in this way. While it was obvious that her father still clung to the old prejudices, I had expected her to be more open-minded. Hadn't she just declared to me that she thought it absurd to judge people not on their actions but on generalised ideas about a group? Perhaps I had misunderstood her meaning.

'I didn't find any more letters, by the way. I searched her whole room. But there was something in the hearth that might be important – she'd tried to burn it but one page escaped the flames. I tucked it inside the book. Can I go home yet?' Sukie raised her eyes guiltily to the Stradas' windows.

'Soon, I promise. And thank you. I'll take the book for now and you can borrow it again when you're back at your own place.'

'I did read some of it. I liked Judith cutting the general's head off.'

I smiled. 'I thought you might.'

'But my favourite was the Book of Esther. They're both about bad men getting what's coming to them. Goodwife Huss would approve.'

I looked at her. Something had triggered a connection in the depths of my tired thoughts. 'What did you say?'

'I said, Goodwife Huss would like it.'

'No, before that.'

'What, the Book of Esther?'

I stared at her open-mouthed for so long that she shook my sleeve. '*Dio porco*, Sukie – you're a genius.'

'Am I? I thought you were having a seizure for a minute.'

'I have to go. Stay where you are for now, I'll come back as soon as I can.'

'I'll keep looking,' she said with a meaningful smile.

'*Be careful*,' I called as she skipped away, but my mind was elsewhere.

In the shelter of the gatehouse, while I picked up my dagger and waited for the boy to bring my horse, I took out the paper Sukie had tucked inside the book. It was creased and badly singed down one side – it must have been balled up and thrown into the fire – but it was clear enough: the words *Oculos habentes non videtis* written over and over in variations on Bartos's handwriting, as the copyist tried to perfect the forgery. I wondered if Katherina had burned other incriminating papers, and for a moment worried that she had been panicked into it by discovering Sukie's theft of the letter. Perhaps it was a mistake to leave the girl in the Stradas' apartments. I hesitated, but told myself I would go back for her as soon as I could. My next task could not wait.

I rode down the hill and across the Stone Bridge as fast as the traffic would allow until I reached the Jewish Town, my head whirling with half-formed thoughts as pieces of the picture swam in and out of focus. Finally, I understood David's last words to me; at least I thought I did. How had I not seen it before? Answer: because it was so audacious that it would never have crossed my mind. Even now, I thought it likely that I had made an absurd leap, which was why I needed to find proof before I confronted anyone with my theory. I paid to stable the horse in an inn yard outside the walls, pulled my hood up and set off through the gates.

I followed the streets I recognised in the direction of the Old-New Synagogue. The town seemed unusually empty; perhaps the whole community was in mourning. Eventually I passed a woman sweeping her step and stopped to ask directions.

'I need to deliver a letter to Benjamin Katz,' I said. 'Could you tell me where he lives?'

'He won't be home,' she said, eyeing me with instinctive suspicion. 'He'll be at his cousin's – they're sitting shiva. Do you want to pay a visit?'

'No, thank you – I'll just leave it at his house.'

'Left, then right.' She pointed. 'The street behind the town hall, at the end of the row.'

I thanked her again and hurried on, relieved to hear that Benjamin would be absent.

His house had a narrow lane running alongside; checking to make sure no one was watching, I slipped down it and climbed the wall, slinging my bag over first and dropping down on the other side. I straightened, brushing dirt off my breeches, and stared in amazement at what I found there.

In the small yard behind the house, someone – presumably Benjamin – had constructed a curious structure: a wooden cube, its sides around eight feet in length, with no windows, though I could see the outline of a door in the face opposite the house. Tentatively, I pushed this open and found myself in darkness. As my eyes adjusted, I exclaimed aloud, forgetting that I was breaking in and ought to be discreet.

One of the side walls was whitewashed, and on the facing side a small hole had been cut out. A shaft of light entered here and was concentrated through a glass disc suspended in a frame from the ceiling, projecting an image of the tree outside on to the blank wall. I knew what I was looking at: my old mentor in Naples, Giambattista della Porta, had written treatises on exactly this kind of experiment with optics and I had witnessed his attempts to build a similar contraption; he called it an 'obscurum cubiculum'. The theory was that any image outside the cube would be focused through the hole and reproduced on the blank wall. The picture would appear in reverse, but could be manipulated by inserting lenses between the pinhole and the wall; della Porta had enthused about the possibilities of this technology, if it could be refined, for aiding our understanding of the properties of light and vision, perhaps even creating images. I was impressed that Benjamin's backyard experiments were so advanced; I wanted to discuss them with him, and had to remind myself that I was trespassing with a specific purpose.

As well as a theatre for optical illusions, Benjamin evidently used his cubiculum for storage; crates were piled up along the back wall. I stepped further in, leaving the door open to allow a little light, and suddenly became aware of a shape at the edge of my vision. I turned, reaching for my dagger, to see the shadow of a man, about six feet tall, in the corner behind me. He remained deathly still; I blinked and realised on closer inspection that he was a two-dimensional figure, and not quite a man – there was something unformed about his shape. A model Golem, I thought, laughing shakily as I breathed out to steady my pulse. 'Don't move,' I instructed him, mainly to cheer myself as I returned to the crates. There was a box of assorted lenses, carefully wrapped in cloth; another of theatrical costumes and props; a screen made of linen stretched over a wooden frame. Under these, I came to a chest containing papers. The top bundle appeared to be the script of a play written in Hebrew; I lifted it out and found beneath what I had been looking for – the papers Benjamin had taken from David's shop. Most appeared to be bills of sale for books, written in German, and I leafed rapidly through them in frustration; I could see no reason why these should be incriminating. Then I came across a note written in Italian, which made me take notice.

Re the copy of Clavicula Salomonis you wanted for your client; I can locate a 1585 Basel manuscript edition but don't think you should take less than seventy th. OS.

Ottavio Strada, surely. I thought of Strada's discomfort when I bumped into him into the underground corridor with his pile of books, his hasty explanation of how David Maier repaired books from the imperial library. Suppose some of those volumes never made it back to the Emperor's collection, but were sold on through David's shop? That would have been a nice little set-up for both of them; I couldn't work out if it made Ottavio more or less likely to have been David's killer, but I could understand why Benjamin had not wanted it to come to light. But when I unfolded the next paper, I knew that the outlandish theory I had formed just now at the castle was correct. It was a letter, written in Hebrew:

My dear Benjamin
This may be the hardest letter I have had to write.
You know that since your childhood I have loved you

like a son, and it was your father's dearest wish and
mine that our families should one day be joined by the
marriage of our children. It is with a heavy heart, there-
fore, that I must tell you this is no longer possible. I
have never doubted your affection for my daughter, nor
hers for you, but sometimes we cannot know the path
that lies ahead, and it seems that Esther, like her name-
sake, is to be the instrument of a greater plan. I know
this will come as a bitter blow to your hopes, but we
must all play our part and accept it with courage and
humility, as my daughter has learned to do. In the
words of Mordecai: 'Who knoweth whether thou art
come into the kingdom for such a time as this?' For
now, I must beseech you not to speak of this to anyone
until the time is right.

   Your loving teacher
   Judah Loew ben Bezalel

I stood motionless, staring at the paper until the characters
blurred before my eyes, as I tried to process the significance
of what I had read.

'Find what you were looking for?' said a voice behind me,
in Italian.

I jolted out of my reverie and whipped around to see
Benjamin standing in the open doorway. He didn't seem particularly angry at my intrusion; he looked too drained by grief.

I held up the letter. 'This is what you needed to remove from
David's shop in such a hurry, I take it?'

He nodded. 'I didn't want it made public. No one else knows.'

'David tried to speak to me when I found him. He said
Esther's name, and something about a book.'

'You said you couldn't make out his words.'

'I didn't understand his meaning at the time. I thought he
was trying to say that Esther was responsible for his death – I
could hardly tell you that.'

'*I* was responsible,' he said sadly, looking at the floor. I could only stare at him in silence. After a long moment he raised his eyes and caught my expression. 'No, I don't mean I held the knife. But I brought about his death. He would be alive now if I hadn't shown him that letter. I was so distraught at the time, I didn't know who else to turn to. I knew he would feel compelled to act. And now . . .' he spread his hands and I saw the pain in his face. He nodded at the paper in my hand. 'You've understood, then?'

'I'm struggling to comprehend it.'

He gave a dry laugh. 'Imagine how I feel.'

'David was trying to say the Book of Esther, is that it?'

'Yes. The Maharal seems to think that he and his daughter have been chosen to live out some modern-day retelling of the Megillah.'

'The story of the beautiful Esther who marries the king and saves her people.' I let out a low whistle, still half-disbelieving. 'The Emperor wants to marry Esther Loew. Is he serious?'

'So he says. They are all as deluded as each other. Not Esther, of course, but what can she do?'

'But—' I hardly knew which question to ask first. '*How?*' was all I could manage.

Benjamin leaned against the wall as if he might collapse without support. 'He saw her from a window. Like something from a courtly tale. The Emperor had purchased a book from Rabbi Loew. David brokered the deal, but he was busy and I offered to deliver it to the librarian, Ottavio Strada. I wanted to go because I had a foolish idea that he might be in a position to help me approach the right person at court.'

'The right person for what?'

He coloured a little and looked away. 'I've written a play. A comedy. When I was studying in Italy, I heard about Leone di Somma, the Jewish impresario and actor who provided entertainment at the court in Ferrara – I thought maybe the Emperor could be persuaded to consider a similar arrangement. I hoped it would appeal to his taste for defying convention. Esther wanted to accompany me because she loves to see the sights at the castle, but she can't walk through the city alone. I selfishly thought it might help my cause – some men respond better to a pretty girl, and this Strada was Italian, after all.'

I thought about Xena's dismissive verdict on Ottavio and the charms of women. 'So – Rudolf saw her from a window, and then what?'

Benjamin sighed. 'Ottavio met us in the courtyard and invited us to see the library. It was generous of him – he was pleased to find that I spoke Italian, and I had never set foot in the palace. We couldn't believe our luck. Esther was in raptures over the library – she ran up and down exclaiming about the books, taking down one after another, while I tried to explain to Ottavio my idea about the play. And all the time, though we didn't know it, Rudolf had followed us in and was watching from the gallery.'

'And?'

'And he was felled by Cupid's dart, apparently.' He could not keep the bitterness from his voice; I couldn't blame him. 'It was Petrarch and Laura, Dante and Beatrice. He was consumed with love for her from the moment he saw her, so he says, and knew he could have no thought of any other woman as long as he lived.'

'He announced that in the library?'

'Oh, no – not then. He stayed hidden. That night, he sent for John Dee.'

'So John knew about this?'

'He was the go-between from the beginning,' Benjamin said. 'Rudolf knew John was friends with the Maharal. He asked John to arrange an audience. The first time the rabbi visited, Rudolf told him he wished for instruction in the Cabala. I accompanied him on that occasion – the rabbi had promised to petition the Emperor about my play and I still naïvely hoped Rudolf might give me a few moments of his attention. But he asked the rabbi to bring his daughter next time. That's when his intentions became clearer.'

'And Rabbi Loew didn't object?'

'What could he say?' Benjamin spread his hands wide. 'Rudolf is the Holy Roman Emperor. Our fate rests on his pleasure or displeasure. You know as well as I do how many Jewish communities have been thrown out of cities across Europe on a sovereign's whim. Rudolf started bombarding Esther and her father with gifts, accompanied by letters in Hebrew that John Dee wrote at his behest.'

'Ah.' That made sense of the dagger and the note. 'At what point did he mention marriage?'

'The third time he saw her. John Dee had pointed out to him the parallels with the biblical story of Esther, and this delighted the Emperor – he loves to think that he is enacting some great destiny. The rabbi had feared that Rudolf wanted her to be his mistress and that her refusal would anger him, but the idea of making her his wife was even more alarming, for reasons I hardly need to explain.'

'Did the rabbi tell him such a marriage would not be licit?'

There was a long pause while Benjamin examined his boots and weighed up how much to say. Eventually he raised his eyes and met mine. 'Oh yes. He told the Emperor that, although it was a greater honour than his family could ever have looked for, his daughter could not possibly marry out.' He took a deep breath. 'And that's when Rudolf announced that he would convert.'

I stared at him, speechless.

'I know. The Holy Roman Emperor wanted to become a Jew. Part of me still wants to laugh when I think of it, it is so improbable.'

'He can't seriously have thought that was a reality?'

He shook his head. 'I think Rudolf lives in his own reality, and no one ever dares contradict him. Rabbi Loew says the Emperor kept talking about universal religion, which is a concept I believe he learned from John Dee, and how their union would be a symbol for all of Christendom, to demonstrate a future in which there were no more divisions between Jew and Christian, Catholic and Protestant. He appeared to have convinced himself that if he married Esther and they combined their faiths, it would usher in a new age of harmony and an end to religious strife.'

'And they would be delighted by that in Rome and Spain.'

He pressed his fingers to his temples. 'Can you imagine? The consequences, when it became known . . . But Rudolf has so little interest in the world outside the castle, he has steadfastly disregarded the possibility that it might not rejoice at his plan, and even Rabbi Loew—' he stopped abruptly, as if he had teetered on the edge of disloyalty.

'What? The rabbi surely doesn't think it could work? That people would accept such a marriage?'

'You remember what else happens in the Megillah, the Scroll of Esther? Her adoptive father, Mordecai, is given the highest office in the land by the king. The rabbi was cagey about the details, but I had the impression that promises to that effect have been made. Esther said the word chancellor was mentioned.'

I leaned against the wall of the cube, stunned by the sheer insanity of it. 'Rabbi Loew must realise that Philip of Spain and the Pope would never stand for it. They would have Rudolf declared mad and deposed instantly.'

'I *know*,' Benjamin said, a wild note of fury creeping into his voice. 'I understood exactly what was at stake. Esther would be accused of bewitching him, the Maharal would be executed for Judaising, there's every chance the whole community could face banishment – it would be presented by our enemies as a naked attempt to grab power. All because one man loses his head over a pretty face and believes he is entitled to whatever he wants. But I blame myself. If I hadn't been so ambitious for the play, Rudolf would never have laid eyes on her.'

'David blamed himself too,' I said softly. 'He said it was his doing. I suppose he meant that he sent you with the book.'

'I tried to talk sense to Rabbi Loew, but he felt the wisest course was to humour the Emperor and hope that his infatuation would burn itself out. His plan was to drag out the conversion process until Rudolf lost interest, but he showed no sign of that. So instead I turned to David – I passed on that letter the rabbi sent me breaking off my betrothal to Esther. I thought David would know what to do.' He rubbed his brow with his thumbnail. 'I knew he had a good relationship with Ottavio Strada, whose sister was the Emperor's mistress. I suggested to him that Strada would think it as much in his family's interests as ours to gently dissuade Rudolf from the course he appeared set on. And now David is dead, and his children—' His voice trembled and fell silent.

'You think Strada killed him?'

'I don't know. I can't see why he would – they did good business together.'

'Stealing books from the imperial library?'

'David never stole anything,' Benjamin said hotly. 'Strada brought him books that had been thrown out, David repaired them and sold them on. Besides, he had done Strada a favour, telling him about the Emperor's feelings for Esther. Why would Strada want to kill him?'

'I overheard him in the yard at the Winged Horse the night he died, talking to someone – I guess it was Strada. David was trying to end their arrangement. Perhaps Strada feared he would tell someone about their dealings with the Emperor's books.'

Benjamin nodded, digesting this.

'Is that your Golem?' I asked, gesturing to the figure in the corner. He forced a smile.

'I've been experimenting with optics,' he said. 'Like a shadow play, but on a larger scale. With a lantern and a magnifying lens, you can project the silhouette of a figure on to a screen. I thought to make an entertainment for the children, but now, with the murder of Bartos, no one wants to hear Golem legends . . . In any case, I haven't quite made it work yet, I need bigger lenses and a more powerful lantern. But I make progress. In different circumstances I would offer to show you.'

'I would love to see it,' I said, thinking that Martin Novak had been telling the truth about seeing a Golem after all. 'But I must talk to Esther and her father right away.'

The substance of Dee's letter to the Maharal had become clearer in the light of these revelations. *Our enemies suspect . . .* I had assumed, and Rabbi Loew had led me to believe, that this referred to the Catholics. But if he was talking about their secret enterprise, that of making Esther Empress (I could still barely comprehend forming that sentence), then it could have had a very different meaning. While the papal nuncio and the Spanish ambassador would certainly be opposed to the idea of any such marriage, if they learned of it, there was a more immediate enemy: the family of the woman she had displaced in the Emperor's affections.

'The rabbi stayed with David's family after the burial this morning,' Benjamin said. 'But Esther went to her house to rest. She sat up with Sarah all night. Come, I'll go with you.'

'How did Esther feel about all this?' I asked as we walked to the rabbi's house. 'I know she is devoted to her father, but surely—'

'Esther knows her own mind,' he said. It was hard to tell from his tone whether he considered this a good thing.

'That's not an answer.'

He sighed; I had the feeling he'd been doing a lot of sighing lately. 'At first she was furious,' he said. 'She was having none of it – but the rabbi impressed upon her the possible consequences of an outright refusal. So she agreed to continue with the visits, in the hope that, as her father reassured her, the Emperor would eventually lose interest before she was asked to make a choice. But Esther is not a woman you can lose interest in easily.'

'No,' I agreed, without thinking. He shot me a sharp sidelong look.

'But recently, she . . .' He broke off and gave a tight little shake of the head, his lips pressed together.

'What? You don't mean – she *likes* him?'

'No. Not in that way, although she says he always treats her with the greatest courtesy and respect – only sees her in the company of her father, has never behaved improperly to her.

404

They talk about art and philosophy, apparently.' He laughed bitterly. 'The thing about Esther – she has always chafed at the limitations of a woman's lot. Since she was a girl, she used to say she wanted the chance to do something of significance in the world.'

'I knew a woman like that once,' I said.

'I suppose it's more common than we realise. Most don't say it aloud, at least not to men. Her sisters would reply, what could be more significant than being a wife and mother? But Esther said that was a lie fed to women so they wouldn't ask for real power.' He kicked a loose stone as we turned into the rabbi's street. 'I fear that she and her father have almost allowed themselves to be convinced by Rudolf's fantasy that a Jewish woman could be accepted as the wife of the Holy Roman Emperor, and wield real political influence.'

'Does anyone else know? In the community, I mean, or in her family?'

'Not yet.'

'And where does that leave you?' I asked as we reached Esther's door.

'Invisible,' he replied, looking away.

The door was opened by a woman who resembled Esther, though broader and rounder in the face, with an infant on her hip.

'Benjamin,' she said. 'Do you want to come in?'

He introduced me to Esther's sister, Rachel, and asked if Esther was sleeping.

'Esther?' Rachel looked surprised. 'No, she went out in a great hurry. A message came for her.'

'From where?'

'I don't know. She threw it in the fireplace, grabbed her cloak and said she would be back soon.'

Benjamin said something forceful in Yiddish; Rachel clicked her tongue and looked disapproving.

'She didn't say anything about who the message was from?' I asked.

'No, but I can look.' She frowned at our expressions. 'The fire's not lit – didn't I say? Come in.'

We waited in the hall while she disappeared into the parlour and returned with a balled-up note. I smoothed it out and Benjamin read over my shoulder. It was written in German:

Please come to the palace urgently (usual entrance) – there is news about the murder of the bookseller. I must speak to you before anyone else finds out.
R

I exchanged a glance with Benjamin.

'How long ago did she leave?' I asked.

'About half an hour? I was feeding the baby when she left and the bells had just struck two. Is everything all right?'

'All fine,' I said, seeing her worried expression. We thanked her and hurried out.

'This doesn't look right,' Benjamin said, flicking the letter, when we were safely out of earshot. 'Esther has shown me notes from the Emperor before. He always insists on writing laboriously in Hebrew – badly spelled since John Dee has been away – and signs himself "Your most humble servant" or something similar. Never "R".'

'Is this Rudolf's hand?'

'I couldn't say. I've only seen him write Hebrew characters. You think it's a trap?'

I thought of Katherina Strada's skill at forging other people's handwriting and my chest tightened.

'I think we need to find Esther before she reaches the castle.'

'If she's crossed by boat, we'll never catch up,' he said, stricken.

'You follow by river, I'll ride over the bridge, I'll meet you at the castle. Do you know what entrance he means?'

'Esther told me they used to go in through an underground tunnel from the Stag Moat that came up in the cellars underneath the royal apartments. She hated it – she said it smelled of death. But it ensured they wouldn't be seen.' He clutched at my sleeve. 'You think someone means to harm her? Who – Ottavio Strada?'

'I don't know. But I don't think whoever wrote this note wants to offer their congratulations,' I said. 'Go, we mustn't waste any time. Do you have a weapon?'

He stared at me. 'I'm a *doctor*. I can't fight.'

'You might not have a choice.'

I spurred the horse across over the bridge, cursing everyone who made the mistake of being in my way as a means of redirecting the anger I felt at myself, for not seeing the whole picture sooner. So Rudolf had fallen in love with a woman who could never be his – something every man has to contend with at one time or another (I thought of Hajek and Magda, my own love for Sophia). But Rudolf was not accustomed to the idea of his desires being denied, and he had convinced himself that the world would bend to accommodate him. A ruler who was more engaged with the political reality of Europe, less closeted away in a tower full of men who believed they could create gold, defy death and commune with angels, would have understood that he could never be allowed to follow his heart in this. A more worldly sovereign would see that, simply by indulging his infatuation with Esther, he was putting her life and her family's in danger. But Rudolf was blind to everything except his own wishes.

I had been blind too, I realised, as I forced the poor beast up the steep incline to the castle. If Esther Loew was Rudolf's obsession, it was unlikely that he would have been so upset by Katherina's dalliance with Ziggi Bartos that he felt provoked to murder. And if Rudolf did not kill Bartos in a fit of jealousy, that left only her father and brother with a motive. Perhaps it was a question of her honour, or to prevent Bartos claiming paternity of her child. And if it was one of the Strada men, then it could only have been Ottavio who carried out the deed, even if both were behind it. If they had been willing to kill to remove one threat to Katherina's place in Rudolf's affections, would it seem logical to them to eliminate another? Did they hope that, with both Bartos and Esther out of the way, the Emperor would find his way back to Katherina's bed? If that were the case, I realised with a sudden twist of my gut, it meant I had left Sukie in the care of a murderer.

I dismounted at the Winged Horse this time and left the sweating animal in the care of Irenka; I didn't want my arrival noted by anyone at the castle. Entering the Stag Moat from the north end entailed a detour around a row of houses and a shortcut over a garden wall, but eventually I scrambled down the bank, under the arches of the bridge that linked the first courtyard to the palace gardens, and ran to the Powder Tower. The iron gate barring the entrance to the tunnel was firmly locked. The ground was so churned up under the bushes that it was impossible to tell whether anyone had passed through recently. If Esther had set off with a half-hour head start, she was almost certainly inside by now.

I returned to the path to wait for Benjamin, and caught an incongruous sound of music: a melancholy old folk tune drifting from somewhere nearby. On the other side of the tower, I found the boy who looked after the dogs sitting on the bank under a tree, playing a wooden flute he appeared to have carved himself. The sound was oddly soothing; even the dogs lay quietly, their ears cocked. The song broke off abruptly when he saw me.

'Hello, your friend's back,' he said amiably.

I looked at him, puzzled, before I realised that he was addressing the small white dog, who had jumped up to nuzzle his nose through the fence at my arrival.

'Have you seen a girl pass by here?' I asked urgently.

The boy nodded. 'Not long ago.'

'Where did she go?'

He pointed with his instrument. 'The tunnel, I think. I heard the gate open.'

'Who has a key to that gate?'

He shrugged. 'Officials. The porter in the Powder Tower, for a start – he's the one who brings the dogs out when they've finished with them.' He jerked his flute at the white terrier. 'It'll be his turn in a couple of days.'

I hurried back to the path – I couldn't think about the dog's perky expression or his imminent fate while Esther remained in danger – and the boy resumed his tune. A few minutes later, Benjamin arrived, gasping for breath as if he had run all the way from the river. I explained that we had missed her, and together we climbed the embankment by the bridge, where the Emperor's silver token gained us entry through the gate to the first courtyard.

I hammered at the door of the Stradas' apartments and it was opened by their young maid. She looked agitated, and told me, in her thick Mantuan accent, that Signor Ottavio was not home; he had gone out an hour ago, she didn't know where.

'An hour?' I looked at Benjamin. That made no sense; Esther would not have been here an hour ago, unless he had spent all that time waiting to intercept her in the tunnel. 'You're sure you don't know where he is? Think!' My tone only served to make her more alarmed. Just then, I heard the sound of a woman's laughter coming from one of the rooms along the corridor.

'*Scusa*,' I said, pushing past the maid, Benjamin apologetically following. I wondered if Katherina knew that her brother had killed and mutilated her lover; she must suspect, even if she had no proof. That might give her an incentive to tell me where he could have taken Esther, although I had my doubts; I knew what Italian family loyalty meant.

I pushed open the door to their small salon and was astonished to see Esther sitting in a chair by the fire, opposite Katherina, holding a glass of spiced wine between her hands. She looked equally amazed to see me, and then Benjamin, and I thought I saw a flash of relief in her eyes. Katherina looked politely puzzled by my appearance.

'Dr Bruno. Back so soon? Were you looking for my brother?'

'Yes, but—' I glanced from her to Esther, searching for some indication of what was taking place here.

Katherina gave an embarrassed little laugh. 'No doubt you find this a strange scene to walk in on. But I thought it would be best if we talked, she and I, woman to woman. Because we are rivals does not mean we must therefore be enemies. I wanted to appeal to her charity on behalf of me and my child.'

Children, I thought. I met Esther's eye with a questioning look that I hoped she would understand to mean: is this true? She took a sip of her wine and smiled back with an expression that said, I have no idea what's going on here.

I didn't quite trust Katherina; though her explanation was plausible, I wondered why she had needed to lure Esther here under false pretences. But at least my worst fears were allayed for now.

'I would like to speak to your brother,' I said. 'Where will I find him?'

'I don't know. He went out.'

'I will wait and walk you home, Esther,' Benjamin said with a firmness of purpose that brooked no argument; I felt a brief pang when I saw the gratitude on her face as she looked at him.

'Who is this?' Katherina asked.

'My cousin,' Esther said quickly, before anyone else could answer.

'And I will take Sukie home, while I'm here,' I added.

Katherina blinked, surprised. 'Oh – if you must. We were just getting used to having her around, she's no trouble. I haven't heard a squeak out of her since this morning – I expect she's hidden away reading somewhere. Are you sure she'll be safe if she leaves?'

I'm not sure she'll be safe if she stays, I thought, but before I could reply, we were interrupted by a noise that sounded like a soul enduring the torments of hell: a low, agonised keening that reached us through several closed doors. Benjamin started towards the door, his physician's instincts pricked by the sound

410

of someone in extreme pain. I had thought at first that it was Katherina's son again, but there was a cracked and haunted note to the sound that could not have come from the throat of a child.

'Please, don't be alarmed,' Katherina said, glancing nervously in the direction of the sound. 'My father has taken a turn for the worse today – Ottavio gave him some of Dr Hajek's tincture to ease the pain, but—'

'It's obviously not working,' Benjamin said, striding towards the door.

'He doesn't want to see anyone,' Katherina said, lurching to her feet as if to stop him. 'Please – my father is a proud man, he would be mortified at the thought of strangers seeing him in this state. The maid will go to him.'

Benjamin hesitated; I watched Katherina. Something was out of joint here; Jacopo was clearly suffering terribly, and yet his son was absent and his daughter drinking wine with the woman who had replaced her. Why were they not at the old man's bedside?

'Now that I think of it,' Katherina added hurriedly, 'Ottavio went to fetch Dr Hajek. I'd forgotten. He knows my father's condition – it would be better to wait.'

It was not the kind of thing you were likely to forget as your father lay in agony; she had obviously just made it up.

'But you've got a doctor right here,' Esther said, gesturing to Benjamin. I wondered if Katherina would object to the idea of a Jewish doctor treating her father, but she didn't get the chance; the moaning came again, accompanied by a sudden muffled crash, and Benjamin was out of the door before the rest of us could respond.

I rushed after him into the corridor; the little maid tried ineffectually to deter us, but Benjamin spoke sternly to her in Italian, which seemed to surprise her so much that she stepped aside and we entered Jacopo's chamber.

The thick curtains were drawn, letting in a blade of dusty light; I recoiled and pressed my sleeve to my face at the smell

411

– a foul soup of vomit and excrement – but Benjamin seemed unperturbed. We found Jacopo lying on the floor by his bed – he had apparently fallen while trying to reach a vessel to be sick into, and in doing so had tipped its contents down himself and on to the floor. With practised speed, Benjamin stripped off his jacket and rolled up his shirtsleeves; I copied him, and between us we lifted the old man on to the mattress. He was unexpectedly heavy, given that his limbs felt thin and frail as a bird's. His skin was slick with sweat and his face had a disturbing greenish tinge. Strings of bile hung from his blood-less lips.

'What's his illness?' Benjamin asked, feeling Jacopo's pulse.

'A tumour in the stomach, I believe.'

He frowned. 'That has not caused symptoms like this to come on suddenly. What has he been taking?'

'A tincture of dwale, Katherina told me.'

He pressed the back of his hand to the old man's forehead. At that moment, Jacopo's eyes snapped open and a claw-like hand shot out and grasped Benjamin around the wrist. He raised his head an inch, croaked a few words and fell back limply as if the effort had drained him.

'What did he say?'

Benjamin shook his head. 'I didn't catch it. Is there any clean water I can give him?'

I cast around and found a pitcher on the sideboard with a little water left; I poured some into a glass and Benjamin held it to the old man's lips. Most of it trickled down the side of his face, but he seemed to have swallowed a few drops, because his eyes fluttered open and he tried to speak again. I rushed around the bed and moved Benjamin aside, leaning – somewhat reluctantly – as close as I could to his face.

'He has poisoned me,' he whispered.

'Who?' He didn't answer. 'Jacopo, it's me, Giordano Bruno. Who has given you poison?' I remembered what Katherina had said about her father's fear of Hajek's medicines. 'Do you mean Dr Hajek?'

412

He sucked in a ragged breath, as if the air were in short supply, and effortfully focused his gaze on me. 'My son, you fool.'

'*Ottavio* poisoned you? How? Why?'

He made a rattling noise deep in his throat that had both me and Benjamin leaping to attention, fearing it was his last breath. It took me a moment to realise that he was laughing.

'For the boy.'

'Which boy?'

I saw Jacopo's eyes flicker to Benjamin. 'Leave us,' he said with a vestige of his old pomposity. Benjamin exchanged a glance with me and nodded.

'I will ask the maid to fetch some hot water and clean sheets for you,' he said to Jacopo. 'And see if I can make something that will counter whatever has done this to you.'

'The Jew can't save me,' the old man said, when Benjamin had left the room. 'I'm a dead man. I can feel it burning me from the inside, squeezing my breath from my lungs. The boy knew what he was doing, no doubt of that. He had talent.'

'Ottavio?' I asked.

Jacopo clawed feebly at his throat, and I remembered Jan Boodt doing the same. All at once, his meaning became clear.

'The boy. You mean Ziggi Bartos. It was *you* who killed him?'

'If there were any justice in this world, I should be made chancellor for doing so. Instead I am poisoned like a rat, the way Rudolf was supposed to die. Give me water.'

'You *knew* about the plot against the Emperor?' I said, tilting the glass to his lips again. He swallowed a mouthful of water and immediately vomited it back up over my shirt. 'Is that why you murdered Bartos?'

'I killed him to protect my family name. Otherwise I'd have let them arrest him for his attempt on the Emperor's life. He'd have been put to the torture and they'd have had the names of his paymasters out of him, which would have been useful. But he'd have said all sorts of other things at the same time. I couldn't have that. It's a hanging offence.'

I looked at him, finally understanding. Erik Moller had been right after all. 'Bartos was Ottavio's lover.' Not Katherina's. I should have considered the possibility after what Xena had told me.

'The sin against nature, Saint Thomas Aquinas called it.' Jacopo's face twisted. 'Ottavio was always girlish, even as a child. When he was a youth I tried to beat it out of him. Mortification of the flesh – cold baths, hair shirts, flagellation. When none of that worked, I had him exorcised. But he persisted stubbornly in his perversion.'

'My God,' I said, amazed at the man's brutality. 'So Bartos told him about the poison plot?'

'No. Ottavio said he was upstairs at the alchemist's lodgings one night when a Spaniard came to the door. Bartos got rid of the man in a hurry but he was cagey about it – wouldn't say who he was or what he wanted. Ottavio was jealous at first – thought it was a rival – but then he became suspicious. He knew Bartos had been working on an elixir, he was secretive about it. Once, when Ottavio picked up the vial, the alchemist screamed at him not to touch it. He made him scrub his hands with white vinegar after. So when Ottavio had the chance, he stole some of this concoction from Bartos without his knowledge and tested it on a dog. Oh, God have mercy.' He broke off, pressing a hand to his stomach, and let out one of those long howls of pain. A fit of retching convulsed him, but there was nothing left to bring up. His breathing was growing faster and shallower, the way Jan's had. 'Don't think I don't see the irony here,' he added, when he could speak again.

I wanted to keep him talking before he lost consciousness. 'So Ottavio worked out that Bartos's *aurum potabile* was poison – how did he know it was intended for the Emperor?'

'Bartos had come into money suddenly. After Ottavio saw what happened to the dog, he challenged Bartos about the elixir. The alchemist was furious, denied everything, told Ottavio he didn't want to see him again. So Ottavio spied

414

on him, saw him meeting San Clemente's thugs, put two and two together. Then he came and told me. He asked for my help.'

'He confessed to their relationship? After everything you'd done to him because of his inclinations?'

'He didn't have to confess – I'd found their letters. I don't allow my children to have secrets from me in this house.' His head fell back on the pillow and his eyes closed. I shook him.

'Did Ottavio ask you to kill Bartos?'

'Of course not. But he was in a quandary. He knew it would be bad. Either he kept quiet, and ran the risk of Rudolf coming to harm, or he reported what he knew about Bartos and the elixir, and had to explain how he'd come by the information. And he knew that if Bartos had nothing to lose, he would drag Ottavio and our whole family down with him. The alchemist had letters in his possession sent by Ottavio, you can imagine the kind of thing. Filth. I told him to leave it with me. I said I would speak to the boy.'

'And while speaking, you slipped a knife between his ribs.'

'It was quick and clean. More than he deserved. More than my son has granted me in return.' He heaved in another painful breath to make the point. 'I learned how to do it in my youth, from a captain in the Swiss Guard. Surprising, the skills you pick up working for the Pope. Although I don't suppose you're surprised – you've been to Rome.'

'Clean? Is that what you call it?'

'He didn't even have time to feel fear. Do you know what they would have done to him in the Daliborka Tower if he'd been arrested for conspiring against the Emperor's life?'

'Cut out his eyes and tongue, you mean?'

He let out that harsh, barking laugh again and another fit of retching wracked his body. 'I can't claim credit for that,' he said, when he had recovered.

I stared at him. 'Ottavio?'

'Christ, no. Ottavio adored the scheming little Ganymede,

he wouldn't have harmed a hair on his head. You want to know how it happened? I may as well tell you, there's nothing you can do. I waited for an evening when Ottavio had an appointment with the Emperor. Katherina wrote a message to the alchemist in her brother's hand, asking him to come to the library. And I was there to greet him.' He paused to snatch a breath. 'But then I had to ask my daughter to help me move the body. That device Ottavio designed to hoist books between floors. Together, she and I hauled him in there and down to the basement, to Hajek's dissecting room. And Katherina saw an opportunity. She has something of an antipathy towards the Jews, for obvious reasons.'

'My God. *Katherina* mutilated him?'

'She had the idea that if we used the alchemist's death to whip the city into a fear of the Jews, Rudolf would see he could not possibly continue to pursue the rabbi's daughter. She underestimates his stubbornness.'

Katherina, who even now was extending the hand of friendship to Esther Loew, drinking wine with her—

'The poison,' I said, shaking his arm. 'The sample Ottavio took from Bartos – did he keep some?'

'It would appear so,' he said, 'since he has evidently given it to me. My condition was slow-moving, Hajek said so. I'd been stable for months. But this sudden turn for the worse – I should have guessed when he brought me medicine. Ottavio won't forgive me for what I did, though the alchemist had already rejected him – even though my son knows I did it to save him from being hanged as a sodomite. Wait, Bruno – there is something else—'

But I could not wait. I rushed to the door, colliding with the maid, who was bringing in a bowl of hot water and linen cloths. I pushed past her and ran to the salon, where Esther and Benjamin were talking in low voices. She was turning the half-full wine glass between her hands; I hurled myself across the room and dashed it to the floor.

'Bruno?' She reared back as if I'd gone mad.

416

'How much did you drink?' I asked.

'A third of a glass, perhaps? What's wrong?' She glanced from me to Benjamin, frightened by the alarm on my face.

'Make her vomit,' I said to him. 'Salt water, or whatever you use, but do it quickly.'

He understood immediately and hurried out in search of the maid.

'Where is Katherina?' I asked.

'She said she had to fetch something and never came back,' Esther said. 'Did she give me poison? Will I die?' She looked up at me, her lip trembling.

'No,' I said. 'I won't allow it.'

She smiled bravely, but her knuckles had turned white from gripping the arms of the chair. Benjamin returned with a tankard, just as another tortured howl emanated from Jacopo's room. I paused to listen; he was calling my name.

'I must find them,' I said to Benjamin. 'Get Esther out of here as soon as you can. Go to the Winged Horse, Greta will give you all you need.'

He nodded, but his attention was all on Esther. I returned to Jacopo; he was clawing at his throat again and his lips looked blueish.

'Before you go after my children, I have something for you.' I approached the bed and he reached for my sleeve.

'Ottavio thinks he has had his revenge. After so many years, he still thinks he can outwit me. Go to the painting.'

I crossed the room to the portrait above the fireplace. 'What about it?'

'Put your hand behind the frame. Lower right corner.'

I did as I was told, and after groping for a moment my fingers closed over a key wedged into the gap between the frame and the canvas.

'The chest,' he said, limply raising a hand towards the one under the window. 'Beneath the ledgers. Hurry, before the Jew comes back.'

'His name is Benjamin,' I said, unlocking the chest. 'He's not

417

coming back. He has other matters to attend to. What am I looking for?'

'False bottom,' he croaked. I lifted out the piles of ledgers and felt around until I found the spring catch. The floor of the chest lifted up and I pulled out a bundle of papers tied in ribbon. Beneath them lay a curved Ottoman dagger with a turquoise-studded hilt, identical to the one I had seen in Rabbi Loew's desk. I picked it up and drew it out of the sheath. It had been cleaned, but rusty traces of blood still clung around the stones and in the tracery on the blade.

'Take them,' Jacopo said. 'All the correspondence between my son and the alchemist. Disgusting, perverted stuff. But useful as leverage. And there are some other papers I took from the alchemist's house in there.'

'*You* searched it? It was you who smashed the place up?'

'Yes. While Katherina persuaded that idiot boy from the kennels to take Bartos to the bridge with her, I went to Golden Lane. I wanted to make sure there was nothing that could incriminate my son, and see what else I might find.'

'And the boy from the kennels – he carried the body, hung Bartos off the bridge and then, what – Katherina pushed him in the river?'

Jacopo fluttered a hand as if such details hardly mattered. 'You'd have to ask her what she did. I know she promised him money if he helped her, and when she came back she said she'd made sure he wouldn't be telling tales. There was thick fog over the river that night, she was in luck.'

'Not so lucky for that poor boy.' Jacopo had been wrong about Ottavio's lack of ruthlessness, I thought; both his children had a streak of it running through their core. He had taught them well.

I flicked through the letters; most seemed to be in a similar vein to the one Sukie had found in Katherina's book – borrowed to copy the writing, no doubt – but one sheet caught my eye. It was a diagram of a design for a bottle with two interior compartments, that could dispense separate liquids; equations

418

marked on the paper indicated the levels of pressure required to force one or other out of the spout. I recalled Ottavio saying he was interested in mechanics.

'Why are you giving me these?' I asked, looking up at Jacopo.

'So that Ottavio doesn't think he has won,' he said. He had begun to shiver violently, even as sweat poured off his brow, and he was pressing a hand to his chest. 'Do what you like with them. Threaten him if it's useful. Just don't harm my daughter – she's with child again.'

'Is it the Emperor's?'

'Of course it is – who else would look at her? Now take them – but first you must do something for me.'

'What?'

'Kill me.'

I stared at him. 'Have you lost your mind?'

'Make it quick. A pillow over my face would be kindest – I won't have the strength to fight you. Or cut my throat. Anything that means I won't die slowly in this agony. I can feel it squeezing my heart.'

'Oh, for God's sake,' I said, tucking the knife into my belt. 'As much as you deserve it, I'm not going to kill you. Ottavio has gone to fetch Dr Hajek.' Even as I said the words, I remembered that this had been Katherina's lie.

Jacopo let out that death-rattle laugh again. 'No he hasn't. He's taken your little girl out.'

I felt a dropping sensation like an iron weight falling through me. 'What? Where?'

'No idea. But she recognised him, you see. I heard her tell him. She said she'd seen him coming and going from the alchemist's house at night. Best not to leave witnesses. Or perhaps he knows it's the surest way to bring you to him.'

I could still hear him laughing as I grabbed my doublet from the floor and ran from the room.

The maid was hovering in the corridor with fresh water. I ripped off my shirt and sluiced the worst of the old man's vomit off myself while she held out the bowl for me, too astonished to speak.

'Can you find me a clean shirt?' I said, drying my chest and arms with a cloth. She nodded; I followed her up the hall. 'Where is Ottavio?'

'He took the child out.'

'But *where*?'

She opened a closet and handed me a linen shirt that I guessed belonged to Ottavio.

'Lion Court, I think. I heard him ask her if she'd like to see the animals.'

'Fetch Dr Hajek to your master urgently,' I said as I pulled the shirt over my head. 'Try the Powder Tower, or the house of Goodwife Huss in Golden Lane.'

'But, Signor Ottavio said no doctors—'

'Jacopo will die without one. Do you understand? So go *now*. And tell Hajek I've gone after Ottavio and the child.'

She nodded, eyes wide with terror. I shrugged on my doublet, slipping the letters into the lining, and ran, my heart beating as wildly as if I'd taken the fruit of the suicide tree.

THIRTY-TWO

Lion Court was an elaborate edifice of white stone in the palace gardens, across the Powder Bridge on the north bank of the Stag Moat. A strong smell rose from it, unmistakably bestial and so thick you could taste it: blood, meat, excrement and something intangibly wild, a scent that humans have recognised as a signal of danger since the time of our earliest ancestors. The hairs on my arms stood up as I approached.

I circled the building, glimpsing the animals through barred windows, until I found the entrance, a porch with Doric columns designed to give the effect of a Greek temple. There seemed to be a worrying absence of keepers. I passed through the pillars into a bare vestibule with an iron gate ahead and a spiral staircase in one corner. Finding the gate locked, I climbed the stairs and emerged on to an open gallery that ran all around the walls some ten feet above the enclosures, from which spectators could view the animals below at a safe distance. The walkway had a roof to protect onlookers from the elements, but only wooden rails on either side to prevent them from falling into the pens. I peered over; beneath me, a tawny wolf sat on his haunches, watching me with shrewd blue eyes as if waiting for me to make one misstep.

'Bruno!'

The sound of a child's voice made me snap my head up; on

the opposite side of the gallery, I saw – with a surge of relief – Ottavio and Sukie standing by the rail, looking down into the enclosure below. He had his arm tightly around her shoulders but she seemed to be unharmed; she looked uncomfortable rather than terrified.

'*Now* can we go?' she asked uncertainly.

'In a moment,' he said, his voice all smiles. 'I need to have a little talk with Dr Bruno first.'

'Let her go, Strada, and we can talk all you like,' I said in Italian. 'You have no argument with her, she's just a child.'

'A clever child who sees things she should not,' he called back. 'How was my father when you left him?'

'He's very sick. He says you've poisoned him as revenge.'

'His illness has affected his mind. Hajek said the tumour would spread.'

'He looks like someone suffering the effects of *cerbera odollam* poisoning,' I said. 'It's known as the suicide tree. Perhaps your friend Bartos mentioned it – he was well acquainted with its properties.'

There was a pause, and then he laughed. 'As soon as Rudolf asked you to investigate his death, I said to Katherina that you'd work it all out sooner or later.'

'Not all of it,' I said. 'I don't understand why David Maier was killed.'

For a moment he looked genuinely stricken. 'No one wanted that. I liked David, he was a valued associate.'

'I'm sure he was. He had the skills to remove the stamp of the imperial library from the books you brought him so they could be sold on, no?'

'I only ever took volumes that Rudolf was tired of, or had written off as damaged beyond repair. No one was harmed by it. Books should find their way to readers, don't you think? Not lie mouldering forgotten in a cellar.'

'David ended up harmed by your association,' I said. 'What happened – did he accuse you of killing Bartos?'

'It's not fair if you speak in Italian, I can't understand,' Sukie said with a little stamp of her foot that made her seem her real age for once. 'I know you're talking about Ziggi.'

'It's not a subject for little girls,' Ottavio said, squeezing her shoulder so that she protested and tried to wriggle out of his grip. 'Watch the lion. Look, I think he's waking up.'

Sukie leaned over the rail, interested, and I shouted at her to stand back. I didn't like the way Ottavio was smiling. He turned to me and switched back to Italian.

'David didn't know who'd killed Bartos, but he was convinced that the overt reference to the Golem was a direct result of the information he'd given me about Rudolf's obsession with the rabbi's daughter. He thought someone was using the murder to turn public feeling against the Jews, and that I was a link in the chain. He was right, of course. My foolish, impetuous sister.'

'But if he had no evidence, why kill him?'

'It was an accident,' he said, lowering his eyes. He almost sounded contrite.

'What? How?'

'David had a crisis of conscience. He was going to confess everything to the rabbi – the fact that he had told me about Rudolf's plans, even our little arrangement with the books.'

'Why then?'

'Someone had warned him that my sister and I intended to kill Esther and he was afraid he had put her in danger. He wanted the rabbi to tell Rudolf.'

'And did you? Plan to kill Esther, I mean?'

He clicked his tongue, losing patience. 'My sister says all manner of stupid things, especially now that she's pregnant again. That grotesque display with Ziggi's corpse did not have the effect she'd hoped. A couple of broken windows in a Jewish school, no more than that. Kat said that if she couldn't incite the city against the Jews, she would have to be more direct and remove her rival. It was just desperate talk.'

'So who warned David?'

'I don't *know*.' He was growing agitated. 'He wouldn't say, and Kat swears she never mentioned it except in private talk with me. But I had to stop David speaking to the rabbi. I couldn't have the Emperor discovering that we knew about him and Esther, that Kat had talked of killing her. There was too much to come out.'

'So you stabbed him.'

'I didn't plan to. We argued on the jetty and I pushed him into an empty boat. Then I had the idea to row him away from the bank and threaten him. But he drew the weapon on *me*. I didn't even know he carried one – it was just a little bookbinding knife. I panicked and tried to wrest it off him, I was afraid the boat would capsize. Somehow, in the struggle, the blade ended up in his gut. It all happened so fast – I was as horrified as he was.'

'I doubt that. Did you know he was still alive when you left him?'

He looked away. 'I should have pushed him into the water and left him to drown, but – I couldn't do it. I couldn't watch a man die. Perhaps my father's right – I lack ruthlessness.'

'You were ruthless enough to give your own father Bartos's poison. Was your sister in on that too?'

'I only told her after I'd done it. She was angry at first, but I made her see it's for the best. All our lives he's been terrorising us. We have no value for him, except in so far as he can manoeuvre us for his own gain.' I could hear in his voice the tremor of a rage that had been building for more than three decades. I needed to tread delicately; he was wound so tight that it was impossible to predict his responses.

'And did Katherina say anything about using the remainder of the poison on Esther Loew?' I asked.

His eyes widened. 'What? No. I told you, I thought all that was just wild words on her part. What makes you think that?'

'Your sister invited Esther to take a glass of wine with her in your apartments. I just walked in on them.'

'I had no idea.' He appeared shaken. 'I suppose Kat could have gone through my room looking for the dregs of the bottle. There was hardly any left. Are you sure? Is Esther—?'

424

'She's in the care of a doctor.' I still didn't know for certain if the wine had been poisoned, but the knowledge that she could only have taken a small dose gave me some hope.

'If you're going to keep talking about adult things in Italian, can I go home?' Sukie said petulantly.

Ottavio tightened his grip on her shoulder.

'Look, Strada, I believe you're telling the truth about David,' I said. 'You're not a cold-blooded killer, not like your father. Prove it by letting the child go.' As I spoke, I began to edge my way cautiously along the gallery, past the wolf's pen, until I was on the side perpendicular to them, above the enclosure of a brown bear with patches of mange, who regarded me with supreme indifference before returning to rocking disconsolately on a stump of wood.

'Don't come any closer,' Ottavio warned. He pulled Sukie to him and crooked an arm around her neck in a chokehold. I saw the flash of fear in her eyes.

'Bruno,' she cried, but her voice was cut off as he increased the pressure; her small hands scrabbled at his forearm.

'Tell me what deal you're hoping to make, then,' I said, keeping my voice steady so that I didn't alarm him. 'Because I presume you brought me out here to negotiate.'

'I need you to tell the Emperor that my father killed Ziggi and David,' he said. 'Say the dead men were both involved in a plot to assassinate Rudolf, say my father was so incensed by the discovery of their treason that he lost control and killed them. As long as you keep my name and my sister's clean. The old man will be dead any moment, it makes sense for him to take the blame. And it's partly true.'

'Rudolf is never going to believe that your father dragged a body to the Stone Bridge or rowed a boat upstream single-handed. And why would he believe a Jewish bookseller to be involved in a conspiracy against him? David would be the last person to want Matthias on the throne.' I moved a few steps closer to the corner.

'That's the clever part,' Ottavio said. 'You tell him David

was Esther's lover, that's why he wanted Rudolf dead. That will dampen the Emperor's desire for her – he won't stand the thought that she's not pure. Two birds with one stone.'

'Christ, Strada, I'm not telling him that. David left a pregnant widow and four children – I won't destroy his reputation or Esther's to save you.'

'I thought you might say that.' With surprising swiftness, he scooped Sukie up – she was such a slight little thing – and swung her legs over the rail, holding her under the arms so that she was dangling over the enclosure below them. She screamed and kicked; I could see he was struggling to hang on to her. 'Will you do it to save *her*? Or would you rather protect a dead man over a living child?'

'Sukie, keep still or he'll drop you,' I shouted. Had he said 'lion'? I couldn't see; it was beyond the end wall of the bear's pen. 'Strada, for God's sake, all right. Whatever you want, just pull her up. You've made your point.'

'Stay where you are,' he said through clenched teeth; he had braced his knees against the rail in his efforts to hold her. 'Did my father give you something?'

I raised my palm to placate him and took another step. 'Lift her up and we can talk about it.'

'I mean letters. My private letters – did he give them to you? He threatened to. He said you could give them to the Emperor so that he'd know exactly what I was, how I had shamed my family all my life. He said Rudolf would never marry Kat or acknowledge her children, knowing her brother was a degenerate, and I would have that on my conscience.' He was shaking, I couldn't tell if it was with rage or the effort of holding on to Sukie.

She squirmed in his arms; one of his hands slipped momentarily and he tried hoicking her up. She let out a piercing scream, scrabbling at his sleeves.

'You make that noise again, girl, and I will let go,' he snapped, in German.

426

'All right, Strada – *enough*,' I said. 'I have the letters.' I moved to reach into my doublet.

'It won't do you any good to draw a weapon – I'd drop her before you could unsheath it,' he said.

'No weapon. Here.' I withdrew the packet of papers slowly and held them out to him, advancing step by step. 'I'll set them down on the walkway and you lift her. Fair exchange.'

'Put them in my hand,' he said.

'You don't have a free hand,' I pointed out, but I moved closer until I was only a few feet away from them and could see into the enclosure below. The Emperor's lion lay sprawled on a pile of rocks, watching the drama above him with regal disdain. He looked underfed and dull-eyed; his pen was no more than twenty feet square and he had worn a path in the dust, pacing back and forth.

'Set them at my feet, then,' Ottavio said, nodding to the wooden boards in front of him. 'And step back immediately. I don't trust you.'

Slowly, I moved forward and laid the packet down. As I did so, there came a noise so shockingly loud and unexpected that I jumped backwards: a guttural roar so deep that it seemed to rumble from the depths of the earth, and it took me the space of a heartbeat to realise that it was the beast below us. Sukie screamed; her body jerked in fear, twisting in the air and slipping from one of Ottavio's hands. She screamed again; he fumbled to catch her, but I heard the sound of tearing cloth as her sleeve ripped from her dress at the seam and she fell ten feet into the lion's pen.

There was an instant of absolute stillness, as if time had frozen. Ottavio and I looked down in horror; Sukie lay where she had fallen on the straw; even the lion seemed paralysed by surprise. The moment passed; Ottavio met my eye briefly, then snatched up the letters and ran towards the stairs. Sukie sat up. She appeared unhurt by the fall, scrambling backwards as the lion stretched out his quivering nose and began to sniff the air between them. I don't even remember making the decision to jump; my muscles seemed to move by instinct, bypassing thought.

The lion snapped his head around as I landed; I remained crouching in the straw, hardly daring to breathe.

'Keep still,' I hissed at Sukie from the side of my mouth; she was cowering against the far wall of the enclosure, but I could sense her wanting to move towards me for protection, when her safety depended on my ability to divert the lion away from her. I darted a quick glance around; there was one iron-barred door on the opposite side, secured with a strong chain and padlock. The only way out, it seemed, was to climb back up to the gallery, but I could not see how we were to achieve that without help. If the girl stood on my shoulders, she might reach to grasp the rail, but it was doubtful that she would have the strength to pull herself up, and even more doubtful that the lion would leave us unmolested long enough to effect this escape.

He took a couple of stately paces towards me as I straightened, keeping all my movements as slow and smooth as possible so as not to startle him. He may not have been in peak condition, but at this proximity he was an awesome sight; muscles taut under his pelt, gold eyes missing nothing. The fur around his muzzle was pale and soft; with his jaws closed, he had a look of long-suffering dignity. At present, he seemed to regard me as a curiosity rather than a threat, but that could change in an instant. One swipe of his paw would take my head off before I had even reached for my weapon. He was close enough that I could feel the heat of him, smell the blood and meat on his breath. He lowered his magnificent head and growled deep in his throat; I felt it reverberate through the ground. Behind me, Sukie whimpered. I stepped to the side, and again; his eyes followed me as I drew his attention away from her. I reached around my back for the dagger I had taken from Jacopo's chamber and held it out, point-first, assessing my chances. The blade looked laughably small in the face of such a creature; could I really hope to inflict sufficient damage with the one strike I would likely get before his jaws closed around my throat?

In the centre of the enclosure, a cluster of boulders had been piled in what I presumed was a half-hearted attempt to make the animal feel at home in this harsh northern climate. I stepped up on to the lowest, still levelling the dagger. Perhaps something in my movement primed him; perhaps the wind changed and he caught my scent; suddenly his lips curled back, revealing a horrifying set of teeth. I watched him coil his energy as if to spring; he let out a noise that turned my bowels to water; Sukie screamed, and in the same moment the pitch of the beast's roar changed. He flinched visibly, whipping around towards his own flank, and I saw the feathered tail of a small dart protruding from the soft crease where his belly met the joint of his hind leg. He let out another enraged roar, his sights fixed on me.

'Roar back,' shouted a voice from the gallery.

I looked up, terrified to take my eyes off the lion, to glimpse Hajek leaning over the rail. He was holding what appeared to be a flute in his hand.

'Spread your arms, make yourself as big as possible and roar at him,' he called. 'Do it now!'

My whole body was shaking; fear had flooded me with a wild energy and every sinew told me to turn and run, but there was nowhere to run to. I had never heard anything as absurd as Hajek's idea, but I had no better option: I opened my arms wide and bellowed at the lion.

The creature stopped, his roar subdued to a growl. I repeated the noise, waving my arms as if trying to signal a distant ship, and he backed up a couple of paces, then began to circle my rock warily.

'Keep up the noise,' Hajek said in an encouraging tone; he seemed almost to be enjoying the spectacle. 'Show him you're a match for him. I don't know how long it will take to have an effect.'

'What?' I called back, between roars, but I couldn't hear his response over the lion's renewed snarling.

I couldn't say how many minutes elapsed while I held him at bay, roaring and waving my arms; each one felt like an hour, but it was probably no more than four or five, and suddenly the animal faltered, its hind legs buckling as it slumped to the ground and lay, whining softly.

'Amazing,' Hajek said. 'I really didn't know if that would work.'

Sukie was curled up against the wall, sobbing; I recovered my wits and rushed over to her, lifting her on to my shoulders so that Hajek could grab her wrists and haul her up over the rail.

As soon as I saw she was safe, it was as if all my strength ebbed suddenly and my legs folded under me as the lion's had; I collapsed against the wall, breathing hard.

'Hold on, Bruno – the keeper's coming,' Hajek called, and I heard the sound of a chain being unwound.

'Did you kill it?' I asked as we trooped back across the Powder Bridge like survivors of a battle – except Hajek, who looked quite jaunty at the success of his experiment.

'Let's hope not,' he said. 'You know about the prophecy? The lion's astrological chart is supposedly bound up with the Emperor's – he won't be at all happy if I've prematurely ended it. But I don't suppose he'd have wanted to let it kill a child.'

'Or me,' I reminded him. 'What did you do to it?'

He held up the instrument. 'Blowpipe and dart – have you seen one? The people of the New World use them for hunting – I'd read about them and tried to make my own. You put a paralysing poison on the tip of the dart, made from plant sap. I used a tiny amount, so he should recover. Of course, you can only fire them at close range, and usually at smaller targets, so this was an ideal chance to test it in real conditions.'

'Glad to have been useful,' I said. 'Did you see Jacopo?'

'Not yet. Their maid came to the Powder Tower and garbled some story about you pursuing Ottavio and a child to Lion

Court and him poisoning his father. I thought your predicament sounded the more urgent, so I took the precaution of bringing this.' He brandished the pipe. 'I suppose I should go to Jacopo now. Take the girl to the Horse – I'll see you there.'

'You need to find Ottavio,' I said, in Italian, so that Sukie would not understand. 'He took a bundle of letters that tie him to Ziggi Bartos, but I didn't see what else was there. Maybe evidence that the Catholics were behind the plot to poison Rudolf.'

'I very much doubt that,' he said. 'San Clemente and Montalcino are far too skilled to make the mistake of committing anything to paper. Ziggi Bartos *was* the evidence against them, and he won't be giving any testimony.'

'We must find Ottavio, with or without the letters, and arrest him,' I said. 'He killed David Maier, the bookseller. He must face justice for that.'

'Needless waste of a life,' Hajek said with such vehemence that I stopped to stare at him.

'Wait – you *knew*? How? Was it you who warned David that the Stradas meant to kill Esther?'

He took a long time to answer. We passed under the arches into the palace courtyard and he glanced up at the windows of the Stradas' apartments.

'I stopped by to check on Jacopo early that evening. The maid let me in, and I was about to enter his chamber when I heard his children inside, arguing. Katherina said something like, "Then we have to get rid of her, it's the only way". I couldn't hear Ottavio's response, but she said, "Ask your friend David when you see him tonight. He can tell us when she's next coming." So I intercepted David that night and told him what I'd heard.' He shook his head. 'I thought I was doing the right thing, trying to protect Esther. Instead, it got David killed.'

'So it was *you* I saw talking to him in the yard of the Winged Horse, the night he died?'

'Yes. I knew that was where they met to trade their stolen books.'

431

'But – you gave him money?'

'I owed him for some books I'd ordered – it was my pretext for cornering him. I ran into Ottavio in the street as I was leaving. I told him if he was looking for David, he'd just missed him. That was a mistake I bitterly regret – Ottavio must have run down the hill and arrived at the river ahead of him. It was my fault.'

'Or mine,' I said, looking at the ground. 'If I hadn't detained David in conversation, he might have reached the jetty before Ottavio and got safely into a boat.'

We stood in silence for a moment, considering how a matter of minutes, of infinitely small choices, could have meant the difference between life and death. Sukie leaned against me.

'I want to see my Far now,' she said quietly.

'I'll find him,' Hajek said. 'You two go on to the Winged Horse, keep away from here for now. I'm going to see Jacopo.'

'Wait, Thaddeus,' I said as he turned to leave. 'You knew Ottavio and Katherina were talking about Esther Loew. So – you knew about the Emperor wanting to marry her. How?'

He smiled. 'John Dee is not the most subtle go-between. Scuttling back and forth between the castle and the Jewish Town, constantly interrupting me to check Hebrew words. In the end I said to him in jest – John, are you courting a Jewish woman? And his face was so stricken, I knew I'd hit the mark. He told me everything and swore me to secrecy. It was one of Rudolf's more lunatic ideas, I must say. I feared there would be a good deal of harm done before he could be talked out of it. It flatters his vanity to think he is re-enacting the story of some great biblical king of times past.' He rolled his eyes and clapped me on the shoulder. 'I must go.'

'Be careful,' I said. 'The Strada children are afraid and growing desperate to save themselves. I think Katherina tried to poison Esther.'

He looked at me in horror. 'My God. Is she all right?'

'I don't know. She's at the Horse with her friend, a doctor. Is there any antidote to the suicide tree toxin?'

'I had not yet had the chance to do much work on the kernels. I was intending to test their properties and effects so that we would know how to counter them – I know only that it affects the heart and the breathing. As I understand it, symptoms are directly proportional to dosage, so if Esther did not consume much, she may be all right. I have other treatments against poisons in my laboratory – I'll bring them to you. In the meantime, you had better pray.'

'I'm out of practice. Here, take this, just in case.' I passed him the Ottoman dagger. 'It's the knife Jacopo used to kill Bartos.'

His eyes widened. 'Ah. The Venetian ambassador always swore blind there were a pair, Rudolf said he'd only ever seen one. Another of Jacopo's perks, I suppose. Don't worry about me, Bruno. Look after the girl.'

THIRTY-THREE

The lion story was growing in the telling; listening to Sukie relay it to Greta, you could be forgiven for thinking that the girl had fought the beast off single-handed while I stood on a rock screaming.

'I was *roaring*, not screaming,' I said with an attempt at dignity. 'Anyway, you were the one complaining there are not enough adventures for girls – it seems to me you've had more than your share over the past few days.'

Sukie took an enormous bite of apple cake and considered. 'Yes, I might like a rest for a while,' she said. 'Maybe I'll write my own book, about a girl who fights lions to save a poor helpless philosopher who just waves his arms at them.'

'Excuse me – I've already climbed up a tower to rescue you, my lady, like a knight from the tales of King Arthur.'

'Very well, in my book I won't make you entirely helpless,' she conceded, with her mouth full. 'Is there any more cake, Greta? It's hungry work, fighting wild animals.'

Greta caught my eye and smiled. It made me think of Besler. Christ – where *was* Besler? I felt a lurch of panic; I had not seen him since the morning, and it was now growing dusk. He had not been back to the tavern either, according to Greta. I would have liked nothing more than to sit by the fire in the quiet tap-room with cake and hot wine, but there was too much still to do.

I climbed the stairs to the first floor and knocked on a door.

Inside, I found Esther lying on a bed, a sickly sheen to her skin. Her chest rose and fell with quick, shallow breaths, just like Jacopo and Jan Boodt. Benjamin sat on a chair beside her, tenderly wiping the sweat from her face with a cloth dipped in cool water.

'What are her chances?' I asked. There seemed no point in dancing around the question.

He raised his head and I saw the strain in his face; in the space of a day, he had had to watch his cousin and the woman he loved at the point of death. 'I made her sick immediately, as you said. I think she has voided most of her stomach by now. But her heart is beating arrhythmically and she's short of breath. The trouble is, there's no way of knowing how much she ingested because we don't know the concentration of the poison she was given. All we can do is wait.'

'Hajek is coming with antidotes. Let's pray they work.'

He dredged up a tired smile. 'What do you think I've been doing all this time? I didn't have you for a praying man.'

'*In extremis*,' I said, 'even a heretic must cling to something. I envy you your rituals.'

He gave me a long look. 'No,' he said, smoothing Esther's matted hair off her brow. 'You don't. Listen, her family will be worrying about her. Sooner or later, the Maharal will discover that she went to the castle and he'll come in search of her. It's not safe for him there with the Stradas around. Can you send a messenger to let him know what's happened and where we are? He must be here with her, in case—' He didn't need to finish the thought.

'My horse is in the yard, I'll go,' I said with a last look at Esther.

As I passed through the tap-room, I saw that Erik Moller had arrived. Sukie was curled into him on the bench by the fire, chattering in Danish, waving her arms and roaring; I presumed this was an impression of me. He caught my eye and mouthed 'thank you' over her head. I nodded and slipped out into the yard. Sooner or later, it would dawn on him that I had taken her for sanctuary to the home of people who had literally thrown her to the lions, and that the danger I had saved her from was my fault in the first place.

Greta followed me out to the stables.

'Here, you'd better take this,' she said, pressing a small green bottle into my hand. 'It's caused enough trouble already.'

I shook it; there was very little liquid inside. 'Bartos's elixir?'

'When the child turned up here clutching her precious silver flask and saying it would make her fortune, Magda smelled a rat. Then you told her it was dangerous and she guessed it was the poison those Spaniards were after, so as soon as the girl was asleep, she poured the contents into this and replaced them with aqua vitae.'

'And you put this in Jan's schnapps.'

'I don't know what you're talking about, Bruno. Jan Boodt died of a bad heart, Dr Hajek said so. And not one person in this town will mourn him.' She glanced up at the lit window on the first floor and her look of defiance crumpled. 'But that poor Jewish girl. If anything happens to her, I shall never forgive myself.'

'You're not to blame,' I said, laying a hand on her arm.

'But I am,' she said, shaking my hand away. 'If I hadn't taken those keys from Dr Hajek, Bartos would never have been able to make his potion in the first place. I only did it because the Spaniards pressured Jan, and he needed the money they were offering. He said he would make my sister suffer if I didn't do as he asked, and I knew what he was capable of.'

'You did what you had to,' I said. 'They'd only have found another poison if you hadn't. How is Magda?'

'She woke briefly and recognised me, so it's to be hoped her wits are not damaged. Hajek thinks her skull is not fractured either, which is a blessing. All we can do now is wait and pray.'

More praying. Benjamin was wrong; I did envy him the comfort of belief. How reassuring it must be to think someone is listening. I felt increasingly desolate as I rode down the

436

narrow cobbled lanes toward the Stone Bridge. Sukie had almost been killed because of my failure to see what had been in front of me all along. Would David Maier be alive now if I had not stopped to speak to him in the inn yard, giving Ottavio time to reach the river first? And Besler – he had come to Prague in my care, and instead of sending him to safety with the English merchant, I had allowed him to be drawn alongside me into this labyrinth of conspiracies and murder. Now he was alone in the city, at the mercy of San Clemente's thugs, and quite possibly the vengeful Count Rozmberk as well, if he learned what his wife had been up to in his absence. On the plus side, I thought, at least Besler would not die a virgin, and I let out an inappropriate, yelping laugh that caused passers-by to turn and stare. God, I needed to sleep.

Rabbi Loew took the news of Esther's condition gravely. I found him at David's shop, where a steady stream of visitors was arriving to see the family. Like Benjamin, the rabbi looked weighed down with grief. I offered to take him to Esther on the back of my horse, but he said he would ask the Jewish mayor to arrange a carriage so that one of his daughters could accompany him.

'Is she in danger?' he asked. 'Be honest with me, Bruno.'

'As far as we can tell, she drank very little,' I said. 'But the substance is extremely potent – no one really knows the effects yet.' Except one man who is dead and another on the threshold of it, I thought. 'Benjamin is with her, and Hajek is on his way – he has remedies to treat poisoning. But – I advise you not to delay,' I added.

'This is my fault,' he said as he put on his coat. 'I let this business go too far. I should have stopped Rudolf when he first told me of his feelings for Esther, explained to him that it was impossible. But how do you say no to an Emperor, Bruno? A man who holds the fate of your entire community in his hands? I feared there could be no good outcome, and yet I persisted in the belief that I could manage the situation. I curse the day he laid eyes on her.'

I was the last person to tell him to have faith; all I could do was embrace him.

'Your boy was here earlier, looking for you,' he said as we parted in the street.

'Besler? When?'

'It was around noon – during David's burial. I saw him standing outside the wall of the cemetery with his head bowed. I think he was praying. Afterwards, he asked me if there was anything he could do to help. I was quite touched. He's come a long way from Nuremberg.'

'In every sense,' I said. 'Do you know where he went?'

'He said he would wait for you at home.'

I thanked him and once again found myself promising to pray for Esther.

I rode back to the House at the Green Mound to find it empty. The horse had been unusually skittish since leaving the tavern, and seemed glad to be home. I left him to be brushed down and fed; Hajek's stable boy said he had seen no sign of Besler all day.

'A message came earlier, though,' he said, leaning back under the weight of the saddle as he lifted it off.

'For me? Who was it from?'

'Dunno. A man all in smart livery brought it. I put it in the kitchen. You smell a bit funny, sir,' he added, lowering his voice as if he were letting me know in confidence. 'It's bothering the horses.'

'Like Hercules, I have been wrestling a lion,' I said, leaving him staring.

I found a folded paper on the table, sealed with red wax and an insignia I did not recognise. The contents, when I broke it open, were short and to the point:

Count Vilem von Rozmberk requests your presence at the Rozmberk Palace at your earliest convenience.

'*Merda*,' I said aloud. That didn't take long; he could barely have set foot inside his own porch before someone had told him that his wife had bedded a young man in his absence. I suspected the sour-faced steward. Was that where Besler was now? The count's men could have intercepted him on his way back from the Jewish Town.

I went up to my room to check how much money remained in our travelling chest, in case there was a chance I could negotiate with the count and buy Besler's way out of trouble. But my purse was running dangerously low, and somehow I doubted that whatever paltry sum I could offer would be of interest to the highest nobleman in Bohemia, when set against the slight to his honour. I sighed and changed my clothes again, although perhaps it would intimidate the count if I showed up smelling of wild beasts. As I dropped Ottavio's shirt on the floor, I wondered if Hajek had managed to have him arrested. He would not need shirts of fine linen in gaol. I confess that the thought pleased me.

I washed my face, buttoned a clean doublet and regarded myself in the glass. It was not an encouraging sight. As I ran down the stairs and picked up my cloak, I heard an urgent hammering at the door. What now, I thought – Rozmberk guards come to escort me in person? Or worse – bad news about Esther, or Magda?

I opened the door to see a messenger in an official livery I didn't recognise.

'Dr Giordano Bruno?' hc said.

'Yes?'

'Are you the employer of Hieronymus Besler of Nuremberg?'

'In a sense. Where is he?'

'In the Daliborka Tower prison. He's been arrested.'

THIRTY-FOUR

The horse was even more reluctant than I was to return to the castle; I had to kick him hard to persuade him back up the hill. The messenger had not been able to give me any further details about Besler's arrest, but I had to assume it was somehow connected with Rozmberk's summons to me. The Daliborka Tower was a dank, hostile turret at the easternmost edge of the castle complex, built into the fortifications at the end of Golden Lane and used as a prison. It was here that the ghost of the young soldier was heard to play his lonely viol at night.

'Breach of the peace,' the gaoler said, when I had paid him to be admitted. 'Public brawling, use of a deadly weapon, attempted murder. Take your pick.'

'What weapon? Was he fighting a duel?'

The man laughed. 'A duel? I wouldn't call it that. Scrapping in the Old Town Square, rolling in the dust, they were. Then one of them pulls out a blade and that's when people screamed for the guard. They're both up there now, looking the worse for wear. Had to put the pair of them in manacles or they'd be ripping each other's limbs off.'

I looked at him, confused. Surely he couldn't have the Count von Rozmberk in manacles?

'Come on, then, if you want to see him.'

He led me up a spiral staircase of dank stone stained with green slime, and unlocked a heavy door. Inside I saw Besler sitting against one wall, his wrists and ankles chained, one eye bruised and swollen shut. Opposite him sat Diego, his mouth and nose bloodied. He gave me a basilisk stare as I entered and swore at me in Spanish.

I ignored him and knelt by Besler, lifting his chin to check for damage. 'What happened?'

'He set on me in the Old Town Square,' he said with a furious glare over my shoulder at Diego. 'He asked me if I wanted to see a magic trick, and I was curious so I followed, and then he clamped his hand over my mouth and tried to drag me into an alley. So I hit him. He wasn't expecting that.'

'I bet he wasn't. You did a good job,' I said, looking at the Spaniard's face. 'I didn't know you knew how to fight.'

'You can't go to the school I attended and not learn how to fight,' he said matter-of-factly. 'I got a couple of good punches in, I think, before he pulled a knife.'

'I can see that.' So the Catholics must have worked out that they had been tricked over the elixir, if they had targeted Besler. 'But you could have been killed. What were you thinking, going along with a Spaniard? You know they're dangerous.'

'I've never seen him in my life,' Besler protested, nodding at Diego. 'Am I to mistrust all Spaniards, just because one or two are your enemies? That sounds like the exact opposite of the tolerance you usually preach, Maestro.'

It was a fair point, but I was too tired to debate. 'Come on, let's get you out.'

The gaoler made the sign for money.

'I've already paid you,' I said, impatient. 'Did I mention that I work for the Emperor? I don't want to have to tell His Majesty that you've detained my assistant for no more than defending himself against a violent assault.' I showed him Rudolf's silver token and the man took a step back, suddenly deferential. 'By the way,' I added as he unlocked Besler's shackles, 'you've got yourself a prize catch here.'

'How do you mean?' The gaoler turned and Besler stood, rubbing his wrists.

I gestured to Diego. 'I know this man. He's in the pay of the Spanish ambassador. If you put him to questioning, he might tell you some interesting things about his work. He might take a bit of persuading, but there could be a reward in it for you, if you squeeze anything useful out of him.'

The gaoler's eyes lit up at the prospect. I turned back to Diego, whose glare could have warped steel.

'Tell your masters,' I said in Spanish, 'that if they have anything to say to me, they can talk to me directly. But if I see you anywhere near this boy again, I will kill you. Same goes for the rest of my friends. Understand?'

He spat a gobbet of bloody sputum into the straw and muttered something I only half-caught.

'*Y tu mamá también*,' I said without looking back.

'It might be better if I didn't come with you to the Rozmberk Palace,' Besler said, slowing his steps as we approached. 'It could be awkward. Besides, I smell like a – well, like a prison cell.'

'I'm well aware of the awkwardness, as you call it,' I said. 'But I'm not letting you out of my sight again. There's another of those Spaniards out there, and I doubt your schoolboy prize-fighting skills would be a match for that one. You'll have to wait in the courtyard. But perhaps this will teach you to think before you drop your breeches in future,' I added sternly.

'Before I what?'

'You heard.'

'I didn't drop my breeches.'

'I really don't need every detail.' I looked at him sidelong. 'That impatient, were you? You didn't even stop to take your clothes off?'

'I don't know what you're talking about.'

'Are you being obtuse on purpose? The *countess*, Besler. Xena.'

He bit his lip and looked down at his boots. 'Don't be angry with me, Maestro – I know you warned me, and I'm very ashamed of myself.'

'I'm not angry, I think you're an idiot. You know she was only after your seed. And now I have to answer to the count.'

'My *what*?' He stopped walking and looked at me, perplexed. 'I fell asleep, Maestro. I drank too much wine, even though you advised me against it, and after the meal she took me to a warm room with a couch, and – that's all I remember. I woke this morning with a blanket over me. And all my clothes on, by the way.'

'You didn't go to it with her?'

'With *Xena*? No, I'd have remembered that. She tried to kiss me, but I was half-dozing by then. I'm not used to strong wine. We always drink beer in Wittenberg. What's so funny?'

'Oh, Besler,' I said, slinging an arm around his shoulder. 'You are ridiculous. *I* could kiss you.'

'Please don't,' he said, alarmed.

I was still laughing when the steward opened the door.

'You again,' he said dispassionately, with a glance at Besler. 'I wouldn't be laughing if I were you.'

I sent Besler to the kitchens to get something cold on his injured eye, and the steward led me to a library that was not as grand as the Emperor's, but equally handsome: high domed ceilings painted with classical scenes, gleaming shelves of dark wood, books on three sides and one wall all of windows, to flood the room with light on a clear day. Outside, dusk was falling. A tall man stood by the window with his arms folded across his chest; he turned as I entered and inclined his head. He didn't look so different from his portrait, despite the three decades that had elapsed; the blond hair barely greying; the moustaches carefully curled; the blue eyes bright and severe. Though he had thickened slightly around the middle, the Count von Rozmberk carried himself like a younger man, with a relaxed, athletic bearing that made me think he must have been an accomplished sportsman in his youth, and probably was still. His assessing gaze swept over me from head to foot. I sincerely hoped he was not going to call me out.

'So this is the famous Giordano Bruno,' he said, in a cultured German with a hint of amusement.

I bowed low. 'My lord.'

'You've made quite the impression on my wife, it seems.'

'I—'

'Yes, I've hardly been back in the city five minutes and she must have mentioned your name three hundred times.'

'I'm honoured,' I said.

'Don't be, she'll have a new favourite this time next week,' he said drily. 'But I am glad to make your acquaintance. How do you find Prague?'

'Eventful.'

He smiled. 'I heard there has been a great deal going on since I've been away. Thaddeus Hajek sent a fast rider to Trebon suggesting it might be time to come back and take the reins for a while. My steward has just been filling me in on everything that's happened in the past few days.'

I kept my face steady. 'Everything?'

'Mm. Murders and so on. Messy business. Tell me something – have you been teaching your memory system to Rudolf?'

'There hasn't been time,' I said. 'He's had a lot on his mind.'

'I suppose so. Good – I would like you to teach me. John Dee says there is no one in all of Europe to match your work in the art of memory.'

'John likes to exaggerate. But thank you.'

'If you will have me as your student while you're in Prague, I'll make it worth your while. You could take lodgings here in the palace if you like, there's plenty of room.' He saw my hesitation and waved a hand. 'Well, think about it. In the meantime, I have a surprise for you.'

He crossed to the opposite corner and opened a door set into the wall, ushering me through and closing it after me. I found myself in a smaller room, also filled with books, and there, in a chair by the fire, his hair and beard whiter than I remembered, but his lined face so dear and familiar, sat a figure so unexpected and oddly comforting that for a moment I wanted to throw my arms around his neck.

'You're safe,' I said in English.

John Dee jolted his head up from the book in his lap and I realised he had been dozing. 'Oh, hello, Bruno,' he said, as if we had only yesterday parted company at his house in Mortlake. His reading lenses fell off the end of his nose and he caught them deftly in one hand. 'Forgive me, it was a long journey, I've hardly slept. Neither have you, by the look of it.'

'I thought you'd been abducted,' I said, hearing the crack in my voice. 'Or worse.'

'Well, I might have been, if Vilem hadn't got me out of Prague. Banished or imprisoned, certainly. He's a good sort, the count. Terrible judgement in wives, otherwise very sharp.'

I shushed him and we both glanced at the door, suppressing our laughter like schoolboys.

'You'd better start from the beginning,' he said, gesturing to a chair opposite. So I told him everything that had happened since my arrival in the city, from Greta turning us away at Hajek's door to the encounter with the lion (which I may have embellished just a little – I was not immune to the power of a good story).

He leaned back in his chair with a sorrowful shake of his head. 'You know, I began to suspect Ziggi Bartos a couple of months ago,' he said. 'I saw him more than once in the company of San Clemente's men at the Winged Horse. He started loitering around the herbalists' floor in the Powder Tower. I feared he was a prime candidate to be used by the Emperor's enemies.'

'Because of his money problems?'

'Partly that. But he had other weaknesses they could exploit. Around the time I began to grow concerned about his association with those Spaniards, I came upon him in the castle grounds in a state of great distress. He was reluctant to tell me the cause, but eventually he confided that someone had been through his lodgings while he was out at the Winged Horse the night before, and taken personal papers.'

'Letters?'

'He wouldn't say. I recalled that, a few months ago, Rudolf had asked me to put a curse on his brother, Matthias. I made an excuse – told him I had never seen a curse work effectively, or some such – and I was relieved when he didn't mention it again. I thought he'd given up the idea. Now I wonder if he asked Bartos instead, and the boy had been foolish enough to set something in writing.' He shook his head. 'Whatever these papers were, Bartos was evidently worried, which in turn made me worried – I suspected they'd been taken with the purpose of coercing him, though of course I had no proof. So when Bartos grew increasingly secretive about what he was working on, then suddenly came into money and claimed he had won it at cards, I thought my suspicions had been proved right.' He turned his lenses between his fingers. 'So I wrote to Walsingham, saying I feared there would be an attempt on Rudolf's life. This was last month. Shortly after that, Bartos began to slander me publicly, so I guessed my letters were being read. I told Hajek I didn't trust his housekeeper, but he swore he could vouch for her loyalty. And despite all the service I had done him in the matter of Esther Loew, Rudolf took notice of Bartos's lies about me. Which was the idea, of course – Montalcino and San Clemente wanted me banished or imprisoned before I could find any evidence to prove Bartos was plotting against the Emperor on their behalf.'

'You carried letters and gifts from Rudolf to Esther,' I said. 'Did you seriously believe that anything could come of it?'

John sighed. 'Of course not. Nor did the rabbi, but in the short term it was a way of remaining in Rudolf's favour. My star had been waning with him since Bartos came to Prague, and suddenly he had a use for me again.' He met my eye with an expression of culpability. 'As for the marriage idea – absurd. But Rudolf did not see why he should be denied. Do you know, he even cited Queen Elizabeth's father as a precedent? He said

446

to me, "If your King Henry can throw off the yoke of Rome to marry a Protestant woman for love, why should I not do the same to marry a Jewess?"'

'Did you point out to him how many people have died as a result of King Henry's infatuation?'

'I did. I reminded him that his uncle Philip is even now amassing a great Armada to bring England back to Rome by force. He rather glossed over that. Rudolf has a remarkable capacity to only hear advice he agrees with.'

'John – you wrote a letter to Rabbi Loew before you left Prague, telling him that your enemies suspected.'

'How do you know that?' he said, sitting upright and gripping the arms of the chair. 'I never sent it.'

'I'll explain later. Did you mean the Stradas?'

'Yes. Katherina guessed there was another woman – I think women have a sixth sense about these things. They know when they've been replaced, even if nothing is said outright. Ottavio asked me if the Emperor had confided in me about a new mistress. I said no, of course, but I could see he didn't believe me. He's a great one for listening at doors, Ottavio – I caught him following me a few times. I didn't realise David Maier had told him the whole story. Poor David. What an awful loss.'

'In that letter, you spoke of danger to B. Did you mean Benjamin Katz?'

He nodded. 'Rudolf has romantic ideals. When he was first stricken with love for Esther – his words – he wanted to find out if she was married or betrothed. Because her understanding with Benjamin was not a formal betrothal, the rabbi told him no. I feared that if the Emperor found out she had a commitment of sorts to another man, he would seek to remove his rival, or punish the rabbi for bending the truth.' He pushed himself up from his chair and moved towards the window, tapping his spectacles against his teeth. I noticed how stiffly he walked now. I hoped that was just the hours on the road from Trebon. 'Ah, Bruno – how are we going to save that poor girl from his obsession? If you tell Rudolf he can't have something, he only digs in his heels – witness this temple to forbidden knowledge he has built around himself.' He peered short-sightedly at his own reflection in the glass. 'If only there were some way to cool his ardour. But he will not listen to any of the obvious arguments. He is convinced he is enacting God's will.'

'I have an idea,' I said. 'But I'm going to need your help.'

THIRTY-FIVE

'Who would have thought it – Zikmund Bartos, plotting to kill me,' Rudolf exclaimed, his face a picture of righteous indignation. He tipped his head back to look up at the stars. 'Of course, we all know who put him up to it, don't we?'

Hajek exchanged a glance with me. 'Do we, Majesty?'

'Yes, Thaddeus, we do. *My brother.*' A small hand emerged from the layers of fur and pointed at us. 'I should have guessed. It's exactly the kind of weasely, underhand trick I'd expect from Matthias – paying a man at a distance to slip me poison, keeping his own hands conveniently clean.'

There was a short pause while none of us mentioned that the Emperor had engaged the same man to put a wasting curse on his brother from a distance.

'Even if Matthias was the intended beneficiary of the conspiracy, Your Majesty,' Hajek said, 'he is in Vienna. He could not have arranged it himself. You need to look closer to home. I hear there is a servant of the Spanish ambassador held in the Daliborka Tower – if he were put to hard questioning, you might learn something useful from him.'

'Good God – you think San Clemente was part of the conspiracy?' Rudolf frowned. 'But he is a great connoisseur of art.'

'The two things are not incompatible.'

449

'Huh. Well, let's have this servant interrogated, see what he'll give up with a bit of persuasion.' He surveyed the night sky again. 'I always come up here when my mind is troubled. I find that looking at the constellations is a marvellous reminder of our own insignificance.'

I stifled a laugh; I thought it unlikely that Rudolf had ever considered himself insignificant. The four of us were standing on the flat roof of the White Tower, which marked the centre point of the long gallery wing facing the cathedral. A brisk wind had driven the clouds away and the sky was vivid with pin-sharp stars and a shining half-moon. Our breath steamed around our faces as the bells of the city tolled for midnight.

The Holy Roman Emperor was wrapped in a thick fur cloak and a fur hat; he looked like a small round ball of fur, as if he were preparing for hibernation.

'Jacopo would often come up with me,' he continued. A wistful note had crept into his voice. 'He told me that in Italy, there are men experimenting with optics and lenses to create a device that will enable us to see the moon and stars as if they are a hand's breadth away. I am sorry that I was too late to reward him for his good service. To think he killed Bartos to save my life!' He shook his head in sad disbelief. 'I still don't understand why he made such a meal of it though. Stirring up fear of a Golem – what did he hope to gain by that?'

'I think Jacopo Strada was no friend to the Jews, Your Majesty,' I said.

'I suppose not. Still, he was a good and loyal servant. Even if he was skimming off my collections. Find out how much money he left, Thaddeus – a portion of it should be mine, in compensation for his theft. And then let him be buried with all honour in the church of Saint Nikolaus in the Lesser Town. I find it extraordinary that his children will not be present.' He looked at Hajek. 'Fled, you say? Are you sure? Where to?'

'The maidservant said only that they packed up and left in a great hurry as soon as their father died. My guess is Vienna – Jacopo had a house there. And then perhaps to family in

Mantua, while Katherina . . .' He paused and discreetly cleared his throat. 'Waits out her confinement. Your Majesty knows she is with child?'

Rudolf grunted. 'If it's anything like the last one, she can keep it in Mantua. Why on earth would she have played those monstrous tricks on me with the eyeballs? What kind of woman would do such a thing?'

'One who felt she could not get your attention any other way,' I said. 'You would not see her, she grew desperate. She chose an extreme way to send the message that you were making a mistake in casting her aside.'

Rudolf narrowed his eyes. 'I hope you don't presume to tell me how I should conduct myself with women, Bruno. Even though I know you Italians consider yourselves experts in that field.'

'I am the last person to call myself an expert on women, Your Majesty. I am merely trying to understand her state of mind.'

'I still say there is something devilish in it. Sometimes I wonder if that child's strangeness does come from my grandmother after all.'

'Women are all quite mad when they are with child,' John Dee remarked. Hajek and I, having no experience, did not contradict him.

'And I suppose Ottavio hopes to evade justice for the killing of the bookseller,' Rudolf continued. 'I never took him for a violent man. What was his reason?'

'I believe it was a dispute over an unpaid invoice,' Hajek said smoothly.

Rudolf sniffed. 'Doesn't surprise me. Ottavio was cheating him, I expect. Inherited his father's chiselling ways. Should I send armed men to bring him back?'

'I think,' John said carefully, 'that the Maier family and the community would rather his death did not become the stuff of pamphlets and interludes in the Old Town Square. If there is a way of dealing justice discreetly, that would be their preference.'

The Emperor looked at him and nodded. 'Well. I will think

on it. For now, let Strada and his sister be banished from my realm, and we will make sure the bookseller's wife and children are well provided for.' He lowered his head. 'I am sorry, John, that I gave credence to Bartos's lies about you. I should never have allowed myself to be fooled by him, I see that now.'

'I have only ever desired to serve Your Majesty's best interests,' John said somewhat loftily. He stood a little way apart from the rest of us, leaning on a wooden staff. With the wind lifting his hair and beard, he recalled the sage Merlin from the English tales of Arthur and his knights. The effect was not unintentional.

'I thought perhaps you served Rozmberk these days,' Rudolf said with a sly glance. 'I should have realised he would have come to your rescue. Tell me – did the angels speak to him through you?'

John glanced at me and I gave him an encouraging nod, invisible to the others.

'Alas, they did not, Your Majesty, much as the count desired to hear them. It seems they will only speak to you.'

Rudolf looked as gleeful as a child who has swiped the last sweetmeat from his playmate. 'I should think so,' he said. 'I am the Holy Roman Emperor, and he is not. Have they spoken to you recently?'

'They have. And they had a most grave message to impart.'

Rudolf's expression froze. 'Well?'

John planted his feet apart and struck his staff on the ground. 'Two nights ago,' he began, in an imposing voice, 'the angel Uriel appeared to me in my shewing-stone, and he related a passage from the Scriptures. It was the story of King David and Nathan the Prophet. Does Your Majesty recall it?'

'Something about a sheep?' Rudolf said, like a student hoping for good marks.

'Exactly so. The prophet came to King David and told him the tale of a rich man who had all the flocks he could desire, and yet when he saw a poor man who had only one little ewe-lamb, he coveted it and took it from him. Of course it was an allegory, for the king had fallen in love with a beautiful woman,

Bathsheba, but she was married, and the king arranged for her husband to be killed in battle so that he could take her for his wife. The Lord God was displeased with him, and told King David that He would take everything from him as punishment for his offence.' John raised his staff aloft. 'I believe the angel came to me with this story as a warning to Your Majesty.'

Rudolf considered this, frowning. 'Hm. On the other hand, was not Bathsheba mother to King Solomon, who was David's heir and the greatest king who ever lived? So, you know. Pros and cons.' He moved his hands up and down, palms upward, miming a tipping scale. 'In any case, the analogy does not hold, because the woman I love is not married. I have not taken her from anyone, much less committed murder. So I think your angels are misinformed, John. Or am I supposed to call you Nathan?'

John glanced at me; this was not how the script was supposed to go.

'She is not married, Your Majesty, but she was promised to another in childhood,' I said hastily. 'You would be taking her from someone who has loved her for a long time. I believe the angel appeared to John with this message for a reason, before you do something that would displease the Lord.'

'I didn't realise you believed in John's angels,' he said with a hint of vexation. 'Or God, for that matter. But you say she loves another?'

I took a deep breath. There was always the chance that this could have the opposite effect and put Benjamin in greater danger. 'I believe she does, Your Majesty. And while you are her sovereign and could command her obedience, love is not love that is not freely given.' I sounded like a bad poet, I thought.

Rudolf wandered away to the parapet and stared out at the spire of St Vitus, deep in thought. Hajek, John and I all looked at one another, each of us willing someone else to speak.

'Could not duty and love be the same thing?' Rudolf said plaintively. He appeared to be addressing this to the gargoyles on the cathedral.

'Perhaps,' I said gently. 'But is that really what you want? Duty, gratitude, obedience, instead of feelings that match your own?' I approached and stood beside him. 'I know what it is to love a woman whose heart belongs to someone else, Your Majesty. It's a particularly cruel form of torture to inflict on oneself.' And one I seem doomed to repeat.

He turned to me, interested. 'And how did you forget her?'

I didn't, I wanted to say, but that would not have been helpful. 'I immersed myself in my work.'

'Huh.' He looked up at the stars again. 'But why did none of them tell me sooner? Esther, her father – you, John?'

'We feared displeasing you, Majesty,' John said.

'Well, I'm not delighted to learn of it now,' he said with a little huff. 'God's blood, I was willing to bring down the wrath of all Christendom on my own head for her sake. But – I will not be the king who takes another man's lamb and leaves him with nothing. Go away, all of you. I need to think.'

'As your physician, I must counsel you to think indoors, Your Majesty,' Hajek said. 'It's bitterly cold tonight.'

'Yes, all right.' He allowed Hajek to guide him towards the stairs. 'But if you cared about my health, Thaddeus, you would not have shot my lion with a poison dart. He's very unwell. You know that if he dies, I will follow.'

'He's not going to die. He has the heart of a lion, as do you.'

'*My* heart is shattered in pieces,' Rudolf said with his customary flair for the dramatic. At the stairs, he turned and looked at me. 'Giordano Bruno – I find myself without a librarian now that Ottavio is gone. Do you want the job? I would give my imprimatur to whatever books you wrote here.'

I was so taken aback, I had no idea how to answer. I thought of that exquisite room with its thousands of volumes, and how it might be to have the run of it, to be the one with the authority to send for forbidden manuscripts from every corner of the known world. Guaranteed patronage from the Emperor – for as long as his reign lasted, anyway. Another part of me wanted nothing more than to leave Prague and its scheming at my back.

'Can I have some time to consider it, Your Majesty?'

'Very well. Don't take too long, though. And you, John Dee—'

'Your Majesty?'

'Tell the Maharal I wish to speak to him.'

'Now, Majesty?'

'No. There has been enough to contend with for one day. Tomorrow night will do. And, John – I will make you my chief alchemist, if you promise me you will not work for Rozmberk.'

John bowed stiffly. 'I am yours to command in all things, Your Majesty.'

'Yes, well,' the Emperor said. 'As Bruno has pointed out, that is a cold kind of affection.'

'Did that work, do you think?' I asked John as I walked with him back to the Rozmberk Palace.

'It's planted the seed,' he said. 'Now we must allow him to persuade himself that giving her up was his idea in the first place. Which he will, in time. He likes the idea of defying the Church, but he baulks at displeasing God.'

'Well, thank you. It was an impressive performance, given how reluctant you were to do it.'

'I don't like lying about the angels, Bruno. It's disrespectful. I know you don't believe in them,' he added, with a hint of indulgence.

'I believe that you believe in them, John, and you are the cleverest man I know, so who am I to argue? You're sure you won't come back to Hajek's tonight?'

'I think I'll stay here a while longer,' he said as we reached the portico of the Rozmberk Palace. 'While I wait to see if Rudolf means what he says. He is notoriously capricious, but you must know that by now. What about you? Imperial librarian – do you like the idea?'

'Ah, God, I don't know.' I shook my head. 'I came here with the purpose of securing the Emperor's patronage, and now I have the offer of it, I'm not so sure. I don't know if Prague could ever feel like home.'

'*Home.*' He looked at me with a mournful smile and laid a hand on my shoulder. 'There's a word that neither of us has been able to say for a long time. I am thinking of going back to England, you know. I've written to Walsingham to see if it would be safe for me now. I miss the old place, for all its faults.'

'So do I. I must go. I've left Besler at the Winged Horse – Greta is patching him up after his bout with the Spaniard.'

John made a face. 'It will be a while before I trust that woman again.'

'She was trying to protect someone she loved. You'd do the same. I suppose Hajek will have to find a new housekeeper now.'

'I rather think he might get himself a wife instead,' John said, pulling me into an embrace that almost crushed my ribs. 'You should follow his example, Bruno. It's not good for a man to be so solitary.'

I walked back towards the gatehouse across an empty court-yard. Frost glittered on the cobbles; from beyond the walls, the lonely howling of the wolves in Lion Court carried through the cold air. I should have felt relieved that it was all over – joyful, even, at the prospect the Emperor had dangled before me. Instead, I felt hollowed out. I thought of David's wife and children. Would it have been better for them if Ottavio had been caught and executed for his murder, or would it make no difference to their grief? Not that banishment was lenient; I knew from experience that exile was a punishment of attrition. I understood John's longing for home all too well. I was mulling on his last words as I passed the cathedral; without warning, a cloaked figure materialised out of the shadows and fell into step beside me. I jumped back, reaching for my dagger, when a familiar Italian voice said, 'Put it away, Bruno – if I wanted you dead, it would have happened by now.'

'You do want me dead,' I said, sheathing the knife. I could see Montalcino's smile glinting under his hood.

'But I want you to repent first,' he said. 'Preferably in public.'

'Repent of what?'

'Of being *you*. I wanted to let you know I've been recalled to Rome.'

'That was sudden. Afraid of what the Spaniard might say under torture?'

'Oh, he won't talk. And in fact, it's been in train for a while. His Holiness is unhappy with my lack of progress in guiding Rudolf back to his Catholic duties.' His mouth twisted and I wondered what had prompted this confession; the failure of his mission was a professional humiliation that he would feel deeply.

'Christ, is he replacing you with someone even worse?'

'Yes, hilarious.' He gave me a reproving look. 'I came to call a truce, actually.'

'What's the catch?'

'No catch.' He reached into his cloak; I tensed again, but he drew out John's notebook. 'Have you mentioned me to Rudolf in your report on the murder of Bartos?'

'No. But he thinks Matthias is involved.'

He let out a short laugh. 'Matthias couldn't plot a bacchanalia in a vintner's. Listen – I will give you this book in return for keeping my name out of any talk of a conspiracy against the Emperor. John Dee is small fry to Rome, and in any case, the damned thing's unreadable.'

'All right,' I said. I knew it would put John's mind at rest. 'But why do you care what is said of you in Prague? You won't even be here. Aren't you going back to breaking people's fingers for the Lord?'

'Since you ask, there is talk of a cardinal's hat,' he said, allowing himself a modest preen. 'So until that is settled, I would prefer not to be associated with an assassination conspiracy, even in rumour. Are we agreed?'

'How do you know I will keep my word?'

'I don't. And yet I do believe, misguided as you are, that you take pride in a sense of yourself as a man of honour. So I do think your word is worth something, if only because keeping it allows you to maintain your belief in your own integrity.'

I could not follow his logic, but it didn't sound like a compliment. Nevertheless, I allowed him to give me the kiss of peace on both cheeks – as sincerely as Judas, I thought – and he passed me the book.

'Well, good luck, I suppose,' I said. 'It must be nice to fail at your job and be rewarded for it.'

'Oh, luck has nothing to do with it.' He touched a finger to the bristles on his cheek, a tic that had always made me want to slap his hand away. 'It's a question of strategy.'

I smiled; I had said the same to Jan Boodt about cards.

'But I make you this promise, Bruno,' he continued. 'When I am cardinal, if you should ever set foot in the Italian states again in your sorry life, I will know about it, and I will have you in front of the Inquisition before you can open your mouth to beg forgiveness.'

'What makes you think I would ever beg forgiveness?' I said, turning briskly away before I was tempted to take a swing at him, which would be exactly what he wanted.

'*Arrivederci*, Giordano Bruno,' he called after me. 'I feel certain that we will meet again. Call it a premonition.'

THIRTY-SIX

'What now, Maestro?' Besler said as we walked over the Stone Bridge the following afternoon. We paused at the plinth where Bartos had hung and looked out across the city, its hundred spires catching the last sunlight as the chorus of bells struck the hour of four. The days were beginning to lengthen, I thought; it was almost spring.

'Now,' I said, 'we must make arrangements for you to return to your studies.'

'What?' He turned, crestfallen. 'But I don't want to go back to Wittenberg yet. I have learned so much here with you these past few days, far more than I did at the university.'

'Yes, but not necessarily the lessons your father is paying for you to learn,' I said. 'I mean, look at your face.'

He touched a finger gingerly to his black eye and turned back to survey the view. 'I will have so much news to tell him in my next letter,' he said. 'Imagine his expression when he hears we are to have dinner with a famous rabbi!'

'I'm imagining it,' I said. 'Listen, Besler – you are a grown man now, as you keep reminding me. If you want to go on working with me, perhaps you need to be circumspect about how much you share with your family. As the prophet Ezekiel said, there is a time to keep silence and a time to speak, and a time *not* to mention to your father that you were nearly seduced by a countess and ended up in a gaol cell for fighting off a mercenary who was trying to abduct you in order to blackmail me. Do you understand? Because if he could see the state of you now, I don't think he'd allow you to continue as my student.' Privately, I thought Herr Besler would go further than that, if he discovered his son's adventures in Prague; I suspected he would ensure the University of Wittenberg had nothing further to do with me, and I did not want to burn my bridges there just yet.

'Yes, Maestro.' He dipped his head.

And how much would I share, in my next letter to Francis Walsingham? It would depend on whether I decided to take the Emperor up on his offer. I imagined Walsingham would enjoy the idea of having one of his people positioned at the heart of the Bohemian court, especially if John Dee was planning to leave; I could make myself useful to England again.

'Well, Maestro?' Besler said, turning away from the river and stamping his feet against the cold. 'Have you made your decision yet?'

'I have decided,' I said, slinging an arm around his shoulder, 'that we deserve a drink. Let's see if Greta will be kind enough to give us one on the house. Though I'd stay away from the schnapps if I were you.'

'You know, that girl at the Winged Horse winked at me last time I was there,' he remarked.

'Irenka? She'd have you for breakfast,' I said, laughing, as we passed under the tower. 'Check she doesn't have a husband first, eh. I'll meet you there.'

'Why, where are you going?'

'There's something I need to do first.'

'A dog? For me?' Sukie leaned on the doorframe, frowning. 'Why?'

'Well, I've rescued him from a terrible fate,' I said. I had expected unconfined delight from her at the prospect of a pet; instead she was looking at me as if there had been some kind

460

of clerical error. Perhaps I had no idea about children after all. The small white dog wriggled in my arms, then reached up to lick my face. The boy with the flute had bargained me up to three thalers for him, which was three times what he'd get for handing him over to the Powder Tower. I supposed it made sense that life should be worth more than death. 'I thought he'd be company when your father's out working. He probably needs a good bath though – he doesn't smell too good close up. The dog, not your father.'

She giggled and held the door for me to come in. The house had been cleaned and straightened since I had last seen it, the broken lock patched up.

'Far! Bruno's brought me a present.'

Erik looked up from the corner where he was fixing a chair that had been broken during the Spaniards' raid. 'You have got to be joking,' he said, eyeing the dog. 'Just what I need – another mouth to feed.'

'He eats anything, apparently,' I said, setting him down on the floor. Sukie crouched to tickle his ears.

'Don't be silly, Far,' she said. 'We don't have to worry about that now you have your commission from the Emperor.'

'What commission?' I said, affecting ignorance.

Erik straightened and brushed himself down. 'His Majesty has invested in the development of my method for refining saltpetre, with a share of the profits if it increases production,' he said, trying to look modest. 'I suppose I have you to thank for that?'

'Thank Dr Hajek. He persuaded the Emperor to look at your drawings. He was grateful for your help in saving Magda.'

'Anyway,' Sukie said, 'we'll have plenty of room for a dog when we move.'

'You're leaving Golden Lane?' I said, surprised.

Erik nodded. 'This place has not been good for our health. I'm taking lodgings in the Lesser Town, now I can afford it. More light. Better class of neighbour.' He crossed the room and shook me vigorously by the hand; I could see in his eyes

461

that he was fighting back emotion. 'If you hadn't showed up at our door, I might still be drinking myself into a stupor in the Blue Elephant,' he said, his voice cracking, 'and God knows what would have become of my girl. I won't forget what you've done for us, Bruno. If there's ever any way I can help you while you are in Prague – you just have to ask.'

I nodded, embarrassed. 'I will.'

'What's his name?' Sukie asked, glancing up. The dog had rolled on to his back in a shameless bid to have his tummy scratched.

'That's for you to decide,' I said.

She considered for a moment. 'Golem?' she suggested.

'I am not shouting that down the street, thank you,' Erik said firmly.

'You're right, he doesn't look like a Golem.' She squinted into the dog's face. 'He looks clever and a bit sad. I think I'll call him Ziggi.'

I caught Erik's eye; he shrugged, as if to say: children – what can you do?

The cemetery in the Jewish Town was a patch of ground barely more than a couple of acres, but crowded with hundreds of headstones tilting at unwieldy angles, like a mouth full of crooked teeth. I followed a narrow path between the graves until I saw her standing motionless in front of one that was freshly dug. We stood for a moment in silence, our heads lowered, then I laid the pebble I had brought on the headstone. Esther turned to me, leaf-shadow playing across her face, hiding her expression.

'It's my fault,' she said eventually, so softly I barely caught the words. 'If I had not believed that I could control the situation with the Emperor – if I had simply said no from the beginning, then David would not have felt the need to take matters into his own hands.'

'Your father blames himself too,' I said. 'But you both did what you thought was right. It's no one's fault but the person who killed him.'

'And he has run from the law,' she said, her anger quiet but potent. 'Along with his sister, who would have killed me too if you had not guessed at her plan in time.'

Hajek's remedies had done their work; over the past day she had recovered enough to be taken home. She still looked fragile, her cheekbones sharper, dark hollows under her eyes. I felt an overwhelming urge to put my arm around her, feel her lean into me. I fought to resist it.

'But to bring them both to trial would have made public the story about Rudolf's intentions towards you,' I reminded her. 'You would have been the subject of every alehouse gossip-monger, every bawdy pamphlet sold in the Old Town Square, every filthy tavern ballad. The repercussions might have been worse than a few broken windows.'

'Oh, I know. I'd have been forever remembered as the conniving Jewess who tried to manipulate the Holy Roman Emperor with my wiles.' She forced a smile. 'I understand I have you to thank for extricating me from the situation.'

'The idea was mine – the performance was all John Dee's.'

'Well, I am grateful.' She let out a shaky breath. 'You know, I never wanted to be the Emperor's wife – of course I didn't, but for a moment I almost convinced myself that I could step up to the role, if it was my destiny. That must sound self-im-portant. But I was fed the story of my namesake from a very young age.' She wrapped her arms around her thin frame, still looking at the grave. 'And in a way I felt sorry for Rudolf. I think he is a very lonely man.'

'Was he angry with your father for deceiving him?'

'He shouted. But the rabbi placated him in the end. Rudolf said—' she pressed a hand to her mouth to stifle a laugh – 'he said he'd been having second thoughts about the circumcision anyway. He hadn't realised that would be a necessary condition of converting.'

'What will happen to David's shop?' I asked, thinking of all those beautiful volumes.

She turned to me, and for the first time I saw the light return to her eyes.

'Well, someone needs to run it until his son is old enough to take over. So I told Sarah I would do it.'

'That's wonderful. But is it—' I stopped, not wishing to be tactless.

'Unusual?' She smiled. 'Yes, very. I imagine it will raise a few eyebrows. But why should I not, just because I am a woman? I know plenty about books – I am my father's daughter, after all.'

Her eyes met mine and I held her gaze for a long moment, as I felt my heart constrict.

'Esther,' I began, 'I—'

'Don't,' she said, laying a hand on my arm. 'Please. I can guess at what you want to say, Bruno. I have seen it in the way you look at me.'

'I have not met a woman like you in a long time,' I said.

She lowered her eyes. 'And you are a remarkable man. Everyone says so. But my path is fixed. If I had been willing to acknowledge it sooner, perhaps none of this would have happened.'

A taut silence unfolded. I could hear my blood pulsing in my ears. Eventually I nodded.

'You will marry Benjamin, then?'

'Yes. It's time. I had delayed because I felt I had a duty to my father, but also because I was unsure.'

'Unsure about him?'

'Unsure if it was really my choice, or merely what I knew was expected of me. But after everything we've been through, I've come to see that Benjamin is as much a part of my family as my own sisters.'

I fixed my eyes on the trees. 'And is that – forgive me, but is that what you desire in a husband?'

She paused before answering. 'I know now what it is to be the object of someone's ardent passion,' she said. 'It's not what the poets would have you believe. I'd rather have something steady and true, that will last. Look, here is my father.' She removed her hand from my arm and stepped away; I felt the finality of it.

I glanced up to see Rabbi Loew making his way through the headstones. He caught sight of us and paused for a moment, as if he divined the nature of the conversation. He lowered his head before David's grave for a silent prayer, then put an arm around Esther's shoulders.

'You should be resting, my dear,' he said, in a tone of gentle rebuke, before turning to me. 'Have you made up your mind about staying in Prague, Bruno? Will you take the Emperor's offer?'

'I told him I will let him know by tomorrow,' I said as we walked towards the gate. 'I needed time to think.'

'It's a prestigious position,' he said. 'And we would like to see more of you, wouldn't we, Esther? I know Benjamin is eager to show you his cubiculum and his light shows too.'

I wondered if Benjamin would be so keen to share his work with me if he guessed at my feelings for his wife-to-be.

'Is he still developing his Golem puppet?' I asked.

'I made him put it away in the attic of the synagogue, until the times are more receptive to that story,' he said with a sad smile. When we reached the street, he drew me into one of his exuberant hugs. 'Thank you for all you have done,' he said fiercely in my ear.

'I wish it had been more,' I mumbled into his coat. He held me for a moment longer, then gave me a hearty thump on the back.

'We'll see you later for supper, my friend,' he said as they walked away, Esther leaning heavily against him. At the gate of the cemetery, she turned and held my gaze.

Let her go, I told myself. It was my fate, it seemed, to fall for women who could not be mine, and if I stayed in Prague, I would need to learn to be satisfied with friendship, to her and Benjamin. For all that, it might be good to live in a place where I could count on friends. But there were enemies here too: San Clemente and his men, not to mention the possibility that Ottavio and Katherina Strada might eventually return from banishment. Rudolf was, after all, notoriously capricious.

If I took the job as librarian, how long would it last? Would I become like the Stradas, like Ziggi Bartos or John Dee, jostling to keep myself in Rudolf's favour, one eye constantly over my shoulder to see who was coming up behind me, fearful of being pushed out by a new favourite? I had no wish to become ensnared in court politics; I had seen too often where it could lead. Nor could I stop turning over in my mind that last conversation with John on the subject of home. Despite Montalcino's threats, I was not convinced that the Inquisition still cared all that much about me beyond his personal vendetta, and Italy was a big place. I would be forty soon; I wanted to see Nola again, and Monte Cicada. Vesuvius, Capri and the sunlight on the Bay of Naples.

I laid a hand briefly on David's headstone and looked up at the last streaks of pink and gold fading over the rooftops of the Jewish Town. As I walked towards the cemetery gate, I took Rudolf's silver token from my purse and flicked it high in the air, watching it spin, glinting, waiting to fall, the outcome still unknown.

In Elizabeth's England, true faith can mean bloody murder…

Oxford, 1583. A place of learning. And murderous schemes.

The country is rife with plots to assassinate Queen Elizabeth and return the realm to the Catholic faith. Giordano Bruno is recruited by the queen's spymaster and sent undercover to expose a treacherous conspiracy in Oxford – but his own secret mission must remain hidden at all costs.

A spy under orders. A coveted throne under threat.

When a series of hideous murders ruptures close-knit college life, Bruno is compelled to investigate. And what he finds makes it brutally clear that the Tudor throne itself is at stake…

Autumn, 1583. Under Elizabeth's rule, loyalty is bought with blood…

An astrological phenomenon heralds the dawn of a new age and Queen Elizabeth's throne is in peril. As Mary Stuart's supporters scheme to usurp the rightful monarch, a young maid of honour is murdered, occult symbols carved into her flesh.

The Queen's spymaster, Francis Walsingham, calls on maverick agent Giordano Bruno to infiltrate the plotters and secure the evidence that will condemn them to death.

Bruno is cunning, but so are his enemies. His identity could be exposed at any moment. The proof he seeks is within his grasp. But the young woman's murder could point to an even more sinister truth…

London, 1584. Giordano Bruno travels to Canterbury for love. But finds only murder …

Giordano Bruno is being followed by the woman he once loved – Sophia Underhill, accused of murder and on the run. With the leave of the Queen's spymaster, he sets out to clear Sophia's name. But when more brutal killings occur a far deadlier plot emerges.

A city rife with treachery. A relic steeped in blood.

His hunt for the real killer leads to the shadows of the Cathedral – England's holiest shrine – and the heart of a sinister and powerful conspiracy …

August, 1585. England is on the brink of war…

Sir Francis Drake is preparing to launch a daring expedition against the Spanish when a murder aboard his ship changes everything.

A relentless enemy.
A treacherous conspiracy.

Giordano Bruno agrees to hunt the killer down, only to find that more than one deadly plot is brewing in Plymouth's murky underworld. And as he tracks a murderer through its dangerous streets, he uncovers a conspiracy that threatens the future of England itself.

A king without an heir

Heretic-turned-spy Giordano Bruno arrives in Paris to find a city on the edge of catastrophe. King Henri III lives in fear of a coup by the Duke of Guise and his fanatical Catholic League, and another massacre on the streets.

A court at war with God

When Bruno's old rival, Father Paul Lefèvre, is found murdered, Bruno is drawn into a dangerous web of religious politics and court intrigue. And watching over his shoulder is the King's mother, Catherine de Medici, with her harem of beautiful spies.

A deadly conspiracy in play

When murder strikes at the heart of the Palace, Bruno finds himself on the trail of a killer who is protecting a terrible secret. With the royal houses of France and England under threat, Bruno must expose the truth – or be silenced for good…

A treasonous conspiracy

Giordano Bruno, a heretic turned spy, arrives in England with shocking information for spymaster Sir Francis Walsingham. A band of Catholic Englishmen are plotting to kill Queen Elizabeth and spring Mary, Queen of Scots, from prison to take the English throne in her place.

A deadly trap

Bruno is surprised to find that Walsingham is aware of the plot and is allowing it to progress. He hopes that Mary will put her support in writing – and condemn herself to a traitor's death.

A queen in mortal danger

Bruno is tasked with going undercover to join the conspirators. Can he stop them before he is exposed? Either way a queen will die; Bruno must make sure it is the right one…